M000217100

Plank Children
Three Furies Press, LLC, United States
Copyright © 2020
Cover credit: Amy Larsen

For more information contact
Three Furies Press, LLC
30 N Gould St
Sheridan, WY 82801
(509) 768-2249
Ebook ISBN 13: 9781950722532
Print ISBN 13: 9781950722549
First Edition: October 2020

Michael Schutz

"PLANK CHILDREN is a labyrinthine nightmare set in an old reform school. Michael Schutz paints the haunted corridors with heavy atmosphere and real characters battling not only the forces threatening them, but also themselves. The dread is so thick you can taste it. Not recommended for the squeamish."

—Jason White, author of *The Haunted Country* and *Isolation.*

"With PLANK CHILDREN, Michael Schutz has delivered another gripping and original tale of horror. St. Hamlin's is a truly wicked locale, bringing to mind Jackson's Hill House and du Maurier's Manderley only even more sinister. PLANK CHILDREN is a tense thrill ride that surprises at every turn."

"A fantastic novel. Intense and unrelenting, not to mention a unique take."

—Mark Allan Gunnells, author of *The Daylight Will Not Save You* and *324 Abercorn*

"Emotionally visceral, relevant, with a powerful resonance rarely seen today. Schutz's unique voice is a breath of fresh air. A must read." – Ben Eads, author of *Cracked Sky* and *Hollow Heart.*

"PLANK CHILDREN slithers into your mind with its haunting imagery, gothic settings, and emotional turmoil. As is his way, Schutz writes details that matter, delivering a pleasurable nightmare."

—S.L. Kerns, author of *The Rut*

Michael Schutz

Table of Contents

Michael Schutz

Acknowledgements

Special thanks to:
The Schutzes
The Hemlers
The Carlsons

Carol, Jason, Lloyd, and Maggie read early drafts and pointed out my blind spots.

Ben and Mark, thank you for reading later drafts and giving your feedback and encouragement.

Edd and Kindra, thank you for your faith during the development of this novel.

For Ricky Ryan

Plank Children
By
Michael Schutz

Michael Schutz

One

Time does not heal all wounds.

Three months in this new crapbox bachelor pad hadn't eased the suffocating void of his boyfriend leaving him after five years.

Nine months ago his nephew—the closest he would ever get to a son—had been scraped off the pavement, and time hadn't done a damn thing to heal that wound, either. Miles Baumgartner had shoved that agony deep into a back corner of his mind, waiting for it to collect dust like the unpacked boxes in his new living room.

The ache refused to dull.

A heavy, happy beat of tuba music thumped through Miles' next-door neighbors' wall. Dressed for another idle day in an old flannel and jeans, Miles sat on his Goodwill couch, laptop on the dinged-up coffee table, systematically liking all his friends' Facebook posts. The bitterness of his morning French roast spurred an angry, wriggling craving for a cigarette.

Smoking was a mortal sin in the dating pool these days, but quitting the habit wouldn't help burn any of that complacency weight he'd gained while with Jeremy—all those decadent dinners with his ex's fellow lawyers from the police union.

Miles scratched his scalp through wild tussles of thinning hair. How to start over at forty-one? He'd lost the knack for first dates, and couldn't fathom maintaining the charade of his best self through second and third ones. Even if he met someone, how long until he and the new boyfriend formed the easy shorthand of glances and gestures that marked true partners? That magic had happened quickly with Jeremy.

And what if his next relationship burned out after another five years? Dear God, he'd be almost fifty.

The end of love was a dying star. That's what he'd told Jeremy three months ago, on the day all the truths came out. Miles hadn't been happy that last year-and-a-half either and sure, he'd swiped through some profiles on dating apps. But it turned out that even though the passion had fizzled, the love lived on. The love between him and Jeremy had collapsed in on itself, shrinking in size, but though smaller, it had the same mass. Same scorching heat. Just compressed.

"A tight hot ball, right here." Miles had struck his sternum with his fist. Jeremy watched from the archway to the dining room, that bored look on his face. The ceiling fan *whump-whump-whump*ed, an intrusive third heartbeat in the room. "If you leave me, all that compressed love is... is going to explode. A supernova of misery and pain and loneliness."

Jeremy had grimaced. "Is that the kind of crap you teach in fifth period poetry?" Then he called Miles a drama queen and left for the gym. Jeremy had made up his mind; he had made it up that first day with the ducks.

Miles sipped his coffee and slammed the ironic World's Best Teacher mug back onto the coffee table. Goddamn ducks.

He scowled at an article about legislation cutting federal funding for public schools.

He scrolled down, and the next post quashed every shred of Jeremy-thought.

Miles reached for a pack of cigarettes that wasn't there anymore.

He blinked, but the photograph didn't disappear.

At five o'clock that morning, his sister Minnie had posted a family portrait—her, her husband Daniel, and Ian posed with tight, congenial expressions, standing on a lawn that he didn't recognize. Minnie's backyard? It was not an old photo, pulled from an album. Certain details placed it as post-funeral. Straight-on but from a few feet away, so not a selfie. He was looking at a recent picture of Daniel with his rugged mountain man face. Beautiful but glassy-eyed Minnie. And their dead fifteen-year-old son, Ian.

Every portrait that is painted with feeling is a portrait of the artist, not of the sitter.

Miles clamped his teeth together until pain zinged from his jaw to his ear. Shaking, he shut his laptop lid, leaned back, and stared at the ceiling. Must have been a cut-and-paste job. Daniel was a closet computer nerd, but he'd outdone himself here. A lot of time and effort had gone into that photo. The attempt to recreate the family was understandable, but posting it on Facebook for the world to see felt a bit much.

He took another sip of coffee. All this time spent licking his own wounds, he'd ignored the unfathomable loneliness his sister must have been going through. Ignorance so glaring that it embarrassed him, shame scorching his chest like heartburn.

He pulled out his phone charger from the laptop USB and stood, leaving the computer and mug right where they sat. In a quick dash through the apartment, he grabbed an extra sweater and threw random toiletries into a small black travel bag. In ten minutes, his old white Chevy cruised up Highway 13 to his sister's house.

Damn, he needed a cigarette.

Miles pulled in behind his brother-in-law's blue pickup and listened to the radio until Fleetwood Mac finished *Go Your Own Way*. He killed the ignition and sat there. Packing up, shacking up—that's all Jeremy wanted to do.

Even so, he missed the fucker. Missed talking with him. Every day—hell, every hour—he expected Jeremy to message him. Miles stretched his legs out and pulled his phone from his front Levi's pocket.

Nope.

Dammit, why should he even care? He had more important things right now.

He pulled himself out of the car. A fist-sized knot in his lower back tightened. Driving five hours without a break had stiffened every muscle, and he twisted and stretched to work out the kinks while brisk air stung his lungs. A week before Thanksgiving, and winter had already rolled in up Nort' in Wabunukeeg, the burg huddled against the shore of Chequamegon Bay at the top of Wisconsin. Daniel had raked and bagged the last of the fall leaves and had arranged the big black Hefty bags along the foundation to insulate the water pipes from freezing during the winter. Miles breathed in woodsy fireplace smoke. The house's blue trim glowed in a single shaft of sun poking through a sky otherwise dark and impenetrable as flint. The last time he'd stood on this driveway, sun and garden smells had filled an April day. An affront to the pall in the house, in the family. Mocking the boy in the casket at the funeral home.

Daniel poked his shaggy face out from the side door. "What are you doing here?"

What a welcome. Miles faked a smile and marched up to the house, extending his hand when he reached the steps to the kitchen door.

Daniel didn't accept the handshake. "Shouldn't you be teaching classes?" New grey streaked through Daniel's thick Swiss hair and curly beard.

Miles dropped his hand. "I took a sabbatical."

Daniel grunted. As long as he didn't start in with his crap that high school teachers had it made. Quips about contractors working in the summers, basting in the heat. But Daniel just propped the screen door open with his well-padded rear end and waited for Miles to squeeze past that Wisconsin gut, crafted over the years by Miller Genuine Draft and cheddar cheese. Sweat and a trace of that beer wafted off the red-checked flannel shirt as Miles scraped dirt off his shoes on the mat in the mudroom off the kitchen. The almost sexual scent of bleach tingled in his sinuses. His sister had been practicing her cleaning therapy.

From deep in the house, Minnie called. "Who is that?"

The screen banged shut. Daniel closed the side door and flipped the lock; he wouldn't meet Miles's eyes. With no lights turned on, all the appliances looked as indistinct as bleary images in a Polaroid.

His sister's cleaning frenzy had stopped at the kitchen. The air in the short hall resisted like water.

"Minnie?" At one end of the couch, his sister had melted into a nest of blankets and pillows. Shades pulled. Curtains drawn.

Daniel hung back. Miles moved a stack of *People* and *Entertainment Weekly* off the couch to the coffee table and sat beside her, in an aura of vodka. The cushions expelled air like farts.

She wore a faded red Badgers sweatshirt and sweatpants. Shadows smeared her face. Glassy eyes vacant. Mouth slightly open.

Waxwork and skeleton seemed to have dark eyes that moved and looked at me.

Yeah, just like Miss Havisham from *Great Expectations*, which he'd taught for ten years' worth of freshmen classes.

It was then that I began to understand that everything in the room had stopped, like the watch and the clock, a long time ago.

The day of the funeral, Daniel had pushed through the mumbling crowd toward him. "She's on the back deck." Frazzled, Daniel chewed on a fingernail. "She left early this morning, drove to the funeral home. Now she's out there, and she refuses to come in."

Miles had sat with her on the topmost step leading from the deck to the lawn. She held a pair of pruning shears, her fingers stained from the marigolds in the beds around that side of the house.

"I can't. I can't. I can't." Minnie had turned her swollen, tired eyes to him. "It can't be an open...." She choked on the last word. When she started again, her voice had become tiny. "I can't look again. I won't." A breeze bent the long blades of grass, shook the flower petals.

Miles massaged her shoulder. "I'll take care of it. I'll make sure it's closed."

"Promise me."

He squeezed her pinkie in their secret sibling handshake. A tear spilled over her cheek, and she let it fall as if to wipe it away meant wiping away Ian's memory. She stood, and brushed off her mom jeans. Mom jeans, but not really. Not anymore.

She'd looked bad then, but she looked worse now. He swept dark bangs off her forehead. "Hey, Min." Her short hair hung stiff, unwashed. Up close, those shadows on her face turned out to be smudges. Dirt? Old makeup? Her frail hand drifted up and fingered the matted hair that hung down just below her ears.

Where was his big sister? The girl whose name he couldn't pronounce so he said *Minnie* instead of *Mindy* until he turned five. The girl who'd beaten him over the head with a My Pretty Pony after he'd snuck into her room and peeled off one of her Corey Haim posters from her wall. She watched his face, her own as starkly disengaged as when they had returned after the funeral. Minnie's courage had forsaken her after sitting graveside, staring at that wound dug into the earth.

Daniel leaned against the wall by the television. Unprompted, he blurted, "That was an old picture, Miles."

"No, it wasn't. Minnie got this haircut after... afterward." A week or so after the funeral, Minnie had cut her long brunette cascade to a chin-length bob. Survivor shame? A new chapter? He had never asked. But the Facebook photo showed her with this short cut.

"Okay, you caught me. I photoshopped it."

That's what he'd thought this morning, but why did Daniel sound like he was lying?

"You did a good job." The shadows under Ian's nose and chin had matched Minnie and Daniel's. Shoulders and legs all seemed to touch. The coloring, pixilation, and angle of Ian's body matched the proportions of Mom and Dad. Eerie, really.

But something had been wrong with Ian's expression.

Daniel munched on his thumb nail, then seemed to realize it and coughed. "Come into the kitchen. I'll brew some coffee."

"I don't want coffee." Miles ground his back teeth together; they shrieked inside his skull.

Minnie's brittle fingers twined into Miles's. "Why are you here?" Her voice was like grinding gears. "You shouldn't be here. Go home."

He dropped his hand to her shoulder, where bone protruded sharp. "Why didn't you call me?"

Minnie sprang forward and grabbed Miles's collar. "I did! You didn't care."

"What ar—" But she was right. She had called when Ian started slipping. Almost exactly a year ago, right before Thanksgiving, Minnie had rung him up, sobbing. The vice principal had suspended Ian for a week after catching him smoking dope. Except for the emotion in Minnie's voice, he would have thought the call a joke. Suspended for pot? Key Club Ian? German Club Ian? The kid wore khakis and polos. Kept his hair short and pomaded and parted like a young executive. Ian's adorable face had never worn a sly look of deception.

"It's this new gang of friends." Minnie had described them: black death metal tee shirts. Piercings. The type too bold to hide their cigarettes from adults. "You should drive up." Minnie had brightened at her idea. "Talk sense into him. He listens to you."

He had agreed. They made vague plans that he broke. Arguments between him and Jeremy had consumed his attention. Now he'd lost them both. Jeremy to Duck Boy and Ian to a stolen car plowing into a bridge abutment.

Daniel spoke around the thumbnail that had snuck back into his mouth. "I told you not to post that picture, Min."

Miles clenched his jaw and glared hate at Daniel. Better to feel anger than sorrow. He turned back to his sister and squeezed her hand with gentle pressure. She'd posted it for the same reason Daniel had made it: time had not healed their wounds.

"They misidentified the body." Minnie blinked rapidly.

"What?"

Daniel started across the room, fast enough to startle Miles. He stopped at the magazine-messy coffee table. His hand went to his mouth, but before he could start biting a nail, he jammed his hands in his pockets. "Fine. I didn't make it. The photo's real." He took his hands out and crossed his arms, defending against the inevitable challenge to his ever-changing story.

Minnie didn't even glance at her husband. "The state police called us two weeks ago. They found Ian at a shelter. He'd been in the car, but it was another boy who died in the crash. Ian wandered off. He's alive."

That couldn't possibly be true. "Start from the beginning." He rubbed a spot high on his forehead. "Please."

Daniel uncrossed his arms and tried hands-on-hips. He didn't interrupt as Minnie carried on. "Ian stole the car, but not by himself. He wasn't driving. This other boy behind the wheel—he was killed. They misidentified the body."

"That's ridiculous. Guys."

He looked to Daniel for help, but his brother-in-law shook his head. "You need to understand, the body that they showed us was... mangled."

They both stared at Miles, their expressions incomprehensible. Did he need to remind them of their worst day? Walk them through burying their son to shatter this delusion and bring them back into sanity? That would be so cruel.

"You didn't photoshop that picture?"

Daniel shrugged.

"You want me to believe it's real? Ian's not dead. That's what you're telling me?"

"Exactly!" Minnie exhaled eighty-proof breath.

"Then who did you bury?"

Minnie deflated back into her corner on the couch.

"Want something to eat?" Daniel asked. "I'll whip something up."

Miles ignored him. Daniel wanted to get him away from Minnie, but Miles had no intention of placating his sister and allowing this nonsense to fester. "Minnie, if Ian were alive—if he came home—then where is he?"

Minnie glanced at her husband. Daniel shrugged the tiniest bit. She said, "They took him away."

"Who did?"

"The court." Minnie bit her lower lip.

This time Daniel demanded. "Come to the kitchen, Miles."

Minnie's eyes glassed back over. Her chest rose and fell in shallow rhythm. Maybe he should go ahead and talk with Daniel. Ask why he'd allowed this fantasy.

"Okay." Miles hoisted himself up from the couch and followed Daniel back into the big, country home kitchen.

"Sit." Daniel pulled out a kitchen chair, and Miles obeyed.

Daniel leaned against the refrigerator. He looked run through the wringer. He again folded his arms over his chest, but instead of scolding, Daniel whooshed out a sad rush of breath. His shoulders slumped. "We'd just gotten a handle on the grief. We were starting to breathe again. And then we get this phone call from the police. They found—"

Miles held up a hand to stop the flow of words. "You're lying. You—" Miles checked over his shoulder, then continued in a stage whisper. "You both identified his body."

"The state police found him—"

"Stop!" This was madness. "If Ian's alive, where is he?" Miles's voice cracked. Goddamn them. This story might make them feel better, but it ripped off the filmy scar over his own pain.

"The state police found him and charged him with the stolen car. Before we could even think straight, they sent him away to some juvie facility. Now Mindy's lost him all over again and can't function."

"Fine. Okay. Want me to play along? Tell me the name of this place."

"I can't."

"Can't? How convenient."

"What do you want from us?"

Miles swallowed hard, needing a moment to calm himself. "Why are you encouraging her?"

"You saw the picture."

"It's fake! You admitted it was fake."

"Honestly, how would we know how to do that?" Daniel slouched to a kitchen chair. He folded his hands as if in prayer and stared into their clasp.

"I know it feels easier to pretend. To ignore. But come back to reality, Daniel."

"Leave it alone."

He'd assumed that Minnie had come up with this idea, and that Daniel had gone along. Had he been mistaken?

"Fine. You win." He stood. "May I use your bathroom before I get going?" Not that he was going far. He'd find a motel room and try this again tomorrow.

Daniel watched his hands as if they held answers. "Bathroom's back through the living room, down that hall."

"I remember."

"Oh." Daniel's thumbnail snuck past his lips. "That's right."

In the living room, Minnie had tucked her legs up under her in the blanket nest on the couch, and fluttery snores accompanied her steady breaths. Miles hung a right, passed by one closed door, and entered the bathroom at the end. He turned on the faucet, listened for a moment, and opened the medicine cabinet. Prescription heartburn pills. Razor. Hemorrhoid cream. Zoloft—interesting but hardly surprising. And Xanax. The two-milligram bars; her doctor wasn't fooling around.

After closing the cabinet, he turned off the tap. He flushed for good measure, but before he left, he caught his own tired eyes in the mirror. He spoke to the old man, a familiar stranger, whom he saw there. "Just let her have this."

On his way back, he stopped at the closed door. Soft clattering from the kitchen as Daniel puttered about. No rustling from the living room so Minnie still napped. Miles opened it up and stepped into Ian's darkened room.

Brewers pennants hung on the walls alongside movie posters: *Kill Bill*, *Evil Dead*—the original, not the remake they'd seen together. Minnie and Daniel had kept the empty bed neatly made. A thin layer of dust coated the low dresser with its scattering of baseball cards. And the sepia-toned picture of Ian and him as gangsters. On their annual touristy visits to Wisconsin Dells, he and Ian would stop at one of those old-timey photo places. Each year they would choose a different period—American

Colonial, Civil War, the Wild West. The high schoolers on staff took them into the back dressing area, musty costumes hanging on racks like a poorhouse fashion show. Last summer, Ian had wanted to play Al Capone. They posed in front of a speakeasy backdrop and in a few minutes... viola! The Baumgartner/Gunderson gang with Tommy guns at the ready and funny money poking out their pin-striped suit pockets.

Somewhere in a box he had kept a similar photo of him and Jeremy heading off toward Gettysburg. That day at the Dells hadn't ended so well. The day Jeremy met his duck boy.

Beside the photo, was the 1959 Corvette model that Ian had built. That was his dream car.

Had been. Had been his dream car.

And there was the baseball, among toppled chessmen. Miles went over and picked up the foul ball in its plastic protective globe.

The force of memory pushed him backward, and he crumpled onto the bed. The mementos of young life weren't the worst reminders. Not even this ball had taken the wind out of him. Ian's lingering smell sapped him of strength: Zest soap and too much Adidas cologne. As if Ian had just popped in to grab a jacket before hopping into Uncle Miles's Prizm to head out and see the new *Leatherface*. At the cineplex, he and Ian used to take pictures of each other making faces in front of the coming attraction posters and standees—Miles on his knees conversing with a gaggle of Minions, Ian lying on his back pretending a scream as a Pixar bulldozer threatened to crush him. Even in the later years, their antics broke through teenaged Ian trying so hard to be cool and reduced him to giggles. All those pictures still lived, on Ian's Instagram.

Miles backhanded tears from his eyes, but fresh ones bubbled up.

With or without Jeremy, kids had never been part of his lifeplan. Ian had come close to changing his mind.

Ian, with that adorable scrunchy face. Precocious. Ferocious love of life. But there was an easy comfort in being the cool uncle, around for some good times, but at the end of a day or a long weekend, his commitment ended.

He flushed with shame.

Ian's silent mausoleum teemed with ghosts. As if he could reach out and catch a second chance.

A cigarette would be heaven right now.

The boards under the carpet creaked, and Miles spun to find Daniel lurking behind him.

"Get out." Daniel's arms hung at his sides, but he rolled his hands into fists.

"I miss him, too."

"Leave. Now." Daniel's fury poured off him, palpable.

Daniel followed him back through the living room, close enough that Miles felt hot breath on his neck. Psychic weight of despair compressed the air in the house, making it heavy as clods of dirt covering a box.

Minnie slurred, "What's going on?"

He bent down into the cloud of booze surrounding her head and hugged her. "I love you, Minnie."

"Miles . . ."

He whispered into her ear. "Please. Tell me what's going on."

"Miles . . ."

She drooped back against the pillows. Miles tore himself away and headed toward the kitchen, quickened his step to get distance from Daniel steamrolling behind him.

"Daniel?" Minnie's voice crackled. With pain? Fear? "Don't do this. Daniel, don't do it."

At the mudroom, Miles pulled at the front door, but it wouldn't open. He looked to his hands. What was he doing wrong? The door wasn't—the lock. He'd forgotten that Daniel had locked the door. The bolt wavered, seen as from underwater. It doubled. Tripled. He wiped away more tears.

Daniel's feet thumped over the linoleum. "Wait up, Miles."

In the other room, Minnie sobbed.

"Wait." Daniel's sour body odor engulfed him; a bulky arm brushed Miles's shoulder. "Get some supper before hitting the road. You look terrible. There's a great place across town."

"I'm not hungry."

Minnie wailed.

"I mean it. You need to find this restaurant." Daniel flicked open the lock, but grabbed Miles's forearm before he could get outside. "Take 13 through downtown, and you'll find it." Daniel tickled Miles's ear with a whisper. "Blankenheim's."

Two

In the car, Miles counted to calm down. Twenty-six... twenty-seven... twenty-eight. When his hands stopped trembling, he went to slide the key into the ignition but his hand was full. He'd stolen Ian's baseball. At some point, he'd taken it out of its protective globe. He placed the ball in the storage between the bucket seats and got the car going. He jumped the curb backing out of the driveway, slammed the automatic into gear and drove until he saw stop lights ahead and turned right on some vague instinct, finding Business 13. A minute later, vacant storefronts in the tiny downtown flashed by the windows. Daniel and Minnie had done well for themselves, but they'd really moved to the boonies. This was worse than where he and his sister grew up.

He drummed his fingers on the steering wheel, wanting a cigarette like a junkie wants a hit.

At the next corner, he pulled into the slant parking in front of an independent grocer with huge bins out front filled with pumpkins and maize. Stickers on the filthy glass door displayed their lotto assortment. A bell over the door jingled as he walked in. It was an older store so the linoleum floors had yellowed; the lights were dimmer than chain stores' high-powered fluorescents. Coolers filled with beer and soda formed the back wall with four short aisles between. This store reminded him of Hauser's just up the street from his childhood home. He and his best friend, Rich, once bought Minnie a soda and then kicked it down the sidewalk all the way home, giggling at the drenching his sister would get when she cracked open the can. By the time they got back, the aluminum had been so dirty, dented, and scuffed that Minnie didn't fall for it.

The young lady in faded clothes and too much make-up at the register popped her gum and looked up from her copy of *Vogue*.

"Marb reds." Miles pulled out his wallet.

Tina—according to her name tag—turned to the cig-arette rack behind her. She knew right where to find the Marlboros.

Miles paid in cash and hurried out of the store, feel-ing a porn-buyer's mix of guilt and elation. Back in his car, he ripped off the cellophane, pulled the box top open, and stuck it under his nose. He breathed in that titillating aroma of fresh tobacco. Twenty new friends. He extracted a smoke and dug around for half a minute in the glove box to find a lighter. His fingers shook as he lit up.

Bitter, foul smoke filled his lungs.

Delicious.

Minnie had given him his first taste of tobacco at thirteen or fourteen. While taking out the trash for Mom one soft June evening, he'd caught her smoking by the garbage bin. He extorted her into giving him a puff. "It's called a drag," she'd corrected him, handing over the smoke.

After only a couple weeks, this ritual felt foreign. A little taboo. He took another drag. On his second exhale, his head spun. His stomach turned. Cursing, he tamped the cigarette out in the ashtray. Blue layers of smoke hung suspended in the car, and as he fanned the waves out his window, he spied a swaying shingle reading *Blanken-heim's*.

Script underneath advertised "Gutes Essen." His stomach recovered from the smoke and gurgled at this promise for good German food. Sausages and sauerkraut. A taste of his youth. A place to chill out and collect him-self. Events since sitting on Ian's bed were a blur.

Daniel's recommendation was stylized like a chalet, white walls and decorative half-timbering. He parked in the wide lot behind and circled around to the front. Inside, a huge central fireplace brought a rush of welcome heat and savory smells of fresh meat. Dark wood-paneled walls glowed golden in the light cast by iron chandeliers. Only ten minutes to three; the dinner rush wouldn't hit for another two or three hours, and no one sat at any of the booths or tables, though across the expanse, at a bar gleaming with mirrors and polished brass, a trio of burly men sat, not together but not far apart, drinking beer from steins.

The barman lifted a hand to let Miles know he'd been seen. After passing a couple words with the drinkers, the guy hurried over. The barman turned out to be a teenager, maybe sixteen or seventeen but definitely not old enough to legally serve liquor.

Barely older than Ian.

"Welcome."

Miles tipped his head toward the bar. "They're getting an early start of it."

"They always do." The kid stifled a laugh. "Just one today?"

"Yeah." Miles followed the kid who had that tall, lanky look so many of Miles's students had these days. Dark hair flopping.

"A booth okay?"

"Perfect." Miles slid onto the padded seat; its back of dark lacquered slats towered high as a medieval throne. A pocket of anonymity. This place reminded him of the restaurant in New Glarus that he'd picked for his tenth-birthday meal. He'd gorged himself on brats until he'd puked on the grassy verge on the way back to the car. A dark chunk had splatted on Minnie's shoe. She'd teased him for years about that.

"I'm Graham, and I'll be your server. Hey, is that your lucky ball?"

Miles looked down at his hand, which held Ian's baseball. "I don't remember bringing this in with me." He set it at the end of the booth. His hand felt lonely without it. Only for a second before Graham handed Miles a huge, hardcover menu with gilt lettering.

Graham set down a goblet of water, ice clinking against the sides. "A couple minutes to look over the menu?"

"Please."

"A drink order in the meantime?"

"Oh." Miles glanced at the bar. A stein of German lager would take the edge off. But he'd promised Jeremy.... "I'll stick with water for now."

Graham nodded and ambled toward the kitchen.

Miles snatched up the baseball, the leather smooth. He fingered the red laces. He'd taken Ian to Miller Park for his first Brewers game. Daniel was a football man and Minnie never cared one way or the other. At eight years old, the boy hadn't even wanted to go. But Miles had guessed right, and Ian had been hooked. There was nothing like a kid's first night game, how the halide lamps lit the field into hyper-reality. Ian's eyes riveted at the grass as green as a cartoon. Players' uniforms glowing angelic white. The boy's mouth opened in awe, as if trying to taste the roar of 35,000 fans. They had driven to Milwaukee once or twice a summer every year after.

Graham set down a basket of warm rye bread with a ramekin of whipped butter. Miles scanned the menu's nearly indecipherable calligraphic script. He made up his mind for the venison Sauerbraten and handed the menu back.

Ian had been a happy, well-adjusted kid. How had a bad crowd lured him in? He'd always had lots of friends. Lots of dates.

A life Miles could hardly imagine.

He and Minnie had been raised in a town marginally bigger than Wabunukeeg, where growing up gay in the Eighties had been a sentence of solitary confinement. Gay men were used as punch lines in movies and TV. Homosexuality was a talking point only because of AIDS, and even that barely trickled out of the Midwest news reports. Miles had endured a lonely childhood. And young adulthood. If any classmates hid their gayness in closets, Miles still had no idea. With no one to date, he'd finagled strained friendships with the guys he liked, eventually scaring them off with too many moony glances.

"Here you go." Graham slid the juicy roast onto the table and knocked the plate into the goblet hard enough that a slug of water spilled over the lip.

"I'm so sorry." Graham turned and raided an empty table of its cloth napkins. "Um...." He looked from the spill to Miles and back again.

"Don't worry about it." Miles plucked the napkins from Graham's hands, but he didn't lay them down. He watched the clear damp stain spread out a couple of inches. Graham asked him a question, but the voice came from a vast distance. He mumbled his thanks and waved Graham off. Heartbreak rushed through him with infected heat.

He'd met Jeremy the new-fashioned way—in the online chat room of Studz, Central and Southern Wisconsin's premier gay dating site. He liked KingVinyl197's pics, so he "smooched" him. Jeremy smooched him right back. Miles couldn't recall his own username, but their first date was etched in his memory. They met at La Paella, a Spanish restaurant with cloth napkins and candles on the table. The sexy young attorney sitting cross-legged in the waiting area looked exactly as advertised. KingVinyl197 hadn't even used an old picture for his profile. Intelligent eyes, young but wise face. His hair that shade of dirty blond that Miles found irresistible. When Jeremy stood, his height proved his claim of six-three.

Once seated, Jeremy handled the wine. "Do you have a Faustino I Gran Reserva 1978?"

Their server nodded sagely. "We do."

Wow. Miles bought Sutter Home at the corner store.

They slipped into an easy dialog about favorite subjects—Fleetwood Mac: yay or nay on Christine McVie?, Hemingway versus Steinbeck, and how Jonathan Demme had made Oscar gold from Harris' awful novels. Things were going great; engrossed in their conversation, Miles scooted his chair forward. And knocked his knee into the table, overturning his water glass. The deluge rushed across the distance. Jeremy's eyes went wide, and he tried to slide his chair away. He was too late. The flood poured into his lap. "Cold!"

"Oh my God, I'm so sorry."

Their server rushed over with a towel. Finely dressed diners watched the floor show with furtive—and a couple of unabashed—glances at their table. Jeremy stood; ice and water fell to the floor. Miles stood, too. "I'm mortified."

For a moment, it seemed their server would kneel and pat down Jeremy's crotch himself, but he passed off the towel. Jeremy swiped a last time and shrugged. "Now we have a story to tell." He laughed.

Their server brought another water glass, and Miles and Jeremy giggled throughout their meal.

Today's spill had already absorbed into the table-cloth. He tossed the extra napkins aside. The sauerbraten's sharp aroma pulled him out of the depression hole he'd fallen into. Before he dug in, Miles checked his phone for messages. Still nothing.

Ian and Jeremy.

Jeremy and Ian.

Twin wounds, seeping loss.

At his post beside the cash register, Graham read a thick paperback by the light reflected off the gleaming top-shelf booze.

Miles coughed into his hand. "I'm ready to settle up."

"Sure thing." Graham set down *Being and Nothingness*.

Wow. How appropriate.

The past is no longer, the future is not yet, as for the instantaneous present, everyone knows that it is not at all.

Halfway down the bar, one of the tap handles advertised his favorite college beer. "I changed my mind." He saddled up onto a bar stool. "Can I add on to my bill?" Screw Jeremy. "Gimme a pint of Point Bock."

"You got it."

Two more men had joined the three drinkers, and now they all huddled together. They'd procured bar dice, and one of the flannel-wearers with a ZZ Top beard slammed the cup down. Shouts accompanied the reveal.

On a thick coaster imprinted with the Blankenheim's coat of arms, Graham set down a heavy stein. Miles drank a long, cooling draught.

"Say...." Miles interrupted Graham just as the kid picked Sartre back up. "Do you know of a juvenile offenders facility around here?"

"Nah, not around here."

Miles sipped. "How about not quite around here? Maybe a reformatory. I don't really know."

"Sorry, I have no idea." He flipped to his page in the paperback.

A short, stout older woman banged her way through a set of batwing doors concealing the kitchen. At the cash register, she punched a couple buttons that opened the drawer.

"Maybe she knows?"

Graham slapped his book closed. He opened his mouth, but the woman turned and spoke first.

"Know what?"

"Nothing, mom."

Her glasses' thick lenses magnified her eyes fishbowl-wide. "What can I do ya for?"

"I'm trying to find the reformatory around here."

"Reformatory?"

Graham stepped up. "I told him there wasn't—"

"You shush." She glared at Miles. "You mean the orphanage?" She trucked up to the bar and pointed a finger in his face. "Whaddaya want with St. Hamelin's?"

The game at the end of the bar stopped so suddenly that her last sibilant rang throughout the empty restaurant. Graham made a show of groaning, but his mom paid him no attention. Miles bowed forward and let her talk.

"We don't talk bout dat orphanage across The Bridge."

He heard the capital letters in the stress of her words.

"Who's dis giving ya trouble?" One of the men— old-man skinny, face deeply lined and tanned from farming—stood from his stool, a cigarette dangling from the corner of his mouth.

"Youse guys stay outta dis!" The woman leaned toward Miles but didn't lower her voice. "But he asks a good question. Who are you?"

"I'm Dan Gunderson's brother-in-law."

"Don't know who dat is." The bearded one stood, ignoring the reprimand to butt out.

Scorn soured the woman's face. Resignation stripped away her heavy midwestern accent. "You ain't got no business up there."

"I didn't mean to offend you."

She shot a withering look at Graham, though it was she who named the secret.

The other four men slid their butts off their seats. They could have been fairytale dwarves: Smoker, Bearded, Balding, Trucker Cap, and Gargantuan.

"Doncha got no sense?" Trucker Cap asked.

They rounded the corner of the bar. Dwarves? More like ogres.

These uncouth hillmen—one would suppose they'd never seen a foreigner before.

Miles's jaw clenched, and the muscles there twitched once, twice.

"What happened there...." The woman's voice hitched. "Was an abomination."

"Why youse comin here to bring up dat old story?" The ash from Smoker's cigarette broke off and dusted the floor.

"I didn't mean any harm."

"No, ya din't mean," Bearded said.

"Listen, I'll just pay my bill and get out of your hair."

Balding spoke for the first time, his face beet red. "Dat's a good idea, den."

"Graham...." The woman backed off. "Take this man's money and see that he leaves." She stormed off, back through the batwing doors, into the alien landscape of tile and bright lights, stainless steel ovens, and orderly racks of gigantic pots and pans.

Graham approached, wary. Maybe gun shy. "Talking about that place gets Mom riled up." He cast a furtive glance at the five ogres who plotted softly among themselves. "But there's nothing up there. My grandpa—well, great-grandpa—died in the accident that shut that place down."

Shut the place down? He itched to hear about this accident, but the men had broken off their conversation, and he didn't want to stick around and find out their consensus.

"Thank you." He over-tipped and retreated, the fives ogres scowling an auger into his back.

Three

A block away from Blankenheim's, the ramshackle Paradise Motel offered Vacancy for $29.95 with COLOR TV/HBO. As good a place as any. He parked, checked in, and walked to room 104. Into an atmosphere of cold pizza and stale beer.

"What a dump."

He froze in place. What a dump. Those words felt familiar. He tried them again.

"What a dump."

Where was that from?

Déjà vu wrapped tight around his head. *"What a dump"... What's that from?*

Oh, wow.

He plunked down onto the foot of the bed. Those were Elizabeth Taylor's lines from *Who's Afraid of Virginia Woolf?* Taylor saunters into her kitchen and declares, "What a dump!" He used to assign Edward Albee's play to his seniors. He loved the Mike Nichols' film. Had seen it a dozen times. Thrice with Jeremy. The story followed a night with George and Martha, an aging academic couple who hadn't been able to conceive children. So they invented a child. A secret fantasy. In the privacy of their home, they loved and raised their made-up son, nurturing their shared narrative with as much devotion as they would an actual child. This particular night, having invited guests over, Martha slipped up and mentioned her "son" after eighteen years.

Minnie had lasted nine post-funeral months before she shared Ian with her Facebook friends. George and Martha had tucked their son away at school; Daniel and

Minnie stashed Ian in a juvenile detention facility because it welded together the accident with what they wanted to believe.

So now what?

Jeremy had been the one person he could confide any secret to or run crazy thoughts by. But his confidante had gone chasing after ducks.

By the end of that movie, George and Martha had beaten each other into emotional wrecks, but they carried on without their fantasy. By the same logic, he might snap Minnie back to reality if he found this St. Hamelin's, captured a few pics with his smartphone, and showed her that her reformatory was nothing but an abandoned orphanage.

But by cracking the delusion, would he devastate her all over again?

Things had to get worse before they got better. Darkest before dawn, and any other stupid axiom that gave him permission.

In the couple hours of remaining daylight, he could zip up to the orphanage, gather his proof, and reason with Minnie and Daniel over breakfast coffee tomorrow. He'd be back home in his rattrap for dinner.

He just needed to find directions—those five ogres hadn't given him time to press Graham for details. He Googled *St. Hamelin's, Wabunukeeg.* The search yielded one result. He tapped and a Wikipedia page loaded, but what he saw there didn't surprise him one bit. A local historian must have started a page, but apart from the title of St. Hamelin's, the rest of the entry remained a template. No information. No citations.

Miles sighed and rubbed his eyes with his free hand. Minnie and Daniel had picked a usefully obscure facility to prop up their delusion.

Miles brought up Google Maps and, on a whim, entered his destination. Huh. Who'd have guessed: a driving route from the Paradise to St. Hamelin's.

Snow flurries fluttered over the parking lot. Thanksgiving next week would feel like Christmas if this kept up. Waiting for the engine to warm up and the heater to kick in, he grabbed his sweater from the backseat and slipped it on. Jeremy used to tease him about his Eddie Bauer clothes, that he'd joined the over-forty club at the mall.

Miles rolled his window halfway down and lit a cigarette. With the car idling, he pulled up Google Maps again and set his phone to talk him through the directions.

On his way out of town, he sped past quintessential Wisconsin landmarks: two taverns and the white, steepled box of a Lutheran church. He hadn't been to church in twenty-three years. Taverns a little more recently. Wisconsin Avenue emptied into Highway 2, where harvested fields stretched on either side—dirt bumps the texture of soda crackers. Soon the north woods took over, and the world darkened a couple shades; temperatures dropped ten degrees. Miles clicked the heater up two notches.

A half hour later, he breezed through Bear Falls— another two taverns and a Lutheran church. The accented voice of his GPS told him to take a left in two miles, and he nearly shot right past the narrow slot through deeper, denser woods. He turned onto the asphalt road, disappearing into a tunnel of trees, branches entwined overhead and forming a canopy. Most of the leaves had broken their tethers to the branches, and in the car's wake, those browned, crisp leaves took flight, twitching and jerking before collapsing back to the road. Underbrush and saplings scraped against the sides of the car. Ahead, shadows darkened the grey road top to a color like charcoal soot.

One moment he bounced along the corridor, and in the next moment the trees and scrub brush came to an abrupt end. He stopped the car and glanced at his phone. He'd lost his internet connection. Ahead lay a trestle bridge of thick wood planks like railroad ties. Decades of rain, snow, and sun had pitted and pocked the wood, drying it out and turning all the planks a brittle grey. It extended fifty yards over an immense gulley. What seemed a half mile down, a white-tipped river cut through the countryside. At the other end of the bridge, the woods started up again.

Open water and heights together. Moth wings of panic frenzied inside his chest. He shut off the heater and rolled the window farther down to get some air.

"No big deal. Half a football field."

Saying it aloud didn't help. The span looked like it stretched for a mile. But he nudged the gas pedal and rolled onto the bridge. The Chevy's tires thumped over every joint between boards. A cigarette would have settled his nerves, but he refused to take his white-knuckled hands from ten-and-two. Instead, he held his breath until the back tires kissed pavement on the other side.

Going twenty miles an hour, his car bumped and jumped through potholes. The forest closed in. The road narrowed, and the passenger tires slipped down off the strip of broken asphalt. He corrected, and the tires on his side whisked through brush. He concentrated so hard on piloting his car that he didn't notice what lay ahead until a break in trees poured fading daylight through the windshield.

On his left, thick woods continued unbroken into the distance, but to his right, all trees had been cleared and the big sky met with a flat grassy field. A quarter mile ahead the road disappeared back into a thick tunnel of trees, but before that lay every nightmare personified.

St. Hamelin's orphanage spilled into the clearing like the Devil's afterbirth. A Romanesque monstrosity, squared bays poked from its façade like Thalidomide-warped bones. Castle walls of brick and stone towered five stories tall. Three unevenly spaced turrets crept up the sides. Spires and chimneys pointed like rotted teeth against the sky. The heavily lidded eyes of attic dormers peered down, but none of the many mullioned windows faced the sinking sun and so stared out, dead.

A sense of insufferable gloom pervaded my spirit.

Miles compressed his back teeth until that familiar pain—like a kidney stone in his face—burst through his cheekbones, spangling stars in his eyes.

"My God, why did I come here?"

He would have turned the car around and fled all the way back home, but he'd travelled here for his sister. And so for Minnie, he tugged the shifter into gear and crept forward. Slow, to not wake the sleeping goliath.

A stink hung in the air, heady and rich like skunky beer. There must have been a paper mill nearby; there were a lot of them up here. As he pulled into St. Hamelin's gravel driveway, he slapped a hand over his nose and mouth. Light snow continued falling and settled in the shallow ruts of the driveway and on the grounds. A thin coating like the dust on Ian's dresser. He pulled up even with the stone portico, ornamental columns at each corner supporting decorative stone molding under the flat roof.

A short distance away, at the edge of the clearing, sat a stout, squat building of red brick, stone, glass, and identical wide concrete steps up to the entrance but without any covering overhead. Shapeless in comparison to the main building, as if the waste matter of a miscarried twin had congealed.

The gravel drive looped around a raised grass knoll and connected back to the road, though a spur shot off toward a weathered wooden carriage house crouched off to the right. Two wings formed an L, and a narrow cupola erupted from the slate roofs where they met. An ancient stone fountain, fuzzy with mold and moss, stood before the half dozen crooked mouths of doors and squinting windows.

A retaining wall of Northwoods oaks, beeches, and aspens pressed against the backs of the smaller building and the carriage house.

All the Poe and the Lovecraft and the M.R. James stories that he loved caught up with him. Miles shut off the ignition, and his mind and belly clenched. He doubled up behind the steering wheel, moaning until the sickness passed. None of the doors or the windows had been boarded up, and every pane of glass remained intact. No kids had been pitching rocks. No bored teenagers had tagged the walls. Maybe the same local historian who had started St. Hamelin's Wikipedia page also maintained basic upkeep?

But for all of that, he tasted bad omens in the air.

An iciness, a sinking, a sickening of the heart—an unredeemed dreariness of thought.

He caught his fingers pulling out another cigarette. Denying himself reprieve, he pushed it back into the pack. True relief would be peeling out of the driveway and watching this place shrink in his rearview. He stashed his Marbs and lighter in the glovebox. He could throw them away later, renew his vow to quit. For now, he unfolded his aching bones from the car. Gravel crunched underfoot as he closed his door. He cupped his hands over his mouth and blew warmth into them. He'd have brought a heavy coat instead of a single sweater, but he hadn't expected this much cold.

A voice boomed. "Hold up there."

A man straight from the Eisenhower administration trucked toward him from the far side of the main building. Crags and creases lined a sixty-something face. His metal-framed glasses hooked around big ears sticking out on either side of his buzz cut.

Miles backed up. "Who are you?"

Bundled in a huge parka, the guy stomped over the gravel. "Who am I? Who are you!" Reaching him, he seized Miles's hand, and pumped it once, twice. "Call me Butch."

Miles glanced down to the odd grip of the handshake—Butch's right thumb was gone.

"How ya doin'?" Butch yelled in his face.

"Fine." Miles tried to pull away, but the man wouldn't let go. Germanic blue eyes sized him up. Butch released his hand, and Miles wiped his palm on his jeans. "I didn't think anyone would be here."

"Me neither." Butch would not step out of Miles's personal space. "Whatcha doin' up this way?"

Shrewd eyes continued taking Miles's measure. Nerve-grating seconds played out.

"I'm looking for...?" Who? He didn't need a person. He needed a shell of a building, evidence of dereliction to photograph. Under the film of snow, the grounds had been mowed and trimmed. No brick nor stone had so much as crumbled off St. Hamelin's, and with no visual decay, pictures of this wouldn't break through to Minnie.

Snowflakes left tiny wet spots on Butch's glasses. "Come on, then. This way." He started off toward the building, limping with an old farmer's walk that Miles had seen a hundred times growing up, with his father at the lumber yard or feed store. Old guys with failing knees, backs wrenched from fifty years of too much hard work for one body.

Miles called after him. "Are you the groundskeeper?"

Butch kept walking.

Miles turned his face to the sky and let the flurries tickle his cheeks. If only the chill would wake him to find that this last year had all been an awful dream. "Wait! Hey, wait up."

Butch reached the front steps. A layer of snow clung to the stone balustrades like exposed layers of fat between bone and skin. Miles ignored his qualms and jogged to catch up, halting at the bottom stair.

Butch scowled down from the top. "You comin' or what?"

"I'll wait." The old guy was just grabbing a snow shovel or a sack of ice-melt salt inside the front doors, right?

"You'll be waiting a long time." Butch crossed the portico, opened up and disappeared through the double doors.

St. Hamelin's blotted out the sky. Should he follow the geezer inside? No one knew Miles was here. Daniel had tipped him off to Blankenheim's, obviously wanted him to find this place, but had no idea that Miles had actually made it.

"I'm going to regret this." Miles moved slowly up the stairs. If he disappeared, Daniel would eventually come looking. And maybe some interior shots would prove abandonment.

The portico swallowed him. Inside, the boards under Miles's feet had no give to them as they should from age and moisture. Butch didn't hand him a snow shovel but rather nodded and started down the hall.

Miles hesitated. Ed Gein had been an old timer, too.

He cursed and took one step, crinkling his nose against the meaty stink. Far worse than a paper mill. A septic tank must have burst. Underneath the top note, a smell like burned dust—Butch must have fired up the furnace for the first time of the season.

"Why do you bother turning on the heat?" Or the lights, for that matter.

Butch stopped at a spot a few doors down. "You need a written invitation, fella?" In the gloom, he looked like one of the ogres from the restaurant. Hunched shoulders, thick body.

The hallway had a musty, disused air that thickened with Miles's every step farther down the gullet. Above wainscoting, the plaster wall darkened to the color of dirt, but nothing looked dilapidated in the lights' dim but steady glow. No broken office chairs or rotting cardboard boxes littered the way. Wooden slat floors hadn't buckled from the damp and cold of passing seasons. The rows of office doors on either side sat plumb.

Still, as he counted lights on his way to Butch, a cryptic sense of isolation wormed into his chest.

An utter depression of soul.

More Poe on his mind. He had tried for years to organize a Masters of the Macabre elective, but for all his love of the spooky, he had never experienced the faintest breath of the supernatural. Wasn't sure he wanted to. But right at this moment, walking down the hallway of St. Hamelin's, a psychic despair half strangled him.

After four lights, he stood next to Butch in front of a door with **Superintendent** printed in bold black on the pebbled glass.

"Here ya go." Butch smiled blocky teeth and rapped his knuckles on the door.

What was this guy playing at?

Miles wanted out. He wanted to suck on a cigarette as his car rolled back over that bridge. He wanted to forget this whole mission and try a different tack. A sympathetic approach might talk reason into Minnie and Daniel. They had surprised him into anger and judgement this afternoon.

From behind the door, a disembodied voice called out, "Come on in."

Butch did.

Miles didn't.

Who could possibly occupy that office?

"Pert near ran into this one wandering the grounds!" Butch moved out of Miles's line of sight.

The man who stood from behind the desk looked a dead ringer for a fat-cat Republican from a 1920's political cartoon. He wore a three-piece suit with notched lapels, the charcoal grey jacket open. The vest stretched at the buttons around his ample middle. A pretentious gold watch chain looped from one tortured button to the vest pocket. His pug nose matched his pink smug lips. He only needed a cigar clutched between two fingers.

The window behind the desk showed the day losing light.

And Miles was losing his grip. Why did St. Hamelin's need a superintendent? It was shut down. Bartender Graham had told him that, right? An accident. A tragedy that riled up Lady Blankenheim.

"Thanks, Butch, I can take it from here." The man tugged the full Windsor knot of his paisley tie.

"Awright." Butch backed out into the hallway, shutting the door and sealing Miles in with a concentration of the noxious burst-pipe odor.

Miles gagged and quickly covered his mouth.

"I'm Superintendent Schramm." The man spoke with the clipped diction of omnipotence. "Have a seat, Mister...?"

Sickness passed. "Baumgartner. Miles Baumgartner."

"Ah, yes."

Miles waded deeper into the stink. The office's low lighting reflected off brass figures and globes between leather-bound volumes on mahogany bookshelves lining the right-hand wall. Along the left wall hung black-and-white photographs in gilt frames, engraved with dates from before he'd even been born. St. Hamelin's boys throughout the years. Now long dead. Miles shivered, despite a small brick fireplace pulsing with fire and heat. After the photos, a closed door that must have led into a secretary's office. Another closed door stood in a recess between the fireplace and the superintendent's gargantuan cherrywood desk.

Without offering a handshake, Schramm sat back into a slat-backed, antique desk chair that squealed under his weight.

"Pardon the smell." Schramm's hands fluttered over his pens on the blotter. "A broken pipe in our septic system." He touched a brass, serrated letter opener. Then a forest-green marble paperweight of a small sphere on a pedestal—looked like a Golden Globe award. The chair squeaked with every fidget. "I'm afraid our man Butch might not be up to the task." All at once, the man's hands jerked off the desktop and gripped the arms of his chair. "We don't receive many visitors out here."

The way Schramm stressed *visitors* made it sound like *intruders.*

"I...." Miles coughed out the frog in his throat. "I'd been told that you closed down."

Superintendent Schramm steepled his fingers and tapped them on his chin. "What can I help you with, Mr. Baumgartner?"

Miles floundered for an answer. What was his play now? He took a seat in one of the two chairs on his side of the desk and crossed his legs. He uncrossed them and leaned forward. "I'm on a peculiar mission."

"Do tell."

A nervous laugh. "I really expected an abandoned orphanage."

Schramm pinned him with piggish eyes. "What business did you have with an abandoned orphanage?"

"Right." His collar seemed to have tightened.

Schramm adjusted in his chair, the rollers drifting him off to the side. He didn't try to get back to center, but he took mercy on Miles. "St. Hamelin's, the orphanage, is indeed no more. Shortly after I took over, we shifted our aim toward rehabilitating wayward youths. St. Hamelin's Reformatory proceeds as a private enterprise. A select few students. We operate with a skeleton crew staff these days."

"I see."

But he didn't. He couldn't process Schramm's brief history lesson because from the instant he pulled into the drive, every moment, every sight, every smell, gave him the creeps. Building up exponentially, until all the bad portent saturated his brain.

"And your peculiar mission?"

"What?" Miles had missed something. Oh yes— Schramm wanted to know why he'd come. Good question. He closed his eyes and took the plunge. "Do you have my dead nephew locked up in here?"

Schramm watched him with the inscrutable expression of a stone god.

All the moisture in Miles's mouth dried up.

Schramm swiveled and pushed a button on an ancient intercom on the far edge of the desk. "Miss Poole, would you please bring in Mr. Gunderson?"

Mr. Gunderson? Why was Daniel here? Certainly not to discourage him. Wasn't the point of Daniel's guiding him to Blankenheim's to help Miles find St. Hamelin's?

The inter-office door *snick*ed. A lilac breeze wafted in, clenching Miles's heart with painful nostalgia. There and gone. A young woman entered—a Grace Kelly pageboy and a simple ankle-length dress and matching grey cardigan with bulging, stretched-out pockets.

Obliged to be plain... no article of attire that was not made with extreme simplicity.

Yeah, she was very Jane Eyre, with a modest prettiness. Pretty but stern. Her mouth condensed into a thin, severe line as she examined him, and her eyes sent a shudder through his core. She stepped out of the way for Mr. Gunderson.

Wrong Mr. Gunderson.

Four

He felt stoned. Baked.

Lifted aloft on a great wave of infatuation and pity.

"I left your baseball in the car." The words sighed between numb lips.

Ian's trouser legs swished as he shuffled toward the fireplace, leaving in his wake a musty smell of tilled earth. The boy who should have been dead halted like he'd found his mark, relaxed in a sort of parade rest, and gazed placidly ahead.

Ian's scrunchy face went blurry. Miles wiped away tears and dried his fingertips on his jeans. How could he feel the rough denim so vividly when none of this was real? But the texture of this moment wasn't dull and all misty and dreamlike. Indeed, his senses sharpened. He transformed into his twelve-year-old self at the Spinning Wheels roller rink on a Friday night, the greasy pepperoni pizza and caffeine from pitchers of Mountain Dew had acted like kiddie-acid, expanding his consciousness to preternatural perception.

Miles sprang from his chair and enveloped his nephew in a desperate embrace. His soul emptied like lungs with the wind knocked out. The reality of Ian filled him back up, and Miles squeezed tighter, drunk on the pungent, bad body odor of him. The solidity of the boy's chest and arms. The heat of breath on his neck.

An insectile drone resolved into human speech.

"Please. Please, Mr. Baumgartner. You're scaring the boy."

"Right. Right." Releasing Ian hurt like warm flesh ripped off a frozen pole. He sat back down, but Ian didn't look scared. He didn't seem relieved either. The boy exuded indifference.

But his almost-son was alive! Technicolor flooded back into his drab world. He absorbed the sight of Ian—his tall thin frame dressed in a navy-blue school uniform as if this were a pricey prep school, a red and gold crest—a Luther rose?—over the left breast, just the knot of his red tie visible over the blazer's top button.

Miles never knew what Ian wore to his grave. Nine months ago, when he'd found the funeral director and passed on Minnie's closed casket request, he hadn't thought to spend a few final minutes with his nephew. One last look. A final goodbye. He had followed the soft notes of organ music and rejoined his family. Peace lilies cloyed up the air. Thank God the coffin hadn't been child-sized.

"What?" Miles blinked to clear his head.

"Alive and well." Schramm repeated.

And looking better than that jacked-up face in Minnie's Facebook post—skin doughy, mouth slack. Eyes caught mid-blink. A wax figure's voided expression. He'd thought that Daniel had photoshopped from a terrible picture.

Daniel's voice floated back to him: *How would we know how to do that?*

"Ian...."

Minnie and Daniel's hogwash had turned out to be true. Ian stood four feet away, healthy but distracted. No misidentifying anyone now. That was Ian's face. Small nose and ears and mouth—that cute, pinched quality as if caught half-grinning, half-squinting. A perpetual flush painted on his cheekbones.

But where was the exuberance? The verve behind his eyes?

Overwhelmed, that was all.

"Ian. I'm...." Astonished. Amazed. Thrilled.

Afraid?

"He's a well-behaved lad."

"Yessir." Ian smiled. Or at least showed his teeth. "Hello, Uncle Miles." Perfunctory.

No doubt St. Hamelin's heavy walls and dark halls oppressed all the young men banished here.

Too fine and fair for the little horrid, unclean school world.

Miles massaged the first pangs of a headache at his temples. Questions atop questions, atop more questions, all wrestling to be asked first. Might he be lucid dreaming? Asleep on the scratchy bedspread in his Paradise room? He wanted Ian to be alive so badly. He would have bled for it. But how could this be happening?

The temperature in the crammed office inched steadily upward. Sweat rolled from his hairline. He'd never felt damp underarms in a dream before. The busted sewer pipe smell grew more intimate, pressing against his skin. That was no phantom.

"Can I have a few minutes with Ian? Alone. Please."

Miss Poole remained silent and still. Ian just stood there. Schramm leaned over his folded hands on the desk, eyeing Miles. Had he not asked that out loud? Discomfort and exhaustion red-lined into anxiety. Why were they just staring?

Schramm dug into his vest and checked his pocket watch. "Miss Poole, why don't you show our guest to the cafeteria. See if Betty could prepare a special supper plate. Give Mister...." He looked to Miles as if he'd forgotten.

"Baumgartner."

"And Mr. Gunderson some time to chat."

Miss Poole glowered with her chill, mocha eyes.

Miss Poole led their procession twenty feet farther down the hallway and into the belly of St. Hamelin's.

At a T-juncture, arched double-doors on the left led to some secret chamber. The three of them hung a right into a wide corridor. Decorative arcading seemed the only interior nod to the fancy stonework of the façade. From Romanesque cathedral to office space and back again. Which was the disguise? Which the truth?

Through the door at the end, they emerged into dusky violet.

"Aren't you supposed to be taking us to the cafeteria?"

Miss Poole didn't turn. "I am."

She led their troupe toward that stout building with the mansard roof that he'd seen from the driveway. A half-pace behind Ian, Miles watched the imprint of his nephew's shoes in the fallen snow. Snowflakes aged Ian's hair into salt-and-pepper. More dotted the blazer's shoulders.

A hundred feet farther toward the woods, smoke lazed from the chimney of a cottage, a pastoral tableau discordant from the brick and stone of the main building. Butch the groundskeeper's house? How many people staffed this surprise reformatory? How many... inmates? Offenders? Whatevers?

They plodded up the stairs and into the brick building. "You walk all the way out here for every meal?"

The foyer opened onto two stairwells, one down, one up. Miss Poole had already walked halfway up the latter. She paused. She didn't look over her shoulder but did turn her head to the profile. "In the winter we use a tunnel from the main building."

"You don't consider this winter?"

She continued up the steps, Ian at her heels. The darkness at the bottom of the downward staircase looked thick enough to conceal predatory eyes. Miles hurried up the stairs after his nephew.

Through an archway at the top of the stairs, Miss Poole hit a switch, and dingy non-fluorescents lit the cafeteria. Same as any. Same as Mari Newton High where he'd taught grammar, essay-writing, and literature to twenty-six years' worth of students. Except Mari Newton didn't boast six rows of tables, four deep. Or twenty-foot high floor-to-ceiling windows. Summers, this cafeteria would have been bright as a solarium. Currently, those windows showed encroaching evening. Cut-outs in the far wall presented the usual buffet style lunch line; beyond, where light didn't reach, clustered the shapes of ovens and refrigerators.

Ian threaded his way through tables until finding the right one.

Miles made a show of rubbing his arms for warmth. "Christ, it's freezing inside." Every exhale floated around his head.

Miss Poole brushed a strand of damp hair from her face. "I'll ask Betty if she can serve you a late dinner." Her eyes caught the light and chameleoned into deep green aggravation.

"I'm sorry to put you out."

She held her cardigan tight around her middle. "Watch yourself." She turned on her heels and left them.

Miles pulled out a chair across from Ian—straight-backed wooden, not a metal folding chair. The funeral home had had folding chairs. Tastefully cloth-covered, but still folding chairs. They had squeaked while the family eulogized the boy sitting in front of him right now.

Ian rested his hands on the table and folded them as if in prayer. "Why are you looking at me like that?"

His index finger was gone.

"I can't believe you're...." Miles resisted the impulse to poke Ian, make sure he was real. "We buried you."

Ian tucked his hands in his lap. "I didn't die in that crash. They misidentified the body."

"I know." He really couldn't stop staring. "Aren't you happy to see me?"

Ian raised one shoulder in a half-shrug. "How did you find me? Mom didn't send you."

"No, she didn't."

"You shouldn't be here."

Miles wrung his hands. The boy sitting in front of him looked like his Ian. Sounded a little like him, too. But even if Ian wasn't happy to see his uncle, shouldn't he at least be surprised? This flat effect unsettled him. If Superintendent Schramm confessed to growing a pod person in the basement and replacing Ian, Miles would have believed it. A shadow lurked behind Ian's vacant blue eyes; a secret veiled by a dead space.

"What happened to you?"

Ian raised both shoulders now, in a slow-motion shrug.

"Just...." Miles opened his hands, welcoming any statement. "Tell me what happened that night. Help me understand."

Ian sighed. "It wasn't my idea to steal the car, but I went along with it. We just wanted a joy ride." No more emotion than in a first table read for a bad play.

The kitchen door swung open, and a plump woman with a face flushed by rosacea marched toward them with a tray. Her pink housecoat flapped around her. Wet tawny hair hung down, limp as scarecrow straws. St. Hamelin's cook let the tray drop to the table. "Hewa gobba dinah."

They both stared at her, but Miles spoke. "I'm sorry, what?"

"Gobba dinah yew too." She slammed down a couple glasses of water before handing each of her guests a plate with two slabs of meatloaf and a runny mound of mashed potatoes, all drowning in brown gravy. Blankenheim's sauerbraten hadn't worn off yet, but even if it had, the aroma off the plate made his stomach seize. This steaming mess would never have passed his lips.

Even so, his manners kicked in. "Thank you."

"Eww welco."

You're welcome. Poor woman had the worst speech impediment he'd ever heard.

She nodded, duty fulfilled, and huffed back to the kitchen.

Ian hunched over his plate, staring at the food but making no move to eat. This would have been Ian's cue to screw his face into mock horror, and they would giggle together. But he didn't.

Their eyes met.

"You need to come home. This is ridiculous. I'll talk to Jeremy—he knows how these things work. Maybe he can make a deal with the prosecutor. At least talk with your lawyer."

"My lawyer?" Ian sat back, that weird emptiness still in his eyes. "I don't have a lawyer. And I can't just leave."

No lawyer? Must have had some lame public defender. Wow. Daniel couldn't spring for a shark in an Armani suit?

"Case worker, then. Whoever's assigned to your case. And believe me, Jeremy knows people. What you've been through—I think you've paid your debt to society. Do you accept your share of the responsibility? Good. We'll work out some kind of deal."

Ian shook his head. "I need to be here."

"What are—" But Miles stopped himself. Ian's stiff attitude; the hesitancy in his eyes—Why hadn't he seen this right away? Ian was ashamed. Didn't want his favorite uncle hearing the details of his downward spiral.

This he could work with.

"Do you know why I teach?"

Ian twitched his head in a little shake of *no*.

"Look, you don't need to be embarrassed. You don't know this, but I was a troublemaker in grade school. Bored, really. I understood the material, but I hated worksheets. College was going to suit me—know the stuff, take a couple tests, write a couple papers. But in those early years, my grades sucked because I didn't do the daily work. I acted out. Small stuff at first—spit balls and fart noises.

"Every year my new teacher knew my reputation: bad grades, detention. By the time I got to middle school, all my frustration had fermented into anger. Another eighth grader—Billy Rubin, never forget that trashy kid—made a crack about some history test. I pushed him. Didn't even think about it. About where we stood. Just pushed him. We'd stopped at the landing going down to the first floor. When I pushed Billy...."

Cottonmouth. This was harder to tell than he'd expected. His hand shook as he brought the glass of water to his lips.

"When I pushed Billy, his heels slipped on the edge of the top riser. His eyes got so big. So scared. He pinwheeled his arms, and I just stood there. I was scared, too. Just as shocked as Billy when he lost his fight for balance and tumbled down the stairs.

"I fractured Billy's wrist. Broke his right orbital bone. That boy limped around school for two months looking like a city bus had smashed him. That earned me real trouble. Not detention or Saturday school that time. The police questioned me. I was court-ordered to see a psychologist every week for nine months."

Caught up by this outpouring of his life story, Miles grabbed his fork and dug in, scooping a giant heap of cooled mashed potatoes and meatloaf into his mouth. It tasted like grey water ladled up from a sewer. He squeezed his eyes shut and focused on chewing. The masticated glop slid down his throat. The fork clinked against the plate as he set it down.

"No one wanted to be friends with me." He coughed. Swallowed to get rid of the paste in his throat. "Teachers had written me off. Your grandma and grandpa grounded me for that entire summer. At thirteen, my life was over. I couldn't even watch TV or rent movies until September. A week into June, I'd half lost my mind. Desperation drove me into Dad's den, looking through his bookcases. I started *Oliver Twist* because the kid felt pretty familiar. I devoured that novel and chose *David Copperfield* next. When I finished that big book, your grandma drove me to the library, and I signed my first library card. I was banned from riding my BMX through the trails, and from hiking along the railroad tracks. I couldn't even go to Bronzeman's Beach. Not once that summer. But my mom would take me to the library anytime I wanted.

"After Labor Day, I started high school. New building. New teachers. Same kids, but except for Billy and his friends, most had forgotten about me. Those new teachers sure didn't know me. They saw me as the kid who read in study hall. My patience had grown over that summer, and my grades improved.

"And then one day around Halloween, as I left Mr. Roberts' World History, he pulled me aside and asked if I could go out to his car and grab a box of notebooks he'd left in there. Mr. Roberts was an older guy, been around forever. Strict but respected. He handed me the keys to his Corolla. I walked out to the teachers' parking, staring at those keys in my palm. Mr. Roberts had trusted me. Implicitly. A teacher had handed over his keys and asked me for a favor. That moment changed my life. I vowed never to backslide into the jerk I had become those last couple of years. I decided I wanted to teach, be like Mr. Roberts and give kids their own chances."

Ian blinked. "What does that have to do with me?"

Holy hell, when had his nephew gotten so dense?

"I'm saying that I made plenty of bad mistakes, but I used them, and they made me what I am. It's why I don't give a damn that you stole a car. You're a good kid. Always have been. You'll find your way back if you can—"

Betty startled him as she picked up both plates. Without comment that Ian hadn't touched a thing and Miles hadn't made much of a dent, she garbled a goodbye and hoofed to the kitchen.

Miles scratched an itch on the back of his head. "Tell me what's going on with you."

Ian gathered his thoughts for a long time. "I laid in a hospital bed for months. I didn't know who I was. No one knew who I was."

Amnesia? The accident scrambling him up that bad could certainly explain a personality shift.

Ian's lips quivered. In effort of holding back tears? Or testing words until the right ones found their way out?

"We just wanted to go on a stony cruise. I was so high that night, everything sounded like a good idea." Ian gazed over Miles's shoulder, as if viewing past decisions play out in the vast emptiness of the cafeteria like clips on a movie screen. "Through the windshield, the world looked like a fish tank. Houses and street lights passed by hazy and weightless. He drove us out to the country, winding through the back roads. It felt like we were going so slow...."

Ian's measured pace matched his story's, and Miles visualized that hypnotic night.

"When headlights swam up in front of us, everything sped up. Like those old baseball clips we used to watch: Babe Ruth fast-forwarding through practice swings." Ian started to sound like himself. "I don't remember swerving and hitting the bridge, but I remember a shockwave like lightning to my head. Gravity turned upside down. Sound was swallowed up. Then I couldn't see, and I remember thinking very clearly: This is how I die. Will I go to heaven? Will I wink out of existence? One way or the other, I'm about to find out."

Life finally shone in Ian's eyes.

Miles leaned into Ian's pause. "What's the next thing you remember?"

The natural flush drained from Ian's cheeks. "I stood on the road in the dark and the quiet. The car, the bridge, everything vanished except for all these trees on either side of me making a tunnel. There wasn't any light at the end of it. I felt more alone than I'd ever been. The silence was enormous. I stood in a bubble surrounded by... nothing. Absolute nothing."

Nothingness lies coiled in the heart of being—like a worm.

More Sartre. Nausea stirred in Mile's belly as Ian continued.

"A fog rose up over my shoes, up to my knees. The trees had spread out, and the fog glowed blue and wound through them like... eddies. Yeah, like eddies in a stream. My body didn't hurt. My body didn't feel like anything. I started walking, but it felt more like floating. Farther and farther along, and whispers spoke through the trees and the blue fog sort of boiled around the trunks. The whispers got louder."

Ian scrunched his face in thought, returning to the nephew Miles loved. The boy with endless iterations of that elastic expression. This one of breathless concentration; his face amazed and confused and concerned like that afternoon they had spent wandering through Ripley's Believe It or Not on the Wisconsin Dells' strip, inspecting dusty-skinned shrunken heads.

"Whispers started screaming. Terrible screams flung at me from the darkness all around, and I knew those screams were the dead, like me, lost and floating."

Ian blinked as if coming awake. He gasped like he had remembered more. He finished in a rush. "I floated up and up, and a nurse was staring down at me through this haze while the screams... the screams kept coming, but then it turned out to be me screaming and coming out of the coma. Only I guess I wasn't because they told me later that all I did was open my eyes, and they knew I was with them."

Miles tried to swallow the lump in his throat, stuck in there like the time in second grade when he chewed up Craig Pfaff's note to him and tried to eat the evidence. That hadn't worked like in the movies—Miss Yenchesky jammed her small hand into his mouth and pulled out all the soppy paper. Ian's story tasted like that note.

"Hiya all doin!" Butch trudged toward them, peering over the frosted-up glasses perched on his bulbous nose. "Dr. Schramm needs to see ya."

Now it was Doctor Schramm?

The tendons in Miles's neck creaked as he looked up at Butch. "We're busy here." His head still walked with Ian through the screaming tunnel. The reality of the shouting groundskeeper felt too harsh an awakening.

Butch dropped the jovial act. "I said Schramm needs to talk to ya."

The animation in Ian's face smoothed over. Whatever more he might have to tell Miles, this interruption had clammed him up.

He hated breaking the moment he had shared with Ian, but he stood, grumbling. "What does Schramm want?"

Butch inched into Miles's personal space and hollered. "How should I know?" But he grinned like he knew exactly what Schramm wanted.

⁂

While night had encroached, three or more inches of snow had accumulated. More continued to fall, no longer light and fluffy but hard and blinding.

Like that *Little House on the Prairie* episode in which a winter storm barreled toward Walnut Grove one Christmas Eve. Miss Beadle bundled up all the kids and sent them home early to beat the snow, but she had waited too long. All the kids died in the blizzard.

Or did he have that part wrong?

Five

"Under whose authority are you keeping Ian here?" Miles slammed his pointer finger onto Schramm's desk, which hurt but he couldn't show it. He had barged in, demanding answers. "Is this compulsory or voluntary? My sister said the court's involved—is this a sentence?"

Schramm surrendered, hands in the air. "We shall have ample time to discuss this tomorrow morning."

"Tomorrow morn—? No. Next time you see me, I'll be with my attorney." He turned toward Ian, who slumped into one of the chairs, disaffected by his uncle's efforts.

"Please, Mr. Baumgartner. Sit. Let us talk like civilized gentlemen."

Civilized? He'd give Schramm civilized. He was going to litigate the pants off St. Hamelin's and its board and the county and whomever else he could think of. Miles turned to storm out, but Butch clapped him on the back. "I almost fergot. I moved yer car outta the snow for ya!"

"Wait. What? You moved my car?"

"Huh?" Butch shouted.

"How did you move my car?"

Butch's grizzled mug broke into a smile as he held out Miles's keys, the House on the Rock fob—a souvenir from a Miles and Ian adventure—clutched between the index and middle finger of the thumbless hand. "Ya left em in the ignition."

Wouldn't Jeremy just love that? He'd be shaking his head at careless Miles.

Schramm answered for Butch. "I asked him to park your car in the old carriage house. Out of the snow for the night."

"For the night?"

"Indeed. You shall be our guest until morning."

The audacity! But Schramm and Butch had caught him off-guard, and his response came out petulant. "I'm not staying here."

"You must." Schramm waved to the window behind him. "The storm is worsening, and we cannot have you mired down in the wilderness. Besides...." A politician's poisonous smile crept over Schramm's face. "You've come such a long way to spend time with young Mr. Gunderson here."

Ian groaned and crossed his arms over his chest. Butch hovered behind.

Schramm rubbed his palms together. "Excellent! Miss Poole will show you to your room."

Schramm rose, and he and Butch herded Ian and Miles out of the office. Miss Poole waited in the hallway.

Should he be outraged? Grateful?

Miles reined in his stubborn streak. Schramm had a point, both about the snowstorm and spending more time with Ian.

He tugged his nephew's blazer sleeve. "I'll make some phone calls, and maybe I can take you home with me tomorrow."

Ian scowled. "I wish you would leave." He sulked past Miss Poole.

"Come back here."

Without a single glance backward, Ian disappeared into the gloom of the hallway beyond the T-junction.

Miles started as Butch wrapped an arm around his shoulders. "Hey, lemme ask ya something!" Butch pulled him into a confidential aside.

"Yes, Butch?"

Butch tilted his chin close to Miles's ear but didn't lower his volume. "Miz Poole sure a fine lookin' thing, ain't she?" Butch winked and slapped him on the back, sending Miles staggering a step.

Holy hell, what a madhouse.

Miles joined Miss Poole a few doors down at a vestibule. In any modern building, this would have been the elevator nook. In St. Hamelin's, the space let onto wide, wooden stairs. His escort didn't wait.

"Miss Poole?" Miles's skin crawled as he set his foot on the first riser. Then the second. "Where are you putting me?"

"Each dormitory floor has a couple of rooms reserved as teachers' quarters."

"Hey, I'm not sharing with somebody, am I?" Why did bad always turn into worse for him?

"Don't worry, they're all gone."

"Gone?"

Miss Poole stopped and glanced back at him "Left already for Thanksgiving break, I mean." She sighed, a bird's breath. "You'll have a quiet night."

Their footsteps thunked as he and Miss Poole followed the twisting stairs up two landings. She led him through a doorway and down a long, dank corridor. Up another flight of stairs. One right turn followed by a quick left. More stairs. All the walls were peeling paint. Each new passage narrower than the one before. Though they ascended, every step increased the sensation of dense, underground air.

After so much silence, she finally spoke. "You don't belong here."

He clung to the railing and caught his breath. "Ian pretty much said the same thing."

Miss Poole stopped on a landing identical to the dozens before; at her back, a door like any of the others they had passed. "You need to leave."

"I'd like nothing more." Miles righted himself. "But your superintendent thinks otherwise."

His lungs burned after all these stairs. He shouldn't have bought that pack of cigarettes.

Crap.

He'd left them in the car.

Miss Poole's eyes shaded to a dark tea color.

"This is the fifth floor of the dormitory." She opened up the door to another deserted hallway, four-panel doors on both sides the entire length down.

Underfoot, a threadbare red carpet, worn shiny down the middle. Frayed edges pulled back from the walls. So familiar. How did he recognize this carpet?

Miss Poole withdrew a huge key ring from her Cardigan pocket. The mass of keys tinkled musically, irritated birds squawking in their nest, as Miss Poole flipped through them with an impatient flick of her wrist. She slammed the correct key into the lock of the door across from the stairwell, and let him in.

Spooky how much it resembled his college dorm. Stuffed into the seven-by-seven room, a writing desk filled a corner under the single window—one fat arc of furniture polish swiped over the desktop. A narrow bed had been made up, an extra blanket folded at its foot. A closet with an accordion door was pulled closed. Opposite the bed stood a tall, thin bureau.

"Nice lodgings for such an old orphanage."

Bleak, dark, and piercing cold, it was a night for the well-housed and fed to draw round the bright fire.

"Hot in here." And mildewy, like when that brutal windstorm knocked a cottonwood limb through the high school library's roof and water-damaged half the books. He parted the stiff, dormitory curtains and looked down into a courtyard. After figuring out the latch, he opened the window and let in some arctic chill. While the radiator at his knees expelled tropical heat.

"They updated this wing in the Forties, so you should find it comfortable for the night. Lavatories are down at the far end. Other than to relieve yourself, don't leave your room. I'll come for you in the morning."

Miss Poole high-tailed it before he could protest. What about Ian? He'd been promised time with his nephew. What was this wait until morning crap?

A lilac mist lingered in her wake. Same perfume that his mother wore for St. Mark's Sunday services. Wearing her cornflower blue dress and those pewter earrings of full-bloom roses that he mistook for cabbages.

Had Miss Poole trapped him in his cell like Jonathan Harker in Dracula's castle? He hadn't heard the *click* of the lock, but that didn't mean she hadn't. The stairwell door slammed closed, and he counted to eight...nine...ten....

His fingertips brushed the brass doorknob. What would he do if she really had locked him in? What *could* he do? The heat from the radiator pulled beads of sweat from his brow, yet the freezing air from the window raised goosebumps over his arms.

The door opened easily under his hand.

Sort of disappointing, after the build-up. He peeked into the hall. A monotone murmur from the rooms, from the unseen children of St. Hamelin's.

He kept the door open. To regulate the temperature, not because this place gave him the heebie jeebies. Not that at all.

The top drawer of the bureau held a couple mildewy towels. The other five drawers proved empty and cleaned with more hasty wipes pushing the dust into the corners. At the bed, he pressed both hands down to test its comfort level. Just a cot—a thin mattress on an old metal frame.

He sat on the edge. What was he going to do all night? He'd never sleep. Ian was alive! And this place.... In the movies he watched with Ian, the spooky houses sometimes glamored their visitors—a sort of hypnosis enticing them to stay and offer up their souls. St. Hamelin's did not invite. St. Hamelin's was cold and hard.

The supernatural comparison did not feel hyperbolic.

A low voltage current coursed through him, giving him what Minnie called the goosies. A disturbance in the Force. The impression of being watched, emanating from the closet. The fine hairs on the back of his neck tingled. He stood, and walked into the sensation. His hand was steady but hesitant, closing in on the handle of the accordion door as if it were a hot pan on a burner. His fingers made contact, and he wrenched open the door, quick as ripping off a Band-Aid.

Holy hell.

His heart jumped into his throat.

A boy no older than ten stood ramrod-straight, gazing up at him.

"What the hell are you doing?"

The boy bared his teeth in some mixture of nervousness and joviality. Big horse teeth overlapped; two lower ones thrust out like bent matches in a book. "I wanted to scare you."

Goddamn. He'd done a good job of it.

"Get out of there."

Teeth stepped out. Miles shirked the impulse to guide the kid out by the shoulder. Miles didn't want to touch him. But Teeth went willingly enough; without a backward glance, he exited and turned down the hallway.

Miles closed the door. Where was a lock when you needed one? With a frustrated grunt, he flopped onto the bed. Dust exploded from the coverlet, encompassing his head in a cloud. He coughed. Sneezed. Sneezed again. And again. One last time. He sat up and wiped his face. Thick, green snot slicked his hand.

He bounded over to the dresser for one of the towels and scrubbed his face and hands. Still gross. He used the towel to open the door, a maneuver that got the slime over his hands again. He headed down the hall, over that familiar carpet. He heard rustling from behind closed doors and faint voices as the juvie inhabitants of St. Hamelin's gossiped or gambled or whatever delinquents did these days. The last door on the right didn't have four panels, but was just a plain flat door. Probably a janitor's closet. On the opposite side, a metal hatch inset into the wall. A laundry chute? Incinerator?

Inside the bathroom—lavatory, as Miss Poole so quaintly put it—enough hallway light spilled in that he didn't bother searching for a switch with his gooey hands.

St. Hamelin's chilly fifth floor bathroom called to mind the London tube stations in James Bond movies. It was the pair of archways straight ahead separating the space into three sections. Miles had flown to England for a literary tour—Shakespeare's Globe, Keats's house, Dickens's Museum, of course—and the Underground didn't have the portent of those spy flicks. In here, black and white diamond tiles made up the floor. Grey tiles were on the walls. The first archway let onto a row on one side of old urinals with overelaborate embellishments, and on the other, wooden-framed stalls with doors ending knee-high off the ground. About a dozen of each.

A window at the far wall let in night's bluish glow, which lit only enough to show a tile curb rising from the floor suggesting that the last third housed showers.

He hung a right, to a bank of sinks.

"Uck."

Half a dozen rust-stained basins with grimy mirrors over each filled the wall. An ambiguous mirror man gazed back at him. He tossed the dirty towel into the first sink, and moved to the next one. The taps wouldn't budge under the heels of his hands. He clenched his jaw and went to the next in line. After a couple good tugs, the cold tap turned with a begrudging squeal. Water, smelling like a dirty toilet, belched from the faucet. He waited while the stream lightened from dark brown to tan, and from tan to almost clear. No soap. He rubbed his hands together. Dirty water sluiced down the drain. He cupped his hands til they filled and patted down his face. Satisfied, he stopped the tap. What a surprise—no towel dispensers or air dryers.

A scuffling from the back of the lavatory made Miles go still.

It seemed to me I had never breathed an atmosphere so vile.

Water dripped down his nose and chin. The scuffle didn't repeat—had he really heard anything? He stepped toward the first archway. "Hello?"

Slurp.

All around him the air hung sour from ancient urinations and defecations. He started past the urinals. Slow. Why hadn't he turned on the lights?

As if I also were buried in a vast grave full of secrets.

If he went back for the switch, he might just leave. Good sense or cowardice? The toilet stall doors were firmly closed, but he knew how those hinges would squeal under the pressure of a stealthy hand.

A scrape. A grunt.

Could have been old pipes wheezing.

Curiosity got the better of him. His steps echoed through the second archway.

A muffled, sloppy sound floated from around the corner to the showers.

The taste of dread—like stale nicotine—coated his tongue.

He called to the hidden recesses. "Hey."

A satisfied smack of lips.

The darkness of an impenetrable night.

Soft, cruel laughter.

His toes touched the moonglow from the window. The drain in the tiled floor exhaled a rank odor that hung thick in the humidity.

A strangled cry burst through the quiet. There and gone.

Perhaps you had better go if you have any friends amongst the savages near by.

He turned the corner to face the showers and was immediately buffeted by a draft. A pair of green eyes pierced the darkness, hanging in the air.

Miles staggered backward.

A sheen in the murk coalesced like cigar smoke blown into a vase. The shape of a boy brought a finger to his lips: *Shhh.*

Miles turned and fled the bathroom. Behind him, a child's laughter rang against the tiles.

He slammed closed the door of his cloister. Dizzy, he leaned against it, his heartbeat pounding in his ears.

"Get a grip." Advice both weak and hollow.

Wind through the open window had turned the room into a freezer. Giving up his post, Miles went and closed it. Outside, snow fell harder and faster.

Okay, so what had he actually seen in the bathroom? He paced to the door and back. Another prank like the boy hiding in the closet. Back to the door, then to the window. Fifth-floor jokesters hazing their guest. He chuckled. Wow. They'd gotten him again. Today had been a long series of stresses, his tired nerves worn to the breaking point. That closet experience had primed him for a more advanced trick.

But how had they done it?

A cigarette would take the edge off.

Eh, the temptation! Good thing the pack was in the car and out of reach.

Miles stripped the bedspread off, bundled the dusty thing into a ball, and threw it into the closet. The spare blanket smelled fresh, and the sheets looked white, clean. He shook out the blanket and flattened it over the bed. He killed the lights and lay down—carefully this time—to rest his back.

He pulled his phone from his pocket to check the time.

And messages.

His back muscles relaxed and leaked pain. He ground his teeth.

What might Jeremy be up to right now? Getting an early start at the bars? Fashionably late dinner? Stretched out on their sofa? Did Jeremy miss him? Did Jeremy think about him at all? Miles had promised Ian that Jeremy would help untie the red tape to freedom, obligating himself to set aside ego and break their silent impasse. He needed lawyer-Jeremy, but who knew—maybe ex-boy-friend-Jeremy might be happy to hear from him.

"Oh, come on." His smartphone lay dead in his hands, and he'd left the charger in the car with his cigarettes.

Too exhausted to care, he reached up behind his head and set the phone on the writing desk. It couldn't be any later than seven or eight, but wouldn't sleep be a sweet reprieve? He was stuck here for the night no matter what, and his plans could wait until tomorrow.

Ghostly luminescence from the window threw a glowing patch upon the opposite wall. Black spots— shadows of the snow—floated over the greying plaster. The radiator ticked, and the burnt dust smell grew faint. Miles closed his eyes and started to drift.

The carpet from the theater!

His eyes popped open. That's why the hallway carpet looked familiar. For their second date, Miles had taken Jeremy to the movies. Cineplexes were great for him and Ian, but he'd chosen the Soglin 7 for the date—a little in-die movie house, with exposed-brick walls for a hip touch. Even if dim lighting fixtures, ratty carpet, and greasy fin-gerprints on the concession counter gave the place a run-down feel. It was that crimson carpet, on which trudging feet had worn a thinning strip, that exactly resembled St. Hamelin's carpet right outside his room.

Miles smiled. That night, they'd broken date eti-quette and loaded up on popcorn, sodas, and over-priced candy. They'd silently agreed on middle seats in row ten. Shane Carruth's *Upstream Color* mesmerized Miles, but he worried that Jeremy's immobile posture came not from rapture but boredom. Neither spoke as the lights came up and credits rolled. Without a word, they emerged from the theater and meandered a few doors down to Café Monet. The bar featured more exposed brick. Burnished Mahogany and art deco chairs. They ordered drinks and found a table in the back under black-and-white photographs of the city. They each sipped, then finally spoke in a rush, words tumbling over each other.

"That was fantastic."

"I've never seen anything like that."

They'd gotten drunk and chatted til closing time.

Lying on this awful mattress in St. Hamelin's, sleep suddenly felt a century away. He rubbed his eyes until the pressure brought white starbursts to his vision.

Did Jeremy go to the Soglin 7 with Duck Boy? Did they feast on gummy worms and Hot Tamales? Did they argue Jung versus Kant until dawn?

Yeah, right.

But what if they did?

Or what if Jeremy made fun of his ex to his new hot piece of ass? All the silly things that they had done while in love became liabilities when broken up. How, over *Survivor* and Taco Bell, they narrated their dinner using Jeff Probst exclamations:

"Miles adding more hot sauce!"

"Jeremy double-dipping his chip."

"Eat that last one. You have got to dig deep!"

Jeremy would fudge the details to make Miles out to be foolish, while those two lay in bed and laughed at him.

Muscles in his cheeks tightened as he ground his teeth. Anger uncoiled in his stomach. He'd be stewing over this all night.

Instead, he fell asleep a minute later.

And dreamed of breakups. Divorce. He wandered a city on fire with his feet strapped into roller skates that he couldn't unlace or remove. Cadaverous hookers huddled in back allies and searched blown-out veins for any viable port to slam heroin. Jeremy waited in some impenetrable distance for him to call, but Miles's fattened fingers couldn't hit the right keys on his phone. Other ex-boyfriends flitted in as substitutes for Jeremy—first it was Ben who waited for his call. Then Brian. Then that jackass, Jim, who'd stolen eight hundred dollars during their torrid month-long affair in Miami. Miles cried out, and from around some far corner Jeremy answered: "I'm here." But when he turned onto the next street, he found only a vagrant in a filthy suit, serenading him with a song about a long-lost home.

He gasped awake.

How long had he been out? The room had gone completely dark.

He wasn't alone. Somewhere in the solid back, someone watched him.

Drakkar Noir surged into the room.

"Jeremy?"

Heartache pierced his gut.

A shadow shape stood just inside the door. "Miles."

"Jeremy."

"None of this was your concern."

Bullshit. "You were texting some other guy." His eyes fought to adjust to the darkness. "Way to turn this around. You wronged me, but I'm at fault for invading your privacy?"

Why did all their conversations curdle?

"Forget this, Miles. I'm here now."

He scrambled out of bed and in a sleep-fog rushed toward Jeremy. Jeremy had come back. Jeremy had found him, come all this way to take him back.

As Miles reached him, Jeremy blew apart and vanished.

"No!"

Vestiges of the dream?

But Jeremy had stood right here. Miles had seen him. His boyfriend's cologne still tickled his nostrils.

"Come back to me."

Loneliness gutted him, and he fell to his knees, an empty husk.

Faraway, almost subliminally, a song unwound. "Onward Christian soldiers / Marching as to war / With the cross of Jesus / Going on before...."

"Come back to me."

Six

Miles groaned and floated up from sleep, holding Jeremy in his arms.

But it couldn't be Jeremy....

He clung to the pillow. Of course. Because Jeremy didn't exist for him anymore. No more blowjob lips to kiss. No more speed bump—their nickname for the skin tag on Jeremy's penis, just below the mushroom head. So strange, though. He heard Jeremy's morning wood slap against his thigh.

A meaty thump.

A heavy slither.

Not against his body—from inside the wall.

Oh, God. Rats.

Miles's eyes flew open, and he scrambled out of bed. He flapped his arms and stamped his feet as shivers wracked him from toes to neck. He watched the wall as if rodents would spill out through a seam. Feeling creepy crawlies on his skin, he pulled out the ladder-backed chair from the writing desk and slouched into it. Good morning to him from this creepy orphanage-reformatory.

He grabbed his phone to thumb the home screen on. Damn. He'd forgotten that the phone was dead. Behind that black screen, Jeremy might have texted him.

His blood itched for caffeine.

And nicotine.

Hunger rumbled in his belly.

Without a bite to eat and legal stimulants, how could he take another run at this Dr. Schramm? He'd like to wheedle out the name of Ian's social worker before noon.

Guilt burned the back of his throat. He should have believed Minnie. All cocky, driving up here to snap some pics and prove how wrong she was. He'd make it up to her by greasing the cogs of justice and shortening Ian's stay. Arrange parole. Probation. Furlough. Whichever term applied.

By sunset he wanted three hundred miles between him and St. Hamelin's—and the rats in its walls.

What if he just packed Ian up in the car and drove away?

Grumbling, he stared at his phone. He felt antsy without the apps and games he'd gotten into without lesson plans and essay grading to keep him busy. Miss Poole had said to wait for her. Screw that. After a few swipes through his hair to tame it into place, he headed out for the stairs.

He descended past one identical landing after another. Had they taken this door? Or the one below? How could his find his way out of this maze?

Paths, paths everywhere; a stamped-in network of paths spreading over the empty land.

He chose at random and entered a hallway. At the far end, another stairwell. His caffeine-deprived head pounded. If he died in these hallways, how long would it take Butch or Miss Poole to find him?

He rammed his shoulder into a door that didn't want to budge and blundered into another passage. Another flight of stairs. At the end of these, a wider, brighter hallway looked like civilization. Or at least the ground floor.

Vibrations shook the air. Footsteps raced. He swung around, and three boys jostled past, their elbows and knees knocking him into the wall.

"Hey!"

Their feet slapped around a far bend.

"Get back here."

Hooligans. He'd bet his left nut that they were the kids who'd startled him in the shower last night. A trail of laughter led him around the corner, just as a door settled into place. He followed into the room.

"Think you're gonna hide from m—"

The door whisked shut, sealing him into a dark cavern of a room. On the one side, ten metal bathtubs ran the entire length on dappled vinyl flooring, each one growing less distinct farther down the line. Metal piping snaked from the wall to the steel tubs. At the nearest one, he bluffed. "I see you guys."

His voice evaporated into the high ceiling.

What looked like high-sided, steel kiddie pools stood in the gloom on the other side. Goose-neck faucets. Temperature gauges.

Why did an orphanage or reformatory need a hydrotherapy room?

In the shadows at the far end, indistinct shapes rose and fell—the kids climbing into tubs and scooching down.

He summoned his teacher voice. "Stop fooling around."

But what if they weren't just messing around? Starting toward them, his stomach flopped with that sinking feeling he always got whenever stepping over that little gap from a jet bridge onto a plane.

"I mean it."

That didn't even convince himself. He passed empty tubs and tanks, and his teeth chattered as the temperature dropped. A figure slumped in the steel tank next to him, and Miles jerked backward, cursing. A shirtless boy stared with hollow eyes; shuddery breaths shook the slats of his ribcage.

"Are you okay? Kid?"

From the front of the room came a squeak like a shoe on a gym floor.

The tubs he'd passed had been empty, but now another emaciated boy stood inside of one, watching him. Across the aisle, a youngster with skin the color of sour milk planted his hands on the lip of a high-sided tank. As he pulled himself up to climb out he slipped, and again that squeal as his feet skidded on the smooth inner sides.

How had he missed these kids?

Both the others swung their legs over and out from the tubs. Their skin had a grainy quality like old Seventies' films. The boy with struggling breath lurched away from his tub, his hips and legs misshapen as if they'd been broken and put back together wrong.

Beastly thing: and he looked as if he was wet all over: and I'm not at all sure that he was alive.

Three new boys in strappy tee shirts and boxer shorts emerged from between tanks, and limped on malformed legs toward him. Some weird interplay between light and shadow gave the illusion of transparency as they advanced, dripping on the floor.

Impossible.

Overtired, that's all. He wasn't actually seeing through them.

Except he was. Right through the boys' bodies to the walls.

Will-o'-the-wisp flickered over the remaining tubs, the tanks, and through that spectral light incorporeal boys sat up, stood up, climbed out. A waif two tubs away turned his tousle-haired head.

Miles froze. "That's a really good trick, guys." He sounded stupid. This wasn't a trick.

A kid in the closest tank blinked rapidly. Dark bags under the boy's eyes distorted his face into a skull with gaping empty sockets. His voice croaked. "Tear us apart."

Miles's flesh prickled. "Stop it now."

Heads snapped toward him.

Just a dream. All a bad dream. He shook his head against what he saw and backed up, but sick boys shuffled forward on spindly legs, surrounding him.

"Tear us apart."

Raised scrawny arms reached to touch him.

"Tear us apart."

Narrow chests fibrillated like sparrows' breasts. Big bruised eyes swam before him.

A gust rattled the windows, infiltrated through cracks and chinks, and whipped through the room, flapping the boys' tee shirts and conjuring putrid smells of illness. They shambled closer, fingers catching on his shirt.

"What are you doing in here?" Miss Poole's voice rang out.

The boys receded with a rustling like cockroaches swarming. "Tear us apart."

Miss Poole stood in a swatch of light from the open doorway. "I told you to stay in your room."

"I...." No sign of the boys. Nightmares banished upon waking. "I got lost."

Though water had dripped off those warped bodies, all the tubs he peeked into on the way to Miss Poole were empty and dry.

"Come with me." She barked the order, and Miles hurried after her into the corridor.

He glanced back to make sure the door closed. He rushed to keep up with Miss Poole, her skirt whisking against her legs in her hurried pace. He checked over his shoulder again.

"Don't stick your nose where it doesn't belong, Mr. Baumgartner." She stopped outside Schramm's office. "It's bound to get bitten off."

Seven

The fireplace heated the raw sewage smell into a tangible presence.

"Ah, come in. Come in." Schramm smiled, accommodating. "Please sit."

Tremors started. Jittery hands. Rubbery legs. Miles fell onto his chair. A white wall of denial blasted through his brain. What he'd seen in the hydrotherapy room could not have been real.

Schramm leaned back and spoke over the complaints of his chair. "You don't look well."

"Your hydro—" He stood on the verge of hyperventilating. "There's something...." He couldn't bear to say it out loud.

Schramm waved a dismissive hand. "I don't believe any of it."

"Any of...?"

"The claptrap you're going on about." Schramm swatted away the idea like it was a fly buzzing around his head. "Overactive imaginations." He plugged his finger into his ear and dug around. "Really, Mr. Gunderson, I'm surprised that you're so hysterical."

"Baumgartner."

"Excuse me?"

"Miles Baumgartner. Gunderson's Ian's name."

"Yes." Schramm pulled out his finger and examined it. A smile pursed his mouth as if sucking on a hard candy. Like he kept a juicy secret. With thumb and forefinger he rolled his morsel of earwax into a ball and flicked it under the desk.

Schramm's flippant dismissal about the hydrotherapy room sounded like bullshit. He hadn't even given

Miles a chance to say what he'd seen. A rehearsed denial as fake as a sitcom's laugh track. It cemented the truth—Schramm was hiding something.

Like a real haunting? Whatever he'd seen, thank God he read Poe and James—a Dreiser man's sanity would have crumbled.

Everything arcane seemed possible in St. Hamelin's. *In this mansion of gloom.*

He sat up. "I assume you're ready to discuss Ian? I want him back to his mom and dad as quickly as possible." Sooner the better. This backwoods haunted house had already eroded his almost-son into a sapped reflection of his former self. "What do we need to get him out of here? Who do I talk to?"

"Oh." Schramm planted his elbows on the desk blotter. "I'm afraid that's not possible." He held up an index finger against any objection. "I called you here to convey some bad news."

Ian was dead. Seeing his nephew was just another trick, an illusion, and his Ian really was dead.

"The blizzard continued throughout the night, and the weight of snow, the harsh winds, collapsed the bridge into town."

"Huh?" The room was so hot. Smelled so bad. "The bridge did what?" Miles crossed his arms and clenched his jaw until the familiar muscle cramp flared.

"The storm damaged the bridge." Schramm sat back and folded his hands, resting them on his belly. "You shall be our guest for a while longer, until repairs are finished."

Was Schramm's amused grin one of those consoling, empathetic, I-feel-your-pain grins? Miles clamped his back teeth, and new, screaming pain jolted from jaw to ear. With measured words, "How long will that take?"

"Obviously, work crews cannot begin until the storm passes."

"That bridge can't be the only way back. The county road running past this place, where does that go?"

"A dead end, I'm afraid."

Miles balled his fists. "How can there be no back roads circling back around to Bear Falls?"

"I'm not a civil engineer, Mr.—Perhaps it's time for Christian names? We'll be seeing so much of each other, Miles. Even if a road presented itself...." That grin widened. "Butch plowed you in."

"What?" A verbal explosion.

"When he plowed our driveway this morning, he...." Schramm chuckled. "Pushed all the snow against the carriage house doors."

Miles blew out tension in a long, whistling breath and forced his hands to loosen. Not a good time for a meltdown. "He can plow the piles away."

"He could, but again, you would still be unable to leave. The bridge, remember."

"I need to get to my car." Nicotine cravings clawed through his veins, worse than ever now that he couldn't get at his smokes. "Give me a shovel, I'll dig myself out."

"You would do well to stay in your room for the duration of your visit. We don't want you getting lost." Schramm's eyes glittered. "Again."

This prick was really enjoying himself.

"If I could just get into the carriage house."

"Miss Poole will take your meals up to you."

"No. I'm perfectly capable of walking out to the cafeteria."

Schramm thumbed the intercom. "Miss Poole. Please show our guest back to his room." He glanced at Miles. "No more wandering for Mr. Gunderson."

"Baumgartner."

Schramm smiled.

Miles stood. "Thank you, but I'm going out for some fresh air."

Schramm watched him like a boy watches a platypus at a zoo. Miss Poole walked through her door, not even trying to hide her distaste. Rather than insisting, Schramm shifted his eyes off Miles and onto her. "Apparently your services are not required at the moment. *Miles* would like to take a walk around the grounds."

"In a blizzard?"

Schramm held up a weary hand. "Some people like to learn the hard way."

Heavy snow blurred his vision on the way down the front steps, but the frosty air refreshed him. In one obscured direction, the road. In another, his cigarettes, in his glove box, in his car, inside the carriage house. Like Matryoshka dolls. He headed that way.

Too much snow for Thanksgiving, but it wasn't unheard of. As a kid he'd spent a few pre-Christmas break weekends making forts and igloos out of early snowfalls.

Christmas. Almost Christmas.

This would be his first without Jeremy. Five years of traditions scrapped like junk. He and Jeremy stringing up lights through the shrubbery. Driving to Olstad's Supermarket, where a section of the parking lot had been cordoned off to sell Christmas trees; ice hanging like ornaments off the branches of the Douglas Firs and Blue Spruces. Their footsteps squeaking on the packed snow as they searched for the tree with a perfect fit for the living room window in their Craftsman dream house.

The wind stung his eyes and made them water.

Time to stop. Christmas memories were dangerous.

Excited voices carried on the wind. Eager for a distraction, he followed a shoveled-clear stone walkway around the side of the building—skirting arches and balustrades, turrets and bay windows—toward the sound.

A gust tussled his hair. His collar flapped. Malicious laughter drew him around a corner into the mouth of an alcove—a wide, ten-foot long notch ending in a metal service door, rust crusting the hinges. With the full height of St. Hamelin's blocking the snow and wind, the clamor of mean joy came louder. Between Miles and the door, Ian and three other boys in St. Hamelin's uniforms gathered, shouting and clapping each other on the shoulders.

Only one of them noticed the trespasser. A red-haired boy, two inches shorter than the others, leveled a stare of scrutiny that froze Miles on the spot. Skin so pale that a tracery of blue veins showed on his neck and cheeks. A hard set to his narrow jaw; wicked little teeth chomped the air. Ignoring Miles, he picked up a dark object from the ground, jumped, and threw it high as he could. The thing clipped a protruding window ledge and tumbled, spinning, back to earth. The boys backed up a step and watched it strike the concrete.

They barked heartless laughter.

The redhead grabbed the object, wound up like a pitcher, and again tossed the thing in the air. The other boys' heads followed the ascent. Ian along with them.

Their heads swiveled toward Miles. The redhead grinned wide-mouthed, lips shining in the cold. A husky boy breathed heavily, the bulk of his chest rising and falling. The skinniest one's face burned with a mountain range of zits over his narrow face. Poor kid.

The object landed with a wet thump.

"What have you got there?" Miles squared his shoulders, stood straighter.

Husky stared with brown, dullard's eyes, his mouth slightly agape. Ian glanced at the brown thing on the ground, up to Miles, then to his redheaded friend. Rocky Mountain Face scratched a couple peaks on his facial landscape. The threesome showed a twitchy energy of guilt. Of being caught. But the redhead puffed his chest out, shoulders back. He did not drop his proud, emerald eyes.

"Well?" Miles forced confidence that he didn't feel.

Rocky Mountain Face looked about twelve. Husky might have been old enough to drive. But the redhead gave off an air of maturity despite the babyface.

En masse, the boys shuffled away a couple feet, toward the back end of the alcove. Miles took a corresponding step closer. When the boys remained silent and kept their ground, he approached the thing on the stone skirt.

Jesus.

"What have you kids done?"

Pity twisted his heart, and he knelt. A rat lay broken on the concrete. Its thick cord of a tail whispered against the ground. Its small round mouth guppied, tongue lolling against busted, overcrowded teeth. Blood matted the fur of its head and neck. Sensing a human so close, the rat found a burst of strength and with flailing limbs, foreleg broken, it flopped onto its other side; then lay spent with limp legs twitching. Its narrow body convulsed. One burst eye dribbled liquid like egg white over its whiskered muzzle.

Disgust formed a bitter scum in Miles's mouth. Just an hour ago, thoughts of rats slithering over each other in the walls had repulsed him, but seeing the cruelty to this animal filled his skull with buzzing outrage.

Down by the door, Rocky Mountain Face and Husky focused on their feet. Honest or token regret? His almost-son's face hardened into a sulking mask.

"This is sick. Minnie and Daniel raised you better than this. You know, this would break your mom's heart."

That redheaded boy's vicious lips parted, showing off his mouthful of tiny white teeth. "So what?" The freckles spattered across his alabaster nose and cheeks lent an ironic power.

Miles curled his shaking hands into fists. "You've got a great life ahead of you, huh?"

A kid so cruel so young must have endured terrible abuse, emotional scars warping him into a dangerous young man destined to land in a place like St. Hamelin's. But Miles failed to summon sympathy for the wearer of that hard, psychotic stare. Redhead's eyes caught some stray light and shone a spectral green like a cat's when they've caught the moonlight.

Like last night in the bathroom.

The boy spat onto the ground, turned, and slapped Ian's shoulder. "C'mon, Gunderson. Let's get outta here."

Ian bristled, but muttered, "Whatever you say, Elijah."

The four of them scampered past Miles to the mouth of the alcove where they disappeared into the swirling white.

At Miles's feet, the rat's runny eye had thickened and gone gummy. Fleas jittered through its fur, but the rodent's sides had ceased rising and falling.

Eight

Holy hell, he needed a smoke.

When he cleared the walls of the alcove, dark shapes blurred by the snow slipped around a far corner. He couldn't hear, but they'd be cheering. Pounding fists. Shouldn't there be consequences for ending a life? Sure, it was just a rat—and yes, he would have laid down traps to be rid of it—but those kids had been so savage. And gleeful. They had a head start, and youth suited them better to wintry weather, but Miles left his smokes for later, tucked his chin, and trudged after them.

This storm had taken a brutal turn. Wind and snow filled in the boys' footprints. He followed the length of the wall at his left shoulder, finally rounding the corner. Far ahead, a brick wing without adornments created a sort of courtyard. He looked up, finding what he figured was his window.

By now Ian and his crass friends would have returned inside, warm and secure behind closed doors. But as he blinked snowflakes from his lashes, a blotch darted from the snow and disappeared around that far bend. Two more danced into view. Taunting him. He had encountered some brash kids in his classes, but where did these boys get this temerity? They sure ran rampant in this so-called reformatory. Miles hustled into the snow drifts to catch up.

At the far edge of the property, a treeline formed a vague grey wall. As a windbreak, it failed miserably. Snow pelted his cheeks, his forehead. He couldn't feel his face any more, and a false sense of heat spread over the skin. Stupid not to have checked his WeatherNow app before driving up here. He would have killed for a winter coat right now. Gloves. He hadn't even pulled on his sweater this morning because the radiator kept his room so hot. Forget about the boys for now—time to get inside and warm up his face, fingers, and toes.

His foot clipped a rock. His stiff arms flailed, but he fell to his knees, sinking into the accumulated snow. A cluster of snow-covered humps surrounded him in ordered rows and columns. What in the world...? He brushed off the lump that had felled him. Not a rock at all, but a wooden shingle planted in the ground. A name and dates had been branded in the wood.

A grave marker.

Trying to count all the mounds was fruitless—white on white in falling snow. But at a glance? More than twenty, less than fifty. He duck-walked to the next nearest and swept it clean. Exposure to Wisconsin seasons had blasted the marker grey and splintered the sides. Moss had stained the edges black. Age and the elements had worn down the burned-in name, and the dates would have been indecipherable if not for snow filling in the shallow grooves. He visored his eyes from the wind with a hand.

Franklin Perry

1940 – 1952

Twelve years old.

He twisted to look over his shoulder. He swiped snow off his brows. No one there. Just St. Hamelin's, reading alongside.

He wound around the closest of others, clearing off names and dates.

Matthew Schultz

1942 – 1952

James Aschenbrenner

1946 – 1952

Ten years old and six years old. His belly ached for these children. Far too young to have died. Then buried like afterthoughts in a field behind their orphanage.

He chose a final marker.

Kurt Hauser

1944 – 1952

What had happened in 1952? Could it have been the accident that Graham from Blankenheim's mentioned?

Wait....

No, not an accident. Disease. The hydrotherapy room he'd found this morning.... The spirits' disfigurements.... Early Fifties would be about right for it. Yeah, a polio outbreak.

He shivered, and not from the cold. More like shock. The corroborating evidence of these grave markers made this morning's visions too real.

Grade-school Ian had once asked him if he believed in the supernatural. In the ghosts and ghouls and super-stitions of all their scary movies. Sitting on the couch in the dark, bowl of popcorn between them, Miles had an-swered no. St. Hamelin's just changed his mind.

Tear us apart.

He had seen ghosts that morning. No use kidding himself. But he knew something else for certain—they weren't monstrous. They had been disfigured by contrac-tures of their limbs. In a way torn apart, like they had said. Their eyes not filled with malice, but desperation. They hadn't meant him harm. Devastated by disease and death, their poor restless souls wanted succor.

But why were they restless if their narrow bones lay in consecrated ground? Maybe it wasn't. Did this chil-dren's cemetery count as consecrated just because they'd been buried under paupers' wooden tombstones, or did more need to be done?

Pastor Boyd hadn't covered all this.

This addition to his belief system hurt his head.

All of him hurt—his toes and fingertips stung; his ears burned; his nostril hairs had frozen, crisp.

Physical pain wore down the mental walls he had built over the last half-year. A frustrated cry screamed from his lips. Goddammit! He would never teach again, not after what he had done. Jeremy would never come back. Jeremy wasn't wasting any time thinking about him, either. Ian hated him suddenly and didn't want to go home even if Miles could figure out a way. Minnie's depression would sink her. Wind blew the anguish back in his face, and clouds of ragged breath pumped from his mouth and encircled his head, like memories he couldn't shake.

Nine

Back in through the side door, the raunchy air choked him. He'd been more comfortable freezing to death outside. He stomped snow off his shoes until his feet splashed in the melted puddle.

Voices argued in Schramm's office—Schramm, Miss Poole, and a young, fey voice. They had left the door open, and he couldn't help but take a few extra steps past the vestibule to try for a peek inside. His soles squelched across the floor, betraying him.

Schramm motioned for him. "Miles, come in here."

If they had kept the door open to expel the heat and stink, it wasn't working. Miss Poole and some anemic boy stood beside the desk. His mouse-brown hair poked up in all directions, spider plant leaves stretching toward the light. Just a little fella. Under five feet tall. A hundred pounds sopping wet. In the St. Hamelin's blazer and trousers he looked like a kid playing dress-up with dad's best suit.

Schramm remained seated as he waved Miles into Miss Poole's heavily perfumed air and toward a chair. "This involves you, as well."

"Yeah?" How could it? He hadn't seen this boy yet. Or the twenty-or-so hymnals piled on Schramm's desk.

The boy turned to him. Behind huge glasses, slightly-crossed big brown eyes flashed terror. Schramm snapped his fingers at the kid, and the boy flinched, blinked, and faced front.

"Go ahead, Miles." Schramm tapped one of the books with the serrated, brass letter opener. "Take a look."

Miles grabbed a hymnal.

The heft, the textured red cover, the slim golden cross etched onto the front all sent him caroming back through time to boyhood Sunday mornings. He held the exact edition that St. Mark's had used. Oh, the daydreams of choirboy classmates he used to have during the sermons. Brad Otay, chocolate brown hair, blue eyes, Midwestern baby-fat body, and juicy butt—the template for his type.

The other three in the office had hushed. Heat flushed his face, and it wasn't from the fireplace. He coughed and opened the book, riffled the pages. The spice of aged, tanned paper reached him. The spine had a break in it, and he let the pages fall open naturally. The Order of Vespers.

A red-blue-orange crayon drawing defaced the printed liturgy.

Schramm watched with greedy eyes. Miss Poole scowled. The boy next to her paled further—had he done this?

Half a dozen plump blue oblongs—people—lay dead, mid-page. Angry red slashes wounded them. Smooth red strokes painted a sea of blood all the way to the bottom edge. Bringing the book closer to his face, Miles studied their circle-faces. Little pink tongues lolled out of frowny mouths.

Miss Poole rounded on Schramm. "Why would Theodore do this? It isn't in his character. You know that."

Miles set that book beside the pile and chose another. How did this involve him? He rifled through the pages, back to front like a flipbook until he found the drawing. A red and grey St. Hamelin's filled the background. At the bottom of the page, a blue and red crayon stickman had been cut to pieces. Arms and legs hacked off. The severed head lay in a big red circle. Above the body, in black letters: MILES.

Schramm fired back. "Come now, Janelle. Chaplain Allen found the boy in the chapel after hours. Holding one of these." Tap, tap, tap—the letter opener again thwacked the cover of a hymnal.

Miles picked another. The crayon brightness of the carnage made it all the more horrible. These St. Hamelin's boys had serious psychological problems. What range of misdemeanors had landed each of them inside this re-purposed orphanage? Letting them run loose had to have been some super-liberal experiment.

Another drawing, another St. Hamelin's. This one with flames bursting out of the windows. An oblong man had black Xs for eyes. Round, brown animals perched on his corpse. The transposed letters above: MILSE.

Theodore squirmed like he had to pee; his face wore an anxious misery completely unlike the haughty expressions of Ian, Elijah, and the other two rat-killers. Janelle Poole might be right about this boy's innocence. He set the hymnal on top of the previous two and grabbed another as the adults squabbled. A petrifying need drove him to examine another, and another, and another of the sketches scrawled over hymns, prayers, and services.

Long black stick-limbs torn off and scattered: miles.

Bold, jagged blood gushed from cuts: Mils.

Grey pencil strokes colored in a stormy sky so furiously that the artist had torn the page to ribbons.

The base of his skull tingled.

Defacing Martin Luther's "A Mighty Fortress Is Our God," an ugly troll named MILLES BUMGARDNER dangled limp from a rope around a tree limb.

"These are drawn by different kids."

Miss Poole stopped mid-stream. Her face cycled through irritation, recognition, puzzlement, gratitude, and once more rage as she turned back to Schramm.

Miles's mouth was an arid plain. "Some of these show real artistic talent." His dry tongue smacked on his upper palette. "Others are just stick figures. Counting the misspellings of my name alone suggests at least five different pairs of hands were responsible."

He tossed his last hymnal on the desk, knocking down a column. Books thudded onto his feet. One opened to a drawing of the Devil rising from perdition's flames, dragging MILES down to eternal torment.

Miss Poole actually smiled. "See? It's a ridiculous charge."

Schramm's face tightened. "Theodore's a bright boy. He could have planned the subterfuge."

"Theodore didn't even have enough time to vandalize all of these."

Schramm's eyes flashed righteous fury toward Miles, but he spoke to Miss Poole. "Time? At St. Hamelin's, all we have is time."

Miles's lips stuck together.

Everything you plunge into time is stretched and disintegrates.

Miss Poole stabbed her finger at the few still on the desk. "Theodore didn't desecrate the chaplain's precious hymnals. You know who did, just as well as I do."

Schramm held up his hands in mock defeat. "Perhaps we'll never know." His attention shifted to Theodore. "Young man. Miss Poole and...." He cleared his throat. "Mr. Baumgartner here make a compelling argument. You will not be escorted to the basement for punishment." He smiled magnanimously.

Theodore deflated with relief. "Thank you, Dr. Schramm." Voice like a squeaky wheel, and his mouth worked hard around the words, chewing each syllable.

Schramm wagged a finger at Theodore and got in the last word. "I'm keeping an eye on you. Behave yourself." Schramm turned to Miles. "What are you waiting for?"

Miss Poole held Theodore's hand on the way to the stairway. Miles kept pace—better another tense walk with her than relying on his memory to find his room.

Loitering outside the arched double-doors at the T-junction, the four rat murderers plus one new platinum blond boy nudged each other and pointed.

The tips of his ears grew hot.

"Hey, Theo!" Husky slapped Elijah's elbow. "Schramm send you to the basement?"

Elijah gloated. Ian looked equally smug behind the redhead's right shoulder.

Rocky Mountain Face cat-called. "Got yerself a new friend? Hey, mister! Ya here to stay?"

Towhead brayed laughter.

Theodore cowered against Miss Poole, earning another round of snide comments.

Mob mentality sickened Miles.

Miss Poole wrapped her arm around Theodore's shoulders and led him into the vestibule.

Husky made eye contact with Miles and mouthed, "Watching you."

Miles bit his tongue. Any rejoinder might be taken out on Theodore's hide. Meek and small, Theodore was a prime target for older bullies. Feeling protective of the boy, he joined Miss Poole on the stairs.

She hadn't softened a bit. She flashed annoyance and sniped at him. "Do you need me to show you the way again?"

"Yes."

Theodore looked up into Miles's face. "I promise I didn't draw those things."

"I know." Miles squeezed the boy's bird-wing shoulder.

Miss Poole tugged Theodore up to the first landing. "Hurry up then, Mr. Baumgartner."

As they twined through the passages, Theodore grilled him in an excited, breathless voice. "Where'd you come from? Why're you here?" Hustling two steps for every one of Miss Poole's, Theodore kept peeking over his shoulder. "Are you staying? Are you here to help me and—"

Theodore bumped into Miss Poole, who had stopped. She bent at the waist until at eye level. "Shush."

The back of the boy's neck blushed. "Sorry."

Continuing through twists and turns jogged only the faintest recollection of their first trip up to the fifth floor. "You'll have to draw me a map so I don't get lost." He chuckled.

She didn't. "Hopefully you won't be here long enough to need one."

Okay then. He shut his mouth and constructed a mental map. He seriously didn't want to get lost in St. Hamelin's.

She told him, "Your room is up one more flight."

He murmured thanks and sure enough, he found his hall. His door.

His? Too much familiarity in that. If he started thinking of this assigned room as home, he'd fling himself out a window onto the paving stones.

From the other rooms, thumps and bumps resounded—the racket of cooped-up youngsters. Were they all bad seeds? Or were those not in Elijah's band of troublemakers sorry for their petty crimes? He closed his door and massaged his eyes until they hurt. He didn't wear anything so analog as a watch, but guessed the time at around nine o'clock. Still incredibly early. Not even close to lun—

What was on top of the tangled sheets?

Through a flurry of dust motes, he studied the shape.

Holy hell.

He retched against the back of his hand.

A dead rat lay on his bed.

Pieces of a dead rat.

He forced himself closer. All four legs had been pulled off the fat, cylindrical body, leaving shredded skin and meat at the wounds. Like the crayon drawing of MILES. A tiny star of reflected light mimicked life in one eye of its torn-off head.

Both eyes intact—it was not the one Ian had helped kill.

It was suddenly so stuffy in here.

He gathered the four corners of the blanket and bundled up the vivisected rat.

MILLES BUMGARDNER.

He carried its grisly weight down toward the lavatory, to the hatch in the wall. Laundry chute or incinerator? Either way, the rat was going for a ride.

The kids quieted in their rooms. So that's how it was. Their bleating stifled. Ears pressed against doors. Would anyone come out and claim their work? Crack their doors for an amused peek?

"Really funny, guys." Speaking to his hidden audience honed a sharper edge to his anxiety. He'd landed on their shit list.

Freeing one hand, Miles wrestled open the spring-loaded hatch. A breath of stale smoke burped out. He dumped the covered rat into the bowels and let the metal door slam closed, a sated mouth. Padded bongs reported the rat's path. His hands and arms itched, and he extended his arms for a look, flipped his hands from back to palm. Palm to back. No lice, no fleas bounced through his forearms' fine hairs. He smelled his fingers. He hadn't touched the rat, but his imagination would drive him crazy if he didn't wash up.

He took one step toward the bathroom; muffled sobs floated through the air behind him. Miles spun around, but the hallway lay empty.

Sniffling.

"Hello?"

He backed toward the hollow wails of a child burbling up the incinerator chute.

Impossible.

He opened the hatch. Glanced over one shoulder and then the next. No one watched, but this had to be another prank. He peered into the chute. "Hello?" The metal throat amplified his word as it rushed down.

Sob. Breath. Sob. Breath.

"Who's down there?"

No answer. Not a sound from any of the rooms.

Could the rat killers have run up so quickly and stolen Theodore from Miss Poole's side? Stuffed him down the fourth-floor chute? Sounded like their style.

"Theodore?"

No more crying.

"Are you down there? Did those boys do this to you?"

The only response was the soft roar of silence. He eased the hatch closed. Behind him, that janitor's closet might have a flashlight. Maybe he could see to the bottom if he wriggled his way halfway into the chute.

Yeah, and then the flash of red hair out of the corner of his eye as Elijah charged and pushed him down through the hatch.

Okay. Terrible plan. But it's all he had.

The janitor's closet was not what he expected. No mops, brooms, cleaners, or rags. No fuse box. No shelves. Not a janitor's closet. Not any kind of maintenance room.

A staircase corkscrewed down into darkness.

All dorm room doors remained shut. No whispers of kids unable to contain their mischievous joy. No more crying from the hatch. No sounds along these stairs. And no assurance at all that this led to the basement and the incinerator. But he had to try. His penance would never be fully paid for his other life—the life in which he'd shoved Billy Rubin down those other stairs—but if these bullies really had thrown Theodore down the chute, Miles had to go pull him out.

He slapped around the chill wall until his palm hit the light switch. A bulb winked on and a second later, exploded like the flash lamp of an old, tripod camera. Deep below, another caught and stayed lit, turning the narrow winding passage into a piss-colored umbilicus. He started downward on the balls of his feet. Quiet. Cautious. The low ceiling offered maybe six inches of clearance. The walls pressed against his shoulders as he descended. No landings or doors to other floors, just the curved way through one and then another ombré glow as one light disappeared around the previous bend, leaving him in darkness for a step until the next light began to show dimly ahead.

Loud and lonely, his footsteps followed him. Sour smells of age and decay hung like vapor. At least he had a break from the sewage stink. He tired of creeping and walked on the flats of his feet. Unlike the slat floors above, these risers had a mushy give to them. With no railing, he ran his hand along the rough wall until a splinter pierced his finger's tender flesh. He swore and sucked on the tip, soothing the spot with his tongue. Tasted of copper and dust.

The next glow drew him forward.

Half a second after his foot touched a stair came its echo. Such a loud report from rubber soles on soft wood.

Step. *(Step)*

Step. *(Step)*

Stop. *(Step)*

In the full dark of one of those dead spots, his breath struck the wall and splashed back into his face. The air felt damp down this far.

For the love of God, Montresor!

Hard to breathe. He hooked a finger into his shirt collar and stretched it. Over his own struggles, was that another's inhale...exhale...?

If someone had followed him, what were they waiting for?

Deep breath and count. One... two....

Paranoia. Too many weird things happening these last twenty-four hours.

Five... six....

Only his only breathing kept him company.

Eight... nine....

Before claustrophobia settled like a blanket over his mind, he got moving and walked through another cycle of light-dark. Light-dark. Light-dark. He rounded a fourth bend, and the passage ended abruptly with an iron door. Above, a bare bulb ticked and flickered a soft yellow strobe.

The handle chilled his fingers, and he gave it a push. Nothing. Again, with more force. The bottom edge scraped a tattoo along the floor, setting his teeth on edge.

He entered a stone chamber, lit by dozens of pillar and taper candles affixed in nests of their own melted wax. Horizontal recesses had been built into the walls, like the bunks on a submarine. Stale decay tainted the air. Instead of the basement, he'd found a crypt.

Framed portrait photographs, not coffins, filled the shelves and the ossuary in the center of the room. The photos gleamed in the light cast from the candles spaced among them. At the first bank on his left, careful not to bump candles on either side, he extracted the closest picture. Hard to see details through the glare on the glass. Degraded photo quality didn't help. He brought the picture up to his nose.

While most of the photos around the room showed one child, this one featured two boys—preadolescent chums with arms thrown over shoulders, smiling resentfully as St. Hamelin's skulked in the background. A couple of the original orphans from the 1940s or 50s, judging from the cut of their trousers and open-throated shirts. And the newsie cap on the shorter one. He set that one back and browsed. He threaded another out through the candles. The somber face, in black and white, of a ten- or eleven-year-old. Grey hair plastered stiff on his head.

All these boys had grown too old to be wanted and adopted by families. Moms and dads wanted young, unsullied children to raise. The boys featured here had lived their lives of quiet desperation in St. Hamelin's, housed and fed, until they aged out of the system.

That is, those who survived the polio outbreak.

He placed the photo back on the shelf. Why were they down here, displayed in a crypt? Complete with candles.

It was a mystery all insoluble.

He scratched the stubble on his chin.

Nor could I grapple with the shadowy fancies that crowded upon me as I pondered.

Someone had created a shrine, and that someone tended their shrine regularly enough to keep candles lit.

Schramm? The superintendent didn't seem the sentimental type.

Nor did Miss Poole—too stern. Cold.

And Butch didn't come across as this creative.

Certainly not the bully-pranksters, though it would be their style to creep down here after him. Planning their next cruelty. Like slamming closed the door and locking him in. He'd convinced himself that the footsteps and breathing had been imagination, but maybe....

He had to stop acting like an hysterical old lady.

But he couldn't shake the bad feeling steeping inside him. This shrine struck him as foul. Evil? That was pushing it, but this tableau raised his hackles.

He reached for a photograph in the next wall. A group shot. Bringing it out, the bottom edge knocked a candle out of its wax mooring. Hot wax spilled onto the vamp of his shoe as the taper fell end-over-end, and sputtered out at his feet. From the photograph that had caused the mess, a dozen St. Hamelin's orphans watched, frozen in a perpetual moment. Faces young, yet old for their age, staring out over a vast wasteland of time. Imagine showing these kids iPhones, the internet, plastic automobiles with rounded corners like alien spaceships.

Would any of these boys still be alive? They'd be....
Subtract 1950; add their age... 80? 85?

He started to put that one back but stopped. He blinked, trying to clear his vision. Shake off what he thought he saw. Whom he recognized. His knuckles went white from holding the photo so tightly. Six or seven of these faces were familiar.

Impossible. Unless....

Tear us apart.

Replace their healthy lithe forms with wasted bodies. Crooked limbs. Sallow faces. Wide beseeching eyes.

Holy hell.

The boys from the hydrotherapy room.

Of course. Who else would warrant placement in a sanctum but children stricken by disease? Tragically dead? Which of these faces belonged to Franklin Perry? Matthew Schultz, James Aschenbrenner, Kurt Hauser?

Whoa.

He knew what this was.

Plank children.

Last Halloween night—not the one three weeks ago, but last year, still at home—between handing out fun size Snickers to trick-r-treaters, he'd been reading Creepypasta on the internet while nursing a Scotch. He found a suitably chilling story about photos just like the ones surrounding him. Post mortem photography. A macabre practice from the late-nineteenth and earliest twentieth century. When a child died, the parents—or teachers, teachers did it, too—took a portrait for remembrance. Dead children propped up on boards—planks—and photographed with classmates or siblings or mom and dad. He'd thought it an urban legend. Most Creepypasta were digital age equivalents of ghost stories by the campfire. But he'd been wrong. Plank children were real. St. Hamelin's had actually done it.

And it pissed him off.

Orphaned. Brought up in this unlovely, unloving place until disease cut their lives short. Buried out in the backyard was the final injury, but the true abasement was being posed and tied to a board and photographed. No wonder they wandered, restless.

Tear us apart.

His hands shook, blurring the faces in the photograph.

Tear us apart.

What if.... What if their spirits roamed not because they were angry about being laid out like trophies down here in the cold, hard heart of St. Hamelin's, but because this shrine kept their spirits animated? That's how these things worked. All those years spent reading horror stories finally paid off. However the voodoo worked, these photographs were the linchpin. He knew it in his marrow.

Tear us apart.

Yes! And those cursed, sick boys had chosen him. Led him down here to set them free of their imprisonment.

He snarled as he threw the photograph to the floor. He stamped his heel on the frame, and smiled as glass broke. He plucked out another, knocking over two more candles. Who cared? With a flick of his wrist, he sent that picture to the floor hard enough to shatter on impact. He went back for a third and side-armed it across the crypt into the middle funerary recess across the way. None of those candles broke free, but a couple of wicks lost their flames, sending tendrils of smoke twisting up.

Inside him, a schism tore open.

He charged and swept his arms through those candles still standing, knocking them and photographs to the stone floor. Crushing them underfoot, he reached to the top shelf and pulled down more photos. He missed one; on tip-toes, he grabbed that and smashed it against the lip of the shelf. The wooden frame splintered at the corner joints. Glass slipped out and landed intact on the pile of destruction at his feet. He ripped the pictures to shreds. He tore the boy's images apart.

Every frame broken. Each photograph sundered or mangled as badly as those poor kids' bodies. He started knocking down the remaining candles, but the crypt lost light fast. He was exhausted anyway, and his heart and blood pressure had his head pounding. Time to stop. His chest heaved. Faint traces of a headache beat like tribal drums in the distance, but as soon as the adrenaline flushed from his system, he would suffer.

A shadow threw itself into the crypt.

Long and thin, the umbra snaked over the floor and up the far wall, followed by the ghoulish shape itself stalking into the stone room.

A figure inexpressibly thin and pathetic, of a dusty leaden colour.

Miles pressed his back against the wall as if he could disappear from this monster.

Thin lips crooked into a faint and dreadful smile, the hands pressed tightly over the region of the heart.

Not a creature, but a lank man dressed in black regarded Miles. A tall mass of blond hair tacked on another three inches of height. Hectic white and red blotches covered his narrow face and ropy neck. Only his hawk nose and large forehead showed clear skin. Miles needed a moment but finally registered the white clerical collar. The chaplain that Schramm mentioned had just caught him.

The pastor's eyes bulged. "What have you done?" A thousand twitches rippled across his face. "What did you do!"

Miles searched for the right words. "There was some kind of Satanism down here."

The clergyman sank to his knees and bowed over the wreckage on the floor as if about to weep.

Should he console this man? "The ghosts—the polio children—it's true."

The chaplain picked up a busted frame. Let it drop. His fingers searched shattered glass. He plucked ripped and quartered photographs and gathered them like a poker hand. A wet, strangled noise escaped his thin-lipped mouth.

"They're lost now."

"No, I freed them."

The man turned his glassy eyes to Miles. "You doomed them."

"Me?" What was this guy talking about? "Wait.... Did you do all this?"

"This?" The clergyman's voice quavered. He stood, a phoenix rising. "This?" He clutched his stack of photo pieces. "I didn't do this. I performed a miracle. You, Mr. Baumgartner, did this." He shoved the pieces under Miles's nose. "Were you not told to stay in your room?" His voice edged up an octave. "You have no right to meddle in our business. Much less...." The clerical collar glowed in the light from the few remaining candles, shone as if with inner, sanctimonious light. A furious red flush spread across Chaplain's face, shading in the uneven blotches on his cheeks.

Miles withered under the drubbing. Chaplain put Jeremy's conniptions to shame—raving at Miles for leaving gobs of toothpaste in the sink or toast crumbs on the counter.

"You are not welcome here, Mr. Baumgartner." Chaplain snorted and threw the shredded photos at Miles's face.

Miles swallowed the castigation into the pit of his stomach where it would inevitably harden into resentment. He clacked his molars together and readied himself to lay into this guy. But Chaplain was right. Miles was a guest in St. Hamelin's. Miss Poole had already made clear that he was only tolerated. And barely. The ritual in this crypt had nothing to do with him or his purpose, Ian.

Not that he would apologize. He shouldn't have meddled, but this scene still stank of indecency.

Chaplain's fingers groped like pincers in the air. "Come with me."

Miles's face tightened into a grimace. He moved, but kept wide of the chaplain's eerily long fingers. With this Man of God breathing warm halitosis at his back, Miles climbed back up the curving stairs, hurrying through the dark patches.

Ten

Elbows on his desk, Schramm massaged his temples. "You've done great damage."

How could Schramm stand the hellacious warmth from the fireplace in that three-piece suit?

"Have you seen what was going on? This chaplain of yours, he.... I don't know. Conjured a spell? It's not just rumors, the... things your people have seen in the hydrotherapy room—" He sounded insane. And he'd almost forgotten what had taken him to the crypt in the first place. "That kid, Theodore—some of the older boys must have thrown him down the incinerator chute. I heard him crying."

One hand parted from Schramm's face to give the stop sign, cutting Miles off. "Do you hear yourself?" A deep breath filled the man's barrel chest. He dropped his hands and tugged nonexistent wrinkles out of his suit vest. "Theodore is safe in his room, I assure you. As for the reliquary, that's Chaplain Allen's business, and you trampled all over it."

How easily Schramm dismissed the astounding. These people lived among spirits and rituals as if it were commonplace. It *was* commonplace here.

"I need to see Ian."

"All in good time." Schramm's face showed a caricature of sympathy. "The blizzard continues." He motioned to the window over his head, to the snow falling hard and fast. He reclined until the chair wobbled on the brink of collapse, and he folded his hands onto his belly. "You will be with us for a while, and you obviously need an occupation while you're here."

"I can't imagine where you're going with this."

But he could.

"Our instructors live across the bridge." Schramm gestured in the vague direction of the road leading away from St. Hamelin's. "You're a teacher...."

How did he know that?

"Honor us...." Schramm's *honor* came out with a peptic snarl. "By taking over English classes until bridge repairs allow our instructors to return."

His guts felt like an aluminum can crushed under a boot.

"I don't know if I can do that." Flashbacks of his last day at Mari Newton High: One by one, his colleagues had stepped into the hall to see what the commotion was; ridicule spread over students' faces as they levered themselves with fingers wrapped around the desk fronts, lifting their butts from seats and peering out the doors. As the volume and intensity of the fracas increased, sophomores, juniors, and seniors he knew filled the doorways, unable to quell their curiosity.

He ground his teeth to stop the memories. His need for a cigarette inched toward a full nic-fit.

"It's the weekend. Besides, aren't you on winter break? Thanksgiving, whatever? Just let me speak with my nephew."

"This is the best option for everyone involved. You need to fill your time. This gives you access to your nephew. Also, our young men have become distracted since your arrival."

"Excuse me? They've been distracted? The boys?"

"You have been a disruption. Look, we have your best interests in mind. No one wants you to cause any more trouble."

"Me?" Miles ground his back teeth harder to keep from saying more.

But screw that.

"You've got juvenile delinquents running around un-supervised, every hour of the day. They scream down the halls, bang crap in their rooms, murder small animals." He pointed at the door between adjoining offices. "They ter-rify that poor little... what's his...? Theodore. They shove him down the incinerator chute, and you worry about me getting into trouble? You have ghosts." He stamped his foot. "Ghosts, for God's sake, and your chaplain holds rituals in a crypt."

Schramm fussed with his lapels. "Taking over a cou-ple classes is the least you could do in exchange for room and board."

"Are you kidding me?" Room and board? His teeth screeched inside his head. Schramm was getting the den-tist bill after this. Lips together, teeth apart. He massaged his sore jaw. "I'm trying hard to be understanding. You were short-staffed already, then this storm popped up. I popped up. But what kind of facility are you running here? Do you have a state mandate? Public funds? I'll play along for now." Not that he had much choice—he was truly at their mercy. And on their bad side. "But come Monday, we are going to sit down and discuss withdraw-ing Ian."

Schramm clapped his hands. "Excellent! Until Mon-day, then. Two classes would be perfect, don't you agree? Teach the boys something before lunch, and perhaps some sort of read-along in the evening. You can start im-mediately."

"Right now?"

"You have somewhere pressing to be?"

Hell yes. He had a lonely apartment with unpacked boxes to stare at. A sabbatical he had to renegotiate. Mes-sages from Jeremy he needed to wait for.

But more flies with honey. "No, I have nowhere else to be."

And the most flies of all with crap.

The squat black vermin that teem in every cranny of this town.

He could pile it on and play nice until Monday. Until his phone woke up, and he made the calls to start lawsuits raining down on their heads.

Schramm thumbed the intercom. A moment later, Miss Poole poked her head in. She frowned at Miles. Turned her disapproval to Schramm. "You asked him."

Schramm busied himself with papers on his desk.

Miss Poole sighed and entered the office, still dressed in the same schoolmarm skirt and cardigan. "I'll show you to the classroom."

"I don't like this idea."

"Believe me, Miss Poole, I hate it."

Leading him through more indistinguishable sets of stairs and doors and halls, she ignored his admission. "You shouldn't have come at all. Now you're sticking around? I don't like this idea one bit."

"If I could leave right now, I'd be gone. You know I can't. Jesus."

She whirled on him. "Don't snap at me." A touch of sadness softened her features. Her face was quite fetching when she didn't glower.

"Hey, I'm sorry."

She tugged at her cardigan. A quick breath to compose herself, and she reached into the nearest doorway and punched an old light switch button. "I'll leave you to it."

"Wait. I'm sorry." But he spoke to her back.

What a jerk. But what did she expect? She'd been disagreeable since sight one. Dammit. He might have blown the chance to borrow her phone charger.

Three big windows let in a wall of the day's gloom. Four columns of student desks, five rows each. Standard issue teacher's desk, older than Methuselah. He could practically taste asbestos fibers from the ceiling tiles. His fingerpads caressed the green chalkboard. Wow, did that bring back memories. Teachers all used whiteboards or PowerPoint these days, but he'd learned writing and arithmetic—if his mangling of numbers counted as knowing math—on a board just like this. He ran his hand over the tray, stirring up powder. He clapped the dust from his hands, and like flour it spread to his flannel shirt and legs. Dr. Volk, the department chair at his alma mater, used to joke that chalk dust poisoning was the number one killer of English teachers.

No textbooks. No lesson plan. This would just be an hour, right? A classroom hour, like a psychologist's hour—fifty minutes. He could bullshit for that long. But which kids would attend? Best guess, the boys he'd seen so far ranged from ten to seventeen. A big age gap.

At the back of the room, a laminate countertop stretched from wall to wall. Cabinet doors lined the front. Possibilities drew him from around the desk. The speckled vinyl floor reminded him of the old county building when his mom would tow him and Minnie along to pay property taxes. Nostalgia squeezed his heart. Summers had lasted forever. From one Christmas to the next felt like a century. When had time begun racing by?

All that passed time weighed on his head, his shoulders, and he groaned to his knees and checked out the first cabinet, far left. One shelf divided the storage space into top and bottom. Nothing in there but a hint of mildew. He jammed that door closed and scooted to the next one.

"Oh." What did he have here?

He pulled out a big cardboard box and let it drop the couple inches to the floor. The sides had gone soft with age and bloated out. He opened up the cross-hatched flaps on top.

"Score."

The smile on his face felt refreshing. He pulled out the topmost book. William Golding's *Lord of the Flies*.

He dug through the rest of the box. Yep, Golding's novel filled the whole thing. And seriously, what could be more appropriate?

He peeked over his shoulder. Still alone. He lifted the book and opened it, stuck his nose into the crisp, yellowed pages. He breathed deep the musky aroma of attics and steamer trunks. His favorite perfume—eau de used books.

"Talking to yourself, Baumgartner?"

Miles slapped the book closed. Rocky Mountain Face leered as he wandered into the room with a couple of other boys—the towhead from before, and a boy with black hair plastered against his scalp but for an Ed Grimley horn in front. The triumvirate glanced about, taking in the room.

Theodore shuffled in, oversized glasses askew. Heart-breakingly fragile, upper arms no wider around than his forearms. All the older boys he'd seen walked around with jaws set, suspicious eyes shifty; they looked like they belonged in juvenile detention. But what in the world could Theodore have done? What family court judge had sentenced this whelp to time at St. Hamelin's?

Slouching in, Ian acknowledged him with a disgusted hiss. "Uncle Miles."

So, this was the new Ian. His nephew hadn't just had a bad day yesterday. A crystalline shard of hope imploded to dust inside of him.

Avuncular duties suspended, substitute teacher Miles lugged the box up to the front. The bottom sagged; a seam popped underneath one hand; the contents shifted, and the moment before the box could rip apart, he slammed it onto the desktop. Dust blew up the sides. He hopped back and saved himself from choking on motes for a second day in a row. Titters rang out at his expense.

Another three drifted in: Husky and one with curly hair as perm-tight as early Justin Timberlake. The other, strikingly pretty; sapphire eyes, features fine as a girl's and face innocent as one of those Precious Moments figurines, but even more delicate—porcelain not ceramic.

"Go ahead and take your usual seats."

Rocky Mountain Face spun in a slow, tight circle face to the ceiling as if marveling at the Sistine Chapel. "We ain't never been here."

"With grammar like that, I believe you." That earned some sniggers. But at a student's expense. What was he doing? "Sit wherever you want to then. Sorry about the lights." The hanging lights were still warming up.

Elijah moseyed on in. He snickered and took the desk behind Ian, who twisted around. They whispered, both glanced at Miles, and quickly looked away as Husky and Towhead found seats.

Miles pulled out a copy of *Lord of the Flies*. "All right then."

A straggler scampered into the room, dark hair poking up in every direction. It was Teeth, the kid from his closet, slipping in his stocking feet; one big toe poked through a hole. Elijah pointed, and half the class laughed, even old Rocky Mountain Face joined in, one of his zits popping and oozing. Teeth stumbled into the seat in front of Ian, his face flushing crimson.

In the front row, Theodore sat completely still in self-preservation—don't join in, try to become invisible.

"That's enough." His first order. Would they listen?

The boys quieted, but the shit-eating grins on Elijah and Ian's faces remained.

This all felt like a lucid dream.

Miles pulled stacks of books from the box and assembled them like Jenga blocks on the desk. With the box emptied, he set it on the floor by his feet. The horde of ruffians watched. Ten rubbernecking faces. Twenty eyes. One hundred fidgeting fingers. An old recurring nightmare pulverized every conscious thought and socked him with the cold-sweat terror that haunted his days leading up to his first student-teaching gig—a classroom full of faces barely younger than his at twenty-five. Would he choke? Could he control a classroom?

He swallowed hard to stall for time. Flop sweat. Then blessed instinct floated up from the neurotic depths.

"I'm Mr. Baumgartner."

"Bum gardener." The curly-haired boy snickered. A hare lip no one had bothered to mend mangled the kid's mouth.

Elijah's eyes glimmered, nudging Miles off balance. Ian slid down further in his seat.

Husky took an opportunity. "Hey, Gunderson—ain't that your dad?"

Ian snarled, "My uncle," and sank even further.

"Nah." Elijah locked eyes with Miles. "It's Theo's new pal. Ain't that right?"

"Settle down."

Elijah raised his voice. "I said—ain't that right?"

Quiet with desperation, Miles's metaphoric knuckles went white upon the slippery reins of his fast-waning authority.

"Theo!" Elijah's green gaze burrowed into the back of Theodore's narrow, unmoving head. "You got a new pal? Huh? Watch out for strangers wanting to get into yer—"

"That's enough!" Miles's timbre startled the whole class to attention.

Except Elijah. A filthy smirk curled his thick lips.

Elijah wanted to challenge him? Bring it. Miles had conquered his fear of student teaching; he could certainly spar with this pint-sized insurgent. In one of his Honor's English classes, he had spent an entire period not saying a word—engaging the spellbound faces by snapping his fingers; rapping the chalkboard; kicking the underside of a desk for an empathic point.

He assayed this new field of students. He needed only to start, and they would settle down

"Everyone, come up and grab a book."

Theodore slid from his seat and took the proffered novel with gentle hands. "Thank you."

Ed Grimley coughed out, "Teacher's pet."

Couldn't even be smart and polite without being badgered. Reminded Miles of sixth grade, of St. Mark's school-wide spelling bee. He'd killed it the first day. Miss Goldman knew him for mouthing off and getting bad homework grades. She watched him with pinched suspicion. How was he cheating? Certainly couldn't be that he knew how to spell. On the opposite end of the spectrum, his classmates teased him for suddenly being a brainiac. For a brief hour on stage that day, he had shone, but no one wanted to amend their verdict of him. The next day, he just wanted the attention to be over, and he took a dive in the semi-finals, spelling 'semaphore' with an F. Peer pressure could devastate a child.

And here they were, singling out the one kid who might be teachable. The outsider. The unjaded.

Teeth unfolded from his seat and loped up the aisle.

Miles handed over a copy. "Don't you have shoes?"

Teeth shrugged and returned to his desk. Now that one of their own had participated, the rest dropped the show of being above it all and slouched on up.

Husky knocked into Theodore's shoulder as he passed. Maybe by accident; a big boy, Husky took up a lot of space. He snatched his book and held it up until it pressed against his nose. *"Lord of the Flies.* Gross."

"Give it a chance. I think you'll relate."

Husky's arms fell to his sides, and his eyes probed Miles's face, searching for any trace of an insult. And yeah, Miles had been thinking about Piggy, but Husky shook his head and when he sat back down, he opened the book and started reading the front matter.

Ian took his copy and grimaced. His transformation into a little punk seemed complete.

Ian's mentor Elijah never took his eyes off Miles. He plucked up a book and lingered for a couple extra seconds. Dammit! He broke eye contact with the boy. He busied himself with opening his own copy. Chapter One: "The Sound of the Shell". Elijah muttered under his breath and slid back behind Ian.

About a dozen books were left. Miles made two neat stacks, lifted them both, and swiveled to put them back into the broken box there on the floor. A long tearing noise broke the newfound quiet of the classroom.

What now?

The ripping came again.

Elijah held *Lord of the Flies* open in one hand. Eyes on Miles, he gripped a page between thumb and forefinger and, with an expression of ecstasy, tore out the page. His lips parted, lower lip fat and glistening. The page fluttered down, arcing gracefully before landing atop a growing pile.

A fuse popped in Miles's head. The children, the desks, the county-building speckled floor all became hyper-real. Like those night games at Miller Park. A familiar, hot ball tightened in Miles's stomach. Blood roared in his ears, a universe of murmuring voices. Deep inside—*deep*—his bright orange rage dragon stirred. It opened its eyes. It growled and shook off weariness from its long slumber inside its restraining egg. Its breath boiled up from Miles's bowels, steamed his heart, cooked his brain.

"Stop that!" He flew out from behind his desk and glared a challenge at the wide-eyed faces.

Elijah's pale moon face stared serenely at Miles as he pinched another page and tore it free of the book's binding. He opened his fingers with a magician's flourish, and the page see-sawed down.

Miles slammed a fist on the closest desk. Theodore yipped. The wooden top rattled, and the welds of the metal undercarriage creaked.

Faces gawked. Mouths hung open, ready to catch flies. *Lord of the Flies.*

Drunk on anger, he advanced between the columns of desks. Elijah's sneer grew closer. Uglier. His fists begged to knock the freckles off that mean, stupid face.

Then someone's foot snagged his ankle.

"Oof."

Miles went down. Hard. Cracking a knee into the floor, he keeled over. His other leg knocked against a desk, which squealed back an inch. Now he lay sprawled at Elijah's shoes.

The class erupted in laughter. Palpable embarrassment pushed him down, defied him to pick himself up and face humiliation. But his rage dragon thrived on childish derision, and it unfurled. Miles rose and brushed himself off.

Elijah set down his stripped book and applauded. Boys were stomping their feet, slapping their desktops. Miles's temper sucked in breath, ready to spit fire. Ian scrunched his face with mockery.

Miles cracked Ian across the face with an open hand.

Immediate silence.

Snowflakes plinked against the window.

Stunned, blank faces watched for what would happen next.

Ian's mouth dropped open. Tears sprang to his eyes, and he backhanded them away. His lips trembled but found no words.

From behind, hands grabbed Miles's shoulder and spun him around. Rancid breath splashed his face. Chaplain Allen, dressed in black shirt and trousers, peered down his long beaked nose.

"Mr. Baumgartner, control yourself." The clergyman shook him viciously.

The bubble of silence broke in a bout of wild chattering.

"I'm...." What had happened? What did he just do? "I'm...." Chaplain had shocked his rage away, leaving him dazed. Leaving him acutely aware of his crime. "I'm sorry."

Tremors started in his fingers. His calves. A tornado whirled and roared inside his head. He spun away and out of Chaplain's grip. He headed for the door, every step heavy. So heavy. Unintelligible murmurs at his back pushed him like a strong wind into the hallway. The minister shouted, "Silence!"

Miles fled into the stairwell.

Eleven

Over-tired. Over-stressed. He didn't mean to do it. He'd never done anything like that before.

Jeremy snickered inside his head.

Blinded by hysteria, he had somehow found his room. He paced from door to window, window to door, door to window, wringing his hands. He'd hit Ian. What was wrong with him?

He needed a cigarette.

He dug his phone from his pocket, caressing it like a charm that could calm. But until he charged it, the charm was powerless. He tossed it onto the writing desk, wincing at the thud as it landed.

What had come over him? He'd slapped a student!

Yet a part of him wanted to chase that rush of anger. He hadn't lost his temper in so long, and striking out had felt as satisfying as an alcoholic trading in his chip for a belt of bourbon. That Ian had been the target felt awful. Inexcusable. But the truth? Might as well admit it to himself; no one listened in on his thoughts. This hadn't exactly *never* happened before.... This was a temper relapse, and that quick sip had tasted wonderful.

Their last months together, Jeremy had put his foot down with an ultimatum, and Miles started seeing a therapist. Anger management. Stress techniques.

And okay, he hadn't been a saint even after the horror of what he'd done to Billy Rubin. He'd brawled at a frat party his sophomore year and landed on disciplinary probation. And he'd seen the inside of a jail cell after a bar fight over a game of darts on his twenty-ninth last-run-before-you're-thirty birthday party. Misdemeanor. Easy to forget.

Miles kept that back from Therapist Joe but did tell how literary quotations popped into his head when stress or anxiety whacked him a good one out of the blue. Joe liked that, encouraged that. But old Joe had more in mind. He helped Miles create the rage dragon—a personification of his temper. See it as a separate being, Joe said. Approach him. Calm him. Now contain him—imagine him returning to an egg. Get him in there. Stuff him in. Check the egg for cracks, and mend them as they occur. "How am I supposed to do that?" With forgiveness.

Another Joe-ism: Would you rather be happy or be right?

Goddamn asshat, that Therapist Joe. The rage dragon visualization was stupid. And being right was what made Miles happy. So there. In fact, riding a rush of anger made him absolutely ecstatic.

Lashing out as he had, after so long, had mainlined a fantastical high. A junkie's first hit of crack after a year of keeping the pipe tucked away. Sex, drugs, gambling, liquor—well, maybe a little Jim Beam—had never been his vices. Anger, though.... A mesmerizing elixir. Yeah, anger was his drug of choice.

A cigarette sure would taste great about now. A complement to the flavor of violence—a fine cigar with a snifter of brandy.

He opened the window, hoping that a cold blast of air would clear his head, but now that he'd popped the cork off everything he'd bottled up, all the turned wine of last year's events poured out.

Last Halloween, he had gone for drinks with his old friend Erin from high school. His first and only girlfriend from the closeted days. Jeremy, being Jeremy, had blown up about it.

"How would you like it if I had drinks with an ex? Maybe I'll call Taylor, see what he's up to."

As if that was the same thing.

As if Jeremy didn't have a harem of cuties as Facebook friends in all those groups he belonged to.

Miles didn't take the bait. He held his tongue and left. Jeremy could have a wild night with his terabyte drive of porn.

A single minute with Erin blasted his bad mood to bits. They shot pool at the Last Resort redneck bar, redolent with the perfume of stale beer. Peanut shells snapped underfoot. Erin fed wrinkled dollar bills into the Wurlitzer for REO Speedwagon hits. Last Resort stocked Woodford Reserve bourbon, and he quickly lost count of how many he'd drunk. That booze went down smooth, flashed fire in his belly, and jolted furry bliss into his brain. He felt laser focus on the billiard table. And they'd laughed like old times. All their goofy accents and invented characters romped. Dear God, he'd missed her. She remembered he loved Funyuns over potato chips; she played their favorite songs on the jukebox; she didn't just finish his sentences, she started them before he could speak the thoughts in his brain. If Erin had a penis, she'd be the man of his dreams.

Afterward, stumbling over his doorstep, the euphoria dried up. The atmosphere back home had built up thick and muggy. Jeremy was watching *Antiques Roadshow.* Kind of, but not really. Jeremy was waiting up for him. Cared enough to wait up, but not enough to marry him.

Miles struggled to hold onto the good, good, good... good vibrations, but Jeremy rose from that stupid sectional couch and shook his stupid head. Exactly the way he had last Christmas Eve on the Ferris wheel.

Therapist Joe's rage dragon breathed fire. "Don't scower at me."

"You mean scowl." With that patented smug look, Jeremy marched up inside Miles's personal space.

Miles hated that.

"Or glower." Jeremy wrinkled his nose. "God, you're drunk."

"No shit, Sherlock."

"What?"

What is that?—Jeremy's words on the Ferris Wheel. Past humiliation skewered, and he said the first thing that popped into his brain. "I hate you."

Not because he did, but because spite tasted sweet on his tongue.

"What did you say?" Jeremy got all up in his face.

Miles swung a drunken punch.

Not much force behind it. Bad aim. Or good, depending how one thought about it. His fist slapped against Jeremy's neck with an ineffectual but meaty *smack.*

Jeremy stumbled backward from shock. Or theatrics. Remorse pummeled Miles, and excuses flooded to mind: he hadn't meant it; he'd pulled his punch; he'd thought Jeremy was attacking him. But instead of crying out an apology, his rage dragon took advantage of his bourbon-soaked brain and roared, "I hate you!" once again.

Jeremy regained balance but kept walking backward until the backs of his legs hit that ugly sectional. He plopped down, perplexed and resentful. Playing the aggrieved party, as if Jeremy didn't have dozens of twinks as his clan members on all those iPhone games he endlessly played. Supposedly played. Because why did collecting wood and gold and merits and other stupid shit require excited bursts of typing?

"I hate you. I hate you!" Miles spun helplessly back in time, stuck on the Ferris wheel, reliving the ignominy over and over. A sober sliver of himself stood apart, repelled by his outburst. Horrified by his screams. "Why don't you leave? Just leave! Get out! I hate you."

After that he must have found his way to bed and passed out. He cried uncontrollably the next morning. Much of the previous night was missing from his memory, but the punch, the yelling, the hate had not hazed over.

"It's okay." Jeremy sat next to him. Held his hand. "I know, I know." But a pall clouded Jeremy's eyes.

They licked their metaphoric wounds and limped on together, Miles trying to believe that Jeremy had indeed forgiven and forgotten. That the scar on their relationship only mattered to himself, who couldn't leave it alone. Who liked to pick.

Time didn't heal sins, either.

They patched the injury with crude bandages of movie nights and dinners at Applebee's. But Miles couldn't go a day without his stomach cramping with self-reproach. Jeremy's smiles had become strained, his eyes critical whenever he thought Miles couldn't see.

But Miles did see.

He agreed to see Therapist Joe. He played along and created his orange rage dragon just to cage it up in a black-speckled egg.

But the damage had already been done. The relationship rotted from the inside out.

Enough remembering. And enough cooling down; he slammed the window shut, and tugged his old man Eddie Bauer sweater over his head. His nerves demanded a cigarette. Saliva watered his mouth. Like a phantom limb, the miniscule weight of those deadly cylinders pressed between his index and middle fingers.

Screw this.

Twelve

"Mr. Baumgartner!"

He was just outside the vestibule, so close to freedom. Underneath the stink, a trace of winter's sterile air filled the first floor. Filled his head.

Schramm stood outside his office. "Let me speak with you for a moment."

"I need some air." The tobacco would be chilled, the filter firm against his lips. The tip would flash and tobacco crackle when touched by the Bic's narrow flame.

"Only a couple minutes of your time."

Had Schramm already heard about the trouble in the classroom? Miles massaged his stiff neck. Could he simply ignore the superintendent? Whatever scolding he was in for—and rightly so, he had to be honest—would be easier with a head buzzing with nicotine. What would Schramm do if he walked away? Lock him in his cloister until the snow cleared and the bridge became passable?

"Miles, please. It's important."

Did he want to be happy or be right?

Fine. Get it over with. He took his now-usual seat as Schramm unhooked his suit jacket button and sank into the creaky chair.

"Look." Miles held up a finger to stop Schramm and get in the first words. "What hap—"

Schramm waved him off. "Some of the children got out of hand. These boys do need discipline."

"Well...."

Was he really off the hook?

The toilet stink of Schramm's office slackened. The maddening heat chugging from the fireplace lessened. Miles relaxed in his chair.

Slightly.

Schramm placed his palms together in old time prayer position. "I must convince you that St. Hamelin's is an institution that demands order."

There was a trick here somewhere. "Really, I overreacted." Miles crossed his legs. "But thank you. I appreciate and accept your apology." Such as it was. He coughed into his fist. Uncrossed his legs and stood. "Thanks for the chat. I should get going."

"Not so fast." An inscrutable flicker passed behind the superintendent's eyes. "You need assurances."

"No, thank you. I'm good."

"Sit down!"

Startled, Miles started to do just that, but he resisted. St. Hamelin's did need order—needed to get control of the inmates running the asylum. But Schramm sure the hell wasn't going to dictate what he did or said.

Yet he didn't turn and leave, either.

He stood in awkward silence, waiting for Schramm to mete out whatever justice would settle the classroom incident. He clicked his tongue and glanced casually around at the framed photos lining the walls. Two dozen black-and-white group pictures. No uniforms, so these must have been the parentless children in the years preceding the changeover to reformatory. He shivered—if he took a closer look, he would recognize the faces of the boys from the shrine. From the hydrotherapy room. And what of the other children in the pictures? Younger ones long ago adopted into a family's love. A new father's alcoholism. A mother's unyielding standards. And those that were cut loose at eighteen? Drifted through Depression-era misery. Or enlisted as doughboys on a boat to Nazi Germany. Most, if not all, dead by now. A wall of death. He squinted. Some of those faces—

"Chaplain Allen!"

Miles flinched at Schramm's welcome as Chaplain strode through the doorway. Now seemed a good time to take his seat again. Of course Schramm's conciliation had been a put-on, and now Chaplain had come to give his spin on what went down.

A frown played over Chaplain's thin lips, like wriggling mealworms. "He's here, Dr. Schramm."

Yeah, sitting right in front of him. Nothing like being talked about in the third person.

Schramm stood. "Bring him in."

What was this? Miles turned, and Chaplain stepped out of the office, returning immediately with Rocky Mountain Face in tow.

Schramm stepped up to take possession and tugged so hard on the boy's navy blazer that the shoulder seam ripped. He clamped a hand onto the boy's neck, pinching until Rocky squealed and gave up fighting.

Chaplain followed in their wake. "I've spoken with the boy. He had nothing to do with the brawl."

Schramm guided Rocky to the side of the big desk and shook his head in that slow, this-hurts-me-more-than-you gesture. Ignoring Chaplain, Schramm spoke to the boy.

"William."

"I didn't do nothin'!" Rocky looked from the superintendent to the chaplain and then to Miles. His forehead and cheeks flushed a crimson that camouflaged his zits.

"Keep still." Chaplain touched the boy's shoulder. "Sir, William is innocent of any wrong-doing. This was Mr. Baumgartner acting reprehensibly."

The fireplace felt hot again, the smell fetid.

Schramm twisted the boy around to face Miles. "Mr. Baumgartner, is William the young man who tripped you?"

"What?"

Rocky Mountain Face drew a deep breath, and Schramm slapped a hand over the boy's mouth so he couldn't speak. Rocky's eyes bulged. He squinted and opened and squinted again. A cipher of winks and blinks? A code for help?

Miles stood. "I don't think so."

Though Schramm held him tight, Rocky closed his eyes and slumped in relief.

As if it could be that easy.

"Take a moment and think about it." Schramm looked up at Chaplain. "Hold onto him."

Looking pained, Chaplain held onto Rocky's other side.

"I don't know who tripped me. But Rocky was sitting in the back row. I'm sure of it. He couldn't have done it."

Schramm threw up his hands like a Roman orator. "Who is this Rocky?" He played to an audience not there. "You are obviously confused. Now sit back down."

The stink in the office worsened with every passing moment. Schramm, Chaplain, Rocky Mountain Face, they all watched him. Schramm's eyes seemed all solid black pupil. A cold bead of sweat dripped from Miles's armpit, tickled the edge of his ribs, and trickled down into his boxers' waistband. His temper started to stoke, but he would never gain control of this situation if he exploded. He needed diplomacy to plead Rocky Moun—William's case. Create an opportunity for Schramm to believe that he'd decided on leniency himself.

"I'll sit when you let that child go." That hadn't come out very diplomatic. He gritted his teeth.

"Admirable of you." Schramm's available arm swept away papers and cleared a space on his desktop. There was a clattering as Schramm picked up some object that Miles couldn't see. "But an example must be made."

"It should be Mr. Baumgartner suffering the repercussions of his actions." Chaplain let go of William.

Schramm glared at Chaplain. "And what are the repercussions for dereliction of duty?"

A terse stalemate played out. Felt like minutes upon minutes upon minutes, but in a blink, a breath, a heartbeat, Chaplain moved to William's back, leaned into the boy, and squeezed a bear hug around him. Distaste souring his face, he grabbed the boy's hands and pinned them onto Schramm's desk.

"Please!" William wriggled in Chaplain's arms, eyes bright with panic—a rabbit cornered by a fox.

Chaplain shook his head. Maybe eased up a little.

Schramm growled. "Chaplain Allen, what does Solomon say? 'Do not withhold discipline from a child; if you beat him with a rod, he will not die. If you beat him with the rod, you will save his soul'."

Chaplain stared down the curved length of his nose; his glacial eyes fixed on Miles.

William barked muffled exhortations.

Time was running out if Miles wanted to stop whatever came next. "It wasn't William. Listen to me. It couldn't have been him bec—"

"Whether William is guilty or not...." Light glinted off the serrated letter opener in Schramm's fist. "Is beside the point. He is an object lesson. For you Miles, but also for you, Chaplain. Bring your dogs to heel. This is still my facility."

A knot in the firewood exploded, and Miles jerked in his skin.

"Hold him tight, Chaplain. And make sure Miles can see. Can you see, Miles?"

More than he cared to. Fireplace flames winked off the brass blade.

"No!" Miles leapt and grabbed Chaplain's arm, but Chaplain swung a hip and knocked Miles off-balance. Miles held on, and Chaplain's grip on Rocky loosened.

Schramm grappled with the boy. "Chaplain!"

Chaplain grabbed the green marble Golden Globe paperweight. With a grunt and a sigh, he cracked the sphere high on Miles's forehead.

Miles's legs seemed to disappear. He fell against the chair, the base of his skull clipping the edge of the seat.

Intense heat jabbed his brainpan. All his limbs went to sleep, like he'd jammed his finger into an outlet.

Schramm shouted. "The boy, Chaplain!"

Chaplain threw the paperweight at Miles's face, and it connected with his eye. Chaplain pushed Schramm out of the way and kneed the backs of William's legs, shoving the boy's belly into the edge of Schramm's desk. He pressed his full weight into Rocky, taking a stronger hold than before. More conviction. Chaplain pinched the bunch of nerves at the base of Rocky's neck and bent the boy's head down. Probably imagining the boy was Miles, Chaplain ground William's cheek into the paperclips scattered on the desk while his other hand held tight to William's right wrist.

"There's...." So befuddled. What did he need to say? "Stop it."

Schramm peeled the boy's fingers apart. "Don't talk yourself into punishment of your own, Mr. Baumgartner."

Chaplain grumbled deep in his chest.

William's feet scuffling against the floor. Chaplain's back, his shoulders, his arm contorted with effort. Schramm gripped the letter opener like a kitchen knife and bent to work.

William's voice shrilled. "Please!"

Miles parroted in a mumble. "Please." He blinked at the two men as they strained. His cranium reverberated like a tuning fork, and his legs and arms wouldn't move. Somehow he needed to get up, drag those men off of the boy. Rocky Mountain Face. The rat-killer. Smartass. William. Now just a boy in trouble. Schramm and Chaplain intent on mauling this scared little kid.

William squealed.

Schramm's face bobbed up over Chaplain's shoulder. A streak of blood on his cheek. Tremors of exertion rolled through Chaplain's muscles, and Schramm bent back out of view. A flash of William's shin kicked out between the chaplain's wide-set legs. Chaplain adjusted. Schramm's arm drew back. Forward. Back.

A thin sound, like sawing through balsa wood.

William shrieked.

Dime-sized spots of blood pattered down onto the wooden floor.

Schramm's arm stroked back and forth.

Miles battled his limbs and managed to sit up. His head spun. Ears rang.

Chaplain's muscles rippled under his staid black shirt.

Black drops the size of quarters. Half-dollars. Now a stream.

William shrieked again, a deafening ululation.

Schramm pulled. There was a wet sucking sound, and he stumbled back a half step. His letter opener had become a crimson dagger held loosely in one hand. A severed finger wilted in the other.

Miles reached behind him for the chair and pulled it close. He levered himself to his knees but had to stop there. Ringing filled his head, high and insectile—summer cicadas tracking August heat-waves of his youth, he and Minnie drifting in their plastic kiddie pool. This was all because of her.

The bloody letter opener clattered to the desk. "Chaplain, mind the floor." A drawer opened; Schramm's head ducked down. Resurfaced. He passed a white cloth to the chaplain.

Chaplain freed a hand and took the measly handkerchief.

William's eyes rolled toward his finger in Schramm's fist. He chuffed, a breathless sound lost between a sob and a scream. His legs gave out; his skinny body slipped out of the chaplain's grasp and crumpled to the floor.

Chaplain knelt and rolled the limp body to face the ceiling. His head swiveled toward Miles, telegraphing contempt.

Rocky Mountain Face's complexion had paled to match the handkerchief. Even his pimples had turned grey. His eyelids ticked, as if he dreamed in REM. Chaplain wrapped the handkerchief around the boy's traumatized hand. The makeshift bandage soaked through with scarlet.

"Take him to the infirmary."

Chaplain slid his long arms under the child's neck and knees and lifted. The boy murmured but didn't wake.

"Oh," Schramm called after Chaplain. "Find Butch and tell him my floor needs mopping."

Still on his knees, Miles smacked his lips, working up enough saliva to speak. "Barbaric."

Schramm disappeared behind the desk and came up with another handkerchief, rubbing at the blood on his fingers.

Miles grappled with the chair, climbing to his feet. His stomach wanted to barf. He swayed.

Schramm picked up the letter opener and wiped it clean. "If you had struck anyone other than your own flesh and blood, you'd be lying in the infirmary next to William." He stowed the blade in the top drawer, and began dabbing at the blood on his desk. He managed only to swirl the puddle around. He sighed and ceased the effort. He stared at the mess. "Obviously, you won't be returning to the classroom."

Miles closed his eyes and concentrated on settling his stomach. If he'd eaten breakfast, he would have lost the battle and vomited. "I...." The office's heat burned his cheeks, but his bones felt cold and tight. They had just tortured a little kid. In front of him. "I understand."

"I hope you do, Mr. Baumgartner." There would be no more Christian names. "With the boys no longer occupied, I'd stay out of their way. If I were you. They'll be angry at what you made me do to Mr. Koehler."

"I didn't—"

"Stay in your room. Miss Poole will bring your meals to you."

Thirteen

He gulped winter air to quench the sick throbbing in his guts.

He hadn't bowed to Schramm's will and gone to his room. He had careened through the hallways to the side door and spilled out into the snow.

How could Schramm have done that?

And a chaplain? That token show of reluctance hadn't stopped him from holding Rocky down.

Gently, Miles touched the knot on his forehead where Chaplain had brained him. He checked his fingers. No blood. The goose egg was enormous, though, and radiated profound bolts of pain through his skull.

He lurched into the snowdrift to his right, bent, and grabbed hold of his knees. Don't throw up. Don't throw up. He squeezed his eyes shut until a tear leaked out. He snuck in a shallow breath. His stomach didn't mind that. He breathed deeper, imagining soothing blue filling his mouth and nose, flowing down his throat. Coating his stomach. Okay. Much better. He opened his eyes.

Snow had stopped falling. Through a thick gauze of cloud cover, the sun shone so weakly that he could stare right up at it. The star hadn't yet reached the middle of the sky overhead. Not even afternoon? All of this in a single morning. Incomprehensible.

Snow devils skittered over the landscape. Way off to his left, these swirling skeins of snow blurred the treeline. The wind carried a ceaseless murmuring.

His veins thirsted for that cigarette.

He started off toward the carriage house and came to a cleared path. Butch and his snow removal. On either side, the snow came up to Miles's knees. As he neared the makeshift parking garage, the drifts grew to hip-height. He wrapped his arms around him, tucked his head, and let the squall at his back nudge him onward. The snowy grass underfoot squeaked like fresh cheese curds. The kind he and Jeremy used to buy at the Mousehouse. When life was sane. When things made sense.

Snow and ice in the ornate stone fountain mixed with decaying leaves floating on stagnant water, turning the bowl into swampy mulch. At the front of the carriage house, the plowed snow towered taller than him—thick at the base and sloping upward. There'd be no digging through that to get at the doors. He would have to find another way in. Between here and the treeline, indistinct shapes dashed from St. Hamelin's main building to the hump of the cafeteria.

The kids?

The sky darkened by a degree and spat flurries. Just like the night of the Ferris Wheel. The Christmas Eve that shattered their relationship. They had kept going for more than a year afterward, but that was the night that started the acrimony signaling the end. Loving the same music and movies and reading the same novels should have been enough. It had felt like enough. He had shopped for weeks, passing over so many clunky men's rings until finding the perfect white-gold band with tactful—masculine—diamond settings. He bought it in early autumn and hid it in his underwear drawer. A week before Christmas, he told Jeremy not to accept any Christmas Eve invitations. Pass on the office party. Decline drinks with their friends. Leave Christmas Eve open and wear the tux from the back of the closet. He was giddy with the secret. Finally the night came; the white limousine pulled to the curb. Dinner at the lakeside restaurant. The horse-drawn carriage to Madison's Holiday Festival. Hopping on the Ferris Wheel, his heart slammed in his throat, but he forced himself to wait until their turn came to pause at the top. He had knelt, the car swaying like it might dump him to the ground. The cold, ridged metal floor dug into his knee. From below, the blinking Christmas lights painted Jeremy's handsome face with red-green-blue-white. He had almost fumbled taking the ring out of his coat pocket. His prepared speech vanished from his mind so he simply asked, "Will you marry me?"

Jeremy's response: "What is that?"

What is that? The hell kind of answer was that?

Jeremy hadn't even taken the ring, much less slid it on. Much less said yes.

Like their first date walking from the Soglin 7 to Café Monet, they didn't speak another word. The bottle of Moët he had set out while Jeremy waited for the limo to show sat in its bucket of melted ice, a cruel joke. He polished it off himself.

Holy Hell, why was he thinking about this now?

He rubbed his arms to warm himself up. Stomped his feet but felt nothing below his knees. The cold ate right through his jeans and sweater. Penetrated through skin to his bones. Were his smokes worth this trouble?

Yup.

He went off-road and doggy-paddled up the snowbank to reach the side of the carriage house. He sunk several inches in the snow that crested up past the windows on the windward side. He could have reached the roof if he wanted. He hiked around the back side of the carriage house. This venture meant more than just the stupid cigarettes, now. They couldn't keep him from his car. His stuff. And screw how petulant that sounded. He was not one of Schramm's delinquents.

A little farther....

There. He'd taken the long way around to the leeward side and found what he needed. Between the piles of snow that had rounded the corners lay a valley where the wind couldn't reach and form drifts. He slid down on his butt to bare ground—a five-by-five canyon of crispy dead grass. Must have been twenty degrees warmer here.

Frost crusted two double-hung windows set about shoulder-height. He tugged his sweater cuff over the heel of his hand and wiped. All that did was mix grime into the frost. Just two panes each, top and bottom. A tight fit. But no turning back now.

He needed that cigarette.

He needed his charger.

He needed to see that his car waited inside. Intact. So easy to imagine his Chevy's hood up, wires cut, hoses sliced, radiator busted like those movies where mutant cannibalistic hillbillies stow their victims' cars out back in a perpetually growing automobile graveyard.

Miles slapped his palms against the cold glass and pushed up. The window didn't budge. Cumulus clouds of breath swam around his head as he tried again. His shoulder ached from the strain of reaching up to the window. His fingers grew arthritic-stiff in the cold.

Was that sarcastic applause buried underneath the wind? Coughing? Maybe obnoxious laughter.

No time for that. Miles pressed his belly against the boards of the outside wall, stood on tiptoe, and inspected the window. The sash lock in the middle of the window— why hadn't he thought of that? He yanked his sleeve further until it stretched and covered his hand. He jabbed a fist at the glass.

Nothing.

He imagined Schramm's face. He cocked his arm, swung like Ali, and the window broke, falling away in jagged dusty pieces. He busted out the remaining shark teeth of broken glass.

No need to unlock it now.

He held onto the lower rail and jumped, pulling himself halfway through the window. He then wiggled on his belly until his waist crossed over, and his balance shifted. Whoa, steady. But he lost it, tipped and nosedived, the floor swimming up to meet him. His heels cracked into the check rail and stopped his fall for a second—just long enough to throw his arms over his head. His feet cleared, and he hit the packed dirt floor, rolling into a half-assed somersault before toppling to his side.

The bump on his head exploded into pain. Thick waves of it that crowded out all thought. He lay in the dirt, curled into a comma, until the agony subsided. He rolled onto his back, huffing from exertion. Forty-one was too old for breaking and entering. Even his fingernails hurt. But he got to his feet.

He stood in a corridor with wide stalls on either side. Wooden support posts ran the length of the aisle until a turn into the shorter leg of the L-shaped building. At the junction, windows looked out onto snow pressed hard against the glass, as if the coach house had been swabbed in cotton. Natural insulation, the temperature in here felt only October-chilly. Pastoral smells of horses and hay lingered even after what must have been decades since the carriage house actually housed carriages.

Farther in, a couple of cracked saddles and a scattering of bridles hung from hooks inside the stalls. Dust and dirt had settled onto the tack—onto the stirrups, halters, reins, and bits, but the neglect felt safe. Peaceful. An undulating metropolis of spiderwebs covered the shallow vault of the ceiling.

Musky animalism grew denser the farther in he went. After the corridor branched off, the stalls had been stripped. Six or seven classic cars and pickups lined both sides. Yeah, he could picture Schramm as a car collector. Those uptight control freaks loved collections—an outlet for fastidiousness. Parked among them, was Jessie, his trusted Chevy.

"Oh, thank God." Finding her here felt even better than that Fourth of July when he'd wandered lost in the

Walmart parking lot for twenty minutes. He caressed her trunk. She was solid. Real.

Hold on. He turned and stared into the dark.

"Elijah?"

Maybe wind stirred from the busted window.

"Ian?"

But it sounded so much like whispers. Shuffling footsteps. Schramm had warned him that the boys would be angry about Rocky Mountain Face's sawn-off finger.

Now with his ears straining, he heard nothing more.

If anything, it had been rats.

A cigarette would straighten him out.

He squeezed in beside a red ZZ Top car. Jessie's door opened right up—Butch hadn't even had the courtesy to lock up after stealing his car. He fell into the comfortable bucket seat. Right there under the radio and ashtray, a beautiful white tangle of cord.

He closed his eyes. "Thank you."

Now if his phone could connect to a cell tower this far north, he would call for.... Help? Fat chance of that. Bridge being out screwed up both directions. As soon as he possibly could, though, he would report Schramm and Chaplain for their abuses. Shut this hellmouth down and barter a probation deal for Ian.

He shut the door and elbowed down the lock. Damn, it felt good to sit in a familiar seat. The whole car smelled like his old life, like coffee and cigarettes and Doritos.

Old life? He'd been at St. Hamelin's for a single day. Time felt mushy here. He'd swear that he had already spent a full month snowbound.

He popped open the glove box and grabbed that glorious pack of Marlboros and his lighter and sat back. With shaking hands, he fumbled open the flip-top box and fished out one coffin nail. The cigarette fit the groove of his two fingers. He planted the filter between his lips. Cold. Firm, like he'd imagined. A deep, secret taste of tobacco. When he flicked his Bic, the stiff wheel produced a worthless spark. Two more flicks of the metal rotors over the flint but nothing happened. Come on, come on. Not this. Not now. On the fourth try, a yellow flame caught and held. He chuckled and touched it to the tip of the cigarette. A burning orange ring ate the paper at the end. Harsh smoke filled his lungs. Such sweet pressure. He held it in like a hit of pot before expelling a huge plume of blue that put clouds of breath to shame. That antsy keening in his arms and legs smoothed out. His hands stopped shaking.

Thoughts came into focus.

He glanced into the rearview mirror. Inadvertently, of course. Not to watch for Elijah or Husky sneaking up on him.

After a third drag, the paranoia fled. He felt truly himself for the first time in over twenty-four hours. Quitting had been a stupid idea. He couldn't give up cigarettes and Jeremy at the same time.

He pulled out the ashtray, tapped, and sucked.

He frowned as his head swam faster. His stomach rolled over, queasy. Okay, so maybe this hadn't been the best idea.

He stubbed out the cigarette.

He stuffed the charger into his jeans pocket.

He checked the rearview mirror again. The nicotine had made him edgy. Still, he pushed the lighter into the box to keep them together and lifted his butt off the seat to get the pack into the pocket with the charger. Done, he slumped back down and waited to catch his breath.

And start a plan.

Was the storm petering out for good or just taking a breather? When his phone charged, he could check WeatherNow, but he had a bad feeling about those ominous clouds over the treeline.

When he climbed out of the car, he punched the lock down. Just in case. The light from the windows had dimmed, and shadows thickened in all the nooks and spaces.

"Storm's a-comin." His Butch impersonation came out flat, and too loud in the stillness. He shut up and re-traced his steps down the aisle of old cars.

He rounded the corner into the corridor leading to the exit window. On either side, the stalls had grown dark. It would be easy for a kid to hide in that murk.

Not the time to think about that. He rushed through the gauntlet, like Ian used to do when they would visit one of the haunted houses on the Wisconsin Dells strip. The real scares came, not when employees dressed as evil clowns and movie monsters jumped out at them, but during the in-between moments, creeping through the dark silent lull from one set-up to the next with no idea when and what the next fright would be.

He grabbed the windowsill. The air tasted thin, and he drank several deep breaths.

Two quick scratches and a thump from a stall behind him.

"Ha. Ha. Very nice." He forced a tone of humor in his voice that he did not feel. "You followed me here. Good for you."

Something like a breath, something like a whisper off to his right.

These kids were relentless.

"You saw what Superintendent Schramm did to your buddy?" He forced himself to turn back to the window. "You want to avenge him? I get that. Go for it. But I didn't do that. That wasn't me."

Maybe a spiteful Rocky Mountain Face—he would never be William—had snuck out of the infirmary. Eyes glassed-over with fever. Hair sweat-plastered to his fore-head. The ragged stump crudely bandaged, blood seeping through the gauze. Come to cut off a piece of Miles.

He jumped and pulled himself up the window sill.

Giggling burst from one of the stalls. Followed by *Shhh*.

He knew that shush.

His sneaker toes ground into the wall as he wriggled like a salamander until his head and shoulders poked out the window. Those gnarly clouds had moved into position directly overhead. Flurries had escalated to full snow, and a gale whistled through the eaves.

Elijah shouted, "Now!"

A quick look behind didn't show a thing except his legs, kicking like a swimmer's. He slapped his hands on the rough outside and dragged his chest over the window-sill and out. With another push, his belly cleared. At his waist, the sweater snagged on a chip of glass still in the frame. He thrashed—a hooked fish—but reached a hand in and slid the knit over its obstacle. He couldn't get his hand out from under his stomach in time, and his upper body tilted down. He started to slide.

One jeans leg caught on something and pulled taut. The cuff rolled up toward his knee. A hard pinch needled his calf. He cried out and struggled at the searing of the flesh high above his Achilles' heel. He jerked his leg to pull away, but the piercing dug in further. Warmth spilled up his leg. He clawed at the wall and kicked madly. His leg ripped free, and he yawped, tumbling from the window and pile-driving his shoulder into the ground.

Amazingly he didn't snap his neck, but the collision knocked the wind out of him. His mouth and jaw worked, but he'd forgotten how to breathe.

Panic shot fireworks into his head.

Was that noise the howling wind or laughter from inside the carriage house?

An inrush of breath finally inflated his lungs. He untangled his limbs and sat on the ground for a moment, gathering himself as the seat of his jeans got cold. No one climbed out of the window after him so he pulled up his pants cuff to check out the damage. Snow blew off the roof and sheets of it doused his head and body. He wiped his eyelashes clear and took a good look at the wound. He swiped a hand across his eyes again. What the hell? He grabbed his leg in both hands and twisted himself into a yoga pretzel.

The gash in his calf formed two distinct arcs of blood-filled dashes.

Teeth marks.

Footsteps crunched toward him from above. He dropped his leg. Around the carriage house corner, a giant shape emerged, walking on the drifts. A three-dimensional shadow of a man loomed above him, head ballooned and rounded, massive shoulders slumping.

"Tryin ta 'scape?" The voice called through the renewed storm. "Won't get far."

Butch. His figure voluminous in the big parka.

"Something bit me!"

Butch's normal shout bested the wind. "Yeah. He does that."

Fourteen

Darkness faded into a muddied yellow.

Large, ill-defined blobs materialized.

Heavy mallet strikes pounded in his head. He wasn't cold anymore. Not lying on the ground either. Had to think.... He'd been sitting on the frozen ground outside the carriage house. Butch had found him, reached out for him, and Miles had started up the drift.

After that, nothing but dead air.

Shoulders aching, biceps sore, he brought his hands up to his face. The bump on his forehead seemed to have grown another inch. He explored the tenderness under his left eye, where the paperweight had hit, until his surroundings came into focus. He lay on a twin bed, but not his. Far off, utensils clinked, a faucet ran. Sickly-sweet smells pushed through the doorway.

He tried to sit up but the mallet inside his skull knocked him back. He ground his teeth and struggled up. He'd been laid out in a room fractionally larger than a walk-in closet, with wood paneling varnished to a dark yellow and dotted with pine knots. The single lamp on an end table at the head of the bed gave off that jaundiced light. No window, and the dimensions of the room really felt too narrow—as if a second bedroom had been partitioned off.

A draft caressed his bare arms.

Bare arms?

And bare chest with its mat of dark hair. He sat naked but for dingy white briefs.

Where were his boxers?

An area of his calf stung, and he crossed his legs for a look: in the center of a red, swollen patch, two blood-crusted crescents indented the skin.

The bite had actually happened.

He stood, squinting as the mallet turned into a sledgehammer. Standing made him feel more vulnerable, a larger target in a strange room wearing a stranger's underwear. No sign of his clothes. No furniture other than the bed and night-table. But a shelf—homemade with varnished boards supported by metal brackets—circled the room. On it, wrapping the walls, stood thirty—maybe forty—glass jars sized from jam-jars to gallon jugs.

He stepped closer. The shelf had been installed high, just above eye-level. Liquid the ocher color of dehydrated urine filled a pickle jar. A brown mass floated inside. Furry. He shifted for a better angle. White spots. A white puff of tail. A fawn—the size of a doll, but apparently real.

His mind felt like an empty thought bubble.

Massaging a crick in his neck, he moved on to the next jar. Suspended in the liquid, a tawny-furred animal the size of a gerbil. Another fawn, this one too young for spots. He spun slowly, checking the other jars. Preserved deer fetuses in all of them.

Wait. Not every one.

In the corner by the end table and lamp, he found a different mass. He went up on tippy toes. A squat baby food jar sat tucked between two larger jars. The glass was chilly as he brought it down to take a good look. He rotated the jar, and a narrow cylinder maybe three inches long bobbed in the formaldehyde. Miles squinted.

Butch's missing thumb.

Butch startled him, hollering from the doorway. "You up for all day?" He chuckled. His eyes flicked down to his thumb jar in Miles's hands.

Miles's face flushed hot. "What happened?"

Butch's aggressive affability shut off. His face turned to stone. "An accident."

"Same accident that took your thumb?" Miles tucked the baby food jar back on the shelf. "Same accident that closed down the orphanage?"

"You could say that."

A string of nonsense words shouted from elsewhere in the house, and Miles flushed hot. What an asshole, now he knew the cause.

Butch snapped back into good cheer. "Look purty good in my drawers!"

Drawwwrs. Like when nine-year-old Ian had gone through his dinosaur phase, roaring to give voice to his plastic T-Rex stomping over the kitchen table, terrorizing his mac and cheese and hot dogs.

Miles crossed his hands to cover his crotch. "Where am I? What happened out by the carriage house?"

Butch picked at the stump where his thumb used to be. "I caughtcha breakin in da garage." *Gradge.* "Ya fainted, and I dragged ya home."

Butch's face projected a perfect blank of innocence. Too much so? He remembered Butch's black silhouette. The bite mark smarting. *He does that.* That's what Butch said. Only a blank space between then and now. How he ended up in this glorified closet in another man's drawwwrs, he could only guess.

"Where are my clothes?"

"Der 'bout dry. Betty warshed them."

"And my things?"

"All yer belongin's out in the da livin' room."

Miles stepped toward the doorway, toward Butch, but the groundskeeper didn't move. Had he turned back into that stony version of himself? Butch watched through his thick glasses for a few seconds. Taking the measure of the big shot from Madison? The tension smelled like a brewing fight. Miles had youth on his side—how often could he say that these days?—but Butch was a hard man. Callused, rough hands. Neck-snapping hands.

Butch scratched his purple boxer's nose and came back to life. "Course!" Butch called over his shoulder, "Betts! Our guest is up!" Back to Miles. "You want a steak to put on that shiner?"

"No."

Butch harrumphed and limped from the room.

Miles hurried after, shrugging off the wretched weight of the room full of dead baby deer. Beyond lay a living room cramped with overstuffed furniture. More heavily varnished wood paneling glowed bronze. Cheap gold flake picture frames hung crookedly. A dozen throw rugs covered the floor. He'd bet his life that the kitchen had been outfitted with those avocado green appliances so popular in the 60s and 70s. A pungent candy smell assailed him.

And when they approached the little house they saw that it was built of bread and covered with cakes, but that the windows were of clear sugar.

Betty emerged from the kitchen, red-faced and panting. "Gobba habba subber ina heh?"

"You want supper in here?" Butch translated. "Or in the kitchen? Out here I can put on the news."

Butch and Betty? First thing around here that made any sense.

Miles found his jeans, flannel shirt, and sweater draped over a cane-backed chair set up facing the stone fireplace. His charger and cigarette pack lay on the seat, next to his boxers and socks, getting toasty. His paltry belongings. What an inconsequential mark he had left on the world.

"Where's my phone?"

"Yer what?"

"Phone. I had it on me."

Butch's eyes narrowed. "I ain't seen no telephone around."

Miles snatched up the charger and cigarettes. Maybe he'd left his phone in his cloister after fleeing the classroom. This entire day blurred. "I need to get going."

"My girl wenta all dis trouble fer ya!"

Betty stared. Butch studied him. Cloying heat from kitchen and hearth burrowed into his pores.

"Something bit me." He grabbed his shirt off the chair. "In the coach house, something bit my calf."

"Prolly caught a nail, breakin in."

Buttoning up, Miles glared. "I remember what you told me. You said, 'He does that." He snatched his boxers. "When will the bridge be back up?"

"Don't you worry bout dat! We'll take good care aya!"

"You've done a bang-up job so far."

"What's that?"

"Nothing." Miles kneaded his boxers. "I'm getting dressed." Grabbing up the rest of his clothes, he burned his fingers on one of the jeans' hot rivets.

"That can wait." Butch's voice rattled the windows. "Yer dinner's comin."

Betty returned from the kitchen, carrying a tin TV tray. She unfolded its spindly legs in front of a massive brown recliner that looked like it fell off a five-storey roof.

"I'm not going to wait. This'll only take a second."

"Sit down!" Not just a shout this time, but a direct order harsher than Schramm's same demand.

He summoned an uncomfortable smile of apology and retreated into the deer fetus room. Under those embryonic gazes, he stripped off Butch's *drawwwrs*. His dick dangled for a moment before shrinking up as if ashamed. His scrotum retreated into a hard ball against his groin.

"Ain't playin with the yerself in der?" Butch called.

Betty jabbered. She didn't seem the type for bawdy humor.

He slipped on his boxer shorts, luxuriously warm. Before he could dress further, Betty chugged into the room. Miles screened his crotch with his stiff jeans. "What are you doing? Get out."

Betty thrust his pack of cigarettes at him, the pack rippled from water damage. He jerked to catch his smokes, and she snatched at the warm pants.

"Stop." He caught the cigarettes. Lost the jeans. He lunged for the sweater he'd thrown on the bed, but Betty beat him to it. His sweater and jeans in her clutches, Betty stormed from the room.

"Come eat yer supper!"

Madness. All of it madness.

At least he had socks and his own underwear, right? He paused and pressed the sore edges of his leg wound. He ran his fingers lightly over the dashes branded into his flesh. Undeniably a jaw imprint. Small. Boy-sized. It should have been impossible to imagine this happening, but he had long since crossed the border of the rational into the territory of the bizarre.

Yeah, he does that.

Elijah had darted out from the shadows, raced to Miles's wriggling legs, and chomped down on his calf with evil glee glittering in those shocking green eyes. He knew it had been Elijah. Not a doubt. Elijah looked like a biter.

He felt a nervous urge to pee.

All he had to do right now was break bread with Ma and Pa Kettle. Then he would scurry back to the relative safety of his room. He took a deep, steadying breath.

"There y'are!"

"She took my jeans."

"Don't sulk."

Passing the chair, he grabbed up his iCharger.

Betty yammered.

Inspired, "Do you have any coffee? Please."

His tucked his cigarettes and charger under his balls as he sank into the busted brown recliner behind the TV tray. Apparently, he wasn't good enough company to warrant the nice tan one. Fine by him. That one sat too close to Butch, and Betty, as she set a steaming mug on his tray and settled onto the quilt-covered couch under the picture window. Feeble light showed around the edges of their bland curtains. Betty kept a scattering of ivies hanging from the walls. Cozy place. But that sugary reek mixed with the savory wafting from the kitchen and triggered his gag reflex.

He blew over the surface of the coffee and sipped. Gah! Cowboy coffee. He chewed the grounds and swallowed the sludge.

Butch watched him. Betty dug into her food.

On his plate: a chunk of grey venison half-covered by clumps of damp boiled potatoes resting on their own moist skins. Could he sit there and wait them out? His stomach growled despite the off-putting smell. Long day. His tank was empty. He took up knife and fork and attacked the steaming mess. With each mulchy mouthful, his stomach rejoiced at hot food.

"Don't my girl do a good job?"

Betty mumbled and flapped an arm to quiet him, but a smidgen of pride shone in her flaring rosacea.

Another forkful, and his stomach gurgled uneasily at the muck piling up inside. He squirmed. He needed a distraction to tamp down a bathroom emergency. He fixated on the fireplace. Ubiquitous black iron grille with matching firepokes. Above the mantel, Butch had mounted a jackalope head to a wooden plaque the shape of Wisconsin.

"Shot that one m'self!" Butch beamed at his prize. Betty slapped his arm, and they both guffawed.

Why did Butch think he had a city boy from New York in his living room? Miles knew all about jackrabbits with buck horns glued to their foreheads. Jackalopes. Give him a break.

A tectonic shift of meat and potatoes in his bowels jolted him to his feet. The TV tray flipped over, and supper slopped onto the rugs as the tray clattered.

"I'm so sorry." He slapped a hand over his mouth and hiccup-burped. Danger passed. "I thought I might throw up."

Butch and Betty glowered.

"Nothing against your cooking. It was—" A greasy belch spilled from his lips.

Butch stood so fast that his knees popped. "Think it's time to put on yer britches!"

"Which is all I wanted to do in the first place!"

Butch's ruddy cheeks darkened.

Miles had used "the tone"—Jeremy's label for his frustrated voice. "If I can have my pants back, I'll gladly get going."

Butch tapped Betty's shoulder. "Fetch Mr. Big Shot his clothes."

Betty spat what might have been profanity, but she rose from the couch and tottered into the kitchen, returning a minute later with his cooled-down pants and sweater.

"Thank you." He snatched them and hurried back into the macabre deer fetus room. The Levi's had tightened up on him. He squatted to stretch the denim. He needed to hurry and get out while his stomach was still satisfied with where it had layered the food, adrenaline, and nausea. He stuffed his tight pockets with the smokes and charger and reentered the living room where a couple hand towels rested over the mess he'd made on the floor.

"Okay. I'll get out of your hair."

"Betts is got some cobbler, take witchya."

Dear God, no. What happened to the consensus that he should leave?

He didn't spare another second. "I can't." He fumbled with the doorknob. Locked. He'd be stuck here all night. Forever. Caged like an animal until he joined the other specimens in the jars—

Butch leaned over Miles's shoulder, a surging smell of dirty *terlet* water belting Miles across the face. "Here ya go." Butch snapped open the deadlock but didn't back off. Miles opened the door, pushing his backside against

Butch, and slipped outside. Where the cold stole his breath away. And furious snowflakes fell. At the far treeline, under the weight of accumulated snow, the branches groaned, distant, vicious sighs.

Fifteen

Jesus Christ. The smell!

Ripped-out book pages littered his room—floor, desk, bed. Pages stuck to the walls. The window. A thick stink of shit gagged him. He wrapped the crook of his elbow over his nose and mouth and charged inside. Wound through the mess on the floor. Found purchase at the window and opened it up. Winter blasted inside, turning his room into an aviary where the edges of pages fluttered like wings. One smooched off the wall and took flight. A second later, an entire flock took to the air. He slammed the window closed.

That godawful smell! Grunting to a knee, he stretched the fingers of one hand into a tripod on the floor to keep balanced. Up close, every torn-out page wore thick brown streaks. No need for a better look. Or smell. Two or three books' worth of *Lord of the Flies* pages had been smeared with feces.

Wow. Just... wow.

The crescents in his calf throbbed. Lub-dub. Lub-dub.

He spotted a dented metal trash can shoved into the far corner under the desk. He duck-walked to it and pulled it out. His knees snapped as he stood. He peeled a befouled page from the window glass and dropped it into the trash can. Went after another. Saliva filled up the back of his throat with the urge to throw up, and his eyes watered.

He cleared the window. Next, the desk where his phone sat pressed against the wall, untouched. Thank God.

Squatting, he pinched torn pages between his fingers and dropped them in the bin. Every few pages, he came across a clean one and used that to compact the growing stack. Why hadn't he grabbed a bunch of toilet paper from the bathroom to wrap around his hands for this work? He'd used up his allotment of towels, and would need to scrounge up a bunch more to scrub the residue off surfaces where the pages had stuck.

"Goddammit."

The trash can was filled to the brim with two chapters' worth of William Golding still glued to the dresser. Four or so chapters on his bed. He threw the remaining pages on the blanket, and wrapped it up as he had the rat.

He would not think about the slippery grit on his fingers.

Titters preceded his walk down the hallway. Boys jubilant behind their doors. Mr. Bum-gardener got what was coming to him.

His dragon stirred.

He tugged open the incinerator's jaw. The squealing hinges matched the resonant frequency of his grinding teeth. First, the blanket swished down. Then he upended the trash can, but he'd stamped the pages down so tight that none came out. Frustration growled in the back of his throat. He shook the can, the edges bumping ineffectually off the corners of the chute.

"Dammit!"

His arms quaked with anger barely kept in check. He banged the trash can against the chute, the hatch, the wall, each crunch releasing bursts of anger and fueling harder and harder strikes. Dents and dings bent the metal. Random pages loosened. Static jittered at the corners of his eyes. He jammed the can in the chute until half the lip was crushed flat. He let it go, and the whole thing clanged down into the incinerator. He snatched back his hands just before the hatch slammed closed so hard that plaster dust blew out from the wall.

Scalding water burned his fingertips. At least the faucet stream didn't smell like shit tonight. Nope, just his hands. Why didn't they have soap! He rubbed his fingers together until they hurt. He gave them a sniff. A trace smell lingered, but each digit glowed pink and clean. He killed the hot water and cranked on the other tap. With cupped hands, he bathed his face. After a couple splashes, the bracing cold loosened the grip of today's living nightmare, and the tatters gurgled down the drain.

He shut off the tap, and looked at Mirror Man's ragged face. Bah. He looked fifteen years older since his peek into Minnie's bathroom. Musky body odor leaked through his freshly laundered clothes. Pressure in his bladder made a good excuse to turn away from his beat-up reflection.

At the urinal, he sighed with relief. Short-lived. A racket blew up down at the shower end, and his stream wilted.

Please, not again.

He tucked himself back in. Bathroom acoustics amplified disembodied voices, turned them into aural ghosts. This time he backtracked and found the light switch at the door and flipped it on.

No trepidation this trip through the archways. He meant to grab the twerps by their collars and drag them into Schramm's office. Let the superintendent deal with these fuc—

He bounded over the shower curb. "Gotcha!"

All the blood rushed from his head. He staggered into the wall to keep his feet.

His entire classroom gathered in the showers. Under the nozzles, Elijah punched Theodore in the face. The small boy backpedaled into Ian and Husky, who flanked Elijah on one side; they slapped him and pushed him over to Towhead and Ed Grimley. Throwing him in a round robin around the circle. Rocky Mountain Face brought a knee up to Theodore's groin before shoving him into Precious Moment's arms.

Precious grabbed Theodore's shirt hem and yanked up so it bound his arms and covered his head like a hood. A hand that could have been crafted of blown glass tightened into a fist and jabbed Theodore in the chest two, three, four times. He stuck his foot over Theodore's ankle—a familiar move—pushed, and sent Theodore dropping to the floor with a slap of bare stomach against tile.

Elijah bent and pulled Theodore's shirt off, throwing it toward Teeth, who stood apart from the others, nearest to Miles, and bounced from one restless bare foot to the other.

Theodore groveled, shirtless, at Elijah's feet.

Miles exhaled an impotent voice. "Leave him alone."

Elijah bared his canines. A signal. The boys fell upon Theodore, kicking and ripping out handfuls of hair.

"Stop!" Miles lunged, but arms wrapped him up from behind.

"Don't think so." Hare Lip's distorted words. Someone had been hiding in the stalls after all.

A helpless baby bird, Theodore shivered.

Elijah clamped a hand on the small boy's shoulder, but his eyes smiled at Miles. "Gotta stick around for this." His fingers dug four divots into the pale, thin flesh at Theodore's collarbone. Elijah squeezed, face strained and flushing with the effort. His fingernails punctured skin. Four bloody rivulets dribbled down the boy's ribs like ladder rungs.

"Sadistic thug!" Miles twisted and flipped Hare Lip off him and into the wall, but Teeth acted fast—lowered a shoulder and barreled into his crotch. A hydrogen bomb detonated in his balls. Saliva flooded his mouth. He went to his knees before he knew he was sinking.

Theodore squawked and beat at Elijah with his scarecrow arms.

Elijah punched the soft spot on Theodore's temple.

The shot laid Theodore out, teeth clacking as he crunched into the tiles. His glasses snapped, one half skittering across the floor. The other half held on crookedly, caught over his ear.

Miles made a move to get to his feet, but the blast radius from Teeth's attack crippled him.

Theodore flopped onto his belly; he scratched and crawled an inch, but Elijah raised and slammed his heel into the back of Theodore's head, mashing the boy's forehead into the slimy tiles. The remaining bow and lens of the glasses crushed into the boy's face.

Miles gasped. "Enough!"

Theodore jerked in a shaky breath.

Hare Lip picked himself up, panting asthmatically.

Ian stared with blank eyes at the boy on the floor, his body just as skinny as Theodore's, but he had a height advantage. And the right friends.

"Go on." Elijah nudged Ian.

Ian glanced from Elijah to Theodore.

Husky looked on with his moronic smile. Precious whistled, low and lascivious. They all held their breaths, eyes hungry.

Miles blew out a slow breath and sat back onto his heels. "Ian, come on." His nephew looked at him. For help? "You're not like them. This is perverse." Miles tried to catch the eyes of the others, all of whom had some degree of legal trouble hanging over their heads to have been here. Maybe that was the key. "This is assault and battery. It needs to stop here, before you dig yourselves in deeper. Walk away."

Elijah whispered like the serpent into Ian's ear. Ian shrugged. Nodded. Whispered something back.

A mental push, an attempt for familial telepathy: Don't hurt this boy, Ian.

Elijah threw his hands in the air. "Go on!"

The vacancy in Ian's eyes deepened as his essence, his Ian-ness, retreated. He skipped forward and landed a fierce kick to the base of Theodore's spine.

Glee sparkled in Elijah's eyes. "Harder!"

Ian paused but didn't turn to Miles for a sign this time. He cocked back his leg and kicked with vile force. A desperate cry broke from Theodore's lips, and he curled onto his side. Ian grinned. Ugly. Elijah didn't need to encourage anymore; Ian reared back and stomped into Theodore's ribs. *Crack.* A flat sound, like the disappointing crunch of a real-life car accident.

Elijah nodded his smug approval.

Miles ground his teeth and got to his feet, although he couldn't stand up straight. He managed a single small step before Husky stepped over Theodore and punched Miles in the dick. Miles folded to the floor in spastic nausea.

Theodore's eyes rolled to the whites in desperate fear. The smell of terror rolled off him—ammonia and sweat.

Elijah licked his lips. "Let me."

Ian and Husky bent and grabbed hold of Theodore. The boy drew his legs tighter to his chest, but Towhead and the Ed Grimley boy knelt and pried him open like a clam shell. Theodore swatted at them. Husky batted away his feeble attempts, but Miles's heart broke with pride that the kid put up some semblance of a fight. As the other three boys held Theodore down, Ian wriggled off Theodore's trousers.

"Don't do that." But words were powerless. He needed to get up and help, but he'd lost all feeling in his body.

Theodore made some bestial sound deep in his throat as Ian tossed his pants into the dank corner.

Elijah flicked Theodore's little worm through his white briefs. Theodore sobbed and curled up again, his spine sticking up grotesquely from his arched back. Husky and Ian unfolded him, and Elijah smacked Theodore's pale belly. His chest. Hard, flat slaps that left instant red handprints. Elijah darted his head forward, knocking against Theodore's middle like a shark. He waggled his head against Theodore's front, hidden from Miles's view. Wisps of orange hair jerking back and forth.

Miles crawled forward. "Stop it."

Theodore's legs spasmed, and Ian lost his grip. Teeth ran up and sat at Theodore's head, trying to get a hold, but Theodore thrashed. Towhead moved behind Elijah and seized Theodore's ankles.

Miles grunted through the pain like an earthquake in his gut. He started to stand, but goddamn Hare Lip pushed him back down and held him. It didn't take much to keep him down.

Theodore's legs and arms flailed. Hands outthrust, his fingers grabbed at the air. Ian went down on his knees and held down Theodore's shoulders. The boy's limbs ground into the wet tiles.

Miles caught a decent breath. "Let him go!"

Theodore cried out. Elijah's shock of red hair shook as his head butted against the boy's belly. There was a sort of gurgling sound. Elijah reared up, mouth covered in gore; he smiled, bits of Theodore's flesh caught between his teeth.

The spinning world ground to a halt. All the air was sucked out of the bathroom. Then Teeth honked a laugh loud as a shotgun blast.

The bite marks on Miles's calf screamed.

Elijah's head dipped down again.

Slurp.

"No!" Miles slid his hands into push-up position and rocketed upward, throwing Hare Lip off of him, but rising squeezed his sore testicles against the tight denim jeans, and he swayed on his feet. He tottered toward Husky at Theodore's legs.

Elijah's head pulled back. A long elastic strip of skin stretched from his jaws to Theodore's belly. It snapped, freckling his face with blood. Juice and meat dribbled over his lips. Off his chin. He sucked up the strand of Theodore's flesh like a noodle.

Theodore convulsed so hard that he sprang free of the boys holding him. The backs of his hands slapped the floor. His heels pounded the tiles. Elijah chewed, swallowed; he crawled and clamped his hands like a vise to Theodore's head. In a blur he cracked Theodore's head down into the tiles. Elijah's chest heaved. He smashed the head again, and all the tension left Theodore's body and the boy went limp and still.

Teeth brushed himself off. Husky helped Ian to his feet. Hare Lip muttered from the shadows. A sociopathic calm over them all.

Ian's slapped Elijah's shoulder. He nodded at Uncle Miles. "What about him?"

"Forget it. He knows he lost." Elijah hawked out a bloody mass of spit and locked eyes with Miles. "You're never leaving St. Hamelin's."

Stomach acid backed up into his mouth. Swallowing his spit burned. Where was his dragon now? Drowned by the nauseous churning from his balls? Shocked into silence? He ground his teeth to shrieking and squeezed his eyes shut, trying to summon his rage.

He failed.

"Monsters."

A scarlet shoreline broke the plane under Theodore's body, from his matted hair and along the curve of his back. The glossy crimson pool flowed toward Miles's feet.

Elijah brushed past. Husky and Teeth followed, Hare Lip right behind. A procession of little league players lining up to slap hands with the opposing team after a game. As Ian slipped by, Miles snagged the sleeve of his bloodstreaked, white Oxford shirt. Ian shrugged off the hold and pushed him aside.

The strength in Miles's knees let go, and he shot out an arm to hold on to something. A wall. Nothing there, and his feet slipped in the sea of Theodore's blood. He went down hard on top of the dead boy, and the slight frame smooshed under his weight. Bone ground against bone. Bones into floor. Miles frantically spat out a backwash of bile as he slid off the body and splashed into the gory puddle.

Someone slapped off the light as he left, plunging Miles into darkness.

The warmth of Theodore's blood soaked into the seat of his jeans.

Sixteen

Had to get out.

Elijah liked to bite....

Had to report this to Schramm.

Yeah, he does that....

Then he'd get out of here.

Odaxelagnia—Ted Bundy had that. Sexual arousal from biting, from feeling skin tension stretch to its tautest, the split-second pause, then the *click* and puncture of teeth sliding through flesh and the juicy burst of blood.

He staggered into the hallway. A cigarette—the taste of smoke—would erase the metallic taint of Theodore's death on his tongue. Clinging to his clothes. Hair, fingers.

Laughter erupted behind the closed dorm room doors. Loud and louder, building up steam. The boys slammed their fists against the doors so hard that the floor shook. Riotous glee ratcheted up into screaming.

"Stop!" The yell tore his throat raw.

Unrelenting, the clamor rammed his brain. He covered his ears. "Stop."

Silence.

Miles opened his palms, cautiously exposing his ears.

The pain overload in his balls, in his gut, hurt with such intensity that it anesthetized. He couldn't feel his dick. It felt like he stood on stilts.

A liquid chuffing rolled up through the incinerator chute.

He marched to the first room after the lavatory. He pounded on the door with the butt end of a fist. "Open up!" They couldn't just walk away from this. They'd murdered that boy. Ian had helped murder that boy. "Get out here now!"

A ripple of laughter behind the door. Another and another—concentric rings of laugher in each room all up and down the line. Rising... rising until the mean, mirthless sound trounced his sanity.

He moved to the next door and clubbed it with the heel of his hand. He kicked the lower panels. Hollow thudding clomped up from the incinerator. The hatch shook. A draft threw septic stink into his face. He pursed his lips, tried to batten his head against the barrage.

Under the bedlam, babbling voices.

Which was the ringleader's room? Elijah was the one he needed. He stomped to the next door and knocked relentlessly. "You think I'm kidding?"

He ground his teeth until neon pain jabbed his head, but the wellspring inside him would not be held back. When Hare Lip or Teeth or Husky opened their door, he would throttle them. Speak some Russian to him, as his granddad used to say. Tune him up. A double dose for Ian.

Triple for Elijah.

His rage dragon bellowed, ravenous.

A single shred of his rational self remained. Time to reign in this fury before he lost himself to it. Was Elijah fueled by a similar, sick instinct?

It was imperative to get downstairs and report all this to Schramm. Make damn sure that the superintendent called the sheriff or state police and didn't decide to chop off arms or legs. Of course, he'd lie about Ian. Tell the police that Ian had nothing to do with the murder. Tell them that Ian had tried to stop it. That would be his leverage to get Ian released while Elijah and his band of fallen caught long stretches in an actual penitentiary.

Unless Ian deserved to be sent away. Didn't he? For his part?

No. Ian had been a good kid. The others were beyond saving, but Ian could still be reached if he got away from here.

While he argued with himself, Theodore grew cold.

Dogs. That's what Schramm had called them. And they were. A wild pack that needed to be put down. His rage dragon whipped its tail. Miles wanted a taste of vengeance as much as he'd ever craved nicotine. He slammed his shoulder into the door, feeding his rancor. He grabbed the knob, ready to twist the thing off if he had to, but the door opened and he rushed inside.

What was this shit?

He blinked furiously to adjust his eyes to the dark because what he saw could not be true. A rage-induced hallucination, that's what had happened. He closed his eyes. He sucked in and blew out quick, short breaths, but his system had reached its boiling point. He reopened his eyes, and nothing had changed.

With the curtains drawn aside, the window showed the blizzard beyond in full force, casting the room in dull light. Cobwebs stuck in ceiling corners arched down the wall to the desk. He had left footprints in a thick layer of dust on the floorboards. Another inch of dust coated the desk. The thin mattress had been rolled in half, showing wide brown stains like liver spots. Chunks of batting poked through ragged holes. Rust riddled the bed frame. Black water stains dripped like blood over the walls.

No one had lived in this room for ages. It was abandoned and gone to rot—his expectation for St. Hamelin's on the drive out. What was this? Rage petered out. He backed out of the room.

What did it mean?

Quiet blanketed the whole wing. Not a cough or a tread. On dead legs, Miles drifted to the next door. The knob chilled his palm. Nothing good lay behind that door, but he had to see.... And he did: broken glass from a shattered window glittering like stars across the dirty floor planks. A spiderweb dangling from the doorsill caught on his head, and a streamer of it sloughed into his hair. He yipped and beat at his head, catching the tender spot from where Chaplain had bashed him. More ugly water stains blotched the walls. The upturned bed frame lay on its back on top of the mattress. One leg had been pulled off and thrown across the room. The curtains had been pulled off and lay in a heap.

The tumble of curtain undulated, expanding-contracting like a heart muscle exposed in a cracked breastbone.

And if you was to walk through the bedrooms now, you'd see the ragged, mouldy bedclothes a-heaving and a-heaving like seas.

He teetered backward.

The folds of fabric opened, and a lean rat shot out. It brushed his ankle. Another squirmed free of the curtains. He tried to jig out of the way, but another and then another came at him, fleeing into the hallway, bodies thumping the walls. The last clawed out, big as a squirrel; its thick tail smacked his foot as it raced past.

The world tilted. How were these rooms broken down into ruin? He'd heard the boys. Heard them in this room right here. In the one before. His blood seemed to actually run cold, quicksilver through his veins. He didn't need to open every door, inspect every room, to know that they were all dilapidated.

St. Hamelin's was a ghost ship.

Where were the outlets?

Nothing under his window but the radiator, ticking crazily. He whirled, stirring a breeze that agitated the stinking air. He dived to his sore knees at the foot of the bed and tugged the cot away from the wall; its four stubby metal legs dug grooves into the wooden floor. On hands-and-knees, he followed the baseboards. Dust bunnies clung to his elbows.

"Where are they?" He needed his phone. He had to call Minnie and Daniel. Jeremy. The cops.

He crawled across the width of the room, grabbed the edges of the dresser and shimmied it back-and-forth, walking it out from the wall. Nothing behind it. Of course not.

"Where?"

The writing desk—had to be an outlet at the desk, right? He scampered to the corner and threw the chair across the room. He felt all along the wall. He ducked to peer underneath. There! One lone two-pronged socket.

Where was his charger?

He jammed a hand in his pocket and pulled it out. He crouched and rammed the plug home. The lightning end tapped against the phone. He was too amped up to get it in. He was going to scream, going to throw the whole damn thing—

It slid in.

He dragged the chair back over to the desk and sat. His knuckles whitened as he held his phone. All his focus trained on the screen, willing the dead black to lighten. For his lifeline to power up.

Why was it taking so long?

He glanced under the desk. Adapter was still in the wall. Did St. Hamelin's old wiring have enough juice running through it? Was that possible? He knew nothing about electricity.

Jeremy had been the tech wizard. Set up their router. Managed their wireless network. Miles didn't know a lick about WiFi and cell towers. He was the weak link, the partner useless without the other.

The door to his room flew open. Miss Poole. "Come with me."

"What? Why?"

The empty battery icon had just popped up. His phone was at least taking the charge. He was so close. How had she known?

"You need to come with me now."

"No." He pressed the power button, praying for the white Apple logo. "You don't know what they did. I saw.... I mean, it was right in front of me."

"Mr. Baumgartner."

"Not until my phone charges. They're not getting away with this." He fixed her in what he hoped was an icier stare than she or Chaplain or Schramm had thrown at him. "Not this. Not this time."

"Phone? What are you talking about?"

Come on. Come on. Why wasn't his phone waking up?

"Miles!"

He stopped. The desperation in the stressing of his Christian name. She wasn't giving off her usual frigid vibrations.

"Leave that." She held out her hand, palm up. A mother, a teacher, calling for one of her children. Urgent, but safe.

A thought burst in his mind like a mortar shell: Chaplain and Schramm would pin Theodore's murder on him. The same way Schramm had sacrificed Rocky Mountain Face for the classroom fiasco.

Elijah's bite on his calf shot a flare up his leg. Not a warning, exactly. His prejudice against Miss Poole melted, if only a little. He set his phone down, pushed it into the far corner where it would be hardest to spot in the shadows should anyone come looking for him.

"Where are we going?"

the closer they drew to the first floor, the more his feet turned to lead. Miss Poole hadn't said another word. A yawning pit grew in his stomach as he followed dutifully behind. He was retreating from the scene of the crime, from that poor boy lying dead. He was walking toward another execution—his own.

"Where are you taking me?"

She didn't bother stifling an exasperated sigh. "I want you to stay with Frederick until morning."

"Frederick? Who's Frederick?"

"Frederick Blankenheim."

"Who?"

"Butch."

Blankenheim? Why did that name ring a bell? And why would Miss Poole want them together? Until morning?

"I've already visited with Butch and Betty. No thanks. I have to get back upstairs. I need my phone."

She stopped and crinkled her face as if listening to a child's nonsense. "What phone? Your room doesn't have a telephone."

He felt that same expression on his face.

She started back down. "Things have started now. Things are happening that you should not know about." They had reached the vestibule. "You know too much already."

"Theodore's murder?" They turned into the hall toward Schramm's office, the last place he wanted to be. "That's what I was trying to do up there, call for help."

The moment froze. "What did you say?"

"Those boys—Elijah... they killed that kid. Theodore."

Miss Poole studied his face. "How do you know that?"

"It happened right in front of me. They killed that little boy." His voice cracked, and tears welled up. "In the showers. They didn't care that I was there they did it anyway knocked him down and beat him and that Elijah he... he bit, he ate—"

"How do you know that?" The color of life drained from her face. She came at him, and he jerked out of the way. "How do you know that?"

His back struck the wall. "I told you I saw it. They just did it. He's there right now." Hysteria clawed up his throat.

Miss Poole's cheeks turned a curdled-milk yellow. Her fingers and shoulders twitched.

"Miss Poole?"

"He promised me." She murmured to herself. "Chaplain Allen promised me." She glanced at Miles. "Chaplain Allen told me it wouldn't happen again. Told me we were safe."

"Miss Poole? I don't know what you're talking about."

Schramm's door opened, and he drifted like some Greek curse into the hallway. "You." He pointed at Miles. "Get in here right now."

Miss Poole blinked her eyes clear. "Miles."

"Miss Poole?"

"Run."

Seventeen

He didn't. Couldn't.

Miss Poole insisted, *sotto voce*. "Run."

His mind was an empty chalkboard.

Schramm's furious impatience acted as a magnet. Miles's feet moved. This was the time to listen to Miss Poole and get out of there. To run for the wicked witch's house. Instead, he drew ever closer to Schramm until he found himself in the office, shutting the door, cutting off his exit. It had all happened in autopilot, so fast.

Schramm stood behind his acre of desk. The scene of Rocky's bloody punishment. "You look a fool catching flies, Mr. Baumgartner."

Those blood-smeared walls, these swarms of flies, this reek of shambles and the stifling heat.

Theodore's broken body flashed through Miles's forebrain.

"They murdered him, and then they disappeared. Their rooms are empty, but I heard them."

Schramm clucked his tongue.

The stink in here was outrageous.

"What does all of this mean?"

Schramm quivered in a belch or a chuckle.

Miss Poole's urging rattled in his head. Every decision he'd made since seeing Minnie's Facebook photo had been a mistake.

"Don't you want to know who's been murdered?"

Schramm shrugged. Was that where Ian had gotten it from? "That's old news, Mr. Baumgartner." Schramm crossed his arms, and his lapels bunched.

"You don't care?"

"I care about your reactions since you've been here. You accepted the specters in the hydrotherapy room so readily. That impressed me."

"I...."

"You outraged Chaplain Allen by tearing asunder his fledgling success down there in the crypt." Schramm wagged a finger, but stopped the second a foul look crossed his face. He hiccupped. He swallowed and composed himself. "Yet you take it all in stride. I find that interesting. I find you interesting, Mr. Baumgartner. Chaplain Allen disagrees with me. Oh, he disagrees vehemently. But I think it's time for you to piece everything together."

Schramm pointed to the wall past Miles. The wall of framed photographs.

Miles glanced over the boys of St. Hamelin's past while he chewed on what Schramm had said. Taking it all in stride. Was that what he was doing? His brain felt like a colander, draining him of sound mind.

"I have always gone to great lengths to keep the truth hidden. Revelation is a new experience." Schramm's fingers twiddled in the air. "This is fun."

"What is this place?"

"I have plans for you, Mr. Baumgartner." He tittered.

Ian turning up alive. Ghosts and shrines. Sawing off a boy's finger. The horrors... the horrors had built up incrementally. Steps. A pathway to some higher truth.

"What's going on at St. Hamelin's?"

But the events here didn't exactly form a path, did they? They built a wall, stone by stone until it encased him.

"Take a good, long look at those photographs, Mr. Baumgartner, and you will understand everything."

Photographs. His life revolved around photographs. Okay. He would play Schramm's game. He backtracked to the first picture just inside the office door. Better to concentrate on these than ask what plans Schramm had for him.

Grainy black and white orphans gathered into three rows on the front lawn, the Romanesque face of St. Hamelin's peering over their shoulders. The engraving plate on this first one read 1951. Four-, five-, six-year-olds sat on the grass, cross-legged—Indian style they used to say. Adolescents knelt in a row behind. Older boys, taller boys, lined up in the back. A scattering of faces from the crypt. Morose faces, all. Defeated eyes. Kneeling at the far end of the center row, a boy with a mouth mangled by a cleft lip stared implacably ahead.

Miles cocked his head, trying a different angle to change what he saw. It didn't help. That boy was Hare Lip. His Hare Lip.

Reality took a greasy slide off-kilter.

He had to be mistaken. Please, please God let him be mistaken. He leaned in, but the boy with a cleft lip remained the boy he knew from his class, from the halls, from the bathroom massacre. And frail Theodore—the cooling corpse upstairs—he posed in the photograph, too. Bottom row, oversized glasses flaring at the camera. A wide and brilliant smile that Miles had never seen on the boy's face.

Schramm stood at the fireplace, grinning. Gloating.

Queasy, Miles stepped and stared at the next photo. In 1952, Hare Lip had aged. New boys had joined, but only half of the 1951 faces remained. A few of them now wore leg braces. The polio outbreak had struck.

In 1953, all the children wore the navy blazers. The young linebacker in the back row was not just any bulky kid. It was Husky. Beside him, a scrawny boy on whose face the rash of acne showed up as a relief map in grey blotches. Theodore, baby-faced yet downcast with misery stood at the edge of the photo, separated from the others by a mere few inches, but didn't that distance relay the whole story about his other-ness? His place in the base-ment of the hierarchy.

But 1953?

Insanity compressed inside his head. Pressure squeezed his whole body like the Gravitron at the county fair—the centrifuge ride he and Ian loved—backs against a padded wall, the saucer spinning faster and faster, stick-ing them to the side. Ian liked to wiggle up the side as the force kicked in, work his way upside down. He would hang there, laughing maniacally. Ready for corndogs the moment the ride stopped.

So many great times....

That was it!

These pictures hanging on Schramm's wall? He knew what they were.

Just like the sepia-toned photo of him and Ian dressed in pin-striped suits, cigars jammed in the corners of their mouths, ready to knock over a bank in 1920's Chicago.

That's what these framed photos were. Tricks.

"Why did you go to all this trouble dressing them up in period clothes? The engravings of the years are a bit much." Hard to imagine that Schramm had such a whim-sical streak.

The superintendent licked his lips. "Come now, you're smarter than that. Think. Piece it together."

Piece it together? This wasn't a game! Theodore lay in an ocean of gore. Rocky Mountain Face had screamed, and Schramm and Chaplain—the chaplain, for Chris-sakes!—had held him down. That plank children shrine. Now the empty rooms. And Schramm wanted to play guessing games.

The pervasive stink pulsed in time with fireplace breath.

Photographed faces watched Miles through what ap-peared to be a great expanse of time. Yet the faces be-longed to boys he knew right now. His bowels gurgled. He grabbed the next group photo off the wall.

In 1954, Hare Lip occupied the back row, far right. Same mouth. Same face. Didn't look aged at all. But his expression looked dulled. Miles got in close, so close he smelled the grime hardened in the pores of the frame. Hare Lip's cheeks had sunken in, and his face froze somehow too smooth. Weird eyes, too. Must have been caught mid-blink because the lids came halfway down so he looked drowsy.

"Like Ian in Minnie's post."

Schramm lowered his chin and watched him.

Enough with these games. "Why are we wasting time? Theodore... Elijah...."

In the picture he held, boys he'd never seen before stared into the camera lens with livid displeasure. But Husky stood with a stoned expression, closed eyes. In front with Rocky Mountain Face, Elijah's hateful glare had been replaced by one dim and vacant. Mouth slack. The boy's red hair and freckles muted by the black and white film.

A faked photo had brought him here in the first place, but that one had turned out to be real.

"You're so close." Schramm touched Mile's elbow, inviting him behind the desk.

In the fetor, the heat, the confusion, he let himself be guided. He sat in the chair molded to the big man's body. Those files Schramm always touched and riffled through lay spread out on the blotter.

"You want me to?"

Schramm nodded.

He still held that last framed photo. He set it aside and opened the topmost folder. He picked up the first page in trembling fingers, and he read.

Paul Schmidt. Date of birth: September 18th, 1943. Okay, a file on one of the orphans arriving at St. Hamelin's. Under the cover sheet lay a series of small, thick squares. He flipped them over like solitaire cards. Photos of Paul

Schmidt. A swaddled baby in the arms of a severe-faced buxom woman. The tiny face peering out from the blankets marred by a cleft lip.

In the remaining photos—faded black and whites with crenelated, white borders just like his mother's baby pictures in the big family album back home—Paul Schmidt grew up in jerky increments and poses. He aged into Hare Lip as Miles knew him.

His rational mind rejected the proof in front of him, but on a higher plane, Schramm's puzzle pieces dovetailed together. Linear thought unraveled.

The next folder held information on Jacob Moore. Date of admission, March 6th, 1953. Birthday of Jacob Moore, May 27th, 1940. Court documents followed. Petty theft charges. A subsequent photo showed Husky's flappable face.

Schramm moaned a hungry sound in the back of his throat. "You always knew that Ian died in that car accident."

Miles shook his head. "No." His head wouldn't stop shaking. "No. The police misidentified the body."

"You don't believe that. You never believed that."

But what did he believe?

He picked up a thin sheaf of yellowed pages held together with a paperclip gone orange with rust. He pried it off, and metal grit pattered onto the papers below. He held the admission form he really wanted. Elijah Yoder. Date of birth November 6th 1941. Admission year 1953. Petty theft. Grand theft. Battery.

His shaking hands sought out the 1954 photo. He lacked the strength to pick it up, so he dragged it across the desk. It featured three of the orphans from earlier photos and the nine boys he knew from here, from the classroom and the showers. The actual orphans he didn't know looked miserable but alive. Elijah and the others looked....

"Dead."

Schramm hissed. "Yes."

He rubbed away goosebumps on his forearms. He had thought the photos of the polio kids in the shrine had been plank children.

Wrong.

How had he missed this? Yes, those boys were dead, but they'd been alive when photographed. The boys in these files, on these walls, had been photographed after death. These weren't stage-dressed vintage photographs. Just look at the waxy skin. How stiff and still they stood— corpses propped up and displayed.

The true plank children.

Elijah, Jacob, Paul....

"Ian." Minnie's Facebook photo—the matching shadows, points of contact. Not faked. And not posed in their backyard. He'd assumed the backyard because he hadn't recognized it. Until now. He pushed himself away from the desk and rose. Daniel really had PhotoShopped Minnie's picture—he'd cropped out St. Hamelin's from the background.

Miles shot to his feet. "How is he here?"

"His mother arranged it. Your sister." Schramm cleared his throat in three quick rumbles. "A breach in our secrecy—someone told her what we could do. She snipped off Ian's finger and brought it to us."

Minnie cut off Ian's finger? When would she have...?

The garden shears Minnie held that day on the deck, before the funeral service. Her fingers stained. But not from tending damp flowers, instead from the make-up-covered hand of her son. That's why she had demanded a closed casket—to hide Ian's hands, folded politely at his waist, missing an index finger.

Miles stepped away, distancing himself from the truth. His back struck the shelves under the office window. By design or accident, Schramm had penned him into the corner.

"Theodore?"

"Killed long ago. What you saw in the showers just now? A reenactment."

His tongue clicked in his dry mouth. "There was blood everywhere."

"Reenactment might be the wrong word. It was real enough, in its own way. Chaplain Allen should never have allowed that to happen." Actual concern creased Schramm's brow. "He needs to talk with that boy."

Which boy? Elijah? Because Theodore was dead. Right? No or yes? False or true?

"Your nephew died. Do you see that now? Do you see?" He pointed at Miles's face. "Yes, you do. The truth shines right there in your eyes."

"Stay there." No more backing up. He clacked his molars together and grabbed the desk chair. His fingers dug into the leather, found the metal skeleton inside. He rolled it between him and Schramm. "They murdered Theodore. Like the rat."

"Yes." Schramm's face crinkled, and he slapped at his chest. "Murdered him long ago." He coughed into his hand. A gust of wind hit the window, and the chill that swept through the office stirred up the worst slug of sewage stink yet.

Miles willed himself not to puke. "Why don't you fix that septic tank?"

Schramm burst into genuine laughter.

"What's so damn funny?"

"Septic tank." Schramm's neck jiggled with mirth. "It's not sewage. It's us!" The superintendent opened his arms to encompass all the residents of St. Hamelin's. "We're all dead. You're smelling our rot." Schramm laughed, high and lunatic. "All of us dead. Except for Betty. She makes sure the lights stay on and the water runs. Mostly for her cottage, but it serves the main building. Oh, she had a heck of a time firing up the furnace when your sister called to warn us you might be stopping by."

"Shut up."

Minnie had sold him out? The Princess Leia to his Luke Skywalker? Kids jumping on the living room furniture, swinging lightsabers until the flashlights broke.

Miles pressed forward, chair as shield.

He'd lost all sensation in his lips. His extremities tingled. Elijah's bite radiated a burrowing sensation. His vision pixelated and broke up into kaleidoscopic swirls. He hadn't thought to bring Xanax; hadn't had a panic attack in months. His hoarse voice sounded like a stranger's. "I want to leave."

"Leave?" The black holes of Schramm's eyes held him. "No one leaves St. Hamelin's."

Schramm burped. A black beetle fell past his lips and struck the floor. The bug trundled over the joints in the boards toward the warmth of the fireplace. Through a smile of black teeth, dirt dribbled out of his mouth. He hiccupped, and a fat writhing earthworm slapped to the floor.

Miles gagged at the expanding reek pouring from Schramm's mouth. He drove the back of his hands against his mouth and swallowed a gout of puke creeping up his throat.

Schramm choked, his shoulders hitching. He tried to clear his throat. His air of giddy madness faltered. He thumped his chest with a fist. A clot of earth spurted over his teeth and landed between his feet.

A maelstrom of panic overloaded Miles. The Facebook photo. Fun and games at Minnie and Daniel's. The abandoned orphanage up and running. Ghosts? Shrines. He'd had a blind spot. An Ian-sized blind spot. He had accepted all the madness—what had Schramm said. Taken it all in stride—the moment his dead nephew walked through the office door. His almost-son had been alive. Of course he had believed it all. Who wouldn't have recalibrated?

A millipede slithered out of Schramm's nostril and tumbled off his chin, over the knot of his tie. One tiny red blemish poked through Schramm's cheek. The bright red irritation spread, darkened, and threw out a webwork of black streaks. A pimple plumped up, and the pus inside bubbled; the skin thinned and popped, squirting gunk with a stench of diseased meat. The ragged edges wrinkled, and half of Schramm's face slid off. Grey teeth showed in a skull's grin through ripped flesh. His jaw broke at the hinge, and his lower palate hung limp.

Miss Poole's voice rang through the tunnels of his mind.

Run.

As if she stood at his side.

Run!

Shouted in his face.

Run!

A coughing fit seized the superintendent, and Miles shoved the chair into his belly, catching Schramm off guard and unable to bat it aside. Miles slipped past and made for the door. He grappled with it, fingers out of sync with each other. Any second, Schramm's rotting hands would slide around his throat.

"There's nowhere to go, Mr. Baumgartner." Schramm had found breath but was bent over the desk as if exhausted.

Miles's fingers still didn't work. He gulped and tried to work up fresh spit.

Schramm's left ear plopped into the pile of grave dirt on the floor.

By dumb luck the door opened, and Miles ran into Chaplain's skeletal arms. The man had wasted away to a desiccated cadaver in oversized black clothes. The skin on his face, neck, hands had tanned and stretched taut against the bone.

Schramm's ruined voice called out. "Nowhere you can go."

Chaplain's finger bones pinched into Miles's shoulders. His tongue-less mouth smacked. Miles kicked at one of Chaplain's legs, and the wreck grunted and blundered backward, losing his grip, and clattered to the floor.

Eight dead boys of St. Hamelin's blocked the hall at the vestibule. Everyone but Theodore. All his efforts had been pointless. He had never stood a chance. Miles's throat closed. The gloom wanted to swallow him, and as the dark rose up, it did not diminish the zeal in Elijah's eyes.

Elijah's dead eyes.

"Get him!"

At Elijah's command, the hellions charged, hard soles clapping on the floor. Even Ian—his almost-son, consumed by some twisted blood vengeance, joined the blitz a half pace behind Teeth and Towhead.

Miles broke from his fugue and bolted for the main doors, the murderous pandemonium behind him coming up fast. He threw himself at the front entrance. Sweat-slippery palms grabbed and yanked, but the doors rattled in place. They'd finally locked him in. His fingers scrabbled over the iron hardware, searching out the mechanism. No deadbolt or latch. Only a keyhole. Where was Miss Poole with her massive ring? She had told him to run—had swapped allegiances in his favor—but she wasn't here for him now.

The throng smashed into him. His face crushed against the heavy wood doors, and he bit deep into the tender flesh inside his cheek. Blood flushed his mouth and down his pipes. The scrum pulled him down and piled on top. His nose flattened into the floor, the cartilage bending to the brink of snapping. He gasped for air but couldn't breathe for their weight and death-stink. Fingers clawed. The bite on his calf thrummed. An elbow stabbed his ribs. His lungs screamed. A knee nailed the bump on his head, and his inner lights dimmed. Consciousness receded. Drowning, he sank, feeling nothing. Thinking nothing.

A fuse in his head popped, and one brilliant shard of instinct exploded out of the inky black. An exit sign in a dark theater, but didn't spell **EXIT**. It flashed: **ESCAPE**.

He bucked. The writhing blanket of boys loosened, and he swam up through them. Mashed his feet into their faces and kept kicking and swinging until the last young arm fell away, and he burst from the heap. Breath had never tasted as sweet.

The scrambling dead still grappled with the empty space where their prey had fallen. But not Elijah—he hadn't even jumped into the fray. The redhead stood right where he'd been at the arched doors, a guardian, sole mission to keep Miles from getting away.

With a yell and a groan, Precious jumped onto Mile's back. A scrawny arm wrapped around his neck. Miles shook like a wet dog, and the boy screamed profanity as he crunched to the floor, amazingly not shattering his porcelain face.

The fallen swarm of boys regained their feet. A flash of white bandage gave Rocky away. Husky's thick shadow stalked toward Miles—Jacob Moore, leading a drive to push him into Elijah.

Miles took off, sprinting at the lone boy acting as safety. He stiff-armed Elijah in the face. The redhead grabbed for him, but fingers didn't catch. Miles turned the corner, and now with nothing but empty hallway in front, he ran to the side door.

Shouts and footfalls followed, hounds fast on his heels.

Miles hit the door full speed. His bones jarred, but the door sprang open. The shock of cold froze his sweat. Torrential snow killed visibility past two feet, but the front drive lay somewhere off to the right, and continuing farther led straight to the gulley and the river.

The door exploded open with the pack of boys.

Wind at his back sped him forward. Toward a wraith, a blue shadow standing in the blizzard.

"Slow down there!" Butch snagged Miles's collar with his thumbless hand.

The knit of Miles's sweater stretched. "Let me go!"

Without a thumb, Butch couldn't hold on, and with a final desperate tug, Miles freed himself. Butch fell over into the snow, knocking Miles down with him.

Miles crawled forward, belly plowing into the snow. Butch snatched at Miles's jeans, the hem, his bitten calf. Miles got his other leg up under him and, a runner out of the blocks, he took off through the blizzard, leaving Butch to pound snow in a tantrum of frustration.

The boys must have gained on him by now, but the storm scattered their shouts and masked their positions. Were they flanking his left? Right? Were their fingers inches away, grasping?

The scuffle with Butch had scrambled his internal compass, and surrounded by this total white-out, he couldn't get his bearings. Snapping wind struck his face, his ears, the backs of his legs, and his chest, not squarely on his back like before. Off course, he could wander into the woods. Those behind the carriage house or even on the other side of the road. Maybe onto the bridge to fall off the broken slats. Or over the edge of the gulley— break his head open on a rock, roll down the slope, and drown in the river.

Phantom voices called from every direction at once.

Disoriented, he simply had to choose. An inch to the right? Two inches left? The cold had numbed his flesh so he didn't even feel the skirling wind strike his bare neck and hands anymore.

Cat-calls whipped through the blizzard.

He put his head down and started off blindly. Every step, he sank a few inches into the snow, soaking his socks. His leg muscles cramped as he high-stepped along, more like climbing than walking. His lower back tightened. He rubbed his arms to warm up, but the friction did nothing. His core temperature dropped, and the snow no longer melted as it hit his skin. It piled in his hair and eyelashes. His teeth chattered until his jaw ached.

Shouldn't he have reached the gulley by now? He would end up at the front steps, Schramm and Chaplain waiting under the portico for him, and if frostbite didn't take any fingers or toes, those two certainly would.

Butch and the boys hadn't found him yet, so they must have been as lost as him.

Unless they weren't chasing him to catch him. What if they were herding him? Intent on driving him over the cliff like buffalo hunters?

His feet felt heavy as cinder blocks. He was too tired to raise them and just pushed forward. The resistance grew. His knees gave out, and he face-planted into the snow. Powder avalanched inside his prolapsed collar, icing his nipples and belly. More shoved up his pants legs. He spat out a mouthful and coughed up the taste of dirt.

But this moment's rest felt good. He was so tired.

So cold.

If he curled up and closed his eyes, he wouldn't need to wait long. He had read that freezing to death was painless. He would just fall asleep. Already, his tingling skin actually felt warm. And really, who would miss him? Jeremy didn't answer any texts. Minnie and Daniel had sold Ian's soul, or however their bargain worked. And he had no job. He'd lied to his sister and Daniel. There was no sabbatical—he'd been thrown out for the bourbon on his breath and the altercation with Jeremy in the hallway outside his class. And for giving Principal Rather a black eye when the man tried to separate them. So similar to his striking out at Ian.

Dear Ian. His nephew really had died that night. He'd been resurrected, but now he didn't even want to leave St. Hamelin's.

Miles had no one to live for.

Voices through the bluster:

"... is he?"

"... see that...?"

"Have you...?"

Elijah, forever youthful and cruel: "Over there!"

Miles swore and hoisted himself to his knees. Who did he have to live for? Himself, dammit.

His body felt like one big, cold bruise. By force of will alone, he found his footing and lumbered ahead, blind and lost, not stepping so much as falling forward. He caught himself two times... three... four, but willpower wasn't enough after all. The fifth time he tripped, he went down. He threw his hands out to catch himself, but his palms didn't hit solid ground. He belly-flopped into the snow, but his hands grasped empty air.

He had pitched forward over the lip of the gulley. Cliff walls blocked the blowing snow, giving a clear view twenty feet below, to swift water the deep color of stormy seas. The river hadn't frozen. Too early in the year, despite the ferocity of this storm.

He shimmied backward, snow spraying over the edge. Over his shoulder, the day had turned to static on a lost television channel. At least he was as hidden from the pursuing cadre as they were from him. He had an infinitesimal time advantage. The vaguest notion of a plan started to form. One quick scramble, and he could slide over the lip into the gulley; he could ford the river.... No, wading across that torrent wouldn't be possible. He would need to make a swim for it.

Did he have enough energy left in the tank for that?

Lying on the ground felt so good. His spent muscles might give out as he scaled his way down. Then the rocks jagging out of the ground would batter him into a concussion. Or he would tire halfway across the water, and as the current swept him away his sodden clothes would weigh him under the surface until he drowned, gasping curses with his last breath. And if by some miracle he managed to reach the other side? How long until the bitter cold hardened those soaked clothes into a shell? He would freeze to death long before reaching Bear Falls.

Excuses.

Just needed to catch his breath for a moment—so hard to do when the cold turned each inhale into nails piercing his lungs. Thighs and upper arms quivered, exhausted, but he lifted himself to hands and knees.

And was knocked down immediately as Husky rushed out of the static and tackled him. Big hands ground his head into the pillowy white. Miles swallowed snow to clear his airway, but more packed into his ears, muffling—not erasing—the panting self-congratulations of the hunting party constricting around him. The pressure on the back of his head and neck eased off. A grip on his bitten calf flipped him, sputtering, onto his back.

Turned into blue shadows by the pelting snow, boys far above him fanned out at his feet. Elijah's flaming hair and eyebrows emerged in startling contrast through the blizzard.

Miles rolled onto his belly and reached for the lip of the gulley. His fingernails dug into the granite, and he pulled himself closer to the edge. His kicking toes threw snow, then grass, then they found purchase in the dirt. He dragged himself forward another torturous inch.

Hands grabbed his ankles and jerked him backward. "Gotcha!"

He squirmed as Butch's long arms reeled him in, a grip hard as steel cables.

Ian scrunched his eyes and nose in disgust. Elijah's cannibalistic lips curled into a sneer. The boys' twisted, mean faces closed in.

Butch flipped him again, replacing the sight of the dead boys for a mouthful of churned mud. Miles choked and spat as Butch heaved him up into a fireman's carry.

Where was his rage dragon? Wake up! But fatigue sucked even the faintest flicker of useful anger out of him like marrow sipped from bones. He relaxed his limbs and lay his head against Butch's back. In a couple minutes, he would be inside, away from the biting wind. He would warm up. Maybe such meager comfort was what St. Hamelin's offered to the trapped souls of boys who'd once lived within its walls.

The white noise of numbness broke, and shivers wracked him.

Eighteen

Raw nerve endings screamed him awake, but blind and as insensate as a corpse.

After an eternity, he addressed the void. "Where...?" But the pain of thawing derailed thought. The pins and needles hurt a thousand times worse than the freezing had.

Pressure on his arm. "You're all right." A crush of lilacs.

He knew Miss Poole's secret, now. Underneath the perfume her body smelled of the same rot as Schramm, as all of St. Hamelin's. Everything was a cover-up. A mirage.

The world lightened from ebony to charcoal to slate.

"Miss Poole?" He tried to face her, but the tendons in his neck stabbed like daggers.

She soothed in a compassionate mother-voice. "Don't move." She petted his head. "You may as well call me Janelle."

A wash of color returned to his surroundings.

As his face warmed, a burning sensation spread over his flesh. His cheeks and nose and the tips of his ears seared. Probably frostbite. Raising his hand took tremendous effort. Ugly red spots marked each chapped knuckle, and they hurt as from a hundred wasp-stings.

"Miss Poole? Janelle? Where am I?" A hospital? Please let this be a hospital in Bear Falls.

"In your room where you belong." Chaplain shouldered Miss Poole out of the way. His self-righteous third eye cast down condemnation.

Even from two feet away, Miles gagged on Chaplain's foul breath.

While he'd been running for his life, maid service had made up his cot with a fuzzy new blanket. Clean sheets underneath. They hadn't thought for a second that he would make it out of here. How humiliating. The whole mess—he had freaked out at their revelations; tried to escape and failed. He'd shown them only weakness. Chaplain pointed his chin toward Miss Poole. "Leave us."

She patted Miles's shoulder. She looked ready to spit, her revulsion at Chaplain more visceral than any she'd shown before to Miles.

"Janelle?" How could he make her stay by his bedside and not leave him alone with Chaplain? "Please." She left before he could come up with anything. Lilac stirred in the air above his face. Home. Childhood. You never knew how bad life could get when idling in the Halcyon days. Now those years were as dead and gone as everything else around him.

Chaplain crossed his arms over his pleated shirt front. His halitosis defeated Miss Poole's perfume. "You and Miss Poole have grown close."

"Janelle hated me until an hour ago." What in the world had changed her mind?

Chaplain studied him. "Your informality is inappropriate."

"Janelle just told me to—"

"Miss Poole," Chaplain corrected. He exhaled through flaring nostrils. "Your disruptions are unpardonable as it is. Do not add lewd intentions toward Miss Poole."

Miles laughed, but that quickly turned into a coughing fit that hurt his ribs. "Lewd intentions? Chaplain, I'm gay."

"Under the circumstances, you should be humbled. Solemnity would do you well, Mr. Baumgartner, rather than such a carefree attitude."

What was he going on about?

"Gay, Chaplain. Homosexual."

Chaplain narrowed his eyes.

"Miss Poole—*Janelle*—isn't my type. I prefer the company of men."

Chaplain's Adam's apple yo-yoed, up and down. "I see."

Didn't look like he did.

Nonplussed, the man of God remained a mighty fortress. "My boys are dangerous, Mr. Baumgartner. Dr. Schramm wants you to stay out of their way. He wants me to pass on the message to stop making trouble." Chaplain seized Miles just above the ankle. Right at the bite. He tugged, hard and firm as Butch's handshake. "I think you should continue to push. Aren't you curious how far we would go?"

Miles ground his teeth against the squeal rising up his throat.

Chaplain let go, eyes merry. Without a further word, Chaplain left him, closing him in the room, but still unlocked and unguarded.

Why would they bother? He couldn't get anywhere. A sort of disgrace wrapped around and through his sinews, infiltrated his cells. He gritted his teeth through the embarrassment and pain and propped himself up on his elbows. The room smelled clean, and a short stack of towels sat on the dresser. The mystery housekeeper even set a replacement trash can in the corner.

Wait.

Where was his phone?

He sat up. It wasn't on the desk.

Hospitality his ass. Pretense to search his room. His fingers combed through his hair, pulling on the ends. He ground his teeth harder than ever, felt a back tooth give, followed by a crunch.

No, no, no, no, no.

He didn't taste blood. No pieces of enameled grit. His tongue poked around. There. A jagged crack in a molar. It was huge. Great, now he had lost his battle with bruxism. How many bad habits did he have to quit?

And he still needed to find his phone.

He flipped to his belly and peeked under the bed. "Ah!" His phone lay on a dust bunny pillow between the cot leg and the writing table leg. He pulled it out. Thank you, thank you Power Greater than Himself.

Sitting on the edge of the bed, he pushed the HOME button. Upper right, the green battery icon had filled in. **100%**. Upper left, one lousy crescent showed the terrible reception.

No notifications beside his messenger app. No one had texted him this whole time? No one at all?

He tapped the blue dialog box to open it up. As the last one whom Miles had texted, Jeremy's smug profile pic grinned out at him in the top slot. But no messages from anyone showed.

His chest constricted. Five years together, and they couldn't stay friends? Jeremy couldn't even bother a random message every couple of days for the pretense? Didn't have the decency to string him along? It would feel less lonely.

He typed: *I miss you. How did everything go so wrong? This is surreal to be apart after all this time. I miss my best friend.*

His finger hovered, at the ready to hit SEND. He read back what he had written. He blew out angry breath and backspaced all the way to the beginning. The cursor blinked... blinked... blinked.

I'm in trouble.

Sent.

He sat without moving, breathing, thinking. Like a statue, as Miss Yenchesky used to say. Storytime on the rainbow carpet: Everyone still as a statue. Had he even evolved that much from the naïve grade-schooler he'd been? He still believed whatever garbage people told him.

He hadn't believed his sister, though, had he? He had gone way out of his lane to prove her wrong, and look where that had gotten him.

The phone chimed. He had a notification! The old joy surged through synapses. It tasted sweeter than ice cream. A pleasing vertigo spun in his stomach, just like when falling in love. Jeremy had responded.

He opened Messenger.

A red exclamation point blared at the end of *I'm in trouble*. Failure to send.

He pressed his teeth together but stopped himself from bearing down. No more grinding. He tapped his message and chose to resend. Nothing more to be done. Pain from his wind-and cold-damaged face and hands subsided, leaving him oddly empty.

A knock at the door straightened his back. No one here knocked; they barged in. He shoved his phone in his pocket. Getting to his feet started the pins and needles again.

Another round of knocking.

"Okay!"

When he opened up, Ian fell into his arms.

"I'm sorry." Ian hugged his waist. "I'm sorry." He buried sobs against Miles's sore ribs. He mumbled, and Miles pried him off just far enough to hear. "They made me. Elijah hates you. All the guys listen to him. You've seen what they do to... to...."

"It's okay."

"To Theo. I had to play along or they'd hurt me, too."

Miles pulled Ian back in and hugged him as hard as his beat-up body allowed. Hugged him like the lost child returned home. Order had reasserted itself. Miles wasn't alone. He wasn't empty and ineffectual. Ian hadn't gone astray at all, only created a ruse. Smart, smart kid.

"I never believed it."

Ian's breath trembled. "I can help you escape."

"I just tried. It's impossible."

Ian separated himself. "It's not. The storm's going to break tomorrow, and I know where you can hide until then. There's a secret way out, and tomorrow when the sun comes up you just follow the river south for twenty miles. There's another bridge."

"I'm not sure I can make it that far, walking through snow so deep."

"They're coming for you tonight, Uncle Miles."

Trying again so soon was the last thing he wanted to do. But it would also be the last thing they'd expect. If the storm cleared, and he had a good head start.... Yeah. Yes, he could make it to Bear Falls.

"Okay." Miles felt a sloppy grin smear his face. It immediately fell away. "You're coming with me."

Ian's face unscrunched. "I have to stay here."

"No. I'm not leaving you behind."

"Uncle Miles, I can't leave St. Hamelin's." His shoulders trembled. "I stay or I die. This is it, this half-life. This or nothing at all."

Nothing?

Like the absolute Nothing at the end of Ian's tunnel after the crash? The tunnel with no light at the end.

"They'll figure out that you helped me."

"They can't do much more to me."

"But...." Theodore's death replayed itself—the string of flesh caught in Elijah's teeth, snapping like a wet rubber band.

A flood of platitudes rushed to the fore, but none of them applied. Miles's feet felt far away and disconnected all the way down there on the floor. He squeezed his eyes closed against waves of nausea cramping his innards. Queasiness passed, and he opened his eyes. Ian's moon-face scrunched in concern. How wonderful to see that again.

Focus.

"How will I explain to your mother that I didn't bring you back?"

"She knows I'm stuck. That was the bargain."

Miles forced his jaw to relax. Lips together, teeth apart, and all that nonsense. Of course Minnie knew the stakes. She snipped off Ian's finger and got him here.

"We need to go." Ian bounced on the balls of his feet. "Elijah's on his way."

Miles probed the cracked tooth with his tongue while he stuffed his belongings into his pockets: phone, charger, keys, lighter, smokes. Just things. All his useless things.

Ian led him into uncharted territory, past unknown darkened rooms and down iron-grated stairs at the back of the building. The deeper they descended, the colder the air.

"Have you tried?" The question puffed out as a cloud. "Leaving? Or did they just tell you that you had to stay?" Liars, all of them.

"Don't make this harder."

Through hallways mottled green and black from mold. Overhead light fixtures spaced ever farther apart until their route reached a uniform level of dim grey.

"Where is this hiding place?"

"The old treatment rooms. Where I hid when I first got here."

They had reached a basement level of bare concrete floors and walls, lights protected by iron cages. A scattering of metal doors. Ian yanked on one, and the hinges squealed like pigs at the slaughter. The sensation of ants crawled up and down his spine.

"I don't want to stay in there overnight."

But Ian disappeared into the space beyond. Nothing to do but follow.

Racks of lights came on, and Ian halted just inside a massive room, a windowless hangar made of moldy,

177

gone-to-black cinder blocks. Ranged over the floor in rows stood silver cylinders, laid horizontally on table legs—a fleet of alien space capsules. Six-foot long metal tubes with twin, round portholes in the sides and hatches open at one end. Across the expanse at the far back of the room, a wide metal door blocked some other, godawful discovery.

Standing among the dust-covered machines, Elijah and the other boys waited.

Someone killed the lights.

"Gonna get you now." The words wisped through a cleft lip.

The sudden darkness throbbed against his eyeballs. It hit him then, what the space ships were—iron lungs. Ian had told him these were treatment rooms, and this one had been outfitted with the state-of-the-art equipment of long ago.

Ian's voice from behind: "I lied."

Miles pivoted, but a fist connected with his kidney, dropping him into a heap on the freezing floor. His fingers curled spastically.

Footfalls as Elijah's goons closed in.

Rocky Mountain Face's shrill scream sprayed spittle on his face. "You did this to me!" Rough fabric grazed Miles's cheek—the dirty bandage, loose and flapping off Rocky's hand. "Get bent!"

A short rush of wind, and something hard and flat slammed into Miles's nose. Wow, he actually saw tweety-birds circling the blank screen around his head. He touched his finger to the drop of blood on lips that felt triple-sized. Rocky had stomped his face. Maybe he deserved it after sitting stupefied and impotent on Schramm's floor, as Rocky's finger stump spurted streams of blood in time with each rapid heartbeat.

Miles got over it. A forced laugh tasted salty, metallic. "I'm glad it didn't grow back."

Husky's mouth-breathing hovered in the air. "Old man don't have nothing left in him."

A kick to the stomach knocked Miles's breath out in a retch.

Teeth's oversized chompers clattered as the boy cackled.

Could they see in the dark, these resurrected plank children? These kids were going to pound him into his own grave. All his tender spots already hurt.

But he could use the pain.

He sipped small breaths and relished the feeling of splinters stabbing his sinuses. It woke him up—forced him to think. No liquid warmth drenching his shirt meant his nose wasn't broken. And no, they couldn't see him. They were relying on where he had stood the moment before darkness drenched them all.

He had a moment of respite while the boys congratulated themselves. So cocky. Accustomed to whaling on frail Theodore. Just like Jack's tribe of boys in *Lord of the Flies* who'd surrendered their humanity to become beasts. Believing they were one with the jungle. Predators. The boys in the book were just schoolboys, who in the end suffered the justice of humility.

St. Hamelin's boys were just the same.

Screw them.

He spit on the floor; coppery ropes of it stuck to his chin. His rage dragon slept, but he could function on hate for a while. He stood. Woozy, he stomped forward to keep from falling down.

"If you assholes think I'm going to run away, you've got another—" He swung a roundhouse punch into the black. His fist connected, and Rocky Mountain Face swore. A thud like a sack of potatoes thrown to the floor. "Ha!" Everyone should know the pleasure of punching a twelve-year-old to the ground. Their gasps were priceless.

But their shock, short-lived.

Scuffling as Rocky got to his feet.

In his brief glimpse of the room's layout, he had seen the iron lungs in four columns and five rows. Same as the desks in the classroom.

"You lied about a lot of things, didn't you, Ian?" He slipped to the left, fanning his hands until he found the cool smooth curve of one of the machines. Extending his reach, he found the next one, and threaded between the first two columns.

"Yeah." Ian's voice came from the spot Miles had just left. "I guess I did."

"You really didn't survive that crash." Miles's hip struck the butt end of the next iron lung in line.

"I already told you that." Closer.

Miles scurried behind the one kitty-corner to the right, and listened to the boys' shuffling.

They had broken into at least two flanks. Husky's panting and the feral smell of Rocky's bandaged hand zeroed in at his back. From the front of the room, Teeth's chattering stalked toward the last sound Miles had made. Tagging along, a faint hint of Adidas cologne, a little like beer. Had Ian been buried in cologne-infused clothes? Or was it nostalgic imagination? Ian had taken him literally, about not living through the crash, but Miles had meant more than that. In the showers, as Ian had joined in on Theodore's beating, Miles had seen his almost-son recede; Ian's kindness had drained away as efficiently as his blood must have filled the channels on the embalmer's table.

Miles stared into the dark where the cologne smell centered. He ducked behind the next iron lung, the one in the position of Ian's desk upstairs in the classroom.

His arms swiped through air; fingers grasping emptiness, trying to find the next column, the next iron lung before he ran into it and the noise called the hunters to him.

A scrape of shoes at his eleven o'clock.

Where was the next machine?

A whistling breath.

His left hand found cold metal. Slapped around it until he made out the rounded edge of a cylinder.

Whisper of trouser legs at five and six.

Patting the surface, he felt his way along the long side.

A squeak of sole against concrete.

He guided himself closer to the back door.

"Hey." Hare Lip stage-whispered.

Miles froze and tried to invoke echo-location.

"Shut up." Husky's baritone, right beside him.

A rivet on Miles's jeans pocket hit the machine. Crap! The clink filled the room like a pealing bell. He hurried into the aisle. His outstretched hands found the next iron lung, but he stayed in the space between, crouched down and making himself as small a target as he could.

"Guys?" Hare Lip didn't have the sense God gave him.

Miles crept down the aisle.

Whisking of shoes several feet behind. Husky and Teeth? They walked on by and were now getting cold... colder... coldest.

According to the map in his head, Miles should have been just about out of the chessboard. He should have removed his shoes and done this in his socks. Miles slipped between the last machines in the two far columns. Sweeping his arms like antennae, he forged through the dark.

Discouraged breaths rasped from the center of the room. Husky? Hare Lip? He'd lost track of who was where.

His open palms slapped a greasy patch of cinderblocks. He'd found the wall.

From the middle of the room, an elbow or knee brushed a machine.

His fingertips grazed the grit and mold of the individual blocks, and he inched toward the back door.

Agitated curses throughout the room, barely shushed.

He had to have been close to that door by now. When he found it, he could take his chances in the unknown beyond, or he could make a break for the front of the room, plunging into the abyss of deep space and hoping that his mental map to the door Ian had led him through was true. And that he wouldn't run into any of the boys searching vainly for him. Either direction, if he snuck through undetected, the boys could scour the darkness between iron lungs endlessly.

His grasping fingers found metal, and he pressed himself against the door. He'd really done it.

"There!"

Ian's voice?

His heart jack-hammered. He ran his fingers over metal until finding a smooth plate that led him to a huge handle. He tugged it two rattling inches before it stopped dead. He cracked his teeth together and ground his molars; a lightning bolt shot through his skull.

Soft-shoe sounds as the boys stopped, turned, homed in on his position.

He gripped the oversized lever and threw it upward, clockwise. It ratcheted up and around past high noon. The door popped open a half-inch. He pushed. Nothing. He pulled, and the door still didn't swing open.

Slow, deliberate footfalls in the dark.

A vision of the door as seen in the light flicked through his brain. Wide. Like Leatherface's kill-room door—built on tracks to slide open.

The boys must have found the edges of the room, footsteps hurried toward him from the side and from his back.

He grabbed the handle and heaved. Grinding along the runners, it slid open. No light spilled out to pinpoint him, but the noise had been immense in the iron lung hangar. He squeezed through and racked the door closed.

Thunder pounded the floor as the boys ran to catch him.

He yanked the handle down, praying that some mechanism would catch and lock. Nothing. The door wanted to roll back open a half-inch.

"We got you now."

"Open up."

He couldn't see, but imagined their fingers wriggling through the gap. Their legs spread, backs arched in combined effort to pry the door wide.

His sweat-slicked palms started slipping off the metal bar. He strangled the handle and threw his weight into the door. The back of his hand knocked against a flange, and he freed the other hand, feeling a seesaw of metal—the latch. With a grunt, he tugged the door in place and flipped the lever. A satisfying click held the door in place.

He backed up into the blackness, keeping the door in front of him as if watching. His racing heart sent blood-red bursts of light pulsing through his vision. Maybe close calls were like a cat's nine lives. How many narrow escapes had he used up? He must have been getting close to the last chance that would break his way.

"Now we're alone."

Miles yelped and shrank against the brilliant light suddenly stabbing his eyes. The first shape that came through—Elijah, standing at the door and smiling in psychotic joy.

What a clever one.

While he had been navigating around the imps in the other room, Elijah had snuck in here and prepared for ambush.

Kid didn't even unlock the door for the others, just sauntered toward Miles.

"You must be great at chess." Where were the exits? Anything he could use as a weapon?

Elijah broke into a smile—a god-honest smile that brightened his face. He morphed into a smart, sincere child—a young man with energy and life and humor. "This is where they experimented."

An infirmary—white tiled walls and floors. A counter with white cupboard doors under and above filled most of one wall. Old jars frosted with age lined the countertop. Long metal poles—IV stands—gathered in one corner like conspirators. A steel table filled the center of the room, surrounded by three of those old-fashioned medical lights with the wide bowls around the bulbs. But like Miller Park where the Brewers played, two walls only came up about six feet; above and behind, four rows of wooden chairs wrapped around that corner.

They stood not in an infirmary but an operating theater.

The atmosphere wasn't one of health and healing; it didn't soothe. It writhed like vipers. The pores of the room—the brittle caulking, nail holes, the individual grains of wood—excreted a rank odor of sweat and terror.

Elijah reached the operating table. "Doctors called it treatment." His breath smelled like burned plastic. He stared into Miles's eyes, reached out and caressed Miles's cheek with cold fingers. "Don't you think they knew the truth?"

Elijah closed his hand on Miles's chin and jerked his head toward the corner. Behind the IV poles, a stout box with a face of knobs and dials sat on a wheeled cart. An early-generation ECT machine.

A remarkable piece of apparatus.

"Electroshock." Elijah spoke with hushed reverence. "That was the kindest treatment. I really don't know if Dr. Schramm ever wanted to discover a cure, or if he just enjoyed hurting the orphans. Tendon transfers. Arm and leg lengthening... and shortening. Nerve grafting. We heard their screams all the way up in our rooms."

The injustice of the procedure and the inhumanity of the execution were undeniable.

Castigation straight out of Kafka. That fit his sense of this room—not a place of medicine at all but a torture chamber.

Tear us apart.

"That's barbaric. Sick."

Elijah stared at a spot over Mile's shoulder, his dazzling green eyes unfocused. Reminiscing? "Chaplain Allen wanted me to show you this."

Miles opened his mouth, though his mind hadn't formed a question yet. Before he could come up with anything, a key scratched at the door. The seesaw latch snapped down, and the door rolled open an inch. Janelle had screwed him—she'd given the boys the keys for these rooms.

All of them. All of them were in on it.

Ian swept open the door. He grinned. Shrugged. "Sorry, Uncle Miles."

"Do you smile like that when you lick Elijah's shoes clean?" That knocked the smug expression off his nephew's face faster than the classroom slap. Deep inside, his dragon licked its chops. Miles barely felt ashamed.

The rest of the crew had joined now. Towhead nudged past Ian, chin down, eyes locked on Miles. Husky's whole body bobbed up and down with each breath. The rest lined up, and they edged forward, riot control cops of this nightmare world. Expressions drained away. Faces drew tight. Emotionless as they were in their photos.

Those taken sixty-five years ago.

Elijah's jade eyes watched with eerie fixity. He gave a sign with an almost imperceptible nod.

They pounced like rabid dogs. Husky clobbered him, grabbed him by the ear. Rocky and Teeth pulled one forearm. Ian and Hare lip grabbed the other; Towhead, Grimley, and Precious swamped his legs. Together, they dragged him to the operating table.

"Hold him good." Elijah's voice came from the corner of the room. By the shock machine.

Husky panted the stink of gravedirt into Miles's face. Fingers poked at his eyes. His ears. Their wiry limbs had steel strength, but he struggled wildly to make them work for it. His calf-bite surged in warning. A hand grazed the sore flesh, and he shuddered. They hefted him up and slammed his butt-bone down on the unyielding steel tabletop.

Wheels squeaked. Closer... closer....

"If you kill me, I'll come back and hunt you all down."

Elijah was at his side, examining. "Let's see if that works out any better for you than it does Theo and his mom."

"His mom?"

A shadow that was Elijah's arm reached across and adjusted one of the lights so it burned into Miles's retinas.

Nineteen

"Monsters!"

Janelle's scream shredded the air. The giant mass of keys jangled, her knuckles white. Face red as fury. She stormed at them fast enough, hard enough, that Elijah retreated to the corner, his motion fluid, floating. The other boys froze still as statues, caught flat-footed and loose-jawed.

A wailing siren, Janelle seized Teeth's wrist. She yanked him off his feet. "You just left him there?"

Teeth's crowded mouth fell open.

"You left my boy on the floor?" She throttled him, rattling both her ring of keys and his awful eponymous teeth. Miles laughed at the hole where that one had broken off in their scuffle. She roared at all the boys. "Get out of here. Leave this man alone."

Miles couldn't stop blatting.

Husky's face hardened from shock into a pout. Guilt? Embarrassment? Rocky Mountain Face had the nerve to speak. "He got my finger cut off!"

Miles whooped manic laughter. "Cut right the hell off!"

Janelle let go of Teeth's wrist and pinched the mass of nerves at the base of his neck. Really gave him the old Vulcan neck pinch. Teeth yelped. Miles slid into hysterics. Janelle flashed him a look so quick that he failed to read it, but it narrowed into hate as she glared at Husky. Never taking her eyes off the big boy, she shook Teeth so hard that his feet slipped out from under him. The boy pedaled for traction. She lowered her voice. "Any of you touch Mr. Baumgartner again, and I'll have Schramm lop off an entire hand." She pushed Teeth to the floor. "You know he would love to do it."

Eight pairs of young eyes goggled.

Eight?

His crazed laughter died. "Where's Elijah?"

No sign of the redhead. How slippery.

Janelle grabbed Miles's hand and helped him off the table. Dragged him, really, with as much force as the kids when they had manhandled him. She marched him like an errant child out of the operating theater. "Let's get you to your room before they decide to come after us."

Derisive laughter erupted after them. "You'll never get away!"

Ian's hyena laugh followed.

"Never get away!"

Winded, trudging up stairs. "Why are you being nice to me now?"

Leg muscles quivered, exhausted to jelly. It was all he could do to keep up with Janelle's cardigan, floating up through the murk like a phantom.

"What do you mean, *now*?"

"You've been...."

"Yes?"

"Kinda bitchy since I got here."

She laughed, a lovely spirited sound. "I didn't want you here."

"Yeah. That's what I'm saying."

"Mr. Baumgart—"

"Just Miles. Please."

"Miles, I wanted you to leave so this very thing wouldn't happen."

"Oh?"

"I hoped you'd get in your car and drive away and never come back to this prison."

Hmmm. Thinking back, rearranging his point of view, had he misread her so completely? Or was she trying to fool him right now? Like Ian. Damn Ian had tricked him, told him exactly what he wanted to hear and walked him into a trap.

But then why would Janelle save him just now?

Maybe she wanted to photograph him for a new shrine.

Paranoia was exhausting.

He halted. Janelle climbed three more steps before she noticed he had stopped following.

"Are you going to hurt me?"

"Why would you think that?"

"You gave them the keys for the treatment rooms."

She regarded him like a slow-witted schoolboy. "I did not. They may have stolen Chaplain Allen's key, or maybe he gave it to them. He prohibited them from touching me or Theo—" She choked on the name, and suddenly he knew.

"He's your son."

And Janelle had found her son in the lavatory shower, naked and broken and...

"And... you're dead, too." Surrounded by death.

Now her skin would melt off her dusty bones. Hair drop out in tufted wads. She'd raise her claws at him. Let loose a banshee scream and swoop down on him. At the witching hour he would wake, a soul doomed to wander eternity in St. Hamelin's.

Benign, she waited for him to catch up.

"I don't understand any of this."

"Come on." She trotted up the stairs.

"Where are we?" It looked like the stairwell leading to his room, but with another flight of stairs ahead, Janelle led him into a hallway. She opened up the door straight ahead, and he followed into her world set exactly one floor down from his. Inside, two beds, two writing desks, two dressers, but not as crammed together as they should have been.

"Wait...." He pointed to the left-hand wall and like checking off a list, swung his finger around to the right-side. "You have a bigger room."

Janelle laughed, polite and refreshing. "Yes, we have a double room."

Janelle's mood change sent his internal gyros off balance. Must have caught her off guard, too. They fell silent. He shifted his weight from foot to foot. He was an intruder here amidst the double furniture. Janelle and Theodore, mother and son—their uncanny connection yesterday in Schramm's office made sense, but the boy wouldn't be coming back now. Elijah and Ian and those boys murdered her son, and Miles felt suddenly overheated.

"It's my fault. They were showing off for me. Theodore died because of me."

"Theodore died because of the filth Chaplain Allen put in those boys' heads."

He didn't want to be let off the hook. "But they wanted me to see."

"The world does not revolve around you, Mr. Baumgartner." She stiffened. "What you saw was an indignity. The real damage was done long ago. Theodore has already found his way back through the fog, and I sent him to hide before coming to fetch you. In case any of the boys split up, or if they hadn't backed down and instead followed us."

"Fog.... Ian spoke of a fog that brought him here."

She waited, but he shut up, and in the awkward silence he checked out the bookshelves affixed to the wall above the second bed. Same boards and brackets as Butch's deer fetus room. In fact, the same sort of patterned rust-and-brown rugs lay on the floor here as in the cottage.

She caught him looking. "Stage dressing for Theodore. We don't sleep anymore, or eat anymore, but a boy needs a home."

In cold-hearted St. Hamelin's. How many scores of people craved eternal life? They wouldn't if they saw the dirty contract they had to sign. Minnie had condemned Ian.

Whatever remained of Ian.

Miles turned back to the books—his favorite company. He caressed the spines. "Great taste." *The Great Gatsby*, *The Catcher in the Rye*, Huxley's *A Brave New World*—he sure could give her some spoilers about the future. "Have you read this?" He pulled free the thick volume of *Ulysses*.

"I'm slogging my way through it."

Miles slid it back into its slot on the shelf. "That's how I felt about reading it, too." These were probably all first editions, bought new at the store. Holy hell—*Fahrenheit 451*. Asbestos cover? He should smuggle this out, not Ian.

Damn. That was harsh.

Janelle smoothed the back of her skirt and slid onto her ladder-backed chair. She had always struck Miles as a sort of throwback spinster, but now that he knew the big secret, Janelle truly embodied the quintessential Fifties' woman. That coiffed hair, the simple cut of her A-line dress, those impeccable manners. But Donna Reed hadn't had the steel in Janelle's eyes.

"When Dr. Schramm made up his mind that you should stay that first night, I did try to talk him out of it."

Easy to guess how that went. Schramm was enough of a lout before adding in the machismo of his era.

"When he had your car plowed in, I was scared for you. I knew then that he would never allow you to leave. I...." Her fingernails clicked as she picked them. "I should have warned you directly, but Chaplain's eyes and ears are everywhere. I did believe you had a chance, until you struck Ian. Schramm gravitates toward violence."

"You mean I endeared myself to him?" Jesus. Now he would never quit nit-picking that moment.

"May I?" He set his tired butt on the second chair, groaning like his old man. He raked his fingers through the tangles of his hair. "Please, tell me what's going on." He wanted to pull his hair out by the roots. "How did all this happen?"

"It's been so long since I've thought about it all in a straight line."

"Start with you and Theodore. How did you get involved?"

Janelle closed her eyes and breathed deep. She spoke on the exhale. "My husband—Theodore's father—died during the war."

She meant World War II. His sanity sagged in the middle like a bed holding stacks of suitcases.

"My parents took us in, but I meant to take care of my son myself. In the spring of 1950, I graduated from the State Teachers College in Stevens Point. Full of high ideals and ready to mold a new generation. A position opened up here, at the orphanage, and that autumn I reported to St. Hamelin's, in one hand a steamer trunk holding all my worldly possessions and in the other, my boy Theodore."

"Nineteen-fifty?" Thinking it made him tipsy. "How old was he then?"

"Theodore?" Janelle gazed into the corner, into the past, and counted. "Seven. He never met his father. Joe took a German bullet in—" She cleared her throat into her loose fist. "Dr. Schramm had just started. Chaplain Allen had been here only a short while. I'll never forget the weight on my soul as I stood in the shadow of this ugly building. Sometimes I think, maybe I'm making that up in hindsight. But no, I did feel the chill of this horrible place."

"That same cold hit me when I drove up. A crushing immensity." He rubbed his hands over his face, as if to wake himself. "I need a cigarette."

"May I join you?"

"Really?"

"Just don't tell the chaplain."

"All right then."

He opened her window as she dug through cabinets self-made from small crates. "We can use this for an ashtray."

She joined him with a mint-green Jadeite coffee cup. Worth a lot of money at an antique store. Flurries splattered into the screen, leaving wide wet blobs like bugs crushed on a windshield. He popped a cigarette between his teeth and turned his back to the open window. With a flick of his lighter, tobacco sizzled, caught fire with a quick whoosh, and he breathed in. Stale from getting wet in the snow and then drying, but none the worse for wear. Sucking down the smoke into his eager lungs brought an orgasmic rush. He blew out a dragon's breath of smoke from his nose and passed the cigarette to Janelle.

She took her turn and loosed a long steady blue stream toward the window.

"If you're...?" Was it rude to remind the risen of their death? "How are you able to smoke?" He held up a hand. "No. Nevermind, I don't want to know. I can't process any more information right now."

"Good." She passed back the cigarette. "Because I don't even know."

The nicotine excited his head. "Look, I have a plan. If I can break into Schramm's office, I can destroy the plank children."

"The what?"

He told her what he had read: photographing fresh corpses tied to planks.

She nodded along. "That's frighteningly accurate." Her fingers asked for the cigarette. "How do we kill what's already dead?"

He smiled at her "we." Janelle had officially signed on as an accessory.

"The photographs are the key. That's how I set free the ghosts of the polio kids."

Her eyebrows raised. "You mean in the crypt? So that's how you made Chaplain Allen so angry." She ground out the butt in the bottom of the cup like an expert smoker. Jane Eyre, his ass. She must have been a wild, wonderful rule-breaker back in her day. Catholic girls had nothing on Lutheran ladies.

"I just need to get at the pictures hanging on his walls. When I destroy them, the plank—those boys will...." Will what?

He had no clue.

And what of Ian? Would what remained of his nephew live on? Or did Miles need to hunt for a print of that picture? Rip him up and throw away his almost-son's life for good and forever?

But that boy wasn't really his nephew any more. He kept forgetting. Hope was the hardest of all to kill.

Janelle nodded for him to finish what he'd been saying, but he had lost that train and jumped onto another.

"Have you ever tried to leave?"

"Of course. Theodore and I ran for the bridge, but as we started across, that fog frothed up. It enveloped us. We kept walking even though we couldn't see. Walking became difficult—it was thick, you see. We continued on, desperate to get away, and the fog finally broke into a rainy mist but when that pulled back, we found ourselves back here at the foot of the front stairs. We tried a couple more times—and in other directions—but we always ended up at St. Hamelin's."

So Ian was right—he lived in St. Hamelin's or he didn't live at all. Miles should have felt relief, the decision taken from his hands. Instead, he felt like he'd just eaten garbage.

"We need to smuggle you out of here, Miles. If you remain much longer, Elijah will kill you. He was always a nasty boy, but after... afterward, he became truly wicked. Dr. Schramm tries to control them, plays his sinister games, but they're Chaplain Allen's boys. It had to have been the chaplain that gave them a key to unlock the treatment rooms. He's got it out for you now, and you don't have many allies."

"Just you."

She shook her head. "Frederick will help you."

"Butch? Why do you keep thinking that he's going to help me?"

"Frederick was a... friend... to me during those bad times. When Dr. Schramm and the chaplain started their experiments with the children who were falling ill." She shuddered.

Elijah had told him the truth.

Janelle continued in distant monotone, picking her way through the minefield of the past. "They started bringing in the troubled boys. Dr. Schramm worked a deal with the county judges so they would sentence juvenile offenders to St. Hamelin's for a kickback. Did you know that this used to be a prison? Long, long ago. St. Hamelin's has always known misery, but after those two took over, real evil soured the ground."

"How did you...?" Best to just say it. "How did you...?" But he couldn't. "What happened to you? You and Theodore? And everyone? I heard about an accident that got St. Hamelin's closed down."

Her hands drifted to her throat, as if clutching for a necklace, a charm, that usually hung there. "Theodore was younger than the new boys, and small for his age anyway." Her eyes begged for forgiveness. "He's a sensitive boy. You've seen that. Those delinquents that Dr. Schramm brought in, they delighted in bullying him." She swiped at her eyes. "Elijah and Jacob. That donkey, William Koehler. They ganged up on Theodore in the showers." She eyed the door. Was she seeing beyond, into the fifth-floor bathroom? "They beat him so badly he—" She hiccupped a wet sob. "He'd been...." She took a trembling breath. "His head had been cracked open, and he'd been...bitten. They left him there, cold and alone. All alone to die. By the time I found him, there was...." Her gaze flitted to the wall above his head, to the bureau, the closet, the waste bin. "Nothing. Nothing I could do."

His brain soaked up her story the way a field thirsty from drought soaks up the rain when it finally falls.

"What I saw in the showers on my floor.... They make him go through it all again? Hurt your son over and over."

"They're not supposed to. Chaplain Allen made me a promise. That was before...." She started nodding. "Before that accident, like you said."

"Tell me what it was."

She coughed, collected herself, and spoke in a rush. "A fire started in the early morning, after midnight while we all slept, and the smoke filled the stairwells, and the floors, and it choked us all even before the flames ravaged everything." She took a deep breath. "It killed us, but we didn't stay dead. We woke up. St. Hamelin's woke us up."

A thousand questions fought to be asked. "How did you wake up? Someone needed to take those photos. Who started this loop if the fire killed everyone?"

"Not everyone. A few boys in a different area were okay, and Betty lived out in the cottage like she does now, so she was safe."

"Wait a minute. So Butch and Betty didn't die."

Janelle glanced to the ground. Her voice was so soft he barely heard. "Just Betty."

So, if Betty had lived on.... His math was terrible, but wouldn't she have been a little girl at the time?

"How young was she when Butch married her?"

"Married? Married whom?"

"Betty. Butch and Betty."

Janelle's laugh broke the unbearable tension in the room. "Oh, dear." Her laugh grew. "Betty...." She caught her breath. "Betty is Frederick's daughter."

Gah! That was disgusting. Father and daughter?
Wait.

Oh... not married at all. Yeah, he saw it now. Butch called Betty his girl. The shows of affection lacked any intimacy. And Butch had ogled Janelle.

He felt so stupid.

Janelle stood. "It's late."

It was. He didn't need to check the time to know it. He felt it. His body was drained. He'd started the day stumbling onto ghosts. Seemed like a week ago. He had woken as one man and would be going to sleep a different person. Possessing a radically evolved perspective at the very least.

Janelle pushed her chair into the knee hole of the desk. She closed the window. The chill had just started aggravating his chapped cheeks and chin and forehead. She stood looking down at him, expression warm. Motherly. She bent and kissed his forehead. "Frederick will help. We'll get you out."

She showed him to the door and gave him a sly wave as he headed for the stairs.

Once in his room, he smoked at the window while digesting all Janelle had told him. He smoked another one after that. He tidied up the sill and threw the butts into the trash can, then crawled into that clean bed. He watched the ceiling for a long time with a headache borne of probable impossibilities.

Twenty

Rats in the walls.

Claws clicked through narrow passages. Fat tails slapped against the drywall. Miles woke with a gasp and beat at his chest and thighs and neck, attacking rats that had chewed through, spilled out, and covered him. He bolted out of bed, hopped from one stocking foot to the other, slapping at his clothes.

But rats were not clawing up his shirt sleeves, or dangling off his jeans, mouths clamped onto the denim. Only tangled sheets and the blanket covered the bed.

A nightmare.

Mostly. Rodents did scuttle behind the walls, and in the midnight stillness, their chittering had nipped into his dreams. Yuck! It was just so disgusting. Those secretive, organic noises were one reason he'd slept fully dressed. Nudity meant vulnerability, and he needed to remain clothed and vigilant.

He yawned. How long had he slept? After yesterday's exertions, he had expected a full night's rest, but dawn hadn't even begun lightening the sky's rural blackness.

The rats squeaked, and he shivered.

Hmm. Not just rats squawking but another, deeper under-sound.

He crept to his door. Pressed his ear against the grain.

Crying.

He slipped out and through the gauntlet of dorm doors, headed for the incinerator. Not a sound from the rooms tonight. He slapped his hands on the wall at either side of the hatch.

Piercing, ragged sobs.

He opened the chute, and the cries amplified. He tried to whisper but shout at the same time. "Theodore!"

The boy sounded hurt.

"Theodore?"

Bawling. High, frantic wails.

"I'm coming for you."

If he could find the right way down.

He jogged out onto the ground floor. Now where? As a starting point this had seemed the best bet. At least he was moderately oriented here. The main floor had to have a way into the basement level. Or levels.

At the arched doors down the hall, movement—dark on darker—drew him forward. Probably a trick of his eyes as they adjusted. But then the doors sighed as they closed.

Curiosity goaded him the rest of the way.

Walking St. Hamelin's endless hallways, climbing up and down these infinite stairways, felt more and more like puzzling through the thought processes in a psychotic's diseased brain. Every room enacted another twisted fantasy. Dammit, he was supposed to be looking for Theodore, and instead stood facing more closed doors. But what if the demented tableau beyond these doors gave up a clue to help the search?

Okay, then. Time to step into one more of St. Hamelin's sick secrets.

At this point, what did another nightmare matter?

He snuck inside....

And entered the chapel.

A couple lights—in back and in front—had been turned on. Probably by Betty, who crossed the communion rail into the chancel.

Shadows shaded in the corners, effectively shrinking the square room. It wouldn't exactly have been huge when lit. Half a dozen short rows of pews on either side of a central aisle.

Miles crouched into the pew farthest back and peered over the back of the bench in front, hoping that either the dark or old eyesight would keep Betty from spotting him if she turned. But Betty kept her head down and trucked past and behind the pulpit—a big black edifice stage left—to an almost concealed door. St. Mark's education kicked in—that door would lead to the sacristy—a room where Chaplain would keep his vestments and communion chalice. All the holy articles. A place Betty had no reason to enter.

She fiddled with a key for a moment. She went rigid and cocked her head. Miles ducked down, clenching his jaw.

A soft snick as Betty opened the door, and he chanced another peek. The groundskeeper's daughter disappeared inside and swung closed the door behind her. He counted off seconds to eighteen... nineteen... twenty.... Hunched, he crept into the aisle and two pews up, third from the front. Sliding in, his knee cracked into the hymnal shelf attached to the back of the pew in front.

He froze.

Held his breath.

Waited for the bottom of the shelf to snap off, for the half dozen hymnals to thunder to the floor. Betty would rush out and catch him; she'd call the alarm in her dialect of gibberish.

But the shelf held.

The day's exhaustion caught up with him, and he rested his forehead on the back of the pew. Seconds passed.

Minutes.

So quiet.

Warm.

He startled awake.

How long had he been asleep? Had Betty left? Thank God she hadn't seen—

The sacristy door clicked open.

Groggy, Miles squatted to the floor. Betty's clunky shoes clomped down the aisle. He hadn't heard them when he followed her in. Must have been too excited. He breathed in time with her footfalls and flattened himself halfway under the pew. Beneath the hem of her house-coat, Betty's cankles approached. He squeezed farther under. Betty's stride bobbed her head once... twice... and she passed out of view.

The lights in back and front winked out. The chapel doors whispered open and a moment later settled shut. He stayed hidden on the floor. She might not have left. Maybe she'd slipped off her shoes. Was right now sneaking up on him. She would fall upon him, grab him by the collar, and drag him to Schramm. Or would she fetch Butch? His holler bursting into the chapel: "Whatcha doin' down der?" Then Frederick Blankenheim would take him, cut him to pieces, and stuff him into little jars to decorate the cottage.

A minute passed. Another. He didn't fall asleep again, and after a few minutes more, it seemed clear that Betty was truly gone and Butch wasn't on his way. He stood and brushed off his jeans. Guess it was time for Betty to warsh them again.

He headed for the front of the church but paused at the chancel. One must be worthy to cross into the sacred sections of a church. He may have turned his back on religion after being condemned to Hell, but Mom and Dad had hardwired Lutheranism into him—and Minnie—from their toddlerhood. St. Mark's from kindergarten to eighth grade confirmation. Weekly church and Sunday school with Wednesday chapel service in between.

A couple grinding swipes of his molars back and forth, and he overcame his indoctrination.

But he hurried as if his feet were catching fire.

All of that for nothing—Betty had locked the sacristy door. He ran his fingerpads over the striations of wood, as if he could read them like braille. Or like tea leaves, divining what business Betty tended to in there.

A spidery sensation crawled up his spine, and he turned toward the nave. Black blotches that may have been Butch or Schramm or any number of the kids filled the back pews.

"Hello?"

Whoever watched him from the darkness, they weren't about to give themselves away.

"Why don't you come and face me?"

The blotches scattered. Jumped into other spaces. They seemed to bloat, then constrict. A great wave of fatigue washed over him. It wasn't Betty or Butch or Chaplain out there. It was stress tricking his eyes.

Eyes that were so tired.

No shapes, no one watching him, but this mounting paranoia was growing like cancer. St. Hamelin's had worn him down. He was cracking up.

But he would have to save the breakdown for tomorrow. Right now, he couldn't keep his eyelids open.

"I'm sorry, Theodore."

As much as he wanted to, he couldn't stop or soothe the crying from the chute tonight. He simply couldn't. He would get lost. He would collapse from pushing himself too hard today. His legs and arms felt heavy. He had to get to bed before he passed out on his feet.

The boy had made it this long without his help.

So heavy.

He dragged his weary bones through the church, to the vestibule. No one assaulted him.

Up the stairs, he prayed to a great silent Nothing to please, this time, please, please no more nightmares.

Twenty-One

Sunlight streamed through the window and painted the backs of his eyelids orange. He woke with warmth on his face, more rested than he'd been since moving to the new apartment. He rubbed crusties out of his eyes. Stretching, he reached backwards over his head for his phone, and every muscle in his body complained. He checked his phone—fully charged, and he'd slept until noon. When was the last time that had happened?

He sat up and crinkled his nose. Old-man body odor coated him like a sour cologne. He had sweated into these clothes a lot since Betty had washed them. He wasn't really going to ask her to launder them, so they would have to do. But at least he could shower. He grabbed a towel from the dresser and stepped into the hallway.

"Oh, dammit."

Cold, wet slop squelched beneath his foot. One sock absorbed the bacon grease and scrambled eggs of his breakfast tray, conveniently left outside his door. His stomach growled and hunger pains almost doubled him over. Of course, it would have been a godawful meal like all the rest, but his body needed food.

Damn St. Hamelin's!

And Betty.

And Schramm and Chaplain with their tortures great and small. Minnie and Daniel for tricking him up here. And Jeremy! Damn him for ruining a great relationship.

A good one.

Oh, hell. A decent one.

He spat on the Soglin 7 carpet.

Walking on the heel of his soiled foot, he limped down the hall. Rooms were noisy. Chattering behind closed doors. Scrapes and scuffles of movement. Even though every single room he passed was empty and trashed. The stink of rot had escalated beyond odious and well into repugnant. He held the towel to his face, the nubs of pilled fabric rough against his nose and cheeks.

In the aquatic stillness of the bathroom, a distant, metronomic plink of water repeated from the showerhead to the tiled floor. Washing away the traces of bloody, bitten Theodore? Or did the stains of the re-dead vanish with the bodies before the lost once more mounted the front steps of their eternal prison?

He diverted to the bank of sinks and pulled off his breakfast-stained sock. He rinsed it, turned it inside-out, and soaked it again. For good measure, he removed the other one. Rinse and repeat. He wrung them out, staring at the familiar stranger in the mirror. He blew out a breath, and Mirror Man's cheeks puffed out like Dizzy Gillespie's. Three days' growth of beard stubbled his face. He ran a hand along the prickles. They pulled the skin and itched.

Staring into the eyes that stared back at him: "How are you going to get out of here?"

Mirror Man didn't know.

Miles stepped up to a urinal. He unzipped, released, and moaned—hamming it up to conquer the silence, but the quiet pushed back. Okay, then. No more procrastination. His bare feet slapped the floor underneath the second archway and over the curb. The floor tiles bore no visible trace of blood, but he smacked his lips and tongue to be rid of the metallic taste, thick as soup.

Grimacing, he stripped. This was wrong. Invasive and disrespectful. But he needed to wash up. No place to set his clothes, so he laid them over the last stall door. Underneath the shower heads, he felt obscene with his dick hanging out. He punched the metal button, and the wall nozzle spat out a sharp spray. Freezing water knifed his tender bits. He twisted the button, trying for warmth. He didn't get it. The water poked and stung like those terrible showers at the public pool so long ago.

He watched the drain, waiting for it to back up and regurgitate blood and puke and mucus. Spewing pieces of Theodore to the walls. Throwing up gore chunky with scraps of flesh.

With a sigh of old plumbing, the pellets of water slackened and stopped.

He turned away from the drain and smacked the button again. This time around the water heater kicked in, and the sudden burst of hot scalded his stomach. He ducked his head under and got his body wet as quickly as possible. His eyes started to burn from the assault.

Enough was enough.

The spray sizzled against the floor tiles as he backed out of the bubble of heat. At the chilly end of the showers, his dick shriveled like a retracting turtle head; balls tightened into a hard shell. His skin had scalded a piggy pink. He was as clean as he was going to get. Clean as the tiles—wiped free of outward blemish but inside the pores, stained beyond the most stringent washing.

"What are you doing in my room?"

Chaplain stood with his back to the cloister's window, hands folded behind him. Dress blacks pressed. "It stinks like cigarette smoke in here."

With his clothes sticking to his damp body, Miles ground his teeth and squeezed his hands into fists around the wet socks he held. He'd wanted to crack the window and lay them on the sill to dry, but now Chaplain's smug face was in the way—composed while Miles's world spun apart. He threw the socks, and they slapped Chaplain in the belly before slopping onto the floor.

Chaplain's mealworm lips grinned. "I've asked the Lord about you."

"About smoking? You shouldn't have."

"Come now. Let's be friends." He let his long arms swing. "Sunday service begins in an hour. You haven't seen our chapel yet."

Was Chaplain screwing with him? Had Chaplain found out about last night's chapel trespass?

Chaplain's third eye passed judgement. "You need to attend."

Miles sat on the bed to tug on shoes over his bare feet. "Oh, I need to? So now you want to bring me into your cult?"

Genuine horror blanched Chaplain's face. He wagged his finger. "You're worse off than I thought if you consider Christianity a cult."

"I'm a captive. Not a captive audience."

Chaplain scrutinized with those beady eyes. Rat's eyes. Chaplain was the king of the rats. "I have prayed about your affliction."

"Affliction?" Miles tried to reach around to loosen where his shirt clung to his damp shoulder blades.

"Mr. Baumgartner. Miles, if I may?" Chaplain sat beside him on the bed. He slid his bony ass closer. He laid a couple fingers on Miles's knee and leaned in, imparting a great secret with that wretched swamp breath. "I was once just as confused as you are."

Miles recoiled from Chaplain's touch. "What am I confused about?"

"At the university—this was before seminary—I roomed with a young man by the name of Floyd Pulvermacher." Chaplain nodded at his own story. "We became instant friends." With his long reach, Chaplain laid a hard, clammy hand on Miles's shoulder.

"Club ties and a firm handshake?"

Chaplain frowned. "Pay attention."

"All right." Miles waved at him to continue but squirmed away another inch. It wasn't far enough.

"Floyd and I ate all our lunches and dinners together. We had a class in common and spent many hours sharing notes and studying. Going for beers after classes." Empty, canned laughter. "No reason to act so shocked, Mr. Baumgartner. I have imbibed in my life. Remember that monks invented beer as liquid bread. I digress. My point is this—I cared very much for Floyd, and yes, soon I grew confused. My thinking muddied. I thought that I loved him... in the way a man loves a woman. See, the Devil tempted me with the same delusion that has led you astray. But I got down on my knees, Miles, and through ardent prayer I heard the Lord's voice and He revealed to me that those feelings were the bonds of a great friendship. Not carnal, as I feared. Not sinful at all, but pure, innocent, deep affection for a dear friend."

Chaplain crossed his arms, satisfied. Was he waiting for heartfelt thanks?

Miles cleared his throat. "You fell in love with your college roommate?"

Chaplain shook his head, perturbed. "No. I'm telling you that it was not love. Not the way you mean it."

"I'm hearing that you're a latent homosexual who has tried to pray the gay away all these years."

Dumbfounded, Chaplain reached for him again. "You misunderstand."

Miles stood before the chill touched his leg. "Chaplain, you seem to be the one misunderstanding."

Chaplain had gone red in the face. He stood and puffed up his narrow chest. "You really are impossible to reach."

"I don't need to be reached."

"Abstain from fleshly lusts which wage war against the soul."

"No worries there. I've no choice but celibacy while I'm here."

Chaplain massaged his temples as though a headache had begun to gnaw there. "Please consider my proposal."

"Wait, were you hitting on me?"

Chaplain smiled, but it looked painful. "You're having fun at my expense. Fine, Mr. Baumgartner, ignore my warnings. All I wish for you is eternal life. That's all I have ever labored for in this institution." Chaplain strolled to the window, lacing together his long fingers. "When I was ten years old, living with my family in Illinois, my mother gave birth to my sister. The Lord saw fit to place challenges in her life." Chaplain stared out into the morning, sounding wistful. Vulnerable. "She was born prematurely. A frail girl, wan and weak, forever back and forth to doctors—her lungs hadn't developed fully, you see. But so concerned were my mother and father with mending her physical body that they neglected her immortal soul." Chaplain picked at his cuticles. "She died before her first birthday, before my mother and father baptized her. Never cleansed of original sin, she did not wake in the arms of Jesus in heaven, but rather she was condemned to the brimstone fires of Hell." Chaplain faced Miles. "I shall never again allow any soul to miss its Glory. I have found a way to preserve life itself, even after death, allowing me another chance to save them all."

"Oh, so that's what's going on here? Soul saving? That includes killing small animals and murdering an innocent little boy? Aren't you supposed to care for the meek? Your boys made a sport of torturing Theodore. They stuff him down the incinerator chute."

"The...." Chaplain squinted at him. "The incinerator?"

"When they're not recreating his death for their amusement."

"Bah!" Disgust turned the chaplain's face purple; the hectic spots on his neck and cheeks shifted like lava lamp flesh. "The murderess has influenced you."

"Murderess?"

Chaplain clapped his hands in joy, a single hard crack. "Miss Poole didn't tell you, did she?"

Miles tensed. "Tell me what?"

"The story of our deaths."

"Yes, of course she did. There was an accident. A fire started—"

"Fire? She sent that imbecile groundsman to kill me and Dr. Schramm while we slept. While she broke into the children's rooms and butchered them to bloody bits with a knife stolen from the kitchen."

"What? No." So hard to speak through the stupor slamming into him like an ocean wave. "That's...."

"That's what your friend Janelle Poole did. The accident was the death of her son. Tragic, yes, of course it was. But an accident."

"I saw it."

"You did not see that night so many years ago. Let me remove the mote from your eye so you can finally see the truth."

Miles grabbed his sweater, the fabric a grounding force. He pulled it over his head, enveloping himself in the comforting smell of armpit sweat.

"You must come to chapel service this morning. The Lord has seen the fruits of my labor and has granted me the opportunity to save you. Almighty God has not turned His back on you, Miles. Do not turn your back on Him. Trust in me, Miles, His emissary." Chaplain's eyes glittered, with madness or the Holy Spirit. "Come to the chapel in an hour."

Miles shook his head, but the words that came out betrayed him. "Yes. Fine."

He just needed to get Chaplain out. Away. Fun and games at Schramm and Chaplain's—they had completed Get the Guest.

Vanish.

A satisfied mantis, Chaplain rubbed his palms together. "Excellent. It will do your soul an eternity of good."

Forcing the words out into the haze: "Uh huh."

"The pair of arched doors past Schramm's office."

Miles had always been a terrible poker player, but he tried to look like he was taking in new information.

Chaplain was so pleased with himself that he didn't pay close attention. "I expect to see you front row center, Mr. Baumgartner."

Lips numb. "Just get out."

Beaming, the chaplain did.

In his St. Mark's days, Miles had been a devout church mouse. Eight or nine years old, sitting in the bathtub, he noticed that he had grown a third testicle. Obviously, the Lord had given him an extra because an accident would soon befall him, and he would lose one of his original two. Excited, he told his mother the story; she checked him out, verified the lump, and took him to the doctor who scheduled the hernia surgery. Boy, oh boy, had he believed. For a time, he had even considered the seminary. Long about sixth grade, he and the new associate pastor had struck up a friendship. Pastor Boyd would take him for frozen yogurt; they would chat pop culture and Christian doctrine. When Miles came out of the proverbial closet sophomore year at college, he thought it only right to tell his friend Pastor Boyd.

Sitting in that sunny office, oversized religious texts bulging from the bookshelves, Boyd had bowed his head in sorrow. "Then you're going to hell."

Shock like he had jammed his finger in a light socket.

He'd expected his friend to rise above strict, conservative Biblical interpretation and offer Christ's unconditional love. The condemnation had crumpled the exhilaration of sharing his true self to Mom and Dad and friends old and new. It had rotted his and Pastor Boyd's relationship that he had so long believed to be real friendship. The censure became a crisis of faith, and he had never sat in a church pew again.

The funeral home's tastefully covered folding chairs didn't count.

Last night when he had followed Betty in here, he hadn't noticed the heady traces of incense. Either too tired or too scared of being caught. This morning, the smell transported him to Ian's service and the intensity of flower arrangements garnishing the casket.

St. Hamelin's chapel looked a miniature St. Mark's holy apostolic church. The burnished pine floors and walls gleamed under six cylindrical, frosted-glass lights hanging from the flat ceiling. A shingle on the wall up front beside the pulpit should have listed the day's hymns, but this one remained blank. With no intention of sitting front and center as Chaplain wanted, he chose the pew second to the back. Settling into one of those hard, slat benches felt....

Comfortable.

The small square chapel was an interior room, and in lieu of stained-glass windows, portraits of Bible lessons hung on the walls. Painted with Rembrandt's deep bloom of light penetrating brooding backgrounds, Daniel prayed on his knees in the lions' den; Shadrach, Meshach, and Abednego turned their frightened faces to God; archangel Uriel wielded his fiery sword while banishing Adam and Eve from Eden. All sinister Old Testament here. No Gospel depictions, except for a haggard Christ suffering on His cross hung on the wall up front. With blood-smeared hands, head, side, and feet. Sunken eyes rolled Heavenward, begging the Father for mercy. How many nightmares had that tortured Jesus hammered into young minds?

Of course the real nightmare—the true sin around here—was Chaplain himself.

Underneath Christ sat a solid slab of altar, covered by a white cloth adorned with gold-stitched crosses. At the far right, the raised pulpit would give Chaplain a crow's nest view of his young congregation. No baptismal font. Huh. Though true that kids coming through here would be a bit old for a dip in the blood of the lamb, but it sure seemed Chaplain's style to drag the unrepentant by the hair—their feet bumping over the wooden floor—toward the Holy Water, drowning the sins that they reveled in.

This chapel hadn't been built for mercy but for softening children's resolves before breaking their bodies in the therapy rooms below.

No one else had shown up yet, so he picked a hymnal from the rack and flipped through the book. No crayon-colored death scenes.

The doors crashed open, and a procession of dark blue blazers marched in, organized and nearly in-step, unlike their rag-tag entrance into his English class. Teeth, Husky, all of them ignored Miles as they filed into the front pews, quiet, just the muffled whispers of their bottoms sliding along the wooden seats. From the back, they sported identical slick-backed hair. Except for Hare Lips's untamed curls. He picked out Husky's fat head. Towhead, of course.

And Elijah's flaming hair.

The smallest head turned, and the lights hanging from the ceiling flashed on the lenses of Theodore's tape-mended glasses, obliterating his expression.

Raised from the dead. Released from the incinerator. Until the next round.

Instead of the chatter and noise that filled the dorm, every one of the boys kept silent. No jocular shoving and pinching. Their Sunday-service behavior didn't fool Miles. Underneath their composure festered the vulgarity he had witnessed inside them all.

Chaplain clacked in with his hard-soled shoes. No black shirt and slacks for the service. The clergyman wore full vestments: voluminous white surplice, a violet stole draped regally over his shoulders.

A wall of blazered backs stood.

Following in the chaplain's wake, Schramm's bulk wobbled down the aisle, followed by Janelle—a pace behind—keeping her head piously down. He didn't know her well enough to tell if she'd been broken or if she merely hid her spark.

Spark.... Had she lied to him about the ravaging fire? Could Chaplain actually have told the truth? Had she murdered the boys who killed her son? The angel of death snuffing eight children?

In Miles's column, boys mashed together as Schramm squeezed into the front row, half his bulk spilling into the aisle. Janelle settled into the corresponding spot in the empty column across the aisle.

Chaplain crossed over the transept and motioned with a tiny wave of his hands for them all to be seated. Miles hadn't stood. Three bodies away from Schramm, Elijah threw a sidelong glare over his shoulder. The visible side of his wide mouth twitched into a carnivorous smile.

Foregoing liturgy and hymns, Chaplain climbed up into the raised pulpit and stared out into the sea of boys—for him, faces; for Miles, backs of heads. Lit by the overhead lights, Chaplain's white robes dazzled. Chaplain's fanatical eyes pinned him. A draft whipped up the smell of stale sandalwood and sage.

Chaplain preached. "And God said to Abraham, 'Take your son, your only son Isaac, whom you love, and go to the land of Mori'ah, and offer him there as a burnt offering upon one of the mountains of which I shall tell you.'"

Chaplain's every word resonated, solemn and powerful.

"So Abraham rose early in the morning, saddled his ass—"

Schramm fidgeted and glanced down his row, but none of the boys tittered.

"—and took two of his young men with him, and his son Isaac; and he cut the wood for the burnt offering and arose and went to the place of which God had told him."

Janelle sat stone cold frozen, fixated upon Jesus' bloody feet.

The corners of Chaplain's wormy mouth twitched in ugly joy. "And Abraham took the wood of the burnt offering, and laid it on Isaac, his son; and he took in his hand the fire and the knife. Abraham built an altar and bound Isaac, his son, and laid him on the altar, upon the wood. And Abraham offered him up as a burnt offering."

Chaplain pounded his fist on the pulpit. "And the angel of the Lord called to Abraham and said, 'By myself I have sworn, says the Lord, because you have done this, and have not withheld your son, your only son, I will indeed bless you!"

Restless fervor undulated through the small congregation. Janelle stayed very still. Had she caught Chaplain's editing as well? Chaplain Allen had left out the part where God stopped Abraham from killing his son; he had changed the lesson that Abraham's willingness alone proved his fealty.

Schramm threw an arm over the back of his pew and pulled his weight around to face Miles. His pink tongue poked out and wetted his lips.

"Well shall ye remember that Cain brought to the Lord the firstlings of his flock and of their fat portions. And the Lord had regard for Cain and his offering."

That was wrong, too. Miles hadn't read his Bible since heading off to the UW, but he remembered that it was the other brother, Abel, who sacrificed the livestock and earned God's favor.

"The Lord said unto Cain, 'If you do well, will you not be accepted? And if you do not do well, sin is crouching at the door; its desire is for you, but you must master it.'" Chaplain swept his hands like a conductor's, whipping his congregation into frenzy.

Miles's left buttcheek had gone numb, and he shifted in his seat.

Janelle shot to her feet. Schramm swiveled toward her. Half the boys shifted their focus to Miss Poole. She didn't meet any of their eyes but turned into the aisle with a tidy, quick motion, head up and spine straight, looking dead ahead as she started up the aisle. Her gait angled slightly, charting a course toward Miles. He stiffened; what was this now? She passed, her fingers flicked, and a small but heavy lump fell into his lap.

Chaplain glowered at her back until the chapel doors swung shut. He trained his scowl onto Miles and raised his voice to a holy roar. "And when they were in the field, Cain rose up against his brother, Abel, and killed him for as the Lord commands in the book of Hebrews, 'Obey your leaders and submit to them, for such sacrifices are pleasing to God.'"

Blood-thirsty murmurs passed among the boys. They squirmed in their seats. Chaplain had just twisted the story of Cain and Abel into an object lesson about human sacrifice, fomenting an atmosphere of menace the level of a Klan-rally.

Time to get out before Chaplain let slip his hellhounds of war.

He grabbed the object Janelle had tossed at him—a key—and tucked it into his pocket as he half-rose, as if a polite crouch would deflect attention. With not much room between pews, he shuffled sideways to the aisle. Chaplain had either finished or paused, and Miles's skin exploded into gooseflesh as Chaplain's eyes tracked him. One half-step more and he would have been out of the pew. So close. Instead he tripped over his toes, and his knee knocked into the hymnal rack. This time, one of the books dislodged and smacked the floor in a puff of dust.

Theodore turned around in open-mouthed horror.

Pews squeaked as boys twisted to look at the sinner fleeing their midst. Hare Lips's drowsy gaze condemned

Miles. Ian scrunched his face in disgust. Elijah's practically slathered.

Instinct screamed at him to run for the doors, but Miles grit his teeth, squared his shoulders like Janelle had, and forced a dignified short walk to the exit.

Chaplain's cadenced voice amplified. "The dog returns to its own vomit, and the sow, after washing herself, returns to wallow in the mire."

At the pebbled glass window of Schramm's door, the cold hard edges of Janelle's key pressed into his palm as he squeezed it. He had to make sure it was real. That it wouldn't disappear. He had told her he needed access to the photographs in Schramm's office, and she had provided. But how long would Chaplain keep his subjects enthralled? Should he worry about Butch and Betty, the wildcards? Janelle insisted they would be on his side, but he couldn't take that to heart just yet.

No matter—he needed to hurry; that service had been for him, and Chaplain might dismiss the congregation now that the topic of the sermon had walked out.

Miles carpéd his diem.

But nerves bested him, and his hand shook so badly that the key danced around the lock. He inhaled deeply and let out a shuddering breath. He had to hurry, but he had to calm down, too.

Again the key missed the mark, nicking the door.

Another settling breath, but now he felt pressured to relax.

He ground his teeth. The nose of the key tapped on the lock once, twice, then slid home.

Thank God.

But the key didn't turn.

Acid reflux burned in his throat.

The chapel doors remained closed. No sounds from inside, but was that good or bad? His jaw locked up, pain zinging up his face. Why didn't the damn key for Schramm's office work?

He unclamped his teeth and swore. Wow, he was dense. He moved down to Janelle's door, and this time when the key slipped in, it turned, and Janelle's office door creaked open.

Lilac air consumed him as he entered. He eased the door closed and found the light switch.

Janelle had about half the space Schramm did. A scarred desk sat in the same position as the superintendent's, though half the size and covered with stacks of books. She had no fireplace, no window, and instead of shelving, old wooden filing cabinets lined the walls. The door connecting the offices had been sensibly closed, but Miles tried it, and it opened right up.

He passed through into the stinky dark of Schramm's office. The fire had died down, and glowing embers peeked between the kindling like rabid eyes.

Miles grabbed the nearest framed photo, but froze before he took it down. Schramm would notice bare walls the moment he walked in. He let the photo settle back against the wall.

Janelle had every key imaginable on that massive ring, but she'd given him the key to her office and not Schramm's. He returned to her office and stood for a moment beside the desk, considering the file cabinets. He strummed his fingers on the red-covered books. He frowned and glanced down. They were all the hymnal desecrated with graphic scenes of his death, moved in here from Schramm's desk.

Those wouldn't be any help. These file cabinets, though.... It made sense that they stored not only copies of those photos on Schramm's walls, but every picture and file for the children of St. Hamelin's. His for the taking without Schramm's knowing.

He chose one of the blond wood cabinets at random and slid open the top drawer. He riffled through the papers inside—yellowed invoices and blurred carbon copies. Fanning them whipped up the same nostalgic smell of the Golding novels when he'd found them in the classroom cabinet.

Inventorying the office, he counted four more cabinets, six drawers each. He couldn't have much time left before Chaplain imparted his final orders to the boys, so Miles hurried on to the next drawer. Only tax records. This was the wrong file cabinet.

A far-off creak.

He froze, a rabbit scenting wolves through the trees.

No further furtive sounds of approach.

False alarm?

Unless the boys had gotten better at stalking their prey.

Either way, he wouldn't leave until he had plank children's photos in hand.

He moved to the next cabinet, where the top drawer held dusty folded maps and land lease certificates. He wiped his palms on his jeans, and used the backs of his hands to blot his damp forehead. He squatted to the middle drawer and thumbed through bills of sale, pages abrasive with sediment. Seiler Farms. Richter Grocery. Itemized lists of eggs and milk and bread and meat. He whistled as he read the dates: February 3rd, 1950... March 25th 1951... December 6th 1952....

Sounds like shuffling papers came from the office next door. Had he been that lost in his hunt that he'd missed Schramm coming back?

Had Mirror Man freed himself? One long leg high-stepping out of that murky reflective surface; a foot finding purchase on the sink; his shadow self winding through the corridors and now hunched at Schramm's desk, helping search for the final solution.

Holy Hell, what was he gibbering about?

The cooling firewood in Schramm's office must have shifted. That's what he had heard. Did he really need to invent new ways to freak himself out? St. Hamelin's had plenty.

And he had wasted more time. He needed the pictures. Now. His mental clock ticked... ticked... ticked. He peeked over his shoulder at Janelle's door. Soon enough, Elijah really would be coming for him.

He didn't have time for every cabinet and every drawer. If he were Janelle, where would he keep the boys' papers?

He passed over the other filing cabinets and went for the one closest to Janelle's desk. He yanked open the second drawer and pulled up corners of papers to see what his gamble had produced.

"Damn right." He smiled at the names. The dates. He grabbed a bundle of pages, once held together by a metal paperclip, now missing. Rust had bled an orange-red, gritty stain on the cover page of Elijah Yoder's file.

A surge of air from the hallway sucked Janelle's door more tightly into the jamb.

Miles blanked. Blinked.

Slapping footsteps left the chapel.

He reached into the drawer and grabbed a double handful of files.

Rowdy chatter echoed in the hall.

He hugged the bundle of papers to his chest and elbowed the drawer closed.

The recently released congregants gathered just outside the chapel doors. It didn't sound like anyone was dispersing. He couldn't leave until the hallway cleared. If Schramm or Chaplain caught him sneaking out, punishment likely meant losing body parts.

The noisy swell finally moved. Miles squeezed his eyes closed and visualized the fading voices moving down the side corridor toward the door out to the grounds. At Janelle's door he inclined his ear against it. Chaplain would likely stay behind in the chapel, but Schramm would come back this way.

He thought it and it happened—the bellows of the big man's breath chugged close. Passed. A lock rattled and hinges groaned, and the bear opened up his den.

Miles shifted the files in his arms, and in sync with Schramm's closing door, he opened Janelle's and snuck through. He kept the knob turned to set the door in place without a sound. No one lagged in the hallway. Free and clear to the vestibule and up to his room.

Another of his cat-lives spent.

Twenty-Two

Miles released his armload of papers onto the writing desk. Had he grabbed useful stuff? Files without photos wouldn't help. He needed pictures of all the boys for this to work. Before he could sit and start digging through, shouts erupted from outside.

Ice had colored the window edges milky white. His first breath steamed up the glass, so he rubbed his sweater's woolen cuff into the condensation to clear a porthole.

Rocky Mountain Face, Towhead, and Hare Lip jumped and shouted out in the courtyard. Husky stomped after them, but their laughter carried, flat and harsh in the frozen landscape. Elijah's red hair caught flurries that lazed through the air. Elijah bent, scooped up two handfuls of snow, and dumped them on Ian's head. Just boys playing in the snow.

What was Theodore doing down there?

The boy's red knit hat with fuzzy ball on top turned him into Elijah's little brother. Mittens encased his hands. He stood away from the others, at the periphery, looking like he wanted to melt into the snow.

Why didn't he run inside before the older boys saw him standing there, meek and mild?

Miles knocked on the window. Theodore's head jerked up; his tiny white face searched for the sound.

Snow dribbled from Elijah's hands. He glanced about. He clapped Ian on the shoulder and pointed his chin to Theodore. Husky and Rocky and Hare Lip stopped bumbling after each other and zeroed in. Mouths opened and closed like goldfish, their speech inaudible.

Miles flung open the window. "Get outta there! Get back inside!"

Theodore bolted. The older boys charged, baying like hounds. For once Theodore's size proved an advantage, and he raced away, quick and nimble.

Elijah sidled up next to Ian, and his thick lips brushed Ian's ear as he whispered. They both looked up to Miles in the window and smiled. Ian's an identical match with Elijah's. Even from this distance, their eyes were cold as the raging river at the bottom of the gulley.

Miles fought the urge to duck down. Seemed like a long time they watched one another in their stand-off. Finally, Elijah and Ian plodded away, heads down and shoulders taut—bent toward a mission.

Giving Miles a new purpose.

The wet blood on the shower tiles, the imprint of the boy's screams, would never wash out of Miles's memory. If he couldn't rescue Ian, he would save Theodore. As long as Miles remained in St. Hamelin's, he would keep Theodore safe. No more reliving those horrendous last moments.

He ran across the room, intent on finding Theodore before the hunting party tracked him down. He threw open the door, and jumped back when a dark figure leapt into his line of sight.

"Janelle!" He dried his sweaty palms on his thighs. "You scared the crap outta me."

"We need to meet with Frederick."

"Theodore was outside. He—"

"Come with me now."

"But Theodore—"

"Is a diversion."

"What?" She sent her son to be beaten up as a distraction?

She grabbed his wrist and pulled him into the hall. "Don't worry. He knows hiding places."

Not so well that he couldn't keep his butt out of the incinerator. And the showers. But Janelle's insistence came with an iron grip. She led him into the stairwell and only then let go. Since rescuing him from the operating table, Janelle showed mettle that he hadn't guessed at in those first twenty-four hours. He never would have believed that the schoolmarm he'd met in Schramm's office was capable of murdering children, but that might have been a failure of imagination. This cold and calculating version of Janelle had no limits.

He had just promised to look out for Theodore, but self-preservation weakened his resolve. "If they're distracted, maybe I could go right now. Ian told me to follow the trees along the gulley until I got into town. Is that true?"

"It is, but Dr. Schramm and Chaplain Allen are watching you too closely. We can slip out to the cottage, but you wouldn't have enough time to get away. Especially now, with the weather clear and not granting you cover."

First he was supposed to wait for the storm to end. Now he had to pray another would blow in. A different story from every player. Considering the other options, he may as well trust her. Anyway, he might need a cold-blooded killer on his side.

Twenty-Three

Two or three more inches had fallen overnight, creating a landscape as sterile as the moon. Cloudless, crystalline blue sky spread out above, but the bitter cold held sway, holding off all sounds and motion of life. No branches moved. No snow swirled up. With no wind, chimney smoke rose straight up from the cottage.

And inside the cottage, Butch sang in a flat, nasal voice. "Oh, muh durlin'. Oh, muh durlin'. Oh, muh durlin' Clementine."

Janelle let herself in. "Frederick?"

The shades were all drawn in the cottage, shrouding the interiors with dusk. Beside the recliner Miles had dined in, a single lamp provided the only soft, yellow light. He'd forgotten about the sickly-sweet smell of the place. The living room fireplace crackled, saturating the room with tremendous heat.

"Lost and gone *fur*-ever, oh, muh durlin'... Clementine!" The song carried to them from the deer fetus room.

"Frederick!"

Butch muttered profanity and clomped toward them. When he saw Janelle, a hearty smile opened on his face. "Ah! Betts, look who's here!" Butch passed gas. "You hear that buck snort in the woods?" He chortled and tottered through the living room, fanning his hand either to disperse the flatulence or to tell Miles and Janelle to take a seat.

Betty's raw face peeped out from the kitchen. She garbled a good-morning. Or groused at their unannounced visit.

"I hope we're not interrupting."

"Not at all! Come in." Butch pointed at Miles's with his thumb nub. "I s'pose this feller wants his breakfast." His brows furrowed. Softly, "What's wrong, Jenny?"

"We need your help."

"We?" Butch didn't shout at Janelle, or squint and turn an ear to hear better.

Janelle touched Miles's shoulder. "I've promised Mr. Baumgartner that we will get him out of here. Theodore and I can distract the boys—"

Butch waved her off. "Now hold on. I don't know 'bout all dat."

"Frederick." Janelle was unflappable. "You know Dr. Schramm and the chaplain have it in for our... friend."

What a warm, non-committal moniker.

Butch's mouth half-opened into a dark empty cavern—he'd taken out his dentures. Were his teeth floating in a tumbler full of Polydent beside his thumb on the shelf? A pine knot exploded inside the fireplace.

"Betts! Go'on out back'n gather up more firewood."

Complaints, but a back door opened—wind howled and shot a freezing tendril into the living room—and slammed shut. The temperature in the cottage dropped ten degrees.

Butch sank into the quilt-laden couch. "Jenny, how is this my business? How is it yours?"

Janelle floated down into the nice tan recliner close to Butch's knee. "You helped me once before."

Butch's face closed off, gruff and uninviting. Janelle let her pitch hang there in the excruciating quiet.

I before him did not know whether I stood on the ground or floated in the air.

Miles chewed his lower lip to keep from speaking. These two had their own customs.

"Yes, I did help, and what did they do?" Butch's up-Nort accent faded to a subtle flatness. "That's why I won't cross those two snakes again." He stabbed a finger at her. "For your sake, Jenny. For your boy's."

Not to oversell it, but this felt like his cue. "I have no right to ask you to stick your neck out for me."

"Got dat right!"

Janelle touched Butch's knee. They traded the glances of a secret language.

Butch stared at the fireplace's black iron screen. He brought his calloused workman's hands together and rubbed them as if he had just come in from the cold.

Did he feel the ghost of his thumb? Did the dead space itch? Did all the boys and adults of St. Hamelin's itch from head to toe—their entire bodies being essentially phantoms limbs?

"I need your help again, Frederick."

Yeah, Butch owed her!

If Miles didn't get outta there, his blood would be on Butch's hands.

Butch couldn't let those assholes win.

But Miles held his tongue. If Butch did this thing, it wouldn't be for any argument Miles could make.

Janelle squeezed Butch's knee. "I know you paid a dear price for helping me back then."

Butch's eyes flicked back and forth as he studied Janelle's face. "Was you and yer boy suffered after that."

"No more than we suffered beforehand."

Butch stared down at his twining fingers. "Weren't always like this." He faced Miles. "Let me ask ya sometin'."

Miles's head weighed a hundred pounds. "Anything."

"Would you put your fam'bly at risk? For a stranger?"

First thought: If he needed Mile's help, yes.

But was that the truth?

"I don't know. I've never been in that bind, but I'd like to think that I would. I didn't know what I would find up here, but I did come for someone else. My nephew is a... casualty. Like all of you."

Butch nodded. "'Preciate yer hon'sty.

The kitchen door banged open, letting in a wallop of cold.

"Gibbe gabba hep. Gibbe gabba hep!"

"'Scuse me." Butch wiggled his bottom, pushed off from the couch cushions, but fell back. "Uff-da."

Janelle started to stand, to help, but one of Butch's knees popped like one of those pine knots, and he got to his feet. He limped into the kitchen to help Betty.

A secret smile touched the corners of Janelle's mouth as she watched Butch's back. "He'll do it."

"Yeah?" Miles hadn't gotten that impression. "I hope so."

And hope springs eternal, huh? If—when—he got out of there, he would be cementing his almost-son's death. Before driving to this cursed place, he'd thought how his mission would kill Ian all over again for Minnie. But now.... Minnie would still believe, wallowing in the absence of her son, yes, but holding tight to the shred of Ian that remained. A flickering flame of hope—like that stupid gospel light they used to sing about at St. Mark's—because she didn't know the reality. The curtain had been thrown back for Miles. If he'd done more in the beginning—last year—Ian would still be alive. If he'd done less and never started this quest, he wouldn't know what had become of Ian. All he had left was a stain of memories, which would eventually fade.

From the kitchen, a metal grate ground open—Betty stoking a wood-burning stove. The *whumpf* and crackle of a fresh log shoved in. Now she could cook another inedible meal.

Betty bustled into the living room, bundled into a faded pink parka that ended just above her knees. She wore the same clunky shoes as last night in the chapel. Harried, she dumped an armload of firewood on the depleted stack at the hearth. She wagged her finger at him and Janelle before her stocky legs carried her back to the kitchen, passing Butch coming in to rejoin them. A draft signaled Betty's return outside to the woodpile. She was a trouper all right. St. Hamelin's last living resident.

Did that mean that she had shit on the *Lord of the Flies* pages?

Butch planted his feet, arms akimbo. "Betts told me that if I'm any kinda Christian, I gotta help you out, Mr. Baumgartner. I s'pose she's right."

The back door creaked and slammed. Creaked and slammed. Butch glanced over his shoulder. "Fergot to latch the door!"

A scream splintered the afternoon.

"Betts!" Butch whipped around. His knee didn't go with him, and he crumpled onto the overlapping rugs.

Miles grabbed hold of one flailing arm. Janelle rushed to Butch's other side and tugged a forearm.

"Betts!" Butch's struggles made it harder to pull him to his feet.

"On three." Miles groaned the countdown.

They heaved. Almost there. Heaved again, and Butch wobbled upright. He lurched into the kitchen.

Janelle ran after, and Miles followed at her heels into a sunny, pastel kitchen. They hurried past a huge wood stove with a full range—not the pot-bellied model he'd imagined. Janelle paused for a beat at the spindly-legged kitchen table, the shiny top and chrome sides like a piece from an old diner. Butch had reached a narrow mudroom, his big blue parka on a wall hook above several pairs of mud-caked shoes and boots on the tiled floor beside a bucket of salt and a snow shovel. Caught by wind, the door screeched open an inch, then slammed.

Outside, Betty shrieked.

Butch rammed through the door, ripping off the top-most hinge.

Miles was last out into a small backyard. A gust whipped up a fine powder of snow into his face. Butch mewled like a run-over mutt. Miles wiped snowflakes out of his eyelashes just as Butch fell to his knees, sinking several inches into the snow beside Betty.

Janelle slapped both hands over her mouth, but that didn't mute her scream.

Writhing in the snow, Betty gurgled and clutched her neck. She lay on a sheet of scarlet. Her feet churned up chunks of snow. Gouts of blood chugged between her fingers.

On his elbows, Butch plowed ahead to reach her. He grabbed his daughter by a thigh and dragged her to him. He scooched around in the snow and laid her head in his lap. She choked out a syllable but broke down coughing. Blood spattered Butch's face like freckles. He caressed her wet hair as blood painted the arthritic knobs of his knuckles.

"Betty, don't you leave me." He pulled her hands up to his chest, covering his heart.

Her body flailed as if possessed. The gash in her neck stretched open. Ragged edges. Strips of flesh. Not sliced, but bitten. Chewed skin fibrillated around the gaping hole with each fading breath.

Butch laid Betty's hands back over her throat, covering them with his own to keep pressure on the wound. Her rosacea-inflamed face drained of color.

Pale.

She choked another breath.

Pallid.

Her glassy dark eyes searched her father's face. She coughed and specks of aspirated blood misted down.

Butch brushed her hair with his gnarled fingers. "No. No. No."

Betty's eyes lost focus, and Butch stroked her face. No longer panting, a single breath shuddered in her chest.

"Betts?" Butch grabbed her up and cleaved her to his breast.

Angry buzzing filled Miles's skull. He couldn't feel his face. "I didn't want any of this to happen."

"Get outta here!" Butch sucked in a mucusy sob. Janelle crouched and wrapped an arm around his shoulders, but he pushed her off. "Just leave!"

Miles had never seen an adult man cry so hard. His own father had only shed tears twice—once when Grandpa died, and then, surprisingly, when he found the family cat behind the couch, cold and stiff. That had been crying, but not like this. Broken up, not broken, like Butch whose snot ran down his chin. Grief burbled out in pitiful, guttural honks.

Betty's mouth palsied. Her legs quivered. She stilled, and from the bottom of her house dress, a yellow pool wet the snow.

Butch howled.

Twenty-Four

Miles fled the cottage.

Butch's wails fractured the pristine landscape, and black birds broke cover from the far treeline.

Miles truly had found Hell, its landscape chiseled of snow and frost and death.

For destruction ice is also great.

Back inside the reformatory, the warmth felt nice for an instant. The quiet, a modicum of relief. Fleeting comfort before St. Hamelin's stinking weight once more crushed him. He stooped under its heft. He breathed oppression like smoky air.

Could he really get out of this alive?

A slushy puddle spread from his shoes. Dead-ahead, the chapel doors formed a pursed mouth. Keeping secrets.

What had Betty been doing in the sacristy?

He stormed the sanctum.

Sacristy door was locked.

Who cared?

He backed up five paces and charged. Threw his shoulder into it, and pieces of jamb exploded as the door broke open with the resistance of balsa wood. He entered the sacristy full speed in a shower of splinters. On loose hinges, the door vibrated like a tuning fork. Trying to stop, he tangled his feet, tripped and fell, skidded, and banged his head into the sharp edge of a cabinet in the center of the room.

His crash reverberated throughout the chapel. Throughout his skull. He might have knocked himself unconscious for a minute or two. He took stock of his bodily damage: a stinger in his neck, aching ribs, throbbing knees. But all his parts moved. Nothing broken.

"None the worse for wear." He picked himself up and brushed off clinging debris. A spot on the crown of his head felt sore and wet. A tender exploration found a cut that felt like a chasm an inch deep. A wellspring of blood pumped out, dripping warmth down the side of his face. Maybe it wasn't so bad—scalp wounds bled like stuck pigs, but he didn't feel faint.

He wiped his face with his sleeve, then held the cuff to the laceration while taking in his surroundings. Same layout as the deer fetus room—floor-to-ceiling shelves wrapped around the whole room except for a sink against the opposite wall. The sink, that was called a.... C'mon, why couldn't he think of it—all those Sunday School hours wasted? Wait, he almost had it. Its pipes didn't lead to the sewer, because holy water couldn't mix with waste water.

Now the old goose egg on his head hurt from pressing on the new cut. He let go and examined his sleeve. Soaked through, but he'd staunched the blood—no more dribbles down his face.

This free-standing cabinet where he'd nearly crushed his head had a specific name, too. It looked like Mom and Dad's old hi fi cabinet, but behind the doors on its front, wide narrow drawers would hold vestments and stoles. Sounded like credenza. Credens! The topmost drawer hadn't been slid completely closed. He opened up the cabinet doors fully and opened the drawer. Only one thing inside.

"Wow."

All his pains and concerns faded, forgotten.

He reached in and carefully, respectfully, pulled out a blue-backed pocket Moleskine—the notebook of choice for Hemingway, which the great author filled while on his endless travels. This one would have come from the exact years of Papa's peak. An English teacher's Holy Grail. He flipped through the pages. Certainly wasn't Hemingway prose. Looked like....

"Holy hell."

No, it couldn't be.

Keeping his place with a finger, he turned back to the cover. No title of any kind. He returned to the saved page. Looked through a few more. Chaplain wrote with a schoolgirl's pretty, looping handwriting.

Miles felt giddy. Like his heart pumped carbonated soda, the bubbles fizzing and popping.

The fallen clergyman kept a journal, and Miles had just taken possession of it. Some of the text was Latin. Some Spanish. The snippets he understood didn't read like mere pablum. This looked like an instruction manual, complete with scribbled diagrams.

He tucked it into his waistband.

Now, what about these shelves?

Same knotty wood and metal brackets as Butch's gruesome room. Same claustrophobic feel, too, the shelving almost coming at him, aggressive. And on those shelves? Myriad glass jars.

Butch and Betty with their jars.

Butch and Betty.... His heart tightened. Had Butch taken Betty inside by now? Janelle would have stayed despite Butch's rage. They had a past, those two. Lovers, if he had translated her innuendo correctly. She would know the right caresses and whispers to soothe him.

Concentrate!

Compared with those holding the fawns, these jars were larger, about the size and shape of the two-gallon lemonade dispenser he'd bought Minnie and Daniel off their wedding registry. A few of these looked larger, some smaller, but all in that range. Smudgy objects floated in snotty liquid.

More dead baby deer?

He approached.

No, not deer. Some other animal.

Incense in one of those drawers couldn't quite overpower a subtle but putrid odor.

Starting to the right of the wasted door, he leaned close to the first eye-level jar. The pulpy mass suspended inside had gone fuzzy around the edges. Loose bits orbited like tiny moons.

More jars on the shelf above. And above that. Even more on the bottom shelves. Every surface shone, polished clean.

Betty had been busy.

In his chosen jar, the formaldehyde turned. Disturbed from his violent entry? The mass caught the motion and rotated, a planet on its axis. The thing inside was round, no legs or tail. A curled hedgehog, bloated over time? But no. The color of the fur suggested a fox, though the preservative leant a witchy hue to all the contained critters in their jars. Continuing to spin, the blob showed the leading edge of a bald spot. The soft underbelly? Turning lazily, the bare patch expanded.

Miles touched the glass. It felt electric, vibrating at a high frequency.

Particles jittered and danced. As the thing inside revolved, a knob poked up at its horizon. Then a bulge. Taking shape. Red speckles dotted the grey flesh.

Good God.

Miles blundered backward, slamming his tailbone into the credens. He clapped his hands to his temples, trying to contain the madness. His head shook—no-no-no-no. He swayed, drunk from the horror.

In the shivering preservative, Elijah's head faced him. The years had softened and widened the gaping nostrils into black caves. Under ginger brows—eyelids frozen open—green eyes layered with milky white death cataracts bugged out. Swollen, discolored lips pulled back in an eternal smirk.

Miles pushed off the credens and thrust himself toward the sink—piscina!—and threw up, his hands closing in a death-grip on the basin rim. Another convulsion ripped up from his stomach, and he trembled head to toe. Bile dribbled off his chin. He didn't dare let go of the sink to wipe the vomit off his face.

Stricken but compelled, he turned back around. So many jars. Now he recognized severed hands curled in mid-grasp. A foot, dirty nails overgrown and curving like knives. Fingers. Stubby toes. An ear. A chunk of skin and hair and flesh from some part of the body he didn't care to identify. A wrinkled penis spun in the slow-moving formaldehyde.

Husky and Teeth leered.

Hare Lip's cleft widened into a mortal wound.

Elijah, his mouth fallen open, laughed in frozen silence.

Twenty-Five

His first full-blown panic attack in months threw visual input into a blender, and the shelves, jars, credens, and the floor spun in a dizzying mish mash of swirling color. He tripped and stumbled from the sacristy and through the church. Caroming off door jambs and walls he managed to find his room and shut himself inside. After that, his brain stopped recording memories for a while.

An infernal chirping called him back to the world, a half-drowned man floating up and breaking the surface. From the number of cigarettes burned to the butt and lying on the window sill, about a half hour had been blacked out of his timeline. Chaplain's blue notebook sat atop the mess of stolen files on the desk. At least he'd done that much right. He rubbed his face to massage away the sleepy amnesia, but the yellow nicotine stains on his fingers burned his eyes.

What was that chirruping?

His phone!

He jammed a hand in his pocket and pulled out his phone. It purred in his palm, a pet coming back to life. The screen lit up, showing the name he had waited so long for.

"Jeremy!" A warm rush in his stomach.

He tilted the phone at the window, hopefully toward whatever distant tower afforded him service. "Jeremy? Hello?"

His ex's voice drifted up from great depths. "Miles?"

"Thank God." A glacier inside him began to melt.

"What's this text about you being in trouble? Where are you? I called your sister, but she acted like she didn't know who I was. She never liked me. If you had invited me to that wedding, she would have met me, and none of this would have happened. But no, you didn't want to jinx anything."

"I followed Ian up here. It's a trap. A Venus Flytrap. Now I can't—"

"Ian? Why are you dragging his name into this?"

"Half an hour past Bear Falls, there's an orphanage. A reformatory now. It's supposed to be closed up, but it's not. I need you. I think I can make it into Bear Falls if I follow the river. I need you to pick me up."

"Are you drinking again?"

"Jesus Christ." Miles shut his eyes. His grinding teeth shrieked. "No, Jeremy."

"Don't bite my head off, you're the one spouting nonsense."

"Not nonsense." Crazy, sure, but not nonsense.

"For what it's worth, I never meant to hurt you. It was supposed to be a fling, you know? A one-night stand. I never meant to fall in love with him."

"This is not about you!" The rage dragon flicked its tongue, testing the air, and Miles's fingers ached to throw a vase or punch a mirror. Do some damage and vent the heat boiling inside his chest.

Regulated breaths. In, out. One.... Two.... In, out. Five.... Six....

He opened his eyes. "Jeremy."

"Did you say Bear Falls? That's six hours away."

A gust of wind blew the spent butts off the sill and onto the floor. The icy draft struck Miles a bracing slap that fully woke him. Another Bible story: Saul on the way to Damascus, the scales falling from his eyes.

"Forget it."

"No, Miles, it's okay." Voices in the background. No. One voice in the background. "For the sake of what we used to have, I'll do this, I'll drive up there and pick you up."

For the sake of what they used to have?

And suddenly a light from heaven flashed about him. And he fell to the ground and heard a voice saying to him....

Not exactly saying, but showing. Their last day trip to Wisconsin Dells, after pizza-lunch at the Upper Crust, after they had taken their Civil War portraits, they had taken the touristy tour of Lake Delton on one of those authentic World War II amphibious vehicles. Ducks. All of those tourist traps hired high school and college kids, their hard, young bodies tanned from their summer shifts outside. Jeremy couldn't reel his tongue back in his mouth, ogling their Duck driver that day—Kyler, a ridiculous, flirty twink. Numb with anger and a beer buzz, Miles hadn't seen Jeremy getting Kyler's phone number after the ride. But it all came out later when he'd snooped through Jeremy's phone. That's who Jeremy had been texting all those months, absorbed in his phone, fingers typing endlessly. The latest message sent by Jeremy just that morning: "I woke up with a hard-on in my shorts and you on my mind." Yet the straying had somehow been Miles's fault; he hadn't given Jeremy enough attention, so what did he expect?

"Miles, did you hear me? Whatever mess you got into, I'll drive up there and get you out of it. It's going to be midnight before—"

"I said forget it. Have a great life with Duck Boy. I mean that."

Did he?

Didn't matter, that glacier inside him had shrunk to an ice cube.

"Stop acting like a child. I told you I'll bail you out of whatever.... Do you need actual bail?" Jeremy breathed sharply into the phone.

"I don't need bail, and I don't need you." Jeremy was out of his life, out of his hair. Out of his business. Seen through this new, enlightened lens, that was a wonderful thing. "I do not need you."

"Then how are you going to manage?"

"On my own."

A freezing hike to the second bridge Ian told him about. If it hadn't been a fabrication. Then miles more into town. A thousand-dollar Uber ride home to boxes stacked in a crappy apartment. Family disassembled. But his life would be his own. Just as soon as he let go of this Jeremy-sized anchor.

"You're not making any sense."

This was the first time, in a long time, that anything did make sense.

"Goodbye, Jeremy."

He hung up and sat in a cocoon of silence. The silence did not asphyxiate.

The phone rattled in his hand. **Unknown Caller.**

"Hello?"

Static belched out, and he yanked the phone away from his ear.

"—iles...."

"Minnie?"

Through the interference: "...bah...ent...hur...iles?" The phone's little speaker crackled. "—iles... wh... you oh—"

"Min, I found St. Hamelin's. I know what you did. I understand why you did it, but right now I need Daniel because the bridge is out—"

The line popped and died.

"Minnie?" On the screen, the counter continued adding time. 00:30... 00:31... 00:32. "Hello?"

Garbled noise sounded like, "Come find me."

"Minnie, you were right. About everything. I should have left this al—"

Crystal clear: "Come find me."

"Theodore?"

Cacophonous laughter, high and youthful, from the other end. Certainly not Minnie, but not Theodore either.

Then: "Strange man."

"What? Who is this?"

The child's voice lowered in imitation. "Who is this?" Then trilled. "Who is this?" A burst of wicked glee. "Strange man. Strange man."

"Stop calling me that."

"Stangemanstrangemanstrangeman."

The line snapped and crackled.

Elijah spoke. "Why did you hang up on me?"

His tongue felt like a dead slug. "I didn't hang up on you."

Elijah over-enunciated. "You don't need me anymore? But I want you to come home."

"You're not Jeremy."

A canticle warbled from the hallway. "*Aus tiefer Not schrei ich zu dir....*" A mournful dirge of iambs.

Over the phone: "Uncle Miles? Come find me."

A lilting voice on the other side of his door: "The best and holiest deeds must fail to break sin's dread oppression."

Ian's soft plea: "They locked me in the basement."

"Just let me leave." Miles slumped against the door.

"Come find me, Uncle Miles."

"I won't tell anyone about St. Hamelin's." Miles cringed at his simpering tone. "If you just let me leave."

Ian's voice strengthened. "You never should have come for me."

"I know that now."

Wind whistled through the line. A fresh blast of flurries spackled the window.

Theodore's reedy voice: "Come find me."

A frenzy of children's voices filled the line, spilling over each other, overlapping.

On the other side of the door, but as clear as if he stood inside, Chaplain lamented. "Out of the depths I cry to thee, O Lord. Lord, hear my voice. Let thy ears be attentive to the voice of my supplication." Chaplain coughed hard and a fine spray of something—spittle? dirt?—pattered against the door. "But no one's listening to you, Miles. No one hears."

From the hall, a mimic of Miles's own voice burbled up as from a deep well. "Come find me."

Nails-on-chalkboard screeched from the speaker, and he dropped his phone. The device hit the floor with a snap. Shit! Praying, he picked it up. Cracks spiderwebbed the screen. He pressed the home button but nothing happened. He poked harder. Solid, ineffectual black behind the white lace of destruction.

Fury quaked in his hands. If Jeremy hadn't called, this wouldn't have happened. Selfish prick. How much was Jeremy going to ruin? Their years together were a damn waste. Therapist Joe had been right—Miles hadn't wanted to marry Jeremy; he'd just wanted to be married. Those years were worse than wasted! Before that jerk, Miles had had a great job. A nice apartment. Friends of his own. And Ian! Ian had been alive before Jeremy. Thought his shit didn't stink. High maintenance asshole.

Miles hooked his arm back and pitched his phone across the room. It punched a hole into the plaster and ricocheted with a crunch. Pieces of plastic case rained to the floor. The phone landed with a dull thunk.

No!

He slid to his knees at the mess. Shards of the screen fell out like puzzle pieces.

"Crap crap crap crap crap."

He stabbed the screen with his finger, and an edge of glass cut him. "Ouch!"

He got to his feet, sucking blood from his fingertip. He threw himself into the desk chair where hard angles pressed his tenderest parts. But what part of him didn't hurt? Escape had never felt so far out of reach.

The stolen files from Janelle's office littered the desk. Felt a century ago that he'd taken them. He attacked the folders. Admissions forms ripped paper cuts into his flesh. Any pages with typing he tossed over his shoulder, and they arced through the air, riding drafts, and slid under the bed or came back at him and clung to his elbows. He sped up, clearing the chaff from the photos.

Where were his cigarettes?

He scavenged through the crap on his desk until he found the Marlboros, not moved at all during his stupor, but buried where he'd left them after the shared smoke with Janelle.

Janelle who, according to Chaplain, had killed those boys. Had she vivisected them, as well? Or had Betty chopped them up and dropped their pieces in those jars?

He patted down the desktop and then his chest, his thighs, until finding the bulge of his lighter in his pocket. He lit his smoke, tilted on the back legs of the chair, and exhaled blue exhaust to the ceiling. His head cleared right up.

He had witnessed the brutality of Theodore's murder, and if it had been his son, Miles would have sought the same vicious revenge. He couldn't fault Janelle if she truly had done what Chaplain charged. But Betty and the jars? Inspired by her husband—father, hard to remember that—but for what purpose?

He jammed the cigarette between his lips and pulled out a photograph. His bloody fingerprints smudged Hare Lip's face. Based on the dates, Hare Lip hadn't come in with the juvenile offenders. He'd been just another orphan stranded at St. Hamelin's.

Tucked into the corner of his mouth, the cigarette bobbed as he puckered and inhaled. His fingers sorted out a stack of smooth eight-by-tens. Smoke blasted from his nose. He collated the pictures, with admission mug shots in back. His random grab contained copies of all the photographs on Schramm's wall, and he laid these out as a timeline. 1951 was either the first time the boys of St. Hamelin's had been gathered into an official reckoning or just the first of this batch. As he knew already, death had come the following year. The drab colors of 1952 captured the atmosphere of anguish. In 1953 another species of death infested St. Hamelin's.

A few misdemeanors had landed the children here, charges that didn't seem severe enough to curse them into the devils they had become. How had Schramm and Chaplain broken them? The operating theater? That cold table. The angry face of dials on the ECT machine.

In 1953's back row, the limitations of black and white blanched the fire out of Elijah Yoder's hair, but the photo captured his pernicious bright eyes. This would be the year that he murdered Theodore.

And that he—and all of them—met their end.

After that? 1954 onward, the stiff dead bodies of Elijah and his friends, trussed onto boards and propped up into place, outnumbered the sad solemn orphan faces. By the following year, those few remaining orphans had disappeared. Had the older boys packed up the younger ones in an exodus out of the sweeping horror? Or had the survivors and healthy boys been killed and buried out back under grave markers?

Miles held the power to avenge them. Time to reset the natural order.

With orgasmic shivers, he ripped 1953 into quarters. 1952 came next. Then 1954. The pieces seesawed down to the floor, in mimic of Elijah's torn *Lord of the Flies* pages from the classroom.

He held Hare Lip's picture. Childhood stolen. Innocence warped. He tore it up and dropped the scraps to the pile growing up along the legs of the chair.

Screw saving the best for last. He rifled through pictures until finding Elijah's smug face. If he hadn't had cotton mouth, he would have spit on it. He ripped it right down the middle. Holy hell, that felt good. He placed the two halves together and ripped it again. He stacked the pieces and tried to rip lengthwise, but photo paper was thick. That was good enough, right? He threw them into the pile.

Two down.... Six more. He needed to destroy every photo, leaving none intact to risk an incomplete job. He scooped up the crenellated-edged pictures from the bottom.

It was a pleasure to tear.

Twenty-Six

No more plank children.

The radiator pinged, sighed a gust of warm air, and died. No more Betty, either, to keep the furnace going.

His fingertips, varnished with blood, had numbed. Slouching at the desk had cramped his shoulder muscles. But these pains were signs of accomplishment. He waded through the scraps on the floor and collapsed onto the bed. Rats thumped inside the wall.

His body thanked him for the respite, but his thoughts raced and he sat up. Janelle must have returned from the cottage by now. He wanted to tell her that he had shredded Theodore's torturers. Chaplain and Schramm still needed to die, this time for real, but he had stripped them of their soldiers. He couldn't wait for her to come to him; he couldn't hold on to news this big.

As he exited onto the fourth floor, Janelle stood halfway down the hall.

Naked.

Her back to him, showing off a huge, round, bare ass, she moved to music only she could hear.

Almost nobody dances sober, unless they happen to be insane.

Some kind of rash or melanoma speckled the doughy, pale skin of her shoulder blades and the slab of her upper back.

A blush warmed his cheeks. He started to turn away, but....

That wasn't Janelle.

His friend wasn't this short or stout. Janelle's simple skirt and bulky cardigan may have hidden her curves, but these extra wide hips in front of him wouldn't have been hers. The strawberry blond hair should have given it away immediately, but he'd been too shocked at the sight.

The woman's gyrations stopped. She raised her hands, jiggling the slack flesh at the back of her arms. Warding off? Inviting in?

Miles backed up.

The woman froze.

His heels scuffled on the floor, and she tilted her head, listening.

Miles pressed his back to the chilly wall at the end of the hallway.

Arms still half-raised, fingers clawing at the air, the woman turned with jerky quarter-steps.

Miles tried to sink into the wall and out of sight. He knew that short nose. That curl of lip. The inflamed red face.

Janelle's door was right there, if he dared make a break for it.

Abysmal black showed in the gaps between Betty's yellowed teeth. She dragged her feet forward. Her heavy breasts swung. The bloodless wound in her neck quivered, and with each step that second, grim mouth murmured inaudibly. Bovine brown eyes rolled in their sockets. A strangled noise issued from the hole in her throat. Her thick thighs rubbed together. Her hairy sex loomed closer.

"Betty?"

Her neck-bite gurgled.

"Betty, please."

Betty lurched another step.

Goosebumps erupted along his arms.

Her lips trembled.

At his side, a flash of black. Something seized him, and he cried out as it pulled him into Janelle's room.

Galloping thuds, and Betty's solid form hobbled into the doorway. The cellulite of her legs shook. She chewed at the air, trying to speak. Her teeth clicked together.

Janelle slammed the door in her face.

She bolted the lock and joined Miles in the center of the room, both watching the door. His mind would snap if fingernails scratched into the wood, a mindless and unstoppable Betty horror, intent on wrapping her hands around his throat, avenging her death.

Miles fell back to the window. "What's wrong with her?"

"She's lost." Janelle concentrated on the door, maybe as unsure as he was that it would hold back Betty. "The confusion takes hours to evaporate the first time. The first few times."

"You didn't mention that you all showed up bare-ass naked."

"I've never seen that before."

Miles pushed off the wall with his butt. "Where's Theodore?"

"He's out playing." Their eyes locked. "Don't look at me that way. I can't keep him cooped up all the time."

He sat on the boy's bed. "No, it's not that." He clasped his hands between his knees. "I came to tell you that Theodore doesn't need to be afraid anymore."

Janelle smiled, but she looked so sad. "I worry about you."

"I mean it. I've ripped up their pictures, just like I did in Chaplain's shrine. The plank children are done."

She studied him. A few minutes ago, he'd felt triumphant, but now he felt like his twelve-year-old self, accused of ding-dong-ditching the neighborhood. He hadn't done it, but Mom and Dad's scrutiny had made him feel guilty anyway.

He chased the confidence he'd had up in his room. "It's only Schramm and Chaplain now. Can you handle them both? Butch certainly won't help me now."

"He will."

"His daughter survived the plague of illness and depravation that hit St. Hamelin's and lived for, what—seventy years?—and now she's dead because of me."

"That's not true."

"Thanks for the sentiment, but you're not that good of a liar. Elijah only killed her because I'm here."

Without the usual smoothing of her skirt, Janelle sat on her bed, facing him. She smacked her palms on her legs and gave one definitive nod. "You deserve to know everything."

"There's more?"

I felt that I must scream or die!

"Frederick came to St. Hamelin's before I did. He'd lost his wife and moved here from Illinois, with his daughter and little else, just like me and Theodore." Her prim etiquette had relaxed so much since sharing a smoke with him. "Seems so strange now—Betty and Theodore were children together, playing hide and seek in the endless hallways."

"Strange doesn't begin to cover it."

And now—again—hark!—louder! Louder! Louder!

She continued in hushed breath, as if speaking too loudly would crush the diaphanous shell of memory. "That first year felt like the fresh start I wanted for us. The children were darlings. Rambunctious, but the older ones helped out. Their hearts were pure, but they had sad souls. By the time they turned twelve or thirteen—so young— the orphans' hope dried up. They didn't trust easily, but I made a difference in their lives." She pulled a handkerchief from the pocket without the keys and dabbed her eyes. "I know I did."

Miles nodded. "I know." He didn't, but he could imagine.

She made the handkerchief disappear up her sleeve and knitted her brows. "I was devastated when they fell ill. That disease spread so fast and struck so hard. Joe— my husband—his death hurt like a broken bottle twisted into my stomach, but then these boys.... After living with so much disappointment, now they battled enormous physical pain. The way their legs wasted away....

The paralysis. I was shocked at how many died. All that pointless death killed something inside me, as well. You wouldn't believe."

"But I can. Putting Ian's casket in the ground buried part of me, too. Sometimes, in the middle of the night, I wake from nightmares, strangled by heartburn. I don't know how much of this drive up here had been to find a cure, but now I learn that you and Theodore have spent my entire lifetime drowning."

She had promised him everything, so he pushed. "Elijah told me about experiments. Medical practices disguising torture."

She stared into the middle distance, and he couldn't read her eyes. Had she known? Had she tried to stop it? Did she think he was accusing her?

Her gaze caressed Theodore's bed, the bookshelves, the rugs. "I still don't know if Dr. Schramm and Chaplain Allen knew each other previously, but when the polio outbreak hit us, they requisitioned the state for all that... equipment.

"The hydrotherapy seemed a good idea. The iron lungs too, I suppose, but they frightened me. They terrified the boys! Encased inside those wretched machines, forced immobile, made to stare up at the ceiling for hours. Days."

She outlined her mouth with the edge of a fingernail, leaving a trail of white from the pressure ringing her lips.

"Dr. Schramm told me it was treatment." She tugged the handkerchief halfway from her cuff but didn't pull it out. "What did I know of medicine?" She picked at a tattered string. "So much was changing, and it all made me uncomfortable—changing St. Hamelin's into a reformatory and bringing in those new boys, the uniforms, all the church services. Frederick said it might be a good thing."

Janelle tapped her teeth with that fingernail. "Dr. Schramm acted the part of a caring, helpful man, but there was no compassion in him. When we would talk, an abyss stared out at me. He just liked to hurt. Chaplain Allen's fire and brimstone sermons hurt the children in other ways. They must have known each other before, right? Otherwise, evil had been drawn to evil, and I can't believe that's possible. The implications are too terrible.

"I was afraid of them, afraid of what I suspected went on in the basement, but I was most afraid of losing my position here. Without recommendations from Dr. Schramm, I might not have found another post, and how would I take care of Theodore then?" Now she did pull the handkerchief out of her sleeve. She held it to the bottom rim of one eye. "The death toll, the faces of the sick children, it all resembled the horror stories that we had heard after the war. About those German prisons."

"Concentration camps."

She dropped her hands to her lap. "Yes."

He'd watched a documentary about crazed Nazi doctor Josef Mengele. Stomach-churning accounts of true-life horror. Stitching twins together. Drowning men by pouring saltwater down their throats. Injecting diseases and watching children die before cutting them up. What exactly had Schramm brought to St. Hamelin's? Elijah said they heard the screams from their rooms.

"I told you that Fredrick comforted me?" She smoothed out nonexistent wrinkles from her skirt. "We were both lonely, do you understand?"

"Of course." Butch had a few screws loose, but back in the Fifties, he might have been more tightly constructed. Making him and Janelle the only sane adults.

"It wasn't long before I was in the family way."

"In the—? Oh." An unwed mother with an illegitimate baby on the way? That would have scandalized a reputation back then. She really might not have found a quality position again.

"When Dr. Schramm and the chaplain found out, they were furious. Well, Chaplain Allen was furious. Dr.

Schramm was embarrassed." Janelle's shoulders quaked. Her exhalations became wet and slobbery. "The chaplain took care of it."

Miles reached out to her from Theodore's bed, a divide too great. Should he get up and go sit with her? Friends and family usually didn't confide in him—he just didn't have that species of magnetism. Only banalities came to mind: It's all right; You did what you had to do.

He chose the least saccharine. "I'm so sorry."

"Theodore started coming home with black eyes, bruises on his arms and legs. I begged Chaplain Allen to intervene, and he said he would, but I don't think he did. Those new boys kept at it, and then.... And then they killed him." Her pitch went higher. "Murdered my boy in the lavatory. Those new boys, those monsters Dr. Schramm catered to." She sped up. "They and a couple of the boys I'd known since I started, ones that they converted. Monsters. I went mad." No longer speaking to him but for herself, edging toward the manic. "I stole a kitchen knife from the cafeteria, and I unlocked their rooms and one by one I slit their throats, stabbed them through the ribs, cut them and sent them to Hades, which was a better sentence than they deserved."

Holy hell, Chaplain had told the truth? Janelle had turned Mr. Hyde on more than half a dozen kids. Holy shit, that was cold-blooded.

Miles slid off Theodore's bed and knelt before her, clutching her hands. Lost in that long-ago moment, Janelle did not move. He felt powerless to calm her rage or assuage her guilt. Maybe he was an unworthy confidante. "It's all over now. They're gone. They can't hurt you anymore."

Except Schramm. Except Chaplain. And Chaplain Allen's fury would be legendary when he learned that Miles had decimated his Christian soldiers.

"Frederick was still furious at what Chaplain Allen had done, before Theodore."

You see her eyes are open/Ay, but their sense are shut.

He had forgotten about her pregnancy, and the horror of Chaplain's abortion. He refused to imagine how the clergyman had scraped it out.

"Frederick wanted his pound of flesh for what Chaplain Allen had done, so he helped me." She squeezed his hands hard enough to shift the bones. "Our bond—he and I—that's why he will help me again now. That grudge is why he'll help you. We did it together, that night. He took care of Dr. Schramm and Chaplain Allen." A trace of a smile on her face. "He choked the life out of Chaplain Allen."

Miles's hands in tow, she raised hers and shook them in pantomime. Did she see Butch's work-hardened mortal weapons only, or did she also see her own, dripping with the blood of children?

What, will these hands ne'er be clean?

Her mouth twitched. Mania drained out of the telling. "Dr. Schramm kept a pistol that we didn't know about. They fought. Frederick ripped the gun away and got him—shot Dr. Schramm in the stomach. After I... finished... I went to find him. Dr. Schramm lay on the floor in his quarters," she sounded wistful, "kicking his heels in the pool of blood. He whimpered as he tried to hold his insides from spilling out. But...." She blinked against a wet sheen on her eyes. "But Dr. Schramm had gotten off a shot—before or after, I don't know, but he shot my Frederick. In the lung, I think. Frederick was still alive, too." Her mouth remained puckered in the little "oo" from her last word. Her eyes ticked back and forth in recollection, but this part must have been just for her. In a minute, she sighed. "With nothing left, I threw myself off the roof."

Were her hands freezing or were his?

Janelle let go when she heaved in a tremendous breath. "Every day I wish that I could close my eyes—that Theodore, Butch, and I—could close our eyes and leave this earth. I am tired and ready to meet Judgement."

Christ, Miles would need years of therapy to pick through the emotional debris of his time spent at St. Hamelin's. He massaged his hands together to warm them up and to buy time to think. Chaplain had told the truth—Janelle had blood on her hands—but the raw, analytical fact of it ignored the emotional context. Janelle had murdered, but she wasn't Lady Macbeth with an insatiable appetite for power.

In a way, Miles admired Janelle.

And was a bit afraid of her.

His chances of getting out of here certainly felt better, but he would be leaving behind Janelle and Theodore—and Butch—to Schramm's twisted justice for their treason.

An uproar outside ripped through the quiet.

An orange glow drew them to the window. Night had fallen as they had talked, but what looked like pulsing firelight spilled into the courtyard. Whatever had caught fire lay around the corner of the dorm wing, out of sight.

A baritone shout.

"That's Frederick." Janelle hurried to the door.

Would Betty still be out there, naked and mad?

He followed Janelle into the hall. Blessedly empty.

"We need to hurry."

Twenty-Seven

A bonfire raged between the tiny tombstones and the cafeteria, whipping flames into curved points ten feet high, expelling a summer heat that melted the snow. Solid black silhouettes cavorted in a bestial dance.

No.

It wasn't possible.

How were they still alive?

The boys kicked their knees up as they revolved, pumping fists into the air. Dancing along with them in an outer ring, their shadows stretched and fattened, thrust against the ground by the blaze, warped into hideous monsters.

He had ripped their black and white faces to shreds.

Butch bellowed from a spot dangerously near the fire, his face lurid in the fireglow.

High-flung flames snapped like sheets on a clothesline and threw mottled light onto Husky, Teeth, all of the lackeys' faces. Orange glinted in their eyes even as shadows darkened eye sockets and mouths like war paint.

He had failed. The photos had not been the thing.

Not gamboling, Elijah stood with Ian slightly removed. The redhead bent, and in a moment straightened, holding an unwieldy armload of firewood.

The devil's dance slowed. Husky and Teeth separated from the others and grabbed hold of Butch's elbows. Butch barked for them to stop, but they dug their fingers into the old man's arms.

With all the boys' rapt attention focused on Elijah and Butch, Miles and Janelle crept closer.

Elijah stepped toward the fire.

"Oh my God." Janelle's shining eyes flicked from the fire to Butch to Elijah. "No."

The cabal hooted encouragement, and Elijah presented the offering, holding aloft not firewood, but femurs. An ulna. Rib bones. A skull tipped back against Elijah's narrow chest, throwing its head back in laughter.

Butch's face contorted with wild screams. Spittle flew from his mouth and fizzled in the heat.

The boys around the bonfire gawped.

Janelle backhanded tears from her face. The tension inside her released like a spring, but the instant her feet pushed off the ground, Miles grabbed her around the waist and wrested her down beside him. "There's nothing you can do. You'd just be caught and tortured like Butch."

Elijah cast his bundle of broken skeleton into the bonfire. Sparks exploded. The base of the fire bloated and blazed yellow. This new fuel of human remains threw flames high, higher, towering over the boys and Butch and Miles and Janelle. So bright that the stars receded.

Glare played on Butch's waxy cheeks and the white scalp visible through his military cut. He thrust his face skyward and yowled. Husky and that snaggle-mouthed bastard let Butch go and retreated to the edge of surrounding night.

The boys watched in rapture.

Butch arched his back, stretched his arms out behind him, and stiffened. Ringlets of smoke coiled out from his work shirt collar. Out of the sleeve cuffs. Small flames erupted along the seams of the shirt and his denim jeans. The bristles of his buzz-cut sparked.

The young savages of St. Hamelin's bounded once more around the fire, leaping and grunting like rutting boars.

Butch's sparking hair caught, and a wildfire raced up over the crown of his head, down his neck, and out along his shoulders. He opened his mouth to scream and smoke poured from his throat, obscuring his head like a caul. He grabbed the thighs of his work jeans and twisted the fabric. His gnarled hands charred. Skin flaked off and drifted on the currents of heated air. A breeze blew the away the smoke, and firelight glimmered in Butch's eyes for a second. A moment. They popped and leaked filmy juice down his face; forehead and cheeks blistered. The bubbles burst and liquified skin ran down his neck and over his chest. The layer of fat beneath the skin glistened and melted like tallow, spilling onto the ground where it spattered like grease in a pan.

Elijah thrust out his hands in orgiastic glory. Ian's face scrunched into a hateful mask of awe.

Miles's fingers cramped—he'd been holding Janelle's arm in a death-grip. He let go and sunk to his knees.

The burned tatters of Butch's clothes fell away, leaving him an upright horror of white bone and strips of red muscle. Bluish-pink organs chugged smoke. The top of his skull sunk in. Arms, wrists, knees stretched like taffy. In the body cavity, entrails blackened. Wrinkled.

Miles dragged in a deep breath of Butch's burned hair and flesh. His stomach clenched. Janelle grabbed his shoulders and wrangled him to his feet. Her face loomed large before his eyes. "Hurry!" She yanked on his arm, and he stumbled after her.

Like Lot's wife, he couldn't resist a last glance over his shoulder. The blackened remains of Butch folded into the base of the fire, and blew apart like coal dust. Fireflies of sparks jittered in the dark, velvet sky.

Boys cheered and minced around the inferno. Elijah scanned the grounds. He knew. He searched the night for Miles, and when their eyes met, Elijah stared deranged malice from under his brows.

Let Elijah Yoder fume all he wanted. Miles knew how to kill him now.

How to kill them all.

Twenty-Eight

Miles humped up the stairs ahead of Janelle. He didn't want company. He didn't want commiseration. It was selfish, but he needed time to think. Tearing up the photos hadn't been enough. For reanimated flesh, destroying their remains was the only way. Just fire, or would crushing them to dust work? More to the point, would destroying the preserved heads and hands and... extremities do it?

He muttered goodbye at Janelle's floor and continued to his room where he grabbed Chaplain's notebook and crashed onto the bed. Now would be the best time to raid the sacristy, but his hands wouldn't stop shaking. His teeth chattered. He opened the Moleskine and read. Rifled pages. Scanned the words, the sentences, losing himself inside a madman's mind, but it was better than hearing Butch's screams rattle around in his head.

Gah, what was that? He set the notebook in his lap, hooked a finger in his collar, and sniffed. His clothes— his pores—had absorbed Butch's execution by bonfire. Woodsmoke, burnt hair, seared flesh had melded on a cellular level with his nostril hairs and would never leave him.

He would never smoke another cigarette again.

He got up and turned off the lights. Lay down and groaned into the mattress. Buried his head under the pillow.

Pretty soon, Jeremy would be lighting their fireplace for the first time this fall.

Tremors vibrated his body like he'd loaded quarters into a sleazy motel's magic fingers bed. He rolled out from under his pillow and stared into the darkness. "Who's there?"

No moon, no stars, no light at all, and in the dark a tall, thin shape waited beside the dresser.

Miles propped up on his elbows and harrumphed. "I knew you'd come."

Mantis arms reached out. "Do you see how deeply you've hurt me?"

"How the hell can you play victim after everything?" Arrogant prick! "Screw off."

The mantis charged, and splashed sour breath over the bed. "None of this was your business, and you trampled over everything. Still, I tried to help you." Another wave of sewer breath. "Betty was indispensable to me. So inquisitive—an excellent acolyte, taking copious notes of every step, every nuance about my process with those sick boys."

The notebook.... That was Betty's.

"Elijah killed her. I had nothing to do with that." But he couldn't muster any conviction; he had already accepted his culpability.

The mantis grabbed Miles's ankles and yanked him off the bed. His butt bone cracked onto the floor. He was grabbed, pulled up to his feet. The light clicked on, and Chaplain's ice chip eyes bore into him. A hard slap across Miles's face jumbled his wits.

"Get off me!"

Chaplain seized his poor excuse for a bicep and whipped him around, face-first into the closed door. "Mr. Baumgartner, I'm so glad that you failed to follow the rules."

Miles's eyebrow cracked against the wood.

They stood in Schramm's empty office.

"Yes. Come in." Schramm's voice issued from the inner door between desk and fireplace.

Chaplain steered him into a dark-paneled hallway, glowing with golden light the shade of good Scotch. A few paces in, Schramm's richly appointed living quarters opened up. Leather furniture with brass rivets. Massive mahogany desk with brass fittings. Hardwood floors polished to a high sheen. At the far end of the room, a hallway's black chasm presumably led to bedrooms, maybe a kitchen.

A sideboard dominated the wall opposite the fireplace where Schramm stood in a strappy white undershirt tucked into high-waisted trousers. Beside him, a spindly-legged contraption. An ironing board, draped with one of his natty shirts. An old flat iron rested on its trivets.

"Thank you, Chaplain Allen. You may go."

Chaplain's hand fell from Miles's neck. He stepped off, a childish pout of dejection on his face.

Watching Chaplain humbled—embarrassed maybe—was worth the roughing up Miles had taken on the way down here. "You heard him. Scram."

"I shall wait in your office." Chaplain backed out the door. A trace of a grin played on those slim, villainous lips. "When you're ready."

When the door shut, Miles faced Schramm. "Ready for what?"

Schramm rubbed his hands at the fireplace. "I just can't keep warm in this old building anymore."

"It's like ninety degrees in here."

Schramm wrapped a thick potholder around the iron's handle and placed it into the fire to heat up. He ambled to the sideboard. "Are you a whisky man?"

"Offering me a drink? I must really be in trouble this time." Schramm had a host of charges to choose from: stealing the photographs, ripping them up, breaking into the sacristy, complicity in Betty's murder wouldn't have been a stretch for the superintendent.

But what sentence did Schramm have in mind?

Schramm poured two fingers of Scotch into Old Fashioned glasses and walked them over.

Miles took the proffered glass of amber. Its impressive weight grounded him in the moment. Schramm sipped, slow and deliberate.

Miles followed suit with a polite quaff. Wow! A powder keg compared to that stein of beer at Blankenheim's.

Blankenheim's!

Holy Hell. Butch was Frederick Blankenheim.... That bartender's long-dead great-grandfather?

Miles gulped his drink, and a mortar blast of heat burst in his stomach. He smacked his lips. "This is incredible."

Not quite as incredible as his woefully belated Eureka moment. Blankenheim's: home of gutes Essen, that scheisse woman, and purveyor of a fabled accident that didn't hold a candle—in a shrine!—to the real cataclysm.

Miles handed over the empty glass.

"How about another, Mr. Baumgartner?" Schramm crossed to the sideboard. "I think it's for the best." He poured another two fingers each. "Under the circumstances."

"Circumstances. Yes." He nodded. His whole body felt freshly massaged. Why did scoundrels always have such good taste? "Circumstances are indeed dire." He stifled a giggle.

Whoa. Better not relax too much.

"I'm glad that you see that." Instead of bringing Miles his drink, Schramm walked over to the desk. The superintendent sure liked his desks and reveled in bloated confidence when behind one. Sounded like a cover for deep-seated insecurities.

Desks and torturing children.

Miles joined Schramm and took his whisky with a polite nod. No reason to escalate hostilities prematurely. They'd get there soon enough. He sipped. Standing so close, in this heat, Schramm's rotting corpse-stink tainted the gestures of civility. Miles gritted his teeth and bore it. Show no weakness.

Last time he'd seen Schramm, the superintendent had drooled bugs and dirt.

He sipped.

Schramm raised his glass high. "I know what you've been up to."

"Watching Butch burn?"

Schramm didn't flinch. "You took advantage of my good nature. Thought you could pull one over on me."

Miles raised his own toast. "Nothing slips past you."

Schramm drank. "This telephone call to the outside world...."

Oh. That.

"Let me see this portable telephone of yours."

"I don't have it."

"You don't...." Schramm slammed the glass on the desktop. "You don't have it?"

Miles hadn't expected this line of attack, and his Scotch-dampened brain slogged along, trying to catch up. "I... I broke it."

Schramm scoffed.

It really did sound like bullshit.

"You have shown nothing but contempt for this institution. Most certainly...." Schramm pounded his drink again onto the desk. "For me. For what I'm trying to hold together."

Miles's buzz reassembled itself. "Your legacy of torture?" He barked a bitter laugh. "Yeah, I saw those rooms downstairs."

"You are mistaken to trust Miss Poole so implicitly. You do not know her truth."

"I do. She confessed everything. And Elijah told me about your experiments."

"They were treatments! I implemented cutting edge technology. Consulted the best medical minds in New York and London to help those patients."

"Those patients were children. Abandoned and discarded, so who cares about them, right? And then you filled their shabby excuse of a home with juvenile delinquents to bully and abuse them."

"That was the only way I could keep St. Hamelin's open."

"What are you a doctor of, anyway? Medicine?"

Schramm glared.

"I didn't think so. You were out of your depth but went ahead and... did things to those kids. The kids you were supposed to care for."

"I did care. I still do!"

"Do you believe your own crap?"

"I am the superintendent here and—"

"You're a sadist."

Schramm flung his Old Fashioned glass into the fireplace where it exploded into brilliant shards. He jabbed a finger into Miles's chest. "I am a disciplinarian!"

Schramm's button, finally pushed.

"You're a psychopath."

Schramm expelled putrescent breath and stood tall. "You have no idea the strength and compromises I needed to survive the Chicago streets of my boyhood. After a box car sliced off my father's leg in the railyards, it was all up to me to earn. My mother was a nervous woman; my sisters took in seamstress work, but the weight fell on my shoulders. Your privileged morality doesn't feed a family of six. Working as a slugger for Dean O'Banion kept the lights and heat on, put food at our table. I worked harder than anyone on that crew to prove myself to those micks. I hashed out new ways to hijack whiskey and gin—that's where the real money was. Adversity toughened me up, made me who I am. You think I like punishing these boys? They need to be put back on course, and Mr. O'Banion taught me how to discipline."

"You are utterly unqualified to run a reformatory."

"Wrong! It is what I know. After those years on the street, I transitioned into local politics. Combating juvenile crime, that was my platform." He stroked his lapels. Rocked on his heels. "I became something of a celebrity, I'll have you know. The National Probation Association invited me to their convention in Atlantic City. I met old Sandford Bates, Director of U.S. Prisons. Dr. Frederic Thrasher and I shared many a cocktail and tête-à-tête. I was appointed superintendent here."

"All of that, yet at the end of the day, you mete out gangsters' discipline."

"Exactly what they needed." Schramm laughed. A wretched sound. How Lucifer would cheer on his sulfur throne. "Have you forgotten that these boys came to me from the courthouse?"

"Where you paid off the judges."

"To choose St. Hamelin's. They were to be sentenced somewhere, why not here?"

"But for petty offenses."

"Delinquents such as these used to be sent to prisons. Even executed for theft! I offered the courts an alternative and the boys an opportunity to straighten out before their crimes escalated."

"But your mobster justice doesn't work! Elijah turned Husky and Teeth and all of them into murderers."

"Husky and...?" Schramm waved off his confusion. "Thank you, Mr. Baumgardner. Thank you for reminding me that I failed. I could not keep that disease at bay. I did not mold those boys into better men. All that I tried to do here failed."

"So, what? You've doubled-down? For God's sake, you cut off a boy's finger!"

"Don't you see what I'm up against? Chaplain Allen's work was supposed to give us all another chance at redemption, but when those children rose again, their... their humanity didn't return with them. I'm two steps behind now. Chaplain Allen has gone off on his own agenda. You've seen how he riles them up. I do what I can to maintain control." Schramm massaged his forehead. "I'm trapped here, too. Just like you."

Parched, Miles drained his second drink. "Why'd you keep me here that first night? I could have made it out. I never wanted to get involved in any of this."

"Didn't want to get involved?" Schramm's fists opened and closed, clenching as if eager to wrap around Miles's throat. "You found us with the intention to take Ian Gunderson away."

"I didn't even believe he was alive until you showed him to me."

Schramm either hadn't heard or didn't care. He slammed his fist on the desktop, and pens rattled. "You brought disorder into this already tenuous situation."

"I didn't mean—"

"It's exactly...."

Slam.

"... what you in*ten*ded..."

Slam.

"... to do!"

SLAM.

"You thought you could extricate one of my boys! Undermine my authority! I was barely holding on as it was!"

He had pushed Schramm too hard, escalated this exchange beyond what he could pacify. The superintendent quaked with rage; his face flushed, and sweat dotted his hairline. Time to retreat before Schramm focused his outrage.

"Dr. Schramm?" Chaplain let himself in, closing the door behind him. Cutting off the exit.

Schramm bowed his head—catching his breath or clearing his mind—and waved Chaplain over. They drifted toward the fireplace, huddling together.

Deciding what to do with him.

Maybe time had come to run, while the two men distracted themselves. The boys might still have been outside celebrating their kill.

Chaplain whispered. "I told you to get rid of him."

But he had promised not to abandon Janelle and Theodore.

Schramm: "Resourceful."

Now that he knew how to kill the dead, Miles couldn't have lived with himself if he left them, subjecting them to Schramm and Chaplain's whims. He had to at least try.

Chaplain clapped Schramm on the back, and the superintendent shrugged off the touch so violently that his undershirt pulled out of his trousers, revealing a patch of belly hair thick and black. Schramm turned back to Miles. His usual pasty complexion returned, and the tip of his juicy pink tongue poked out to wet his lower lip. "You understand what an invaluable caretaker Frederick's daughter was?"

"Honestly, I don't."

Chaplain shook his head, oh-so-disappointed.

"Betty was vital to our continued existence, but she was getting up there in years. You asked why I kept you here?"

"Yeah." But he no longer wanted to know.

"I thought you'd make an ideal replacement."

He sobered up. "Replacement?"

"We need a living agent. A proxy."

Or maybe he felt drunker. They wanted to keep him as their Renfield? "You seem to be doing just fine on your own."

"Chaplain Allen and I manage most operations just fine. The world has more or less forgotten about St. Hamelin's, and the locals keep their distance. However, occasions do arise when a representative must drive into town. A few years ago, a snooping journalist fellow telephoned us repeatedly. He wanted to write up some sort of biography. We couldn't have that, but nor could we invite him up to dissuade him. Best not to give a curious mind any sip at all—just look at what happened with you! Betty drove into town, and she put a stop to the biography."

The unfinished Wikipedia page on St. Hamelin's?

"You want me to do your dirty work."

"Mostly you'd be an insurance policy, should our Chaplain's efforts hit a snag."

"You mean tend your illustrious collection of boy parts in those jars?"

Chaplain stamped his foot. "He can't be trusted. This is a mistake. I smell his sin and arrogance."

Disheveled, scratching his chin, Schramm walked to the sideboard, fixed two more Scotches, and brought them over. "There are benefits for you, as well."

"What would those be?"

"Remaining here with the ones you love." Schramm held out the glass.

Miles took it. "The ones I love, huh?"

"Ian, of course. But I am also thinking of Janelle and Theodore Poole."

To buy time to gather himself, Miles knocked back the generous double.

Whew!

Schramm took his in a long, slow quaff. "You have grown close to Theodore, that is obvious." Schramm's glassy eyes considered Miles for a moment. "Curious though, your affection for Miss Poole."

"Is it? Curious?"

"The boys I could understand, but such interest in the woman is unusual. For a queer."

Alcoholic vapor swam in his head.

A queer.

Boy, that last drink really warmed him up.

Not just queer, like gay. A queer. Like *a fag*.

His rage dragon whipped its tail, and Miles popped a jab at Schramm's chin. Sloppy. He missed, smacking his knuckles into one doughy cheek. The skin rippled. Schramm faltered a step, probably more surprised than hurt, but who cared? Finally striking back at that prick felt amazing. "Ha!"

Amazing only for that second.

Chaplain bear-hugged him from behind. Bastard swept his ankle, pushed, and laughed as Miles fell to the floor. Above, Chaplain's face glowed with the exact sentiment Miles had just felt about Schramm.

"Fine." Miles picked himself up. Tried, at least. His elbows failed, and he collapsed back down, tasting a bit of dust that had blown up. Schramm had pickled his brain. Down on the floor felt nice.

In the ether above, Chaplain and Schramm discussed. "Are you convinced now?"

"We need him, Chaplain. Your brat killed Betty."

"This one provoked Elijah into acting."

"You worry about your dogs; I'll take the fire out of our new man here. Just help me."

Hands hooked under his armpits, and Miles made himself go slack. Partly passive resistance, but mostly the booze and how Chaplain had knocked him off-kilter. They threw him down by the ironing board. He landed with his full weight pressing on his right arm caught at a bad angle. The Scotch kept the pain at bay, but also got him pretty pissed off about being slapped around.

He rolled off his arm and snatched Chaplain's pant leg.

"Really, Mr. Baumgartner...."

Chaplain bent to pry off his fingers, and Miles swung his tingling arm. Chaplain dodged and chopped the side of his hand into Miles's throat.

Miles sputtered.

Schramm planted his foot on Miles's shoulder. "Mind yourself! I would like us to come to an understanding." A pestle to a mortar, Schramm crushed his shoulder blade into the hearth.

That was one hell of an understanding. He gritted his teeth. Never let them see you hurt, right? But he couldn't bear it. A squeal jumped from his lips.

Schramm stepped off and snatched a shiny object from his desk.

A sick déjà vu swept over him.

"No." His jugular beat, swollen and full. "There's no need for that."

Schramm brought over the serrated letter opener.

Chaplain knelt beside him, grabbed double fistfuls of his hair, and lifted his head. He slammed the right side of Miles's face into the hearth and ground his cheek, his brow, into the brick. Chaplain chuckled into his left ear, the exposed one. The one hearing the sandpaper-swish of brick scraping off skin.

Rocky Mountain Face's screams echoed down the chambers of memory. The scent of the boy's blood overpowered Butch's smoky death.

Schramm hunkered down, holding the letter opener like a scalpel. Its gruesome length flared in the firelight. "I wouldn't toe the line after this, you don't want to know what I'll take next."

"You—"

Chaplain squeezed his throbbing carotid, silencing him.

Schramm grabbed his ear and tugged.

The warm blade bit into the membranous skin behind the ear. The teeth carved an arc down the backside toward the lobe.

A noise started in the back of Miles's throat. A consonant sound groaning on and on.

Schramm pulled the ear away from the head. "Get his chin."

Chaplain planted a hand over the side of his mouth, his chin, and squashed the lower third of his face.

Miles's vocal cords vibrated as the sound in his throat went up an octave.

Schramm reset the letter opener to the top of the ear. He pressed it in the shallow groove he'd made. His tongue popped out in effort, and he sawed into the connection between ear and head.

Miles mewled; his mouth flooded with the metallic taste of fear. Blood or saliva dribbled down his throat, and he choked. He gurgled the thick juice, and slimy strands of it drooled over Chaplain's hand.

Schramm moaned in pleasure as the blade cut deep into the cartilage.

A creaky scream wrenched from Miles. His head felt like a lead balloon, not even part of him.

Schramm bore down. The blade dug deeper. Miles counted saw-strokes.

One.

Miles screwed his eyes shut. He couldn't stop blubbering.

Two.

He kicked. He flailed. But Chaplain only pinned him harder.

Three.

Ripping screeched through the ear canal where it wriggled and writhed like an earwig burrowing toward brain meat.

Tug.

A long slow cut.

Pop.

A release of pressure.

Chaplain released him, and Miles slid his head off the hearth and curled into a ball. Standing over him, Schramm dangled his miserable ear. Blood trickled from the red, ragged edge and dappled his face.

Thank Christ it was over.

"Hold onto this, please." Schramm set Miles's bloody chunk of ear into Chaplain's palm. Chaplain receded into darkness. Schramm loomed over him, large as God.

God said, "It's almost over."

Almost?

Miles forced his lips to move. "No more."

Schramm disappeared from view. Maybe Schramm would just stay gone.

Maybe he would bleed to death and be done with this bungled life entirely.

Schramm returned, holding an implement of pain far worse than the letter opener.

Miles draped an arm over his head. He tried to shrink into himself, but he couldn't vanish.

Chaplain pulled his arm away.

Schramm towered over him, omnipotent.

Glowing orange-red, the iron pushed explosive heat at the side of his head even before the hard metal connected.

A supernova burst into his flesh. The meaty stink of burned skin unfurled into the office. Exquisite agony blinded him, and Miles's throat went raw with his inhuman wail.

An eternity later, Schramm held up the iron for Miles to witness.

Every nerve ending in his body had been flayed.

Schramm smiled beatifically. "All done."

Miles passed out.

Twenty-Nine

Dark.

...never should have come for me...

Damp.

... the rat's burst eye dribbling over its whiskered cheek...

Cold.

...Theodore's hot blood soaking into the seat of his jeans...

Hard.

...never should have come for me...

Was he dead?

He blinked but still couldn't see.

Misery blossomed on the left hemisphere of his head. The tang of his own burned flesh coated his tongue.

Had they killed and resurrected him? Was this vague, hangover malaise the same fugue passing for thought in dead Betty's head during her lost, naked wanderings?

The lights still hadn't come back on. They'd either blinded him or stuck him down a deep well.

Or incinerator chute.

Scratching sounds, out beyond the full reach of his bruised senses.

"Hel—" He coughed; his mouth tasted like plaster. "Hello?"

Scritch-scratch. Scratch.

Hard surface under his butt. Rigid surface at his back. He was sitting in a chair, slumped to the side so his uninjured ear pressed against a rough, grainy surface. Raising his arm hurt his shoulder. His pulse sent shocks of pain into his ear-hole. *Beat-beat-beat.* His fingers traced the wall's rough whorls and striations. They'd stuck him in a wooden box, the sides old and spongy. He pressed harder, but it wasn't rotted through. It held.

Scratch-scratch. A low moan.

He stood, and his head banged against the top of the box, the low ceiling. *Beat-beat-beat* in his ear. He dropped back into the chair. With fingertips, he examined his noggin. The cut from hitting the sacristy's credens had reopened. Probing down an inch, he encountered cloth—Schramm and Chaplain had wrapped up their handiwork. The beating pain so filled his head, the side of his face, that he hadn't noticed the bandage—thick, not light and fibrous like gauze. Too big for one of Schramm's hand-kerchiefs. Spare undershirt? Most of the cloth had gone stiff—Schramm had cauterized his brutal surgery, so it probably wasn't blood.

Seepage.

Stomach juices leapt to the back of his throat. He swallowed, which triggered a stronger urge to gag. He screwed his mouth into a little O and tried some Lamaze to calm himself while his guts argued, but his expelled breath hit the close walls and came back at him.

What if they'd buried him alive? How much air did he have left?

He shimmied his chair away from the wall and reached out to find the other side. Less than his full wing-span. They'd stuffed him into a coffin?

The most terrific of these extremes which has ever fallen to the lot of mere mortality.

His insides knotted up.

But if he was upright, then they must not have buried him. Just put him in the St. Hamelin's version of a time out.

The scratching started up again. Who else had Schramm and Chaplain tucked away?

"Hey, out there."

Phlegmy gargling answered, breaking down into harsh, chuffing barks. Not the sort of noise a human boy would make.

"Who is that?"

Calling out threw the *beat-beat-beat* into overdrive, drowning out all sound.

What was he supposed to do—serve out his time here, while he healed enough to make his next escape attempt? Could Janelle even help him anymore, without Butch?

What if that was Janelle down here with him, struggling to speak because her tongue had been severed from her mouth?

"Janelle? Hello?"

There was maybe some thumping in answer, but he couldn't be sure.

Hell, even if she was okay, Schramm and Chaplain— and the damn boys—would never be distracted enough now. What a joke. He laughed and tasted blood—he had screamed his throat raw during his torture. He bit his lip. All plans were over. All bets were off. There would be no more running away.

That son of a bitch Schramm.

Schramm and Chaplain both.

Sick freaks with power over the weak. Did they think they could break him with suffering and humiliation? Bad move. They had just served up steak and potatoes for his rage dragon. Yeah, it rolled over like a dog demanding a belly rub now.

Miles smiled, here in the dark where no one could see. The pounding in the side of his head stoked the fire inside.

"Mr. Baumgartner?"

Miles jerked and teetered backward in the chair, hitting the wall behind.

"Mr. Baumgartner?"

Frantic scratching,

Miles banged the chair's front legs down on the ground. "Theodore?"

Bestial grunts.

What the hell rooted around out there?

The voice returned. "They hurt you."

Miles swallowed the drainage clogging his throat. "Yes."

Just please don't ask how; he couldn't bear replaying it in his head. He couldn't think about it anymore, let alone speak of it. And the pain eclipsed all known words; he would need to invent a new vocabulary just to come close. He stared at the invisible walls of his prison. Quiet. So much quiet, for so long. Had he finally lost his mind?

"Mr. Baumgartner?"

Certainly sounded like Janelle's son, but Elijah and Ian were so clever. They had tricked him before. Gotten the jump on him too many times already.

Madness—the compulsion to speak, the urgency not to.

He broke. "Where are we?"

Scraping, like rat teeth chewing through wood.

"In the basement. In the punishment boxes."

The what?

He groaned. He didn't even want to know.

A string of ugly snorts.

"Am I dead?"

"No."

Definitely Theodore's voice. Did the boy sound closer? Hard to tell, Miles heard with only one ear. The aural equivalent of depth perception ruined after losing an eye.

"I can let you out."

"Yes." It was Theodore, right? "Yes, please."

The click of a padlock. The furtive metallic slide of the shackle through the latch loops. Hyena screams of rusted hinges. Narrow shafts of light outlined a door's edge. Probably not a lot of light at all, but after the black totality, his eyes watered from the brightness.

Standing kick-started the *beat-beat-beat* in his ear.

His ear-hole.

Where his ear used to be.

Had to get accustomed to a piece of him existing in the past tense.

Beat-beat-beat, a paroxysm demanding he sit his ass back down. He was halfway down to his seat when his rage dragon snuffled. Miles stayed on his feet, but this agony would have to recede a couple of degrees before he could move. If only the edge dulled a little, he could take a first step. A bare minimum truce. Enough to get him above ground. Back to his room upstairs and the wasted effort of photos littering the floor. Then the full-force anguish could overwhelm him.

He ground his teeth until they squealed loud as those old hinges. He made it to the opening, then a loud *crack* popped in his jaw. Another molar split down the middle. He bumped his head stepping through the doorway, and wasps swarmed in his skull. He bent his knees an inch for clearance. His tongue explored a jagged peak of tooth. A piece of it rolled around in his mouth, immense as a boulder. He spit it into his palm. Size of a grape nut. He threw the granule, and it struck the floor with a meaningless, tiny *tink*.

"Watch your step." A blurry figure about the size and shape of Theodore.

A trickle of blood coursed down Miles's face from the reopened gash in his scalp. He blotted it with the heel of his hand and took an exaggerated step out of the—what had Theodore called it? Punishment box?—and planted his foot on solid concrete. Stale air, but fresher than he'd had in the suffocating space he had left. He turned to examine the true nature of his cell.

A child's school chair had been set inside a free-standing structure like an ice fishing shanty.

Jeremy had flown them to San Francisco for a vacation three years ago. He'd eagerly shown Miles around South of Market, the seedy twin of the Castro's gay Xanadu. SOMA's claim to infamy? Leather bars where hairy, burly, shirtless men held skinny, smooth, barely legal boys in literal leashes. Jeremy was dying to take them into Powerhouse, where guys could screw, suck, snort, and smoke in a series of back rooms. A little like those opium dens in period television shows. Jeremy knew exactly where to go and what he'd find. The basement of Powerhouse had stalls exactly like these. Almost. There, wide inviting holes had been drilled into the sides.

Thank God these were solid-sided.

High in basement rafters like whale bones, warehouse pendant lights shed blurry, yellow illumination every six or seven feet. In the gloom, a dozen more punishment boxes exuded foul auras. Makeshift solitary confinement for misbehaving boys. Definitely a Schramm and Chaplain invention—locking cowlick-headed innocents into filthy little rooms. For hours? Days?

One more detail to stash into a far back closet in his mind. Into a shanty of his own making where he could lock away all this St. Hamelin's depravity.

Theodore showed off one of his mother's keys before slipping it into his trouser pocket, an earnest smile on his dorky face. "I figured they'd lock you down here with... them."

"Them?"

"Shhh. They're already awake."

The zinging in his head had deafened him, but now that Theodore pointed it out, scratching and moaning bombarded them on every front.

Unsure about his volume control, Miles tried to whisper. "Who's them?"

Theodore's soft hand slipped into his and tugged him along. Every few feet, they passed thick wooden support beams that gathered darkness behind them. Mothers holding back their children from dashing out. His skin crawled. The passage felt alive with bated breath and keen eyes.

"So...." He cleared his throat, and his head thrummed. "Who else is locked down here?"

"There were other boys, before us."

"Yes, I've seen them. The kids who died from polio. The kids in the tubs."

"Nuh-uh. After them. Between them and us, Chaplain Allen tried all kinds of different stuff on the sick kids before they died, but they came back deformed and brain dead and so Mr. Blankenheim built the boxes, and Chaplain Allen and Dr. Schramm locked them away down here."

"As... as punishment?"

"No, just to get rid of them. But now Schramm locks us in the empty ones if we get in trouble so we can hear those mutant kids. They can smell us, and they wake up and try to dig their way through their own boxes to get at us. Mom tried to stop him from doing it, but Dr. Schramm is crazy. He likes doing shi—stuff like that." The boy bounced on the balls of his feet, anxious. "We should hurry."

Another support beam watched them pass.

What did Chaplain consider failures? Had the black magic written in his notebook raised the boys as desiccated, mouldering monsters? Or had corpses sat up, fresh as schoolboys on the first day of summer vacation, but with zombie mash for brains? Just how damaged had they been when cast off into the basement like the beasts confined to the woods of Dr. Moreau's island?

That scratching.... A sentient boy locked in a shanty without the strength to batter down the door. Dehydration chapped his lips. Thickened his spit into paste. Starvation snarled in his belly as he ripped his fingernails out pawing at the shanty walls. His screams echoed throughout this basement's endless chambers. No one to hear except the masonry.

"Stop it."

Theodore turned around, looking crushed. "I'm sorry. I'll be quiet."

"No, not you."

No, Theodore, not you. The dead boys left to rot.

All these years, surely one—maybe more—had managed to claw through or under the walls of his punishment box.

His shoulder brushed another post. He checked over his shoulder. Now he was the impatient one. "Can we hurry?"

They did, propelled into the far reaches by the slathering cast-off children stalking in these shadows thick as stage curtains. Awful beasts limping along, slobbering over gnashing teeth.

Miles tripped over his feet and collided with Theodore. The swathed gash in the side of his head roared.

"Are you okay, Mr. Baumgartner?"

No, Theodore. He wasn't okay. He was so far from okay, he needed a map to find okay's neighborhood. "Let me catch my breath for a minute."

Theodore was a smart kid. His face brightened, almost genuinely, as he changed the subject for Miles. "Mom said you saw our room."

"Yeah." He renegotiated the compromise with his body: an adequate tolerance to the pain while he followed Theodore out of the basement.

"Mom likes to keep our room just like it was. It's silly, but it makes her feel better."

"Moms are like that." The hurt subsided enough to draw him back from the precipice of passing out. Miles motioned for them to start walking again. "What time is it?"

"Eleven."

"Oh." Finally, some good news. Good-enough news, anyway. "It feels like a lot more than a couple hours passed."

Theodore scrunched his face, and nostalgia—Ian!—twisted Mile's stomach. "It's eleven in the morning."

"What?"

"It's Monday morning."

Impossible.

In such surroundings the mind loses its perspective.

Battling the ephemeral now....

Time and space become trivial and unreal.

... In addition to bodily abuses.

And echoes of a forgotten prehistoric past beat insistently upon the enthralled consciousness.

Beat-beat-beat.

How long had they wandered these blasted basement rooms now? Schramm and Chaplain really were Lovecraft's Elder Ones, confounding Theodore's spatial cognition. They couldn't be lost. They mustn't be lost!

Misery infected St. Hamelin's like black mold. Loose strands of anguish floated like asbestos in the air inside those so-called treatment rooms and around the punishment boxes. But even in these anonymous stretches, a singular desperation seeped from the concrete walls and floor. Oozed from the joists and rafters.

The degradation of Chaplain, Schramm, and the plank children had sifted through the admin ward, the dorm wing, even that classroom, and it all settled where he and Theodore now tread, stirring it all up.

His gripes of the past months were so small. He'd suffered a bad breakup. And *suffered* was hyperbole. A minor mental breakdown at work had gotten him banished, but he and Bob Rather were friends so he hadn't been fired. Suspensions could be lifted. Even this gobsmacking pain of his severed ear would dissipate. He'd bear the scar forever, but didn't scars lend dignity—or mystery—to an older man? Scars were badges of trauma survived.

Theodore took them through an archway and toward a grey patch of a doorless entryway. Hope of leaving the underground?

Yeah... hope.

Hope had died along with Ian that spring. Losing Ian had been his real and true torment. Oddly enough, as bad as things had gotten after he'd found St. Hamelin's, action—forward progress—had helped him figure out a truth. No, time didn't heal all wounds. But experience did. Shuffling through his apartment in his bathrobe, bemoaning his fate had only nurtured despondency. The cure? Get out, live life, form new memories. That's what healed wounds. Not waiting for the clock or the calendar to erase the hurt. The horrors of St. Hamelin's were a bitter medicine, but he no longer gave a shit about Jeremy. And at least he was in the process of letting go of Ian— the boy haunting St. Hamelin's was but a wan remnant.

They reached a door, a pale-yellow glare on the iron. Theodore rattled another of his mother's keys into a large lock. This door swung open quiet and easy as if on oiled hinges. Theodore vanished into the full dark of the other side.

The smell of mechanical viscera—oil and grease and fuel—knocked into Miles. "Wait up."

A sun burst into the room, and he threw his hand up to shield his eyes. He struck the knot on his head, and the brilliant explosion of pain weakened his knees.

Theodore stood with his hand on an old push-button light switch. A bizarre structure of black iron filled the huge brick room. A steampunk God in his throne room.

"What is that?"

Looked like the nose of a steam locomotive had been dropped into this hole in the ground.

Theodore confirmed. "The furnace."

With Betty absent, the squat cylinder lay dormant.

Metal-grate stairs led to a catwalk above the bleak heart of St. Hamelin's. Two dozen pipes, thick as his arm, poked out of the ancient barrel and stretched around the room and up into the ceiling—its vast network of capillaries and veins circulating beneath the reformatory's skin of stone and mortar, lathing and plaster. Dials protruded out the side of the iron ventricles; gauges bulged from the ugly vessels—Frankensteinian efforts to monitor the monstrous system.

Behind the furnace lay a wooden pen filled with coal, the polluting fuel that could once again warm the blood of the beast. Miles shivered in the cold chest cavity. Schramm could run this thing himself—or have one of the kids do it—but maybe he planned on freezing Miles out of the dormitory and into his new home in the cottage.

"How—"

What? How to resuscitate this thing? He didn't want to learn—even if Theodore knew, which he doubted. One way or another, he was getting out of here before a dead furnace became a real problem.

Out through the door in the opposite wall, he followed Theodore into a big space, smelling of old root cellars. Dim yellow glowed from fixtures far overhead. From St. Hamelin's shifting, settling weight, heavy cracks zigged through the concrete walls, interconnecting like highways on a map. Thank Christ no more punishment boxes had popped up, but several feet away lay a huge patch of bare dirt. Some warped idea of a garden. Then it came clear. A wide section of the floor had been hammered up, and piles of busted stone lay in several piles like tribal grave markers. Smooth, rounded stones lay scattered. Mounds of excavated earth lay like the humped backs of breaching leviathans.

Famous vaults... which possess the horrid property of preserving corpses from decay for centuries.

Theodore squeezed Miles's hand. His voice trembled. "This is where we're buried." The boy stared, transfixed, at the gaping wound in the floor.

"We?"

"Me and my mom. Elijah and...." He swallowed hard. "And what's not in the jars."

"You know about those?"

Theodore nodded. "Miz Blankenheim buried all of us in the basement alongside her dad."

Miss Blankenheim?

Betty.

"She did this?" He trembled. Nearly seventy years ago, a broken-hearted young girl had discovered the bodies of slain friends and classmates and.... "This is where they dug up Butch's bones for that bonfire?"

A rhetorical question.

One by one, she had dragged them, lifeless, limp, down stairs, their heels cutting twin rails through dirt to this basement. That little girl picked out a hammer from her father's tools, and she broke up the concrete. Took up a shovel and dug. Would she have worn fuzzy yellow work gloves? Or had her hands opened with blisters, popping ugly like overcooked pepperoni, red and greasy?

Those round, smooth stones had made up the cairn Betty had assembled for her dad.

What strength.

What courage.

He felt puny. Softened by modern convenience, and American laziness. Back home, he drove two blocks to the corner store. A heated apartment was a quarter-turn of a dial away. He didn't even need to open the door to grab the newspaper from the stoop; after the timer on his automatic coffee maker brewed his first cup, he sat on his ever-widening ass and flipped through apps to find out the happenings of the world.

Even without supernatural manifestations, St. Hamelin's was a world he fundamentally did not understand. Could never understand. Intellectually, yeah, of course. But he didn't have an iota of the muscle memory of these people who had lived during St. Hamelin's frozen piece of time.

Several two-by-eight boards stood propped against a cracking wall about twenty yards away. He shuddered so hard it mimicked convulsions.

"And those?" He pointed toward the planks on which the dead children of St. Hamelin's had been posed for their final photographs. "Who took the photos?"

"Chaplain Allen and Mister Blankenheim. They came back first."

Of course. Betty had raised her father and then her mentor. Pig-headed Chaplain would have stood the murdered children next to the living orphans who'd remained—no wonder the living faces had been scared!—photographing the plank children, even though he must have known he needed the remains, too. Did he do the dirty job himself? Or had he left the wet work to Betty? Chopping them all up, storing some pieces in the chapel before burying the rest in the basement?

"The real ones started running away. Dr. Schramm didn't bother stopping them." Theodore tugged on his hand. "I don't like it down here."

"Me neither, pal. Let's get outta here."

And lay down. Rest, if not outright sleep.

Great idea, but time was speeding back up as the invisible spokes keeping St. Hamelin's together had begun snapping out of joint. Butch and Betty both died—each in their respective ways. Elijah and his boys were spinning out of control with Miles as their new prey. Schramm wanted to keep him here forever, and Chaplain wished him either "cured" of homosexuality or drawn and quartered.

Chaplain himself looked on the verge of a nervous breakdown.

Yes, they had maimed Miles, but they were also falling apart, weren't they? If he applied more pressure, he could sneak out of here in the resulting chaos.

He'd kill for some ibuprofen. Literally strangle someone for a couple Vicodin. Holy Hell, to tend the dressing wrapped around his head he'd have to rip apart the clotted blood and dried juices that had sealed the wound. His kingdom for a sterile ER, and a handsome young doctor sticking him full of the succoring sting of morphine.

He and Theodore crossed the wide expanse and ducked through another doorway. Distance between him and the graves should have eased his mind, but every step waded him deeper into a charged atmosphere. The lighting cast the world in an odd sheen like those washed-out early black and white movies. Cobwebs thick as ivy clung to the walls. At the far side of the room, a big foreboding iron box sent a metal chimney up and into the ceiling.

"This is where it is!" Aghast and triumphant, he grabbed Theodore's shoulders and turned the boy around to face him. "This is where they trap you. Seal you up."

Theodore's big eyes blinked. "What do you mean?"

Miles pointed. "The incinerator. I've heard you crying through the chute in the wall."

Theodore squinted one eye, looking up at him as if he spouted nonsense. "I've never been inside the incinerator."

Like a Novocain drip jabbed into his jugular, a freezing numbness spread through his head, down his neck, swamping his torso and legs with liquid lead.

...hollow wails of a child burbling up the incinerator chute...

Theodore watched him with the innocence of Botticelli's Madonna.

...muffled sobs floated through the air...

Anesthetized feet carried Miles toward the incinerator. Its cold bulk taunted him. The edges of the loading door smirked, becoming Elijah's face.

He crouched.

"Mr. Baumgartner?" Theodore was a gnat buzzing faintly. "Are you all right?"

...when Dr. Schramm and the chaplain found out, they were furious...

He slapped his palm on the cold and silent mass of metal.

...the chaplain took care of it...

He couldn't feel the handle when he grabbed it.

...sob...breath...sob...breath...

He took a knee and steadied himself.

...the Chaplain took care of it...

He yanked it open.

...a liquid chuffing...

Inside, cold ashes gave off the faintest of campfire perfume.

...the Chaplain took care of it...

In his mind, he had seen Chaplain strapping Janelle onto the table in the operating theater, and—angry, spurned, begrudging his transgression—scraping out the offending mortal sin.

...piercing, ragged sobs...

Chaplain had not aborted Janelle's unborn baby.

...bawling high, frantic wails...

Lying on a bed of ashes, the charred-black skeletal remains of an infant.

Chaplain had taken care of it, all right. Had brought the wriggling, crying baby down here and laid it inside. Or had Chaplain just carried the child down the hall from Janelle's room and thrown it down the chute?

...hollow thudding clomped up the incinerator...

Up? Or tumbling down, banging into the sides of the chute as it fell?

The incinerator had built up enough heat to consume skin and hair, organs, arms and legs and the less dense bones, but the arch of spine remained. The twin, curving racks of ribs. The skull, which fit neatly in his palm.

Thirty

"Mr. Baumgartner?" Theodore stood on tip-toes, looked over his shoulder. "Did you find something?" His voice went higher. Frantic. "What did you find, Mr. Baumgartner? What is that?"

When had he slid his hands under these fragile remains and pulled them out? The bones weighed nothing, but meant everything. Holding this precious horror, his nuclear anger could only be a trifle next to the fury possessing Janelle in the moments, minutes, hours, days after Chaplain's atrocity.

He laid the half skeleton back down upon the ash. He closed the incinerator so Theodore wouldn't see.

"Go find your mom."

"What are you gonna do?"

Him? He might pound his fists into the incinerator door until he crushed every metacarpal to powder. Or break into hysterical sobs. Maybe his molten anger ball would finally hit critical mass. What would that look like?

If St. Hamelin's kept pushing him, they'd all find out. Her infant discarded like trash. Her son beaten and cannibalized. What he wouldn't give to travel back in time to help her slaughter the real butchers.

Hell had better be waiting for them all when he unwove Chaplain's spell.

"Tell your mom to meet me in the chapel. Tell her that it's time."

Theodore stared, his face open and kind. A child who even now just wanted to comfort his new friend.

Friend.

Friend was good.

Friend was great. He wasn't an uncle anymore. Wasn't a boyfriend or husband. Felt further away from fatherhood than ever. Soon to be a disowned brother. But a friend? Now that was something special.

"Hurry. Don't let the other boys catch you."

Theodore did as he was told and ran to the closest door, leaving it open in his haste. His spry footsteps clapped up stairs, growing fainter every second as Miles crouched there alone, bowing his forehead to the cold metal incinerator to stop the room spinning.

His fists clenched. He fought the urge to grind his teeth to calcium dust. He choked down his violent fantasies. Packed them tight as a glutton's meal.

His hips started to complain. His lower back ached. He stood and lightly pressed the disgusting mass of shirt bandage to satisfy an itch gnawing in the skin.

Meltdown successfully contained.

Theodore would need time to find his mom. Janelle needed time to work her way down to the chapel. And he could use some time to fine-tune the idea building inside his brain. When he finished, he would head out immediately, but he hadn't forgotten the cold. How it had chewed through him. Dressed like this, he would be useless within fifteen minutes—shivering, teeth chattering and chipping away.

Lucky for him, he knew where to find a winter jacket.

All that remained of the bonfire was a steaming wound in the snow. Residual Butch-skin and hair still stank. Thin, twisting ropes of smoke curled upward to dissipate into the backdrop of a mean grey sky. Beyond the treeline, another tempest gathered. He might live through the next couple of hours only to die of exposure in the next blizzard.

But better that than hunker down until morning, spending even a single, unnecessary minute within those walls.

Like Janelle had done, Miles walked right into the cottage. He halted. A kinetic energy filled the cottage, like a downed wire snapping and sparking on the curb. A feeling like Betty had just left the living room. He'd forgotten that she wandered, somewhere, on the grounds.

He knocked on the door jamb. "Hello? Anyone here?"

No answer. And no telling if she would or could answer if she lay in her bed. Or dusted her father's jars in the deer fetus room. The fire she had stoked moments before her murder had gone cold. Whatever potpourri made the place smell like the witch's gingerbread house had also died. Lessened, at least.

He fought the urge to search the cottage. His mission was strictly in-and-out.

He tramped through the living room, passing the overstuffed chairs, the television, treading on the overlapping rugs where no one living would set foot after he was gone. He reached the mudroom and pulled down Butch's parka.

"Sorry, Butch." Miles encased himself in the big coat. Cloth lining warmed him. He knelt to browse the boots on the floor, but the truce he'd made with his ear expired, suddenly and completely. Razor wire drilled through his ear canal.

He plopped down on his butt.

The light in the small space grew incredibly bright. Then went very dark.

The agony waned, but he didn't expect any miracle during his last hours of battle.

He dug through the boots. Betty's were too small. Butch's too big. He'd find their bedroom and take some of Butch's socks to help protect his feet on his trek to Bear Falls. He found a pair of gloves and stuffed them in the coat pockets.

"Hello?" A male voice cut through the mad ringing in his ear.

Now who the hell was this? He stood—tightening that razor wire—and clutched the coat collar tight.

"Hello? You left the door open." Bootsteps trod into the living room. "Aunt Betty? Grandpa Fred?"

Aunt Betty? Now was not the time for surprises. He was almost out! He walked through the kitchen to meet the voice. They saw each other at the same time. Both stopped. Face flushed from the cold, the gangly young man looked familiar, but from where? Not from St. Hamelin's. Elsewhere.

The guy's mouth fell open. No wonder. Miles was a stinky stranger with wild hair sticking up, three-days' growth of stubble, wearing the filthy, flapping tatters of a gore-stained shirt around his head.

The young man's eyes widened. "You found Ian."

"What?" How did this guy know? "Yes, I found Ian."

"What did you do with my aunt and grandpa?" The young man's nostrils flared, and he took an aggressive step closer.

Aunt Betty. Grandpa Fred. Miles snapped his fingers. "You're the bartender from Blankenheim's." What was his name? "Graham!" Ha! He knew he knew it. "But how...? What do you know about my nephew?"

Graham's face paled. "Ian's here?"

"Yes, Ian's here. How do you know about it?"

"After all my mom's stories...." Graham studied his palms as if they held the storyboards to whatever tale he was piecing together. "And Grandpa Fred...." He blinked and looked up to Miles. "When I told Ian's mom, I really didn't know if it would work."

"You know my sister?" Miles cleared his throat and held up the teacher's hand—the command for a whole classroom of rowdy youths to shut up and calm down. Through his pulse throbbing in his throat, he spoke like a rational man. "Explain this to me. How do you know Ian? How do you know his mom?"

"Shit. It was my fault. We were just going to joyride. It was my idea. The whole thing. Stealing that car. I was so high. I lost control and the car was going so fast and we crashed and his head hit the windshield and, oh, the sound it made, and I blacked out and when I came to he was just slumped and bleeding and—"

"Slow down." Miles advanced on Graham, meaning to comfort him, calm him, but Graham mistook his intent and stumbled backward into the living room. Graham's shoe snagged on the edge of a rug, and he sprawled into the crappy recliner. Mind reeling, Miles followed him into the other room, but the fear and confusion on Graham's face stopped him.

"Graham, I...." Breathe. Just breathe. "I don't understand."

But he did.

"You talked to Minnie? To Ian's mom?"

"Uh-huh."

"You told her what St. Hamelin's could do—bring back the dead."

"That's the family story. My great-grandfather died in that accident, along with all those kids, but this place brought them all back."

Graham didn't know the whole truth, but it wasn't Miles's place to dissuade him from the cozier version of his familial legacy.

"All she needed was a small part of him. A piece of flesh. She gave me—"

"His finger."

"Yeah." Graham stared, transfixed. "It really worked? The stories are true? What's it like here? Do you know my aunt and grandpa?"

"I don't know where to begin." Miles offered a hand and helped Graham to his feet. "But first you have to tell me how you got here. Is the bridge repaired?"

"Repaired?" Graham looked taken aback. "Nothing's wrong with the bridge."

"But the snow. The bridge collapsed in the snow."

"No, it didn't."

Holy hell, he was so stupid. "They... lied?"

"Are you okay, um... sir?"

Wow, they had duped him good. He had never even thought to question the story of the bridge being out. "So to get here, you just...?"

"Drove."

He felt an acute shame like he'd swung for the fences but hit nothing but air on a wicked curveball.

Forget it. He had a getaway driver now.

"Graham, I need your help with something."

They had to walk single-file in the narrow shoveled strip to the side door.

"Where are my aunt and grandpa?" Graham shouted to be heard over his shoulder. Just like great-grandpa Butch.

"About that...." He needed this kid focused, not mourning Aunt Betty. He'd break the news once they were on the road. "What are you doing up here, anyway?"

"My mom pays for Aunt Betty's expenses. Electric. Phone bill. I have her groceries in the car."

"Your mom knows about all this?"

Graham shrugged. "Yeah."

"Who else knows? What about the five dwarves?"

"Who?"

That's right—Graham had no idea about Miles's nickname system, about Bearded, Trucker Cap, and the rest. "Those guys at the bar the other day, who wanted to kick my ass."

"No one outside the family knows about this, but most everyone in town is upset by the accident. They don't like talking about it—and don't like how it upsets my mom." Graham whipped around. "She'll kill me if she finds out what I did. You can't tell her."

"Deal." If he happened to meet Graham's mom again, the last thing he would ever do was talk about St. Hamelin's.

"Hey, are we actually going inside?" They had made it, but Graham stood apart, keeping his distance.

"Of course."

Graham craned his neck, looking up the solid grey slab of St. Hamelin's.

"You've never been inside?"

Still gazing upward, mouth hanging open, Graham shook his head.

"Do you know about the kids?"

"They haunt the place."

Miles tugged Graham's sleeve to make the young man look at him. "It's not that simple. Listen, there's a darkness here that I don't think you understand. There just isn't time to explain." And if he did, Graham might not stick around. Besides, divulging all the details wasn't necessary. With an extra set of hands, Miles could sneak in, burn those twisted fuckers, and get out before the Devil even knew what he'd done. "It's not fair of me to involve you in this, but if you help me, this won't take any time at all."

He shut up and let the weight of silence sell the deal.

Graham nodded. "Yeah. Okay." He followed Miles inside.

With its heart stilled, St. Hamelin's didn't hold onto heat. The first floor was a walk-in freezer. The architectural adornments in this corridor made Miles sick. He couldn't wait to never see it again. But Graham's mouth hung open again, wide eyes bedazzled. "I had no idea."

"Not the wreck you expected, huh, kid?" Boy, did that take Miles back.

They reached the chapel doors, and a crunch blasted from down the hall. Chaplain, in full white vestments, exploded from Schramm's office, the door slamming into the wall so hard that cobwebs parachuted off the ceiling. Even in the distance, in the shadows, Chaplain's face flushed with scarlet rage. His wormy lips writhed. His vestments billowed and turned him into a wraith flying at them down the corridor. His hands twisted into talons; he pointed a clawed finger at Graham but thundered to Miles. "Is this your *lover*?"

The indictment hung in the air with the gravitas of Old Testament condemnation. Miles pursed his lips to ask What? Who? but in the end could only stand flatfooted and stunned speechless.

Chaplain lunged at Graham, who screamed and blundered backwards. Too slow. Chaplain grabbed his flannel shirt collar and yanked him into the chapel; one skater shoe flew off and bounced on the floor like a rock skipped across a lake.

Before the doors swung closed, Miles rushed after. The undertow of Chaplain's violence caught him, swept him partway down the aisle until he skidded to a halt halfway to the waiting nightmare.

All the lights blazed. Walls glowed, golden. The cold hadn't penetrated the chapel, and Miles shrugged off Butch's parka and tossed it into a pew. But he didn't take his eyes off the row of rigid plank children in front of the altar. Seven perfect little gentlemen, hair combed, wearing spotless, crisp St. Hamelin's trousers and jackets. The boys didn't acknowledge their chaplain, or the young man tripping and sputtering in his grasp. They stared straight ahead, impervious to Janelle a few feet away, pyramiding red hardcover books like charcoal briquettes next to the pulpit.

Chaplain pulled up just shy of the communion rail, a dumb and dumbstruck look on his face. "What is the meaning of this?"

Damn, Janelle's caustic sense of justice was impressive. Her distraction—the hymnals from her desk, the ones with the gleeful drawings of his mutilation. They had separately come to the same solution. She opened the last hymnal in her hand and placed it at the peak of the small mountain.

Chaplain shook off bewilderment. Ire replaced confusion, and he crossed into the chancel, Graham hollering and clawing at the long hard fingers holding him. With his free hand, Chaplain knocked Janelle to the floor.

Her flash of surprise hardened into loathing. Good. Her well of hatred ran vast and volatile, and she would be a better ally when mad.

Ignoring her, ignoring the hymnals at his knees, Chaplain spotted Miles—his congregation of one—and raised his voice to sermon pitch. "How do you like my flock?" He hurled Graham to the floor at the plank children's feet.

The boys still did not react. The pallor of faces went beyond pale and into blue. Their unresponsive eyes held the same stoned emptiness that had been on Minnie's face as she'd sunk back down into the couch when he'd last seen her.

Same as in their pictures.

Bereft of smirks and leers and kicking and shoving, the fiends had reverted into true plank children—corpses propped up on the wooden boards from the basement. The planks rose a few inches over their heads. He hadn't noticed that at first. Hadn't seen the lengths of rope cinched under arms and around chests, tying them straight and upright to their posts.

Graham floundered on the floor below the seven dead children as the madman in clerical robes climbed into the pulpit.

Seven children?

He shouldn't have needed a head count to see the obvious. No Elijah. These knocks to the head must have muddled his brain if he failed to notice Elijah's burning bush of red hair missing from the lineup.

The cogs and gears of his plan spun and whirred to keep up with the evolving endgame.

"Young man?" Janelle picked herself up.

The Blankenheim heir goggled at the menagerie above him.

Miles's legs felt like stilts. He would topple if he tried to walk. "Graham!"

Dazed, Graham turned toward his voice.

Janelle grabbed Graham's arm and heaved. Graham had never been inside St. Hamelin's; Janelle would have made sure never to be seen. With her lover's great-grandson in tow, she met Miles at the pews.

"What did they do to you?" She reached for the horror of his bandaged head.

"Schramm cut off my ear."

She winced in empathy, and mercifully did not touch.

"What's going on?" Graham a groggy dreamer, waking.

Miles didn't like the blank slate of Graham's face. "Graham, snap out of it."

Graham's Adam's apple bobbed. He stared at the side of Miles's head. Looked to the chaplain who had grabbed him and thrown him to the ground. Breath heaving, he looked again to Miles. A glance to the children. "What's going on!"

"Don't worry about it now." He took Graham's hands and led him into the closest pew. Sat him down. "When we're back in town, I'll buy you a drink."

Graham watched his face, which was good, but the guy was out of it. Fine. He had all the help he needed with Janelle setting into motion whatever was up her sleeve. As long as Graham didn't beat feet out to his car and burn rubber back to town, stranding Miles. He patted Graham's shoulders. "We'll have a good stiff drink." Or ten. Or a hundred. Just as soon as he and Janelle ended Chaplain's mad reign.

Simple.

Thirty-One

The chapel doors flew open, and Theodore tripped into the center aisle. Behind him, Elijah carried a lumpy burlap bag. An actual potato sack. He shoved his armful into Theodore's back to spur the boy on. The contents of the sack clattered.

A familiar sound.

Graham gaped, his color draining to match the plank children's. Nothing in that young man's life of reason and order had prepared him for today, despite the years of family legend and monthly visits to the mystical St. Hamelin's to restock Aunt Betty. Was it hitting home that through all of those years, dead boys had stood at their windows, watching him?

Miles passed Janelle the key to destruction. She palmed it, and her hand barely brushed her cardigan as she pocketed it.

Miles loped up the aisle toward Elijah and Theodore.

From the pulpit, Chaplain cleared his throat.

Good God, what now? Adrenaline hit Miles's veins to fend off the plank children if they broke from their trance and rushed him. But the boys remained still, and the reverend's piercing attention focused only on Elijah, his prized acolyte, with pride glimmering in his iceberg eyes.

Theodore ran to his mom and threw his arms around her middle, hugging her tight. Janelle cooed mother-sounds to her boy and smoothed his hair. Kissed his forehead.

For the moment, Elijah waited contentedly with the unwieldy sack near the back of the chapel.

"What've you got there?"

Elijah's answered with his slick grin.

With Janelle and Theodore reunited, Miles turned away from Elijah, done with that one for now. His skin crawled as if the vile redhead wasn't just throwing daggers into his back but swarming bugs. The squeeze was on—Elijah stationed at the chapel doors and Chaplain mere feet from the sacristy, where Miles needed to go. What role the plank children would play, he couldn't guess, but with unease drying the spit from his mouth, he headed toward Chaplain's chessmen.

Husky's plump body anchored the middle of the row. Frozen, half-dead, half-alive, the whole row was a ghoulish criminal lineup, with Rocky Mountain Face at one end, his pitted skin a newsprint grey; on the other end Hare Lip's loose jaw stretched his cleft lip into a snarl.

Chaplain's flashed a genuine but chilling smile. "Beautiful, aren't they?"

"Not the word I'm thinking of."

"Mmm...." Chaplain's face softened into that condescending *I understand your troubles, my son* clergy-expression. "Do you see these young men as the Christian soldiers they are? Do you see what I have accomplished here? Do you?"

Do you? See?

"Soldiers?" He spat on the chapel floor. "Those aren't soldiers. They were barely delinquents at the start. They came to you as troubled boys, and you warped them. You told me that you wanted to save souls. That was your holy calling—no child's soul left behind. So, what is all this? Chaplain?" He twisted the title into an insult.

Not a flicker of doubt in Chaplain's eye. Miles would have to needle him harder. Chaplain had an anger monster of his own—it had peeked out through the clergyman's eyes four or five times now. Four or five moments of Chaplain getting sloppy. Just a hairline fracture, but Miles only needed a little. Once he had hold of the thread—to mix his metaphors—he'd pull until Chaplain unraveled into a Tasmanian Devil. Then he'd match Chaplain, temper for temper.

The reverend would lose.

For now, Chaplain kept his cool. "You want to know what all of this is? This is my life's work come to fruition." He puffed his chest—a proud father, a maniacal scientist. "Did you know that Christian holy days are so scheduled to replace pagan rituals? Rites of dead religions?" Chaplain's hands found the edges of the pulpit. Not letting go, he pointed a finger at Miles. "I bet you did know that. You are an educated man." His preaching tone ramped up. "In my travels, searching for Truth, I studied those pagan rituals. I did not discard, did not disregard, the heathens' practices. Willful ignorance of what came before was what led the Catholics astray all those centuries ago—seeking to cleanse the past with their Crusades." He slapped an open palm on the pulpit. "There is only one true God but myriad paths of worship. Who is Thor but our Savior? Odin but our Father? Loki the Angel of Light—Lucifer, cast down after playing the ultimate trick?" He breathed deep and cast his eyes Heavenward.

"Get to the point, Chaplain."

"The point?" Chaplain's composure faltered. His pitiful anger tried to stare Miles down.

The rage dragon did not drop its eyes.

Chaplain did. He knew it, too, and to cover, he worked his way down from the pulpit. He posted up at the end of the plank children row, his ballooning robes a stark contrast to Rocky Mountain Face's narrow shoulders, the navy-blue St. Hamelin's blazer a tight box on his lank body.

Chaplain pressed his thin lips together in a narrow white line of disdain. "You're missing the beauty of this." He gestured at his plank children. "The best way to save souls is to never allow them to die. The Indians of the Pacific Northwest were right to fear photography. Oh, it does nothing on its own, but combined with charms from whom the Haitians named Bondye, the results were startling." His expression hardened. "As you saw in the crypt."

"Haitian? You're talking about actual voodoo?"

"Precedent exists, during the plagues of Egypt. Exodus Chapter Seven, Verse Eleven. 'Then Pharaoh summoned the wise men and the sorcerers; and they also, the magicians of Egypt, did the same by their secret arts.' I studied those secret arts." Chaplain fingered the fabric of Rocky's blazer cuff. "I saved some of those sick children from damnation—until you ruined it all—but preventing spirits from entering the afterlife wasn't enough. Preservation of flesh—that was the goal. I told you what a quick study dear Betty Blankenheim was? The idea for the jars came from her, borrowing the concept from her father, actually. Did you have the chance to see his beautiful fetuses, collected from pregnant does that met a cruel fate?"

Crazy. Every one of them, even Janelle, though she was Miles's kind of crazy. Maybe the children had lost their minds by wiling away their first sixty-plus years of eternity within St. Hamelin's, but the adults' insanities began in the Fifties, when Chaplain, Schramm, Butch, Betty—and yes, his friend Janelle—had been young and fitted in their proper time. What was it about the Midwest? Gein, Gacy, Dahmer, all the real nuts came from here.

"Too bad your experiments failed."

"Failed?" Chaplain's hand snapped away from Rocky's blazer. "Open your eyes! Show respect for this miracle."

"You've preserved life, but those boys are rotten."

"Rotten?" Smug satisfaction erased off Chaplain's face.

"Soulless."

Chaplain stepped forward, a vein pulsing in his forehead. "Soulless!"

Ah, he was getting close now. Satisfaction bloomed in Miles's stomach, warm as Schramm's Scotch.

"I see flesh." He made his way down through the transept. He rested his hands on the communion rail. "But these boys' souls died with them the first time. You've created nothing holy."

Chaplain threw his hands in the air, swatting away the criticism. "What do you know? The lot of you—an adulteress, murderess, and her sniveling son?" He pointed at Miles. "And you. An abomination who dares bring his sin—" His finger swung to Graham. "—into this sanctuary."

"He's not my boyfriend, you ass." Miles belly-laughed, to irk Chaplain further. "Don't you recognize Betty's nephew? How much goes on around here that you're blind to?"

Out in the pews, Janelle gasped.

Chaplain glowered at Graham, the ladder lines on his forehead straining.

"You label Janelle a murderer. Me, a sinner." Miles rummaged through Sunday School memories for a verse. "How dare you cast stones when your own house is in disorder?"

Chaplain in his vestments quaked with boiling rage.

A hymnal flew past Miles's ear, pages rattling in its arc toward Chaplain. Miles swung around. Janelle grabbed one of Graham's hands and guided it around Theodore's much smaller one. She plucked another hymnal out of the rack, stepped into the middle of the aisle, and flung the book. She had a good arm; the book clapped into the floor at Chaplain's feet alongside the first missile. A blizzard of dust motes jittered like the sparks over Butch's bonfire. Janelle ducked into the opposite pew and grabbed an armful. She pitched the topmost, end over end, and it banged into Chaplain's shin.

"Stop this puerile display at once." Chaplain rubbed the spot where the hymnal had connected.

Janelle laughed, a single hard "Ha!" She advanced, chucking a hymnal high. A second book zinged immediately through the air, low and flat.

Chaplain ducked the first, and the second connected with his face. "Fuck." He went down to one knee.

Elijah threw down his bag with a clatter like hollow bowling pins. Whose bones were those? Elijah sprinted down the center aisle and wrapped Janelle in his arms. Janelle twisted, slipped free, but Elijah caught the hem of her cardigan and leaned all the way back, keeping Janelle close.

Graham dropped Theodore's hand and bolted toward the scuffle in the aisle. He body-checked Elijah into the oak back of a pew with a sharp *crack* of breaking wood or Elijah's arm.

Elijah couldn't pale further than he already was, but he hit the floor like he'd fainted dead away. Yet he didn't let go of Janelle's hem. Graham pried Elijah's fingers off the sweater, and while the redhead lay dazed, Graham sat on him. Neither had much weight to them, but Blankenheim had the slightest advantage in heft and maturity. Elijah was out of the fight for a while.

Throwing hymnals, Janelle worked her lilac breeze up beside Miles. "Don't just stand there." She pelted a hymnal at Chaplain's face. "Go!"

Chaplain duck-and-covered, fleeing to the other side, away from the sacristy.

Under Janelle's covering fire, Miles darted into the chancel. He slipped by the plank children. Like sleepers who dream with lids only partially closed, thin slivers of their eyes showed white. Clay figures with the breath of life stored inside their lungs. Of course, they were more like sleeping rattlesnakes. Chaplain had charmed them into this line, and Miles sure the hell better finish before they wakened to fulfill their ghoulish purpose.

In the aisle, Elijah wriggled out from under Graham and skittered away. Graham scrambled and lunged, dragging Elijah backward, collapsing on the boy and pinning him down once more.

Out of ammunition, Janelle rushed to the front, toward the original pile of hymnals she'd laid.

Chaplain's arms fell from their protective shield over his head. He crouched under the painting of Job's trials. The cords in his neck strained. "What gives you the right...?"

"Gives?" Her face flushed from exertion and her own building rage. "Anything I want, I need to *take*." She extracted what Miles had given her from her pocket. "You taught me that." The hanging ceiling fixtures reflected off the lighter's hood. She flicked the spark wheel and touched the flame to the open book on top. The brittle paper caught, unfurling a thin, steady trickle of smoke.

In the row of plank children, a flutter.

Miles's leg prickled from the bite mark that branded him. Seconds bled from his internal clock. He double-timed it to the sacristy door—Butch's last task for St. Hamelin's must have been to hang a new one, but he hadn't gotten around to planing the edges. An eighth of an inch too big, the door was wedged into the frame, leaving the lock useless.

Breaks were still falling his way.

He tugged. The door popped open like a cork, and a muscle under his right shoulder blade *twang*ed as if plucked. His right arm spasmed. Reinvigorated, his ear wound throbbed.

He willed that crap out of his mind.

The credens had been closed up, so Chaplain must have noticed his notebook missing, but nothing else had been moved or hidden—jars sat undisturbed on the shelves. That bravado would undo him today.

From its place, Elijah's umber-haired head watched him.

"Say goodbye, kid."

Puffy lips pouted.

He slid his hands over the cool, smooth glass. His palms and fingerpads tingled. The short hairs on the back of his neck stood up. Preservative sloshed as he picked it up. The weight irritated the scapular muscle he'd just pulled. Jostled, Elijah's head turned away, sly.

He carried the jar, formaldehyde shivering and lapping up the sides. Elijah's head tilted downward in disapproval. Miles cradled the jar against his chest to secure it. Now Elijah's head felt too close. The chill of the glass like breath. He ground his teeth, and another tooth imploded. A shard lodged into his gums, and blood squirted onto his tongue.

Miles lugged the jar into the chancel. His arms shook, not with strain but from a swell of anger. He stood abreast of the row of boys, who remained still as sentries.

Wait.

Had Teeth's dish-water grey smile widened?

Had Husky inclined his face toward the sacristy just the tiniest bit?

They all seemed to have moved a fraction of an inch in the minutes he'd been gone.

Janelle knelt beside her fire. She tore hymnal pages from their bindings, balled them loosely, and stuffed them into empty spaces among the piled books. The wadded paper sprouted tiny flames. Those tiny flames engorged. Multiplied. A haze steamed out from nooks and crannies.

Chaplain edged toward her.

Flames snapped and rose as the fire found its breath. It chewed into exposed pages, and the haze thickened into a black cloud, lifting off toward the ceiling.

The row of dead boys quivered.

Prone underneath Graham, Elijah's eyes locked onto his own head in the jar. "No!" His fingers dug into the floor, and he bucked Graham off his back. As he scrambled, he kicked Graham in the tender arc under the eye at the side of his nose. Getting to his feet, he snatched up his bag of bones and limped toward the front of the chapel.

"Elijah." Chaplain's attention vacillated between the bag and the fire.

At the front row of pews, Elijah paused. His gaze flitted from the jar to Miles's eyes. The boy shifted his weight from one foot to the other; the contents of the sack clacked. Elijah looked to the fire. Smirked.

Miles stood closer, but he had to fish out the head. Elijah could simply pitch the whole bag. But whose remains did Elijah have in there?

Chaplain charged, shouting incoherently. He lowered a shoulder into Janelle, and they both fell, sprawling, their legs knocking into the burgeoning bonfire. A third of the pile sheared away in an avalanche of sparks and ashy pages. The pyramid of books wounded, the fire sputtered.

"No!" Miles looked up just as Elijah's focus jumped from the damaged fire to him once again.

Chaplain's robes covered Janelle like fallen sails. They grunted and brawled, rolling; their entangled limbs cracked into the pulpit, sending shivers up its wooden sides.

Should he help? He felt like he should help. His biceps quivered from the weight of the jar.

Janelle and Chaplain hit the chapel wall, shaking the portrait of the fiery furnace.

Right. The jar was more important. In his arms, Elijah's head still rotated in waterlogged slow motion, like the first time revealing the brow, the nose, the chin. Elijah's wicked smile preserved on the wide mouth. But hadn't the eyes been open before? The sides suddenly felt greasy, slippery. The jar slid a half inch through his hands. He juggled his grip to cradle from the bottom. Inside, the boy's eyelids popped open. Lips parted.

Elijah screamed. "Put me down!"

Which Elijah? He didn't even know.

The jar slid another half inch. Behind the glass, the head bobbed in the sloshing liquid—Elijah nodding. Miles shuddered and lost his hold.

Elijah in the aisle jolted forward from the front pews but stopped at the communion rail. The burlap sack dangled from one hand.

The jar slammed upright into the floor with a solid thud. Preservative hit one side like a wave pool. Elijah's head bounced against the glass, and the jar teetered. Tipped. The sealant around the top cracked, the lid popped off, and the jar vomited its stinking contents. The head thumped end over end. Liquid chugged out, hit the edge of the fire, and a giant *shushhh* blew upward with a swarm of sparks like flaming gnats. The fire hissed and burped. Shrunk into itself for a second before the formaldehyde fumes went up with a brilliant pop of flame and stink, a devil's breath that blew Miles backward into the row of boys on their boards.

Their blazers and trousers rippled in the shockwave. The narrow slits of their eyelids snapped wide open. Waking, they shuffled against their planks—a sound like riffling through pages and photographs. Addled glances at Miles, the ceiling, the fire.

Agog, Elijah stood at communion rail.

Graham closed in, but began to watch the roiling smoke spread across the ceiling.

Miles scooped up Elijah's cold, slippery head. He gagged as bile hit the back of his throat. He quaked convulsively and tossed the sodden mass like a hot potato into the burning pile. Hymnals shifted like a campfire really getting going for the night.

Elijah screamed and hit the floor.

A mean orange light glowed inside and among the hymnals. Heat ripples shimmered above the covers like they were hot tarmac. The head rolled off into a puddle of flame where the preservative had ignited.

Elijah dragged himself up into the chancel, over steaming floorboards. Flames tasted the edges of the pulpit. Sediment irritated Miles's eyes, and he burst into flushing tears.

Elijah pushed up to his hands and knees and crawled toward his head. On his actual face, his freckled cheeks reddened. The skin darkened. As his severed head scorched, his own face started a monstrous sunburn. He grabbed up his head from the embers, scooched back, sat on his heels, and cradled it against his chest.

On their planks, the other boys wrestled against their ropes. Their fingers wriggled; shoulders shook as they twisted. Their eyes cleared and came to sharp life. Behind them, flames swept up the linen altar cloth, gorging on the fabric.

Janelle pushed Chaplain off her, her hair frizzed, the Cardigan torn and stretched out of shape. Her busted lower lip dribbled blood down her chin. She backhanded it off. Chaplain rose more slowly. Scratches bled battle stripes across his face. He picked at his robes, grabbed the bottom hem, and pulled the vestments up over his head, leaving him in his cassock. Balling up the robes like so much trash, he cast them into the flames engulfing the pulpit.

Low, blue flames boiled over the varnished walls of the chancel. Out of the thunderheads of smoke on the ceiling, flames poked. The paintings of saints melted, and brightly-colored strips of canvas dripped to the floor.

"Janelle. We have to get out."

Smoke churned from the wooden slats as they blackened. The smoke filling the chapel thickened into dense fog. Miles yanked up his shirt, exposing his belly to the heat of the blaze, and covered his mouth.

Muffled, he cried out. "Janelle!" He plunged a hand into the smoke to take her hand, but she pointed over his shoulder.

"Watch out!"

Elijah emerged through the smoke, his sunburnt face the same red as the beating heart of the fire. "Say goodbye to Miss Poole and her little brat."

Chaplain bolted forward. "Don't!"

Elijah flung Theodore and Janelle's remains into the fire. He shrugged at Chaplain. "What?"

Theodore ran through smoke and flame to join his mom. She went to her knees and held her boy close. The back of his head, the backs of her hands, blurred with white smoke. She wrapped her arms tight around Theodore and stood, picking him up and holding him against her shoulder. He laid his head on her breast, his eye catching Miles; he smiled as the side of his face fell away like a chalk drawing blown into dust. Jan looked like a chalk drawing blown into dust.

Janelle mouthed *Thank you*. Or maybe she spoke. The fire rumbled so loud.

From their feet, ribbons of fire swept up their legs, clothing them in a blinding conflagration. As if an atomic wind hit them, they blasted apart into powder.

Miles turned away. His insides felt cored out.

The plank children were breaking out of their bonds, but Elijah didn't help them. He ran into the sacristy, still holding his own severed head.

Let him do his best.

Miles hurdled down past the communion rail. An ocean of fire drenched the floor. A fiery path blazed into the aisle, around Graham's feet.

"Those...." Soot cracked along the edges of Graham's mouth. "Those two people just died."

"They're free now."

In thickening smog, the boys at the front of the chapel were indistinct shapes.

Chaplain shrieked and blundered past the blazing tower that used to be his pulpit. Like the ash rained down upon Pompeii, a thick coat of talc covered him head to toe.

Cremated Janelle and Theodore, settling an old score.

A coughing fit seized Miles. Head swimming, he doubled over and grabbed his knees. His mouth filled with a viscous clot of phlegm. He spat it out.

"Graham?" Sweat streamed down his cheeks. Down his sides. "Graham, we're getting outta here." The cauterized flesh from his severed ear absorbed the intense heat, turning that whole side of his head into a furnace that he could not pull away from.

At the pulpit, a pale light penetrated the smoke— the Chaplain-form. From the inside out, a glow pressed against the suffocating second skin, like a lightbulb behind a silk screen.

One of the ceiling lights snapped from its mounting and whistled to the floor, shattering into a billion sharp pieces.

The bottoms of Miles's feet were getting hot while he stood in the aisle with Graham.

The glow diffusing through Chaplain pushed through pores in the shell. Cracks appeared. Fissures widened. The dusting chipped and fell away, leaving Chaplain a martyr burning at the stake. He beat the flames on his chest, muttering a stream of obscenities.

Miles took Graham by the shoulder, led him through this oven. Orange flames snapped through the smoke like lightning through storm clouds. Another ceiling light whistled to the floor. They barely scrambled out of the way.

Thirty-Two

Every thing that may abide the fire, you shall make it go through the fire, and it shall be clean.

Why did people talk about the cleansing properties of fire? There was nothing purifying about this loathsome thing. Alive—breathing, eating, multiplying—it growled. It belched smoke and shat soot. St. Hamelin's desiccated wooden construction laid itself out as a feast for this wild demon.

Towing Graham along, Miles coughed and gagged his way through the fire's throat. A juicy string of spit dangled from his lip. It whipped off as he pulled Graham close and shoved him first through the chapel doors.

A smudge on fire, Chaplain staggered to the nave, smoke swirling from his passage. He fell to the floor. Hopefully he suffered, grinding flames deeper into his flesh as he floundered, gasping for final breaths. Were those his screams? Or joints coming undone? Smoke coalesced once more into a solid, rising mass, burying Chaplain forever.

Miles dragged contrails of smoke into the clear air of the hallway where they shredded and drifted away. Chapel doors wouldn't hold back the fire for long. Already, heat butted through them.

Graham pulled out his phone. "We have to call somebody." His shaking fingers kept hitting the wrong numbers for his lock screen password. "The police. Fire department." His teeth chattered.

Soon enough, Miles's own adrenaline rush would crash. He needed every precious second. "Forget the fire department. It's just us now."

Smoke seeped from the narrow crevices between the jamb and the doors. Graham stepped farther away. "Then let's go."

"Just one thing left to do."

Graham's basset-hound eyes pleaded.

Maybe he had done enough. Janelle and Theodore would never be raised again. He could quit while ahead, flee and never look back.

Tempting.

But Elijah had saved his head, and the rest of the plank children would right now be carrying their jars to safety. Or maybe they didn't even need to. Those jars held only pieces; most of their skeletal remains lay buried in the basement grave. Monsters would continue running St. Hamelin's.

They needed to pay for the evils they had committed.

"Miles Baumgartner!" Schramm's baritone cut a path through the crunching fire. Through Miles's missing ear and bandaged head. "What is the meaning of this?" He tromped down the hallway, flapping his hand to clear smoke from his face. A face that darkened to an unhealthy indigo as he hurried his weight down the hall in that three-piece-suit he must have died in.

Graham sighed. "Thank God."

Miles held Graham's trembling hands. "Listen up." But Graham was watching an authority figure approaching to set everything right. Miles pulled Graham's chin down to face him. "Hey. Go out to your car. Wait for me there."

Graham's eyes wandered back to his savior in the swanky business suit.

Miles shook Graham's hands as if they were craps dice. "Pay attention. That man's no good. Wait in the car. Don't leave without me."

Schramm slowed. Stopped. "You did this." He wheezed and doubled over in a coughing fit. No dirt and beetles this time.

Miles nudged Graham to get moving, but Blankenheim didn't budge.

A black wall of smoke blew open the chapel doors. Flames curled like fingers grasping for purchase on the lintel. The compression wave of heat rocked Miles back on his heels. The stink of a thousand housefires disgorged into the hall.

Chaplain teetered out. Singed edges of the cassock flapped in tatters. The front pleats smoked. His neck had charred like the skin of grilled sausage. Blisters pocked his face. Around them, his melted skin shined, smooth. His eyebrows and eyelashes had burned off. His true self revealed—a horrid disfigured devil. His eyes rolled, wild and mad. He smiled, and burned patches of skin cracked open. "Sodomite!" The word rasped from his smoke- and flame-ruined throat. "The Lord has brought His judgement."

"Janelle started the fire, you idiot."

"Behold and lo...." Chaplain's voice crackled as he raised his volume. "...the smoke of the land goes up like the smoke of a furnace." He broke down in sobs or cackling laughter that wracked him til his legs buckled. From the floor, he lifted his face. Bared his teeth.

Graham hadn't moved from Miles's side.

"Go to the car!"

"I'm not gonna leave you here."

An ungodly crash resounded from inside the inferno. More pendant lights falling from the ceiling, or the ceiling itself?

"I need to get to the basement. You'll slow me down."

The walls on either side of the chapel scorched to a dusty grey.

"Sinful nation." Chaplain's voice breaking apart. "Laden with iniquity. Offspring of evildoers." He gasped and got to his knees. "You have forsaken the Lord." Wailing, he launched himself at Graham.

"Get off!" Miles started for them, but Schramm seized him from behind.

Chaplain dragged Graham toward the chapel.

Miles horse-kicked backward; his foot connected, and Schramm's restraining hands fell away.

Graham screamed, and Chaplain wrapped an arm around his neck, choking off the sound. An intimate embrace, they waltzed backward toward apocalyptic heat. Graham dug fingers into Chaplain's arm, but the reverend was too damaged already and crossed the threshold into brimstone. Smoke folded over Graham. The doors closed and sealed them in.

"You condemned that boy." Schramm nursed his inner thigh, where Miles hoped he'd left one hell of a bruise.

"What did you say?"

"Meddling." Schramm *tsk-tsk-tsk*ed.

The rage dragon snapped.

Miles shoved both his hands into Schramm's chest. The superintendent faltered backward with a rancid *oof*. Miles clasped his hands together in a mace of flesh, and swung. He missed high, striking the hard bone of Schramm's forehead. His hands flew apart, knuckles smarting. The rage dragon spit flame, raising Miles's anger into a freebased high. He closed in and belted Schramm in the ear. He punched the idiotic grimace off Schramm's face. Cartilage crumpled, blood exploded out the nostrils and Schramm's whole nose, beet red, swelled to twice its size.

Miles shrieked with mad laughter.

Hands cupping his broken nose, Schramm backpedaled, tripped over his polished wingtips, and crashed to the floor where he curled into a protective ball.

Miles charged the chapel doors and wrenched them open. His eyes snapped closed against the smoke. A couple feet in, heat formed a tangible wall that he couldn't break through. Orange light pressed against his closed lids. He opened his eyes just a crack, and tears welled up in defense, spilling over and cutting channels through the grime coating his cheeks.

A jet stream of smoke rushed past, pouring out the open doors. In the dusky layers of sediment, Chaplain stood not far, Graham in a headlock, throat crushed.

"'And the king's counselors saw that the fire had not had any power over the bodies of those men....'"

Graham's wild, pleading eyes bulged. Chaplain sneered with the effort of squeezing harder, and Graham's face darkened from red to crimson. Graham's feet lifted off the ground, and his color deepened to maroon. Graham's feet beat against the smoke. Spit clung to his shuddering lips. His hands fell away from Chaplain's arms.

Chaplain dumped Graham to the floor.

"'The hair of their heads was not singed, their mantles were not harmed....'"

Miles ran farther into this smelter's heat, his skin feeling loose and melty.

Graham's chest heaved, and he coughed up thick drool. His eyes rolled. His mouth moved; maybe he spoke, but if he did, Miles didn't hear.

Graham's chest did not rise again.

Miles snaked an arm under the young man's neck, the other under his knees. He lifted, but his shoulder gave out, and he had to lower Graham back to the floor. Breathing hurt.

Chaplain pulled Miles to his feet, and his lips peeled back over dirty teeth. "'God smote the wicked.'" His vocal cords were destroyed by the hellfire he'd waited for his whole life.

"'And no smell of fire had come upon them!'" Chaplain opened wide his arms, accepting the judgement of his Lord God. But Providence made a liar of him as damnation spun him into a pillar of fire, consuming his speech before devouring meat and muscle with ferocious appetite.

Miles retreated. The air he pulled into his lungs thickened like wet concrete. His mouth tasted like charcoal. He held his breath but smoke had already gotten in. So dizzy. His legs numbed. His head floated as his numb legs summoned the muscle memory to walk him back into the hallway. Haze undulated down both directions and filled the corridor to the side door. Singed hairs on his arms and back of his neck stung like red ant bites.

No sign of Schramm. The coward inside the brute had shown himself, and even the high and mighty superintendent had run away.

Reason screamed at him to do the same, but the rage inside him burned hotter and brighter than the chapel. Crippling weight of death and destruction landed on Miles's shoulders. That feisty Blankenheim woman had lost her son today, and unless Miles finished the job, Graham's death would mean nothing.

His dragon growled to him that Schramm would never have abandoned St. Hamelin's. Schramm's duty was preservation of the horrors here, and that meant only one place he would have gone.

Miles hurried to the basement entrance that Theodore had brought him out of.

He had digging to do.

Thirty-Three

Miles ran down the stairwell, blessedly cold and clear. Scant comfort. He needed to dig up makeshift graves before Schramm had a chance to pull out all the bones and hide them.

How much of a head start did Schramm have?

The whirlwind of these last hours made it hard to think. He'd only been inside the chapel fetching Graham for a few seconds. A minute at the most.

Not very long. Could he have done more for the boy?

Elijah's formaldehyde-soaked head flashed through his mind. The soggy, loose skin simmering at the edge of the fire. Red hair smoldering

And the real Elijah gaping at him, at the fire, watching himself burn.

Made Miles laugh.

Made him scream.

In the incinerator room, he refused to look at the big oven. Just standing this close made his gorge rise. Crying erupted from the metal box. Obviously an infant's. How could he have mistaken that wail? He hurried away from the hitching scream, slicing through the atoms jittering in the air from Schramm's path minutes ago.

His footsteps marked the time, pounding out seconds.

Still in a suit jacket, Schramm knelt at the wide swath of earth where St. Hamelin's secrets had been buried. Dirt clumped in his tousled hair, caked into the creases of his knuckles. He turned his twitching, manic face at the noise of Miles's entrance.

That which you mistake for madness is but an over acuteness of the senses.

Schramm watched Miles for a moment, eyes vacant, then bent to his excavation. Stretching out, his belly pressed into the tilled dirt, he raked his fingers through the earth. He grunted and pulled a long bone free from the shadows thick as a funeral shroud. Schramm set it upon a skeleton cairn of ulnas, tibias, and femurs.

Schramm swiped a hand through forehead sweat, leaving a pitch-black streak.

"Where were you going to take them?"

Schramm didn't slow.

Miles ran and slid to his knees beside him. Schramm glanced over but continued digging. Miles shoved his hands into the dirt and started scooping. His fingers found the pebbled ridge of teeth in a jaw. He extracted a skull and laid it to his right. He went back in for more, stirring a fecund odor into the musty basement. Miles grabbed and pulled free a child's arm bone. He dropped it on top of the skull. He jerked forward into the earth, tugging out pieces of Husky, or Rocky, or Hare Lip.

Overhead, the rafters squealed, a long, pained cry like slaughtered pigs. Dust and debris sifted down upon Miles's upturned face, specters of suffering whipping down through the air. He spit to clear his mouth.

Schramm craned his neck and watched the ceiling. "What is that?"

Miles had heard those words before, a hundred lifetimes ago.

Miles opened his mouth to answer, but thoughts cooked to steam and evaporated. One... two.... He fought for focus. Four... five.... At six, he snapped back, fully conscious. Between them, he and Schramm had exhumed an impressive amount of grisly remains. But was it nine boys' worth? Plus Schramm himself and Chaplain?

The ceiling groaned, on and on, a never-ending, warbling moan, vibrating in his bones. A second violent cracking spewed chunks of ceiling.

Schramm's superiority complex would have insisted the man dig himself up first. Which meant that his bones were vulnerable. And surely, enough of each boy had been exhumed by now, piled up here on the cracked concrete floor. Exposed.

Let St. Hamelin's kill itself. Miles scrambled away on hands and knees.

Schramm stared dumbly up as a ragged tear split a foot-wide gash in the heavens above. Burning rubble fell. The ceiling shook, loosening one of the thick ancient rafters. One end swung down, a lever that ripped off its other end, and in a firework-display of sparks spitting through the schism in the chapel floor, the ceiling beam pile-drived into Schramm's upturned face.

His head exploded in a shower of chunky gore.

The ceiling buckled with a demonic roar. The floor of the chapel tilted into the ceiling of the basement, and in a rain of Hellfire, slabs of wall and flooring crushed and buried Schramm's headless corpse.

Hot wind slapped Miles's face. Kicking and pushing, he slid farther backward, scraping skin off his palms on the rough floor.

The breaches overhead yawned wider. Another and another rafter broke off and slammed into the floor, cratering the concrete with their impact. Falling over each other like giant pick-up sticks, they pulverized the piles of bones as they landed.

The apertures above opened wide, and figures clad in white flame spiraled down—angels expelled from Heaven.

Not angels.

Plank children plummeting from the chapel hit the pyre with splashes of flame. Raw screams barely heard over the conflagrant bedlam of St. Hamelin's, eaten from the inside out.

Miles grabbed hold of a joist and pulled himself to his feet, tearing new abrasions in his hands.

Burning bodies rolled off the rubble pile. Miserable, grasping death reached out arms with skin burned off. He didn't recognize any of the boys as they dragged disintegrating bodies toward him. Gasping. Eyeballs black. Moaning. Begging for more life? Pleading for death? Trying to pull him to the fire?

Miles kicked at them. They wailed and writhed over the ground, skin and tissue melting. Consumed by fire, they left carbonized stains in vague human shapes.

Coughing threw barbs in his slice-and-diced ear canal and spangles in his vision. He shuffled through the thick gout of smoke, toward the door that would take him into the incinerator room and from there, above ground.

Tears washed out some of the smoke and dust but couldn't keep up. Miles rubbed his eyes to clear them, but that ground the particles into his corneas. Blinded, he swatted at the air, so thick that walking felt like swimming. Away from fire. Away from St. Hamelin's final wave of death.

Wails still rang in his head.

You are a silly little boy.

Janelle's baby had bawled into the night with only its basic bone structure left. Had the plank children burned thoroughly, torched to oblivion?

Mucus coated his throat. Following an insectile instinct to scurry from noise and heat, he pressed on for cleaner, cooler air. But he should have come to the incinerator room door by now. He checked over his shoulder. The cloud of smoke, still building mass, rolled after him. So easy—too easy—to image Husky and Teeth, or Hare Lip, Rocky, shambling after him.

Just an ignorant, silly little boy.

The true horror back there? Graham's charred shell, an innocent discarded among the wretched dead. Growling, he tramped further into unrecognizable reaches of the basement. He'd missed the door, taken a wrong hallway. Gotten himself lost.

There was no need to panic.

St. Hamelin's had fooled him before, turned him around. He'd always found his way.

Absolutely no need to panic.

Every breath hurt deep in his lungs, but he stepped up his flagging pace.

In another twenty or fifty feet, narrow windows crenelated the top of the foundation walls. Snow covered the ground-level windows, but enough meagre light shone through to light his way. He'd been right not to panic. He'd kept his head and come through it all right.

Except that nothing looked familiar.

Walls narrowed into a passage, and light faded as he went. At the edge of what illumination remained, the corridor rounded a bend.

No other option.

Don't you agree? Aren't you just a silly little boy?

He turned the corner into total darkness. After several paces, the cold pressing at his back felt alive. Squirrely.

Were those footsteps?

He glanced over his sore shoulder, and against a backdrop of pitch black, orange spots danced.

The boys?

He'd been right to worry. Towhead or Husky followed at a distance, crispy, embers glowing in the husks of their bodies.

You'd better run off and play with the others. They think you're batty.

Or were the light bursts imprints of the flames against his retinas?

Or imprints in his mind, flames that he would never forget?

Each step rocketed agony into his ear canal. Every stride tweaked his back. The beating his body had taken these last days caught up with him. Even if the path ahead were lit, he couldn't have seen through the pain overtaking him.

What are you doing out here all alone?

He picked up the pace and gritted his teeth. A shriek of shearing rock filled his head, and he spat out another grape nut of tooth.

Aren't you afraid of me?

His flesh crawled, sensing disfigured plank children in relentless pursuit.

Calm down, calm down—repeated as a mantra. He felt untethered in this total blackness. Weightless. Maybe he wasn't moving at all. The air felt loose. Vast. If he went to his hands and knees, at least the sensory input would keep him company.

There isn't anyone to help you.

Footsteps or his pulse or the relapsing *beat-beat-beat* from his ear chased him. He'd been right about the footsteps in the stairwell to the crypt. He had shushed his instincts then, and Chaplain had snuck up on him.

Fancy thinking the Beast was something you could hunt and kill!

Those orange flashes weren't flames burnt onto his eyes. Or into his memories. Or even boys on fire. No, that was red hair, singed but aglow. Elijah's head. Floating in formaldehyde. Floating in the darkness, inches from his face right now.

You knew, didn't you? I'm part of you? Close, close, close! I'm the reason why it's no go? Why things are what they are?

He wanted to tear the skin off his face, the feeling of being watched had become so unbearable. Scopaesthesia—the psychic staring effect. What was the name of that blond Abercrombie guy in freshman psychology he'd had drinks with? If he'd settled down with—Matt, Matt Miller—none of this would have happened. Change in the timeline. Butterfly flaps its wings....

Manic thoughts.

But the last time he'd felt eyes upon him, he'd also been right.

He spun his arms in futile search for a wall or a support post or a doorway to orient himself.

Get back to the others and we'll forget the whole thing.

Where was the way out!

St. Hamelin's had swallowed him up just like the whale had gobbled Jonah.

Cement filled his chest. His lungs burned. He choked and coughed and choked again, hacking until his mouth tasted full of old pennies.

Were his eyes open or closed?

His shoulder bumped a hard, flat surface. His hands explored. A wall. He followed it, sliding his palms along what felt like mortared stone. The roughness opened up the tears and slices in his hands that had glued closed with dried blood.

You know perfectly well you'll only meet me down there—so don't try to escape.

Had Elijah fallen through the chapel cave-in?

My poor misguided child, do you think you know better than I do?

Or had Elijah gotten the jump on all of them and fled. Always the sneaky one, always one step ahead.

I'm warning you. I'm going to get angry.

Still feeling his way along the abrasive wall, his fingers hit a bump. With both hands, he made out a ridge. Rectangular. His fingers fluttered. Found a switch. Flipped it. And then there was light; and the light was good.

D'you see?

He chuckled. Grimaced at the ghoulish sound of it. Yeah, he saw. He squinted against the brightness that overpowered him after the void. In the huge chamber, a dozen or more support beams threw crisscrossing shadows. No punishment boxes, thank God. Green-black mold furred the walls. Across the room, mostly buried under fungus....

A door?

Yes.

A door meant an exit.

He jogged—the sudden glut of relief compensated for his ear wound pounding with every stride.

The way out.

Of course, the door wouldn't open, would it? Why would St. Hamelin's let him go now? It wouldn't budge. The lights would douse. St. Hamelin's would avalanche down upon him and seal him in forever.

With the rats.

With the children.

We are going to have fun on this island! So don't try it on, my poor misguided boy, or else.

He swiped away slippery mold and attacked the latch. The door opened with the pop and sigh of a broken seal. Miles checked over his shoulder. No ghosts. No zombies. No half-living abominations. The plank children had burned. He'd made it. He turned back around, to his way out.

Elijah's green eyes floated there in the dark.

Thirty-Four

"No...." He was so close. "No, you're dead."

"Of course I am. And I hid my bones before digging up Butch." The eyes darted forward.

Miles jerked back, ready for teeth to clamp down on his forearm. Or neck. Elijah's bite tearing through flesh and ripping out an artery.

A string of ceiling bulbs flickered on overhead, dirty yellow and dim through their coat of grime. Elijah's broiled face stood between Miles and a narrow stone corridor. Some kind of service passage.

Why did he hear Janelle's voice inside his head? A story about a tunnel.

No, that was Ian.

Right?

Elijah had lost or abandoned his jacket. Soot striped his Oxford shirt. Cigarette-burn-sized holes dotted the fabric. And his neck. His collar had ripped most of the way off. Glistening blisters pebbled his brow and nose and swept down the right side of his face. His ear had burned off—a taste of justice there—along with most of his red hair. Where the fire had torched his severed head, the black shredded skin on Elijah's own left side looked like a marshmallow held too long in the campfire.

He still carried the head, tucked under his arm.

Elijah now looked like the warped, twisted monster he'd always been on the inside, but he did not look beaten. Both eyes glared, livid and brilliant through the peeling mess of his face. Delight. Hunger. He flashed teeth, like he would literally eat Miles up.

Tunnel.... Ian's tunnel had no light at the end. But it was still Janelle's voice that spoke. What about a tunnel?

Then he had it. That first afternoon, back when Janelle had seemed to hate him, she'd told him about a tunnel from St. Hamelin's to the cafeteria. This had to be it, right? He'd found his way out, underneath the fires above. The only obstacle? Elijah.

Miles screwed his face into a war mask. Rolled his fingers into fists. He beckoned his anger.

But all it did was snap and crackle, a dud firecracker.

Joy lit Elijah's face; he'd seen the frustration. He smiled, and dead skin sloughed off his chin. A patch of white jawbone showed.

That fucking smile.

Those biting teeth.

The boy crushed and tore rodents apart like it was a party trick.

The rat-killer tortured kids smaller and younger than him.

Had beaten and bitten Theodore to death in the showers.

Dammit. It was no use. Where his anger had nestled all his life, Miles found only a pathetic fizzle. His rage had finally depleted. Now. After all those years, his rage dragon had spewed the last of its vitriol, deflated, and died.

Elijah smelled blood in the water, just as sure as he stood there blocking Miles's route. But Miles stood tall. Elijah had no limits to cruelty, but he was no more than a bully, bullheaded and ignorant. Couldn't even be bothered to read the novel Miles had handed out. Nope, he'd just destroyed it. Kid really could have related to that book. Could have learned something.

Miles's temper had enslaved him for years, he'd overcome it once. He was smart. Educated. He read anything he could get his hands on.

Anything.

Anything at all.

He unclenched his fists. "You should have read *Lord of the Flies*, instead of ripping it up."

Elijah scoffed, that dismissive-disgusted sound universal to all teenagers.

Could Miles remember what he needed? He glared down and stood toe-to-toe. "I used to be the same way, but I changed. Ian knows this story." He looked down his nose at Elijah's wrecked face and tried a smirk of his own. Felt good. "I read anything I can find."

Elijah tightened his grip on his severed head and cradled it close against his side. A flicker—of doubt?—flashed in those eerie jade eyes. Still no anger, but a resuscitating fusion of joy and anxiety expanded inside Miles. The twirling-stomach pleasure of the roller coaster's first plunge over the edge. Miles had him. Elijah hadn't thought of everything.

Elijah fidgeted. "Stop smiling like that."

"I only read one book while I've been here, but it was a page-turner."

A complicated twitch of Elijah's lips—sneer... frown... bravado... fear.

"Did you know?"

The voice of a small child. "Know what?"

"Betty Blankenheim helped Chaplain with your...." Miles flapped a hand at Elijah and stressed the disgust of the next word. "Experiments."

Elijah fell back half a step. "'Course I know."

"Yeah? Did you know she wrote it all down? All the prayers to say over your remains."

Miles darted forward. Elijah twisted away, protecting the head in his arms. Miles pushed Elijah in the back, hard. "Everything done can be undone."

Elijah's feet tangled, and he fell to the ground with a frustrated yelp.

Good. Miles needed just a little bit of time. What he said was true, but Betty had filled the Moleskine cover to cover with her flowing, looping script. Page after page after page with what he assumed were prayers or curses or incantations. But in languages from around the world. Many with foreign alphabets like Cyrillic.

Elijah clambered to his feet, one of those disjointed toys that reassembled with the push of a button. His arms and legs flapped loosely before stiffening into place. The boy just couldn't stand to lose the upper hand; he started toward Miles.

Truth was, he hadn't exactly pored over Betty's notes. He recalled a scattering of meticulously recorded instructions. He summoned the pages to his forebrain like photographs to examine. Extraordinary illustrations had been sketched above and below the phrases. Some of the lines had looked decidedly Hebrew. Others what he took for Greek. A notation on one of the first implied they were the very words Christ spoke to Lazarus, calling him back to the living.

The last thing he wanted to do right now was raise the plank children up from their ashes.

Think, dammit, think. Some of the phrases had to be spells to stop the dead.

A snippet of Latin floated up like the answer inside a Magic 8 Ball. He recited the words.

Elijah kept coming.

No more retreat. Miles rushed Elijah, going for the dismembered head. Elijah pulled, but Miles grabbed the ears. Elijah squealed. Softened skin tore off the head, and left Elijah holding a limp mask as Miles snatched the skull from the boy's arms. He spat a line from the note-book, misshapen words straining his tongue.

Elijah's actual eyes popped wide. Then his jawbone set, and those eyes narrowed into savage focus.

And just like that, Miles had it—the last drawing in the book had been hands placed on the reawakened dead's earthly remains, sinking into a hole in the earth.

The illustration could have meant the opposite—the rising up from the grave—but it was the only phrase left that he remembered.

Miles wrapped both arms around the head. He clutched it tight to his chest, and the skull compressed like he'd squeezed a red rubber kickball. He shuddered, wave after wave. He gritted his teeth against the urge to throw the thing to the ground; his stomach lurched as he spat out broken tooth chips. Blood dripped onto his lower lip.

"Yimakh shemo ve zikhro!"

A single drop blood fell to the floor, the hallway so silent it *plink*ed. How long did he have to wait? How many times to repeat it? Command it over and over like Father Merrin's demand in *The Exorcist*.

Elijah's chest expanded... deflated... hitched, gulping for breath but failing. Stress lines creased his brow. His mouth flapped like he was chewing gum—chewing oxygen to get it down. Confusion flickered in his eyes. Then a sharp glint of panic. His throat worked, lips fell open. Furious eyes found Miles, and Elijah lurched toward him, but it looked like his feet weighed a hundred tons. He swayed like a reed. The emerald green of his eyes faded. The last scant dregs of resurrected air left in his alveoli expelled in a soft, long exhale like a whispered secret.

Miles stepped back until the rough, cold wall of the tunnel chilled his shoulder blades.

Elijah twitched. He belched a heavy shot of ammonia into the stale air. His shirtsleeves filled out. Trouser legs ballooned. Seams unraveled. Hems of shirt and pants frayed. The fabric thinned, threadbare. Just rags now, his shirt and pants moldered and fell away. Naked, he bloated. Belly rounded. Arms and legs fattened into sausages. His neck expanded like a goiter. Face and hands tinted a muted orange. He broke wind—a rank, dumpster smell . The orange tint spread over Elijah's whole body. His eyeballs clouded, white. The boy's skin shrunk, and what hair remained on the right side and back of his head lengthened. His fingernails elongated into claws.

Miles held the dismembered skull tighter, and juice squeezed out, dribbled over his hands, and puddled onto the floor. He shivered from lips to toes and threw down the leaking gourd.

Elijah's coloring deepened into an orange-green. Like an eggshell, the face on the boy standing in the passageway crackled and shot through with a fine filigree of cracks. Black dandruff flaked off. Like grilled bratwurst, the skin on his arms broke open, and green goo leaked from the lesions. His skin ruptured up and down both legs. Thighs. His neck. His eyeballs shriveled and fell backward into his skull. Moribund green liquid glugged from the goggling eye sockets, nostrils, ear holes, mouth. Farts and burps blew out of Elijah, but Elijah wasn't really there anymore. His standing corpse had sped through the levels of advanced decay that the actual boy would have—should have—cycled through seventy years ago.

Elijah's remaining hair fell out in sheets. His face ripped in half horizontally at the nose; the upper half slid off the back of the head like a shower cap. The lower half dropped away, and his upper jaw protruded with a fantastical horse overbite. Worse than Teeth. Dark viscous fluids pooled at Elijah's feet as the organs inside his body cavity liquified.

The puddled syrup sped toward Miles like the tide. He side-stepped, sliding his back over the tunnel walls. The rancid smell overwhelmed the cramped space, and he retched; he flung himself forward and threw up until only bilious foam from deep in his guts wetted his lips. The nausea didn't pass, and the mucous from all the smoke inhalation hadn't slackened either. He should have taken off right then and there. Freedom was his, but Elijah's time-lapse decomposing was too damn mesmerizing.

Skin on the torso, arms, legs, changed from orange to deepest purple and pulled taut as leather on his bones. His belly caved in. Pelvic bones burst out at his hips. Necrotic skin around his ribcage tore down the middle. Ribs poked through. Spinal vertebrae broke the surface. Elijah's hide ripped at the elbows and knees and crumbled to dust before it could hit the tunnel floor. Only random patches of blackened skin hung off the shoulders, the waist, a couple ribs, like tattered rags.

How was this thing still on its feet? The bones rattled. Life left in the boy skeleton? Consciousness? No.... No, it couldn't be sentient. A mind trapped in that horror would be too abhorrent a fate even for Elijah, whose skull tipped back on the spinal column, jaws widening, widening, and though Elijah no longer had his thick lips—had no lips at all—his mouth distended, yawned beyond reason, and a terrible klaxon blared through the tunnel, rising in pitch and volume until it shredded the world.

And the skeletonized Elijah took a shambling step forward.

We shall do you.

Miles bolted away down the tunnel.

See?

Elijah's shriek pelted his back.

Do you.

Miles barreled through one bulkhead and then another, ramming himself down St. Hamelin's ugly gizzard. Mesh-shielded light fixtures shed just enough glow to fatten up his shadow.

Underneath the ululating scream, Elijah's bones clacked as he trailed Miles.

See?

Madness spilled from his own mouth, dissonance underpinning the strident note from wrecked Elijah. Dizzy, Miles ran out of breath. His smoke-raw throat felt like he'd swallowed glass. But Elijah's tortured cry ramped up, higher. Squeaking. It was close. Elijah was close.

All the little hairs on Miles's arms and neck prickled under the pressure of pursuit—a cyclonic force stirred the air around his good ear and bad. But it came from ahead, not behind. Squeaking. Squeaking! SQUEAKING! and a barrage of impacts struck his ankles, his calves. A brown, undulating river of rats bumped and nipped and scrabbled up and over his feet. Whiskers twitched, and furry necks strained in their hurry. A thump and a clatter from several feet away as the rodents took down Elijah's ragged corpse. Not as close as he'd thought—not near enough for breath to fall on his neck—but so, so much closer than where he had left Elijah when he took off down the tunnel.

He trudged against the current, glancing over his shoulder just to make sure.

Had to be sure.

The mischief of rats writhed in a rounded hill. With no meat for the rats to nibble, the gnawing susurration had to be their crooked teeth chewing bone.

Rapt, he ran his bad shoulder full-force into a metal door. The pain was worth it. He'd found the exit. He slumped onto its pitted surface. He'd found it. He'd found the door out.

And if it wouldn't open?

There was no bashing this door down. Even if it had been wood instead of pocked iron, he lacked even a morsel of physical strength. He was spent.

He would have to turn back.

No, he hadn't come this far to give up or turn back. The rats had found a way into the tunnel; he would find a way out.

He caressed the barrier between him and escape, delaying the inevitable. He didn't even want to try. His luck had run out, he felt it—a taunting emptiness in his bones, his blood, his cells. And the rats had certainly found ingress through cracks and crevices too narrow to even comprehend.

He couldn't wade through the pieces of Elijah's corpse. This door would open. It had to.

Sure. And if the cafeteria building wasn't behind it? What if another section of tunnel waited? And another after that. St. Hamelin's final trick, trapping him in an endless underground hamster tube. Graham's car would sit parked in the long arc of the gravel driveway, gathering snow. And rust.

He grabbed the handle and pulled.

Nothing.

He howled.

Cut his throat!

What if the rest were after him? Elijah had kept coming. Why hadn't he checked that Rocky and Teeth and Husky and every damn plank child had burned to tar? Janelle's infant son had bawled through eternal night from the incinerator with only a few baby bones remaining.

Spill his blood!

How could he think that he'd wiped clean every stain from St. Hamelin's?

Do him in!

How much longer until St. Hamelin's unraveled his mind? He would glom onto the scraps, but after five years... ten... twenty, his sanity would be grains of sand sifting through his fingers.

Screw this.

No more doubt. He stomped out the desperation bubbling up from his guts. He howled again, but in triumph. The bastards had burned. He'd seen them. Smelled them.

And if he was wrong? Let the emptiness devour their cursed shouts! He was outta here. There was always reserve in the tank.

He overlapped his hands and grabbed tight to the door handle. With a barbaric yawp, he threw himself backward. The door resisted, but he strained. He gritted off the jagged remains of his back teeth. The muscle below his right shoulder tore with a dazzling lightning bolt, and the door ground open a foot, maybe a foot-and-a-half. Fresher air slapped his face.

He squeezed his ruined back through and into the dead-quiet, cold cafeteria building.

His syncopated progress echoed as he limped along, listing to port just like Butch. The staircase ahead led to the front door, only the top visible from this angle, but it glowed with winter light. He climbed two stairs before his legs folded; his butt hit the third step with a sciatic jolt. He swallowed hard. His body sang every note and chord of pain and anxieties. Time for another truce. He was fresh out of negotiations, and if he had to, he would drag himself up these stairs by his fingertips until they bent—white creases in the pink—and splintered off at the quick.

He didn't know how long he sat there, but the fingernail method wasn't necessary. He pulled himself upright with the railing. Brittle as some grandfather, he climbed the stairs and reached the door to the outside. A moment to savor the bubble of peace. Silence. No sensation of great evil watching over his shoulder. Was it truly over? Once behind the wheel of Graham's car, he needed only one hand to steer and one foot to hit the gas and rumble over the bridge that they had so easily suckered him about.

His mouth and throat burned, and more gooey sputum built up. He leaned into the door til it opened and stepped into the blessed cold of pre-Thanksgiving winter.

And knocked into the boy who blocked his path.

How had he forgotten about him? The corners of the young mouth curled. Eyes gleamed under a furrowed brow. Tongue licked the bottom lip. The last boy. The only boy whose bones were not buried in the bowels of St. Hamelin's. The one boy left to stop him.

Thirty-Five

Miles scooped up snow off the parapet and shoveled in double handfuls. The melted water soothed until he could speak.

"It's over."

Ian shook his head. "Nothing is over."

The white-covered field all the way to the bridge stretched free and clear. Like a meerkat poking its nose out its hole, his brain sniffed for the scent of danger. The dirt taste in his mouth might have come from the snow he had eaten or from the smoke in his lungs. It may have come from the billows pouring from St. Hamelin's proper over his right shoulder.

"Is there any way to save you?" He ate more snow.

"Ian died months ago. You don't know who I am now."

He did know, but... "He has to be in there somewhere. Ian? Yes? Come on. You've forgotten, is all. Forgotten our movies. Our trips. Your parents. Your friends, your clubs, school, and... and.... You had everything. You—"

"That's what you thought?" Ian jiggled his head, as if startled. "The kid you knew was miserable and lonely. Teacher's pet? Key club? Chess club! Yeah, he was a real social climber. The second he found an in with a group that could stand him, he shed his skin, wove himself a new persona. Wake up. What high schooler gets his kicks hanging out with his lame uncle?"

"You don't mean all that. Stop talking in the third person."

Ian hung back, his heels at the first step down. Not an aggressive stance. Not a retreat, either. "The boy you knew broke that night, in the crash. Emptied out. The world was a vacuum? He was a vacuum—his stomach, his chest, an eviscerated pumpkin waiting for the candle to light the new, carved face."

"You have Ian's imagination. You use his words."

Again, that shrug. Ian watched the heavy Romanesque façade of St. Hamelin's. His gaze shifted, toward the alcove where he had helped kill that rat. "Remember the road with black walls I told you about?"

"Of course." The image he'd been obsessing over for days—his almost-son, floating through a cannonade of screams down the unlit tunnel.

"There was no light because there's nothing after death." He turned his beautiful eyes upon Miles. "The big nothing. Nothingness. The chaplain knew it. Didn't you ever wonder why he didn't just baptize the kids who came in?"

The conspicuous absence of a baptismal font....

"He stopped saving souls long before I got here. He was just spitting in the face of the final abyss. I would have fallen into the void at the end of that road and winked out of existence, except that ropes, these... spider-web strands shot out and stuck to my wrists and ankles, my neck, marionette strings glistening like wet silver, but there wasn't any light so I don't know how they were shining."

"I take it back. Don't talk like you're actually my nephew."

"You never got to hear Chaplain Allen talk when he wasn't pontificating. His greatest fear was returning to eternity. How he had stood at that precipice, looking down, and he saw that his body had been erased, but his consciousness continued sharp and clear as he tipped over the edge. Fully cognizant but powerless and floating in darkness like an astronaut out for a spacewalk if his cable broke. Forever. No heaven, no hell, but a great, empty eternity."

Faith aside, eternity had haunted Miles as a parochial-school child. Contemplating God's existence before the world, before time. God had always been there. Always was longer than billions and trillions and zillions of millennia, and it worked both before and after. Hundreds of nights as a child he had been scared to fall asleep. Terrified that he would be swallowed by the Neverending.

Ian brought him back. "Guess you damned him right back there, didn't you?"

What had Miles said to Chaplain in those last minutes before the fire? That Chaplain had brought back boys without souls. Here was one of them, a boy—a thing—that looked like his almost-son admitting to the truth of Miles's worst terror.

But was this boy telling the truth or weaving another deception? All these years, Miles had thought he'd lost his faith, but perhaps he had only fled the dogma.

Ian nodded as if he knew his words had shaken Miles to the core. "Chaplain Allen hauled me out of Nothingness with those strands. Same way that cafeteria lady had saved him. He brought me to the bottom of those front steps. St. Hamelin's was magnificent, Valhalla rising through the clouds. When I walked inside, it filled the emptiness inside me." Voice soft with remembrance. "It filled me right up. Tasted like hamburger left outside for a week in the middle of summer." Ian looked him dead in the eye. "It's an acquired taste." He nodded again, so pleased with his telling. "But I hate being told what to do. The chaplain and Dr. Schramm were full of themselves, and Elijah was worst of all, bossing those jerks around. But you got rid of them for me." His mouth creased in a lopsided, arrogant smile that Miles's Ian never could have come up with. "Thank you, Uncle Miles."

"Don't call me that anymore."

Why did he always need so much time to learn life's lessons? This revenant beside him bore only passing resemblance to the boy who should have been his son. It retained a scattering of Ian's memories like photos left behind in a box under the bed after moving into a new house. Scraps. Ultimately meaningless.

"I belong here."

"You sure do."

Ian's adorable scrunchy face departed for good. The ugly leer replacing it erased any trace of the kid Miles had taken to ball games and movies. This thing had shed the identity of who it had been in life and extinguished that pure spark of soul.

A gargantuan crunch ripped through the day as St. Hamelin's roof imploded. A mushroom cloud of smoke and debris belched from the damage and hung over the stonework shell.

Miles sighed. "People will come now. Investigate."

"No. Our reputation will keep the locals away."

Ian was probably right. Eventually the fire would devour all the combustibles and starve itself out. The real question: Was St. Hamelin's burning, dead and purged, to the ground? Or was it molting? Would St. Hamelin's lick itself clean and live on, revived by the plank children's eternal voices?

"It's not my problem." Had he really said that out loud? Whatever. It was true. None of this concerned him anymore. Ian—his Ian, the real Ian—was gone. Janelle and Theodore had disintegrated and blown apart, free. Of that he had no doubt.

He was finished here.

Equal measures of sorrow and relief took flight off Miles like released doves. He felt lighter. Maybe a little too empty, but time—no, experience—would fix that. He flapped his hand toward the main building. "It's all yours." He brushed past the body that looked so much like a boy he once knew.

He found the eroded path that Butch had cut between buildings. No one followed, but a voice so much like Ian's called to his back.

"I left you a little surprise."

Butch and Betty's cottage huddled against the woods like a pet abandoned at the side of the road. Frightened. Insignificant with both its people gone.

A coughing fit shook him nearly to his knees. He spat out a thick wad of green goo. Taking a breath started another round of hacking that rattled his brains and started up his ear's *beat-beat-beat*. When he could breathe, he dug his pack of smokes from his pocket. He crumpled the whole thing into a ball, and tossed it away. No more sucking on smoke. Ever.

Around the front of St. Hamelin's peeked the nose of Graham's blue Accord. A few steps more and Ian's last gift came into view. The car's hood yawned wide open. A dusting of snow lay on the engine. At the front tire lay the short fat snakes of radiator hoses.

He chuckled.

The distributor cap sat in a depression in the snow.

He laughed, though it felt and sounded like grinding glass.

For good measure, all four tires had been not just slit but gouged.

He exploded into raucous mirth. Laughing the last laugh because he couldn't have used the car anyway. The keys were right now a melted slab in whatever remained of Graham Blankenheim's pocket. He grabbed snow off the roof and shoveled it down his throat. So cold. So good. A winter coat lay on the passenger seat where Graham must have laid it when the heater kicked in on the drive over.

The lining chilled his arms as he slipped it on. It would warm up in a minute. He pulled up the hood and started off in the direction of the road.

Behind him, pillars of smoke streamed from St. Hamelin's.

He would probably hit Bear Falls before dusk. Did they have an Enterprise car rental? It would be a long drive home. And a long time putting all of this behind him.

Maybe he didn't want his teaching job back. Not right away. What was that saying? Everyone has a novel in them? English lit majors, especially. Time to give it a try, see if he could do it. A novel about a grieving man snowbound in an abandoned orphanage. Trying to save his family but saves himself instead. He could write about the terrible secrets buried there. And all about the plank children.

Yeah.

Sounded pretty good to him.

He stuffed his hands into the parka pockets and hiked toward the bridge through flecks swirling through the air like the plastic bits in a glass globe.

The flurries could have been snow, could have been ash.

Michael Schutz

About the Author

 Michael Schutz was born and raised in the frozen tundra of Wisconsin, where the macabre tales of Ray Bradbury and Stephen King kept him warm at night. He's seen way too many horror movies to be healthy. He is the author of the novel Edging, and his short fiction has been featured in Crossroads in the Dark II, III, and IV, Ravenwood Quarterly, Dark Moon Digest, and Sanitarium. He lives with his three, naughty cat-children in northern California. You can keep tabs on him at http://michael-schutzfiction.com

Praise for EDGING

"A surreal psychedelic dream of horror, confusion, and just pure fear of the unknown."
—Nev Murray, *Stitched Smile Magazine*

"The characterization makes this novel a real stand-out. Schutz has the impressive ability of quickly sketching out believable back stories."
—HorrorTalk

"Wild book... Fear is the purest emotion. In EDGING Michael Schutz shows you just how bad a trip it can be. Pain and pleasure, reality and perception—sometimes it's the same side of the coin."
—Richard Thomas, author of *Breaker* and *Tribulations*

"EDGING is a hallucinatory ride through a nightmarish landscape. If Jim Thompson and William S. Burroughs were to collaborate on a novel about dark psychedelic drugs, murder, and the supernatural, this would be the result. A fantastic and dark read that really does linger in the mind long after having read it."
—Jason White, author of *The Haunted Country*

"EDGING is a wonderful accomplishment. It evokes the early shadow of King, but Schutz's voice is unmistakably his own."
—Terry M. West, author of *The Night Things* series

From Three Furies Press:

https://threefuriespress.com/

A Flutter of Darkness
Jason LaVelle

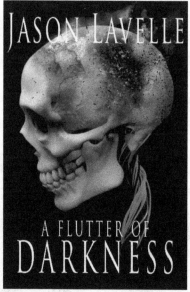

A flutter is a gathering of butterflies. Elegant, ethereal, inspiring joy and wonder. But not all butterflies feed on flowers and light. Some are drawn to decomposing bodies and trickling pools of blood. Some, are drawn to darkness.

This collection of short stories and novellas is the perfect place to admire those creatures. Whimsical and beautiful, splattered with terror, these stories show the darkness that lies hidden within us all.

Pathosis
Jason LaVelle

JASON LAVELLE

PATHOSIS
Book I of the Dying World Chronicles

A sloppy extermination. Evidence mismanaged. And all of America is at risk.

Coast Guard Lt Emily Brisbane is in charge of a strange ship at her dock. Everyone on board has been ripped apart. Even more disturbing, some of the bodies show teeth marks. Human teeth marks.

Before she can conduct a full investigation, she needs to clear the ship of aggressive spiders attacking her investigators.

Jack Wolfgang has seen a lot of strange things in his pest control job, but nothing like this ship. Picking through the bloody decks is bad, but spiders who hunt men is just too much. The government lady isn't paying him to risk his life, so he does the bare minimum before heading home.

The Suffering
Robert Cano

After twelve long years of ongoing warfare between the Fae and the Satyrs in her kingdom, Devani is finally heading home. The war was on the doorstep of her father's land when she was sent to stay in Yor'lon, where the king and queen were supposed to treat her kindly. The war has shifted now, and it is time to go home.

But the princess soon finds herself in a position she never expected, especially so close to returning. Struggling against death itself, her will to survive is overwhelming. She finds a way to freedom and relative safety, but at what cost and for how long? It seems the gods have other plans for Devani.

Augur of Shadows
Jacob Rundle

Destiny. Adventure, Prophecy.

Grief-stricken, seventeen-year-old Henri moves to New York City after he loses his father. Vivid dreams and visions lead him to meet a wise young man, Simeon, someone who means more to him than he wants to admit. He also reconnects with an old friend, Etlina.

The three of them venture on a journey to fulfill their intertwined destinies in order to bring forth a cataclysmic event that's meant to hold back the Primordial Evil.

With guidance from supernatural beings, Henri and his friends will do what is needed to save the world from the Old Ones.

Road to Jericho
Mark Reefe

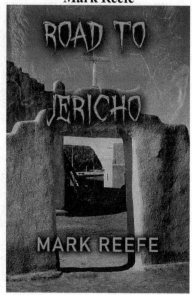

No good deed goes unpunished.

Finn McCallan is a genuinely good man. The type of man who steps in and helps when he sees a dying woman. But his good deed draws the ire, and interest, of the devil whose plan he thwarted. Wearing the mask of a human named Leonard, the devil tricks Finn into a deal, which leaves him marked.

The brand in the center of his right palm isn't the worst of it. His eyes can see the true face of everyone he encounters - frightening him more than anything in life had prior.

Now no matter how far he runs, how determined he is to lay low, calamity seeks him out.

Torturing him, testing him, provoking him. Destroying everything good in his life. He will not be allowed to live a peaceful life until the bargain is fulfilled. To what end?

And for what purpose?

Only the devil knows, and he's not telling.

Shattered
Frank Martin

Prophet. Savior. Freak.

Gifted with visions and voices of the future, Jonathon Chambers has always been special. But that information comes with a price. His gift is also a curse, tormenting John and leading him to a life as a patient under the care of Dr. Scott Houseman. As World War III rages across the globe, Dr. Houseman struggles to treat John's unique and perplexing condition. But the world has other plans. A whirlwind of events sucks the doctor and patient into a race against time. Half the planet believes John to be an oracle. The other half views him as a threat. And stuck in the middle is his doctor, a man who only sees a sick young boy teetering on the edge of madness and willing to do anything to keep him safe.

Michael Schutz

Michael Schutz